Drantc

VLG – Book
Vampires, Lycans, Gargoyles

By Laurann Dohner

Drantos by Laurann Dohner

For most, a plane crash means the end of life. For Dusti Dawson, it's just the beginning...

Dusti and her sister Batina survived the crash, thanks to a couple of brothers who are equal parts menacing and muscled. She'd be grateful…if they hadn't turned out to be delusional kidnappers, who believe Dusti's grandfather is some monstrous half-breed creature bent on murder. Turns out Vampires, Lycans, and Gargoyles do exist—and they've been crossbreeding to form two hybrid races. Drantos, the man Dusti can't stop lusting after, is one of the most dangerous of all.

VampLycans Drantos and Kraven were sent to eliminate a threat to their clan. But when that threat turns out to be mostly human women, clueless of their lineage, plans change—especially after Drantos gets a taste of Dusti's blood. Now, he'll die to protect her. Even if that means walking away from everything he knows to keep her at his side.

Is her strong desire for Drantos reason enough to endure danger coming from all sides? Or should Dusti cut and run the first chance she gets?

Author Note: VLG stands for Vampires, Lycans, Gargoyles…and breeds in between. Living in Alaska's harsh, pristine territories, these creatures live and love fiercely. These are their stories.

Dedication

Always and forever - I have to thank MrLaurann. He's my hero in all ways. He took those vows of 'in sickness and in health' and stuck to them, big time. He's always had my back and my front. I love you, baby. I couldn't do what I do, without you.

Kele Moon - Not only is she the best friend a person could ever have but I love her like the sister I always wished for. We're family in my heart. She rocks as a critique partner too. Now she's holding my hand and steering me through a new adventure in the wonderful world of writing.

Kelli Collins - I was nervous and scared going out on my own. You were there for me. Thank you for being a kickass editor and giving it to me straight. You made this book so much better. Always a fan!

Most of all, I'd like to thank you, the people reading this. I was a housewife with a love for writing and I had a dream. You made it come true. You have stuck with me through every obstacle life threw at me. I might write slower but I'm still here! Thank you. I hope you enjoy this new series. Happy reading.

Drantos

Copyright © December 2015

Editor: Kelli Collins

Cover Art: Dar Albert

ISBN: 978-1-944526-01-6

ALL RIGHTS RESERVED. The unauthorized reproduction or distribution of this copyrighted work is illegal, except for the case of brief quotations in revies and articles.

Criminal copyright infringement is investigated by the FBI and is punishable by up to 5 years in federal prison and a fine of $250,000.

All characters and events in this book are fictitious. Any resemblance to actual persons living or dead is coincidental.

Table of Contents

Chapter One

Chapter Two

Chapter Three

Chapter Four

Chapter Five

Chapter Six

Chapter Seven

Chapter Eight

Chapter Nine

Chapter Ten

Chapter Eleven

Chapter Twelve

Chapter Thirteen

Chapter Fourteen

Chapter Fifteen

Chapter Sixteen

Chapter Seventeen

Chapter Eighteen

Chapter Nineteen

Chapter Twenty

Chapter Twenty-One

Chapter Twenty-Two

Chapter One

"Brace for impact!"

The pilot's voice sounded high-pitched for a man, his fear obvious.

"Tighten your belts, remove all sharp objects from your pockets, and bend forward."

Dusti clutched her sister's hand tightly while her heart beat erratically from adrenaline and terror. She turned her head to stare into Bat's terrified blue eyes. Her older sister, usually so calm, appeared as panicked as Dusti felt. Bat's aloof attorney façade had fled, replaced by sheer fright.

The small plane engines droned loudly as the cabin shook violently. The overhead compartments rattled, a dull background noise that made the grim situation more realistic. Dusti peered through the window to her left. It revealed dense foliage far below, a testament that they'd flown far from civilization.

The pilot came back on the speaker to make another announcement, as if telling the twenty-some passengers the plane was going down hadn't been bad enough.

They'd reached Alaska, but it seemed they'd die there too.

"Mayday, mayday!" The pilot yelled now. "This is Brennon Twelve. Mayday." The plane took a sudden nose dive after a loud *pop* tore through the cabin. "Fuck!"

People in the seats around Dusti cried out and one woman in the row behind her frantically began to pray aloud.

It was just a guess, but Dusti figured the pilot wasn't aware he'd left the microphone on as the conversation between him and his copilot was broadcast throughout the cabin via speakers.

"Pull up, Mike! Fuck, she's fighting me. Help!"

"I am!" the other pilot responded. "I don't see a place to land, do you? Christ! The yoke feels like it weighs a thousand pounds. We're going to break apart before we ever hit the ground."

The nose of the plane leveled off somewhat but the plane was definitely losing altitude. Dusti glanced out the window again to notice the trees had become more defined now, instead of similar to a distant carpet of green bushes. Her gaze swept the ground to confirm there wasn't a clearing within sight for the pilots to try to use as a runway.

"I'm so sorry," Bat whispered. "This is all my fault. I love you."

Hot tears filled Dusti's eyes when she turned her head to lock eyes with her sister's fearful gaze. "I love you too—and don't you dare blame yourself."

"Fire in engine two," one of the pilots yelled. "Shit! The extinguishing system is offline. It's not responding. We're only twenty miles out but we're not going to make it to the airfield."

"Level off," the second pilot harshly demanded.

"Got it." The pilot cursed. "Do you see anything? Do you?"

"It's just trees. We're going down too fast. Why in the *hell* aren't they answering? I know it's a tiny airport but Jesus! Where are they? Maybe we lost communications and they aren't receiving our mayday." The copilot sounded both angry and frightened.

"Damn those cheap bastards for not giving us a backup system," the pilot hissed. "Shit! We're definitely going down. Seventeen hundred feet and falling." He paused. "Sixteen hundred." He paused again for several long seconds. "Fifteen hundred. Oh damn!"

"It's been good knowing you, Mike."

"You too, Tim. Drop the landing gear but I don't know why we should bother. We're going to be shredded to hell and back." There was a pause. "Oh shit. *Cut the mic!*"

Movement from the aisle startled Dusti when two tall, massive-bodied men wearing leather jackets and faded blue jeans suddenly stumbled next to their seats. They used the chair backs to keep themselves upright on the slanted floor of the plane by gripping the edges.

She immediately recognized them from the Anchorage airport. She and Bat had to change planes there to catch the smaller connecting flight. The two burly men had stepped out of one of the bars they'd passed while walking from one concourse to another. To Dusti, it had seemed as if the guys were following them. She'd even pointed them out to her sister, fearful that the men might be planning to mug them.

Bat had laughed, assuring her airport security was too tight for that to happen. Dusti had kept glancing back though, nervous. She remembered thinking how big and threatening they'd looked at the time.

Now they were right in the aisle, so close she could almost reach out and touch them.

The one in the lead turned his head to peer directly at her. Dusti stared up into a rugged, masculine face displaying strong cheekbones. His thick, wavy black hair fell to his shoulders, brushing the front of his leather jacket. Generous lips were curved into a frown, but it was his seriously dark blue eyes—framed by long black eyelashes—that held her attention the most.

He moved quickly to slide between the small space where she and her sister's legs were and the backs of the seats in front of them. He stepped over Bat to plant his body between Dusti's feet.

She watched in stunned shock as the other guy, almost a twin in sheer body mass to the first one, wedged his frame literally between Bat's spread legs and the seats. Dusti's confused gaze returned to the man whose crotch now hovered in front of her face. She felt his jeans pressed against her bare legs from the knee down, where her skirt didn't cover them.

Her first fear resurfaced, that they were about to be mugged, but that didn't make sense. They were all going to die when the plane crashed.

"What—"

The one in front of her cut off her words when he turned his head to look at the other man, this one with short, spiked black hair. "Good luck, Kraven. Love you."

"Love you too, bro," the other man replied.

"I'm Drantos," the long-haired guy informed Dusti when he looked down to hold her stunned stare. "We're hopefully going to save your asses by protecting you with our bodies. We might survive this if we don't blow up or get ripped apart on impact like the pilot thinks." The cabin shook violently and he swayed on his feet.

"I'm hoping he's wrong about that."

Dusti was mute and definitely confused. A gasp from Bat drew her attention.

As she turned her head, she was too horrified to do anything but watch as the spiked-haired man leaned forward, slid to his knees and shoved Bat's legs farther apart to fit his hips between the cradle of her thighs.

He grabbed her sister, jerked her against his chest, and then wrapped his arm around her back in a tight hug. She heard a click as the stranger unfastened her sister's seat belt, and then he clamped a hand around Bat's thigh. He yanked it up until her knee was bent enough to nearly touch her shoulder, then used that arm to hug around Bat's back, too.

He had totally covered her body with his, smashing her against the seat.

Bat's cry of alarm jostled Dusti from her stupor. She recovered enough to find her voice. "Let her go!" They weren't muggers. They seemed to be rapists.

Like they didn't have enough to be afraid of before?!

Dusti lunged to attack the bastard assaulting her sister. She tried to claw at his arm but two big hands grabbed her wrists. Her full attention returned to the huge bastard who quickly slid to his knees between *her* legs, his hips pressing against her inner thighs. The move pushed the bottom of her skirt high up on her lap.

He moved fast for such a beefy guy. Dusti screamed but it didn't stop his attack. He held her wrists together with one of his hands, shackling them, while he used the other to shove her feet up on the seat. It kept her legs spread wide apart to make room for his hips. His body nearly crushed her to the seat when he collapsed against her.

Her mind instantly filled with horrified thoughts. *Am I really going to be raped before I die? Is this asshole serious? I've heard men joke about wanting to go out nailing a woman but this can't be happening. These assholes are really going for it.*

Screams suddenly filled the cabin that hadn't come from Dusti, the noise so piercing it made her remember the plane was about to crash into the rugged Alaskan wilderness.

The man assaulting her shoved her hands at his crotch to pin them there when he pressed more of his weight down, trapping them between the seat and his jeans. He let go of her wrists and it gave him the freedom to grip both of her legs near the knees and force them up against her chest until she sympathized with a pretzel. His jeans were rough against her inner thighs and his belt buckle painfully dug into her panties.

His two strong arms locked against the sides of her thighs as he reached around her body too. He adjusted her under him in a way that made her comprehend *her* seat belt had been unfastened as well. He wouldn't have been able to yank her to the edge of the seat otherwise.

He gripped one of her ass cheeks and tucked his head down on top of hers, to force her chin lower, until her forehead smashed against the cool leather of his jacket. She struggled but he effectively held her in a tight ball, his bulky body keeping hers trapped between him and the seat.

All hell broke loose in the next instant.

Dusti screamed when she felt both of them being violently flung forward. The plane must have hit the trees. Shrieks rose in the confined cabin and air blasted through it, whipping around as though they'd been tossed into a wind tunnel.

The sick feeling of being thrown rolled through her as the plane bounced before it brutally slammed into something again. The belly of the plane hit hard enough to toss their entwined bodies back against the seat.

His heavy weight crushed down on her until breathing became impossible. She swore she heard an animal growl next to her ear when the screams in the plane cut off after the horror of the initial impact. *Maybe everyone has died*, her dismayed mind considered.

The strong arms around her tightened even more as the plane violently bumped over the earth. An image flashed through her mind of them skidding across the ground, mimicking a sled from hell.

An explosion ripped through the cabin, deafening her with its intensity, a second before they were thrown sideways.

The man holding her didn't let go, and his body must have hit something solid and unforgiving. The force of the impact reverberated through his body right into hers. He grunted loudly, as if he'd had the air forced from his lungs.

She didn't know which direction was up or down anymore, just continued to experience swift movement and blinding terror until everything came to a lurching stop. Her back hit something soft before the man's heavy weight squashed her once more.

Dusti couldn't move. She was too stunned to do anything but wish for air while it sank in that she'd survived.

The stranger's hand on her ass eased its bruising hold when he lifted off her a little. She heard him gasp in a breath and his upper chest pressed tight to hers when his lungs expanded. The second the pressure eased as he expelled the air, she gasped in her own lungful.

She slowly became aware of sensations. Her ass hurt from the man's near-sadistic grip on it and her chest ached a little, probably from him crushing her a few times. She also realized one of her knees painfully throbbed.

Dusti took another deep breath and smelled the leather of the jacket under her nose. The texture of hair on her tongue made it apparent that either some of her long blonde hair or some of his shoulder-length black mane had ended up inside her mouth. She promptly spit it out, not caring who it belonged to, but just wanting it gone. His head lifted off hers.

Panic shot through her instantly as things came into focus and she glanced to the right. They were actually still in her seat—but the one next to hers no longer contained her sister or the spike-haired stranger.

Her mind refused to accept that Bat's disappearance meant she hadn't survived.

Her gaze lifted more to stare beyond that empty seat. She gaped as she saw the other side of the plane.

The cabin wall across the aisle had been torn completely open to reveal trees and blue sky, in place of windows and overhead bins with stored luggage. The jagged, torn metal of the fuselage was splayed obscenely to reveal the scenic view. Something had demolished that side of the plane.

The guy who still held Dusti slowly eased more of his weight off her when he leaned back a bit to look around too. Distress made her focus on him instead of the certainty that her sister had been thrown from the plane.

Blood marred the man's face from a cut on one of his pronounced cheekbones, an injury a good inch long. He wasn't classically handsome, too rugged and masculine to ever be considered a pretty boy with those dominant features. He needed a shave too, since stubble showed on his lower jawline, his chin, and shadowed his cheeks. His dark gaze swept across more of the plane than she could see while scrunched down inside the seat, where he still kept her pinned.

"KRAVEN?" He roared the word, his voice harsh.

"Fuck," an equally cavernous male voice responded, sounding close. "We're alive. Did yours make it?"

The stranger lowered his chin to peer into Dusti's dazed stare. He studied her from face to chest, and finally locked gazes with her again. "She's alive."

"I hate flying." Kraven sounded irritated. "I mentioned that, right?"

The man continued to watch Dusti and he actually smiled. "Several times, but we're not flying anymore, are we? I don't mind flying but I hated the crashing part. I bet you wish you were still in the air right now. Quit bitching and let's see how bad the situation is. We survived. That's all that counts in the end."

"Get off me. You're crushing me!"

Relief swept through Dusti at hearing her older sister's aggravated voice and it tore her from her traumatized state. "Bat? Are you okay?"

"Dusti! Thank goodness you're alive. Are you all right? Get off me, asshole! You weigh a thousand pounds. I need to check on my sister."

"Maybe I *would* get off you if you weren't gripping my dick. That's not my thigh you've been clutching in terror, woman," Kraven snarled. "Let go!"

"Ewww!" Bat squealed. "Get off me! My hand is trapped there, damn it."

The man still pinning Dusti to her seat chuckled. "Did I introduce myself? I'm Drantos."

"Let me go. Please get off." Dusti hated the way her voice trembled enough to make it sound more like a feeble plea than a demand.

He arched an eyebrow. "That's all you've got to say to me after I saved your life? I believe this is where you're supposed to say thank you and tell me *your* name."

Dusti was still suffering from shock but this had to be the strangest conversation she'd ever had. "Your belt buckle is digging into my…um…" She tried to wiggle her hips away from his but it only caused more discomfort. The metal object pressed against her panties pushed in deeper, causing her to wince.

He jerked his hips back to put a few inches between their bodies but he glanced down. His smile turned into an outright grin. "Sorry about that. I hope I didn't damage you down there. That would be a crime. I love bright red, by the way. Is that a thong? I can only see the front."

Her mouth hung open and she gawked speechlessly until she realized he continued to stare at her exposed lap. She shoved at him with her hands, pushing hard against his massive chest, and tried to put her feet on the floor to scoot back in the seat and away from the obviously deranged pervert.

He let her go, still grinning as she grabbed at her skirt to shove it down the tops of her thighs to regain her modesty.

The sound of a sobbing woman filtered through Dusti's shock-hazed brain and her jumbled thoughts. Other noises slowly penetrated and she became more aware of her surroundings when Drantos rose to his feet to loom over her, no longer touching as he stepped aside to stand in front of Bat's empty seat. He surveyed the plane, his features set in a grim expression. Dusti heard soft whispers then someone cursing from the back of the plane. It sank in that the four of them weren't the only survivors.

She peered up at Drantos, since he kept her trapped in the row with his body planted between her and the aisle. He sniffed the air, made a distasteful grimace, before peering over the seats in front of them. He turned his head, staring down at the floor of the aisle.

"Are you going to just lay there on top of her or are you going to get up? It's no time to take a nap, Kraven."

"Go to hell. I think she crushed something vital when she squeezed my dick. I'm trying to recover. She's got nothing on a cock ring, that's for sure."

Drantos shook his head. "You're going to give her a bad impression if you don't watch your mouth."

"Like I give a damn what she thinks," Kraven grunted as he climbed to his feet.

Dusti stared at the other man when he appeared in the aisle a row ahead of where she sat. His black hair looked worse for wear, some of his spikes crushed flat on one side of his head. It gave him the bedhead look of a punker gone bad. Maybe a punk biker, considering the leather jacket he was sporting. He frowned down at something below him.

"What are you? A masseuse?" He lifted his chin and shot Drantos a dirty look. "I swear she crushed my dick."

Bat struggled to her feet, her blonde hair in a messy ponytail now that her neat bun had been loosened from the crash. She glowered at the man, who gave her that angry look right back. "Why did you grab me like that? What the hell is your problem?"

"I was *protecting* you. I'm Kraven. You can thank me later, by the way."

"Thank you?" Bat gawked at him. "You'll be lucky if I don't have your ass arrested for sexual assault, battery, and…hell, bad hair! Move out of my way. I need to check on my sister." Bat tried to shove him aside, her gaze locking on Dusti. Relief showed on her features.

Dusti forced her body to move and she tried to stand but Drantos held out his arm, holding up a hand as if to tell her to stay. She stared up at him.

"Could you please move? You're in my way."

He arched a black eyebrow at her. "My brother can take care of your sister. He's in charge of her now. You just stay put while I deal with this mess."

Shock rolled through Dusti again. *In charge of her?* His words played through her mind. They left her even more confused as her gaze flickered back and forth between the two men standing just feet apart, with only a seat between them. They both had tan skin, huge bodies and black hair, but she wouldn't have previously pegged them for brothers.

Now, as she stared, she started to see some similarities—the strong bone structure for one and the generous lips for another. The spiked-haired guy had light blue eyes though instead of dark.

"Help me," a man called from the back of the plane. "Please, help!"

Drantos sighed. "I've got it." He inched out from between the seats and into the aisle. "Kraven, watch them and keep them both where they are. We've got dead bodies in here, and panicked types who I never trust not to go crazy in a crisis."

Kraven nodded. "I have the women."

"Have this, you jerk." Batina sounded riled still.

Dusti flinched when her sister nailed the unsuspecting guy in the chest with her expensive footwear. Kraven staggered back in astonishment and Bat lunged around him to reach her. Dusti rose to her feet on trembling legs, a moment of wooziness making her see spots, but she pushed the sensation back to hug her sister.

Bat clung to her tightly, both of them enormously relieved the other had survived.

Dusti pulled back enough to get a really good look at her sister's face. There was a red mark near Bat's right temple. It wasn't bleeding but it looked as if it might become a bruise. Her complexion was unnaturally pale but Dusti figured she probably had that in common with her. They'd just been in a plane crash, for God's sake.

"It's okay, Bat. I'm okay. Are you hurt?"

Bat eased her hold on her a little. "Nothing a good drink won't fix. I'm so glad you're okay."

Dusti gave a little nod but then looked away from her sister to stare in dismay at the cabin around them. Injured people were still strapped in their seats, but worse, a guy lay sprawled in his seat across the aisle next to the torn-away section of the fuselage. He was bloody and definitely dead. No one could be missing an arm that had been sheared off at the shoulder and survive. Bright red drenched his chest and lap—fresh and wet looking.

Dusti heard someone gag, only to realize she'd made the sound herself as bile rose.

Bat grabbed her face by cupping her cheeks. It jerked her horrified gaze away from the sight and forced her to stare at her sister instead. "Look at *me* and not that."

Tears welled in Dusti's eyes that she tried to blink away. She stared into her sister's gaze, very much resembling her own since they looked so similar. "Oh God!"

"I know," Bat crooned. "We survived though. We're Dawsons. We're tough, remember? Just take deep breaths. In and out. Remain calm."

Dusti didn't feel very tough at all. She was in shock, and she knew it. It was difficult to think, a surreal feeling fogging her mind. Too many awful things had happened in a short timeframe and everything seemed a nightmare at that moment. It helped to concentrate on her sister's face. Bat caressed her gently with her thumbs.

"It'll be fine. We both made it. We're okay." Her sister always knew how to keep her head—if not her tongue—in a bad situation.

"Sit down," the spiked-haired man ordered harshly. "And I'll spank you if you hit me with another shoe, you little hellion."

Bat released Dusti's cheek without missing a beat to raise her middle finger at the guy behind her. "Take a hint and get away from me, you perverted bastard. You should have picked another woman to molest."

Kraven, if that was his real name, stepped closer. He looked dazed when Dusti glanced at him. He didn't seem like someone you could be rude to without dire consequences, but her sister dealt with the dregs of humanity and didn't seem overly concerned. She was used to stressful situations. Plus, her sister could be a first-rate bitch. That's how she'd made partner at her law firm by the age of thirty-three. She defended the worst criminals, and had made a name for herself as a cold-hearted ball-buster in the courtroom.

Her reputation *out* of court had become even worse. A man had hurt Batina when she'd been younger so she avoided relationships now, treating all men equally—as if they were dog shit.

"I saved your life," the clueless man said, not knowing he'd probably regret it. "I covered your body with my own to *protect* you, Cat."

"It's *Bat*, you moron. B.A.T." Her sister turned her head to glare at him. "Back off, asshole. I refuse to deal with you right now. Can't you see my sister is freaked-out? I'm trying to calm her down."

"Crazy as a bat or bat-shit crazy. It fits," the big guy said.

Dusti saw her sister's nostrils flare and knew she had to act quickly. Her sister had a tendency to be harsh with her words when it came to men. The spiked-haired guy was bodybuilder-size, had to be at least six feet four, towering over them. The last thing she wanted was for him to attack Bat. The full-time bodyguard that usually stuck near her sister wasn't along on the trip to intervene.

"Let it go," Dusti ordered. "Let's help the injured."

Bat's blue gaze narrowed when she turned her head to stare at Dusti again. "He's irritating me and he felt me up!"

"That's the least of our worries."

"You're right. I'll ignore the big ape just for you this one time because I'm in shock too. I hope I'm not as pale as you look. You're doing a hell of a ghost impression." Bat cringed. "I shouldn't have said that, considering the circumstances. Sorry." She took a deep breath. "Let's help out. People are hurt. Just breathe and focus on that, okay?" She released Dusti to reach inside her inner jacket pocket and then whipped out her cell phone.

Dusti felt a rush of relief. Her older sister was always the one to remain coolheaded in a crisis. They needed help, and Bat was obviously thinking the same thing. "Do you think you're going to get a cell phone signal out here?"

Bat flipped open the case. "I hope so." Her mouth curved downward into a frown a second later. She spun suddenly to glare at Kraven.

"You broke my phone with your gorilla-sized body." She shoved the phone upward to show him the crushed face, parts of the broken screen falling to the cabin floor. "You owe me a new one. Give me yours."

"It's in my bag." He pointed up to where the overhead cabinets had once been. "Wherever that is now."

So much for that plan.

Bat was confronting the spike-headed guy yet again, who stood way too close to Bat as he argued back. Dusti turned away from them both. Kraven was the one who had grabbed her sister before the crash, after all, so Dusti figured if anyone deserved to be a target of Bat's anger, it was him.

She got her first glimpse of the back of the plane and her heart nearly stopped.

"Oh God."

"I know! I can't dial 9-1-1."

"Shut up, Bat," Dusti whispered. "Look. Oh my God."

Bat moved beside her and clutched her hand, which hung limply at her side. Her warm fingers laced with Dusti's while they both stared toward where the rear of the plane had once been.

A big, craggy hole glared at them from five rows back, the tail section just gone—along with a few rows that had contained people.

The dreadfulness of it hit Dusti full force as she stared at the line of broke trees and scarred ground the plane had created when it had been dragged along the forest floor. A body remained still strapped into a lone seat in the near distance. It had broken free from its twin and the rear of the plane. No one could have survived that. The poor victim resembled bloody hamburger wrapped in soaked red clothing. It was impossible to tell if it had been a man or a woman.

A big body suddenly stood in the aisle, blocking Dusti's view of the dead person a good fifty yards away. Drantos's expression looked grim when he lifted a hand to run his fingers through his shaggy mane of hair. His lips twisted into a grimace as he approached Dusti. Their gazes remained on each other until he stopped a few feet in front of her. He shifted his attention to look at his brother behind her.

"There are ten survivors besides us in the cabin. Most of them will make it but I'm doubtful about a few. One of us should go hunt up the back of the plane to see if any of those people made it. We also need to check on the pilots."

"Fuck," Kraven sighed. "What a damn mess. I'll go search for the tail section of the plane." He paused. "You watch the bitches. The one in the dress suit is a terror, so don't turn your back on her."

Bat squeezed Dusti's hand painfully as she turned her head to glare at Kraven. "I'm going to rip off your nuts if you call me a bitch one more time."

Dusti jerked on her sister's hand. "Batina Marie Dawson, enough!" Hot tears filled her eyes when her sister met her gaze. "I know bitchiness is your defense mechanism when you're scared or mad but please *stop*! I can't deal with it right now."

A wave of dizziness hit, making her knees go weak. She swayed on her feet.

Bat grabbed her before Dusti collapsed. Her sister struggled to hold her upright until two strong hands gripped her. She opened her eyes to see the big guy, Drantos, lifting her until she was cradled against his chest.

"Where's my purse?" Bat asked, clearly panicked. "It's black. I need it!"

"I'm okay," Dusti whispered. "It's just a dizzy spell."

"My purse, you big gorilla! Move out of my way. My sister needs her medication," Bat yelled.

Drantos frowned while he stared into her eyes. "What's wrong with you?"

He was strong, easily holding her in his arms while he stood in the aisle. She appreciated that he'd prevented her from falling on the floor and taking her sister down with her when he'd swept her off her feet.

"I've got a rare form of anemia. It's bad sometimes and makes me dizzy. I have iron shots in my purse but Bat keeps a few of them with her, too, in case of emergency."

He paled a little, lifting his face to stare at someone behind her. "She's defective. I think we saved the wrong two women."

"Shit," Kraven cursed softly. "They were the only two single females aboard. I was positive they were the ones Filmore sent for. That blows every theory we had."

Shock tore through Dusti while she stared up at the man holding her. "You know my grandfather?"

He swiftly looked back at her. "You're Decker Filmore's *granddaughter*?"

She nodded, feeling a little stronger and less lightheaded. Maybe it wasn't her anemia kicking her in the ass but just the shock that had gotten to her. She'd also been battered around and nearly crushed by the big man who currently held her. "He's my mother's father. We were on our way to see him. He's terminally ill."

Rage tightened the man's features, making Dusti feel more fear than when the plane was going down. He looked *really* scary.

"That's a lie. That bastard will never die until someone takes him out." He jerked his head up to glare at his brother. "We've got the right women. I never saw *this* coming, did you? Granddaughters? But we can stop him now that we're the ones who have them."

A soft growl came from behind Dusti, making her startle at the chilling animalistic sound Kraven had made. "I wouldn't have risked my neck to save one of them if I'd known they were related to him by blood. Now we're going to have to kill them ourselves."

Terror struck Dusti as she stared into Drantos's furious blue eyes, which were fixed on her. He blinked once, then twice. His plush lips pressed tightly together to show his displeasure. He finally looked away and shook his head.

"I don't kill helpless women, and you aren't going to either. I know it's tough to get a good read in here, what with all the blood and everything else filling the air, but they smell just like the other passengers." He paused. "You know what I'm saying. You're just angry and it's been a bad day. We'll find out what they know and crush that bastard's plan. We'll use them against him. They're his blood, even if it *is* faint enough that we can't pick it up. That means they'll be valuable to him."

Kraven glared at her and his nostrils flared. "How can they be his blood?"

"We'll figure it out later, after we deal with this mess, but do you know *anyone* who would purposely claim to be a relative to that bastard unless it was the truth?"

"I found it!" Bat rushed to them, gripping her purse. "Hang on, Dusti. I have some of your shots."

Dusti flashed a terrified look at Bat, trying to convey that things were much worse than just being in a plane crash. She tried to catch her sister's eye but Bat remained too intent on finding the iron shots, digging inside her purse with one hand. She jerked out a small black case with a grin.

"Here it is. They aren't broken."

Dusti glanced at Drantos, only to discover him glaring down at her. She and Bat were in a lot of trouble.

Her grandfather was rich—and she had a sinking feeling they were about to be held for ransom.

Can this day get any worse?

Drantos watched the sister inject the woman in his arms with a small syringe. Then he looked at his brother, attempting to conceal his rage and dismay.

These women were the granddaughters of their worst enemy. He knew his brother hated Decker even more than he did, which was the only reason why Kraven would even contemplate killing the obviously helpless sisters.

Decker Filmore had sent a woman to seduce Kraven months before, and then she'd attempted to murder him. She'd failed, but it had left his brother with a hair-trigger abhorrence toward any females associated with Decker's clan.

Drantos didn't blame him for being leery. It would be unnerving to have a woman attempt to stab him in the heart during sex.

Still, one thing was clear. The ultimate fate of the sisters wasn't to be decided until he found out what they knew.

He'd hate to have to kill them. But that didn't mean he *wouldn't* if he was left with no other choice.

He peered down at the one he held in his arms. Dusti. She had pretty blue eyes, confusion and fear shining clearly in them. It was easy for him to read her emotions, but he couldn't make sense of either. Decker *had* to have warned them that they might be met by the enemy. She could be faking whatever physical flaw she seemed to have just to appear weak. It could be a cunning game they played, hoping to get him and his brother to let down their guards. They wouldn't escape, if that was their plan.

Dusti had said her mother was the tie to that family, and he tried to remember details about Decker's daughter, but Antina Filmore had run away from her father shortly after her mother's death. Nobody had heard from her again. It was assumed by Drantos's clan that the girl had known or suspected her own father had murdered her mom, and she had also likely known what he had in store for *her* future. Antina had never resurfaced.

It was possible she hadn't told Dusti or Bat the truth about their grandfather. Did Antina want to save herself from the fate her father had planned for her badly enough to offer up both of her daughters instead? She could have sent them herself, making some kind of deal with Decker. He wasn't the type to forgive anyone for what he'd consider a betrayal, but he'd bargain for something if he wanted it bad enough. The bastard was totally ruthless.

Drantos studied the woman staring back at him with fear. She trembled in his arms and a sudden sense of protectiveness hit him.

She was the best actress he'd ever met, if it was indeed an act. Then again, she really might not know what her grandfather had in store for her—but Drantos could guess.

Decker would use his granddaughters to begin the bloodbath he so desperately wanted.

Chapter Two

The large bonfire kept the darkness surrounding them at bay. Dusti inhaled the scent of leather coming from the oversized jacket wrapped around her. She tracked Drantos's movements when he strode closer to the fire pit he'd dug. He'd made sure she hadn't had a moment alone with Bat since her sister had given her the iron shot. As a matter of fact, he kept her at least ten feet away from all the other passengers, who huddled around the fire he'd lit before the sun had gone down.

Drantos had carried Dusti off the plane and made a camp while Bat and Kraven had helped the injured off the damaged aircraft. Both pilots had died and there were no survivors in the tail section. Kraven had gone to look while Bat had been ransacking the plane for blankets and supplies. Drantos constantly watched Dusti, and her sister had gone right along with his plan to keep them separated, agreeing that Dusti should lie down to avoid fainting. Bat was worried about her.

"Don't say a word about what Kraven and I discussed—to your sister or anyone else," Drantos had warned.

She'd taken the threat to heart. He was a big man, muscled, and probably had some kind of criminal history that would be terrifying if she knew the extent of his rap sheet.

His dark gaze fixed on her from across the small clearing while he crouched by the fire, adding broken branches to the flames. The harsh expression on his face scared her but she remembered that he'd said he didn't kill women. He'd even removed his jacket to wrap it around her to help keep her warm.

That has to mean something, right? How bad can the guy be if he would worry about me being cold? Then again, don't forget there are always people on the news being interviewed about how the serial killers they were friends with are such nice guys. But there are witnesses. He can't kill us all. Well, he could, so maybe he's just playing nice for right now.

Bat walked out of the woods with Kraven. He carried a bunch of cushions that they'd removed from the plane, while Bat clutched the handles of a few small suitcases. The two had worked together for the past couple hours. It shocked Dusti, frankly. Her sister was abrasive at best around men so she'd expected yelling and a little bloodshed to ensue.

Bat smiled encouragingly at her after she dropped the suitcases and approached. "How are you doing? Your coloring is much better. You hadn't taken your shot in a while, had you?"

Dusti shook her head, glancing toward Drantos. He was watching her. She was afraid to speak.

"Damn it, hon. You know better. Your body needs the iron it can't produce or you get all chalky white and go unconscious. You're supposed to take one every other day at least, even if you're feeling fine." Bat reached into her dressy suit jacket to pull out a small black case. "I've got good and bad news. The bad news is your purse is toast. It was torn up when it was batted around during the crash. The good news is I found your shots. The case protected them from breaking." Bat crouched down to hand over the container. "Don't lose those, Dusti. I mean it. I only have one of your shots left and you have the five I found in your purse. I'm certain we'll be rescued soon but we both know these need to last us until we return to California."

Dusti decided this might be the only chance to speak to her sister alone. "Bat, we're in trouble. I—"

Drantos suddenly appeared next to them, sporting an unhappy expression.

Dusti stopped talking, terrified that he might have overheard her whispered words. His gaze narrowed on her in silent warning. She tried to appear as innocent as possible by holding his stare for a few seconds. He didn't seem to be buying it when he continued to give her a dirty look, so she swallowed hard, breaking eye contact.

"Don't worry," Bat assured her. "We're going to be rescued. They'll have a fleet of planes searching for us in the morning. That's procedure when a plane goes down. I just hope the emergency beacon is working. I believe they're usually a part of the tail section. That will help them pinpoint our exact location." Bat peered up at Drantos. "I forgot to ask your brother how bad the tail section was damaged when he went looking for it. Do you know? Is it possible the beacon still works?"

"I don't know." The big man shrugged.

"I should ask Kraven." Bat glanced around, seeming to search for him. She waved her arm to get his attention then focused on Drantos again. "We're safe from animals with the fire burning, right? It will scare them away? Dusti and I don't want to end up having to take rabies shots."

Dusti bit back a groan. Bat had clearly mistaken her few words for worries about them not being found, or being in danger from creatures in the woods. Dusti was more concerned about the two brothers. It wasn't possible to correct her with Drantos right there, so she just shook her head. "I'm sure that won't happen, Bat. Thank you for finding my shots. I didn't like that purse anyway."

"We found some snacks and water bottles on the plane," Kraven announced, joining them. "I'll pass them out to the survivors."

"They were talking about the emergency beacon from the plane." Drantos stared at his brother. "How it'll make it easier for the plane to be found. You tracked the tail section. What do you think?"

Kraven shook his head. "I'm sure it didn't survive. The tail was completely destroyed."

"You don't know that for certain," Bat argued.

Kraven narrowed his eyes, fixing them on her sister. "It hit a tree and was wrapped around it. Everything in that part of the plane is smashed to hell and back. I checked for anything I could salvage but it was a lost cause." He turned his attention back to Drantos. "I'm going to go hunting. Everyone could use some fresh meat."

"Sure you are," Bat muttered.

Kraven glared at her. "What?"

Bat stood and faced him. "What are you going to use to hunt with? Your bad manners? Maybe you can just talk to the animals and they'll commit suicide."

Kraven inched forward to glare down at her sister with an intimidating-as-hell look. "I told you to shut up. We have an agreement, remember? I don't whip your ass if you keep your lips sealed together."

Bat opened her mouth but she held her tongue, to Dusti's amazement.

Her sister actually backed down. It was something that never happened, *ever*. But now, Bat just nodded silently and brushed both of her hands down her tailored skirt. She looked everywhere but at Dusti or Kraven.

A smirk twisted Kraven's lips before he winked at his brother. "I'll be back soon. I'm going to scout while I'm out there to see just how fucked things are."

"I'm sure rescue crews will be searching for the plane at first light. They're going to have to fly out of Anchorage. The smaller airport won't have helicopters. And with no place to land, the best the planes will be able to do is help with the air-spotting." Drantos sighed. "The question is, do we leave on our own or wait for help?" He darted a glance around the group by the fire. "They're helpless if we walk out of here on our own. I'm afraid they won't be found and will die from exposure. Not one of them has survival skills. I asked."

"We'll worry about it later." Kraven shot a glare at Bat. "I'll be back." He turned on his heel to march out into the darkness.

Bat watched him go before turning her attention to Drantos. "Are you sure it's safe for him to be traipsing around the woods at night? We didn't find a flashlight or anything to use as a weapon. Aren't there wild animals around here that we should be worried about? The fire is here, not out there. He won't be able to see them but I'm sure the same can't be said for anything that might attack him."

Any hope Dusti had of warning her sister died when Drantos settled down crossed-legged right next to her. Only inches separated her hip from his knee. It was probably intentional, to remind her of the warning.

He shook his head. "We live in Alaska and were raised not too far from here. We know what we're doing. It's not unusual for us to hunt at night and nothing out there can hurt Kraven. Trust me on that one. He'll be back within the hour and have something for us to eat."

"I couldn't even find a real knife, just plastic ones." Bat carefully sat down on a cushion and tucked her skirt neatly around her legs. "How will he skin it? I guess he could try to tear off part of the plane. Some of it is pretty jagged and sharp."

Dusti wanted to scream in frustration. They were in danger but her sister seemed fixated on how someone would get them food. Bat didn't realize missing dinner was the least of their worries. They may have survived a plane crash, only to become victims of two men who had something against their biological grandfather. It just wasn't fair or right.

Drantos reached inside his boot and pulled out an impressively large folded switchblade. "He's got one of these."

"But those are illegal to take on planes," Bat sputtered. "How did you get that past security to smuggle it onboard?"

He arched a dark eyebrow. "We have our ways, and the smaller airports are more lax about rules up here. It's common to carry weapons when you're flying in and out of smaller airports. It's life in Alaska. Don't worry about it." He shoved the knife back inside his boot. "He'll be fine. He's going to bring back something tasty to eat and then we'll all get some shuteye."

Bat turned her head to peer at Dusti. "Help will find us tomorrow. I bet they're already putting together a huge search party to look for us as soon as the sun rises. We'll be rescued in no time and will arrive at our grandfather's house by tomorrow night."

Dusti noticed Drantos tense up next to her. Her heart raced but she said nothing, afraid he might hurt Bat if she did. He and his brother looked like real badass thugs with their muscular bodies and dark looks...and they *did* dress as though they were bikers. They kept switchblades inside their boots, for cripes' sake. Nice guys didn't do that.

Then she noticed something else when she studied his handsome features.

"Your cut is gone." She stared hard at his once-injured cheek.

He frowned. "I washed my face. The blood wasn't mine. I'm assuming it splattered on me from someone else in the crash."

Confusion had Dusti shaking her head. "It was cut. I saw it myself."

"Do you see it now?" He cocked his head toward the firelight to show her that side of his face better. "It was just blood, not even mine. It wiped right off."

Dusti let it go. She'd been traumatized at the time and must have just assumed he'd been cut when she'd seen the blood. He obviously didn't have a mar on his skin.

Bat sighed. "I'm really sorry I dragged you along, Dusti. You'd be safe inside your apartment right now, watching one of those lame shows you love so much if it wasn't for me. I...I manipulated you into taking this trip. I knew you'd insist on coming with me as soon as I told you who I was planning to visit. I didn't want to go alone, and I thought it would be nice to spend some time together since this is technically my vacation."

"It's not your fault. You didn't know this would happen. No one could have. I *did* insist on coming, remember? We know each other well. I've manipulated you a few times into doing what I wanted. We've never kept track before. Stop beating yourself up. Shit happens."

"You made me go watch a few movies with you." Bat teared up. "Big difference. I might have been bored but we were always safe."

"The neighborhoods weren't the greatest," Dusti reminded her. "You were always pointing out that we could get mugged, carjacked, or murdered when I took you out. Flying is supposed to be safer than driving."

Drantos cleared his throat. "You were on your way to visit your grandfather?"

Bat seemed to get her emotions under control. "Thanks, Dusti." She turned her attention to Drantos. "Our grandfather is terminally ill and he wanted me to come say goodbye to him. He's a mean old bastard but he's the only family we have left. He and Dusti never got along, so he didn't bother to invite her, but I told her I was going to see him. I'd hoped she could make her peace with him before he dies."

"Why don't they get along?" Drantos's tone sounded casual but Dusti knew better.

"Oh, as I said, he's a tough old bastard. Our mother ran away from home as a teenager and moved to California, where she met our father a few years later, and they had the two of us. When we were young..." Bat hesitated, thinking. "I must have been seven and Dusti about five when our grandfather showed up at our front door. He'd somehow found out where we lived. We moved after that, but we still saw him again when we were about ten and twelve. He invited me to visit him for the summer but he didn't want my sister to go. I guess he just didn't like the way Dusti refused to speak to him, or maybe he thought she'd be a pain in the ass."

Bat chuckled, winking at Dusti. "You always *were* a brat. She pitched a fit to stop me from going with him, so I stayed home. I didn't want to go by myself anyway. I didn't know him that well."

"He was cold and he never talked to me," Dusti informed Drantos quietly. She focused on her sister. "He gave me the creeps. It wasn't that I didn't want you to go spend the summer in Alaska. It was that I didn't want you to go with *him*. I still think something is wrong with that guy, like maybe he's a pervert or something. Mom always refused to talk about why she ran away from home except to say he planned a life for her that she wanted nothing to do with. If you'll remember, it was *Mom* who refused to let you go anywhere with her father. That should have spoken volumes that something is really off with him. She flat-out told us to have nothing to do with him and we moved both times after he showed up. It was obvious she hated him. Maybe he tried to molest her. He was too nice to you."

"She would have just told us if that were true."

"She always tried to protect us, Bat. I'm the quiet one, remember? I tend to watch people," Dusti reminded her sister. "And Mom seemed almost afraid when he showed up. She wouldn't even talk about the birds and the bees until we were teens and already knew everything. Do you *really* think she was going to explain perverted sickos to us when we were that young?"

Bat fingered her jacket hem. "It doesn't matter anymore. He's rich and dying. We're his only family that I know of. I think it's a good idea if we spend a little time with him."

"What she means is," Dusti looked back at Drantos, "she hopes he'll leave us something in his will. I don't want his money. I hope when he dies, they stuff it all up his ass and he takes every dime with him."

"Damn it, Dusti." Bat shot her a glare. "You live in a crappy-ass apartment, barely scraping by. I tried to talk you into going to college after I graduated but you wouldn't go." She switched her attention to Drantos. "She's seriously pissed at our grandfather. Our parents died the year I turned eighteen and I tracked him down via phone. He refused to send us any money. We had to sell the house to survive. I had just started college full-time, with a heavy study load, and we had to use the money from the house to support us until Dusti graduated high school. We couldn't afford college for both of us at the same time, so when I graduated, it was supposed to be Dusti's turn. She worked to help me finish law school and I wanted to do the same for her, but she refused to go."

Dusti turned her head to stare directly into Drantos's dark gaze. "We haven't seen that asshole since we were kids. We're not close to him and he didn't send us one cent in all those years we were struggling. He doesn't care about either of us. I don't think he would have even called Bat if it weren't for the fact he's dying and probably trying to be nice for once, thinking he'll earn some brownie points to get him into heaven." She shot a dirty look at her sister. "Not that it will work. That bastard is going straight to hell."

"You're right. He *is* an asshole but I'm still hoping he leaves us something in his will. Why should it go to total strangers?" Bat huffed. "You say *I'm* the negative, jaded one. You have more compassion for strangers than you do for your own family. He was our mother's father."

"He's an asshole who had plenty of money but didn't step in when we needed help. We had to sell the home we lived in with our *parents*, Bat! We survived on peanut butter sandwiches a lot of times and lived in hellholes just to have a roof over our heads. What kind of jerk lets that happen?"

"Blame me," Bat whispered. "I probably made bad decisions. Maybe there was another way to get by that I couldn't think of at the time." Tears filled her eyes. "I should have sent you to college first at least. I would have made it easier on you if I had just let go of my dream."

"You earned those scholarships, Bat. I wasn't letting you waste the help they offered." Dusti looked away, hating to hear Bat's guilt one more time. There was no reason for it. "Just stop. We've had this argument a thousand times. I'm not mad at you. You're an awesome attorney, even if I think you're working on the wrong side of the law. You're doing what you love. I'm just pissed that our grandfather could have sent money to help us out. He's rich enough that it wouldn't have been any skin off his nose. He didn't."

She looked back at her sister. "He deserves to die alone and miserable. We shouldn't even be here because neither one of us owes him a second of our time." She curled her hands in her lap. "I don't give a shit about the money. I like my life just fine the way it is. I'm used to struggling. It builds character."

Bat smiled. "You remember me saying that, huh?"

"All the time, usually when I was bitching about whatever lame job I had to deal with in high school." Dusti smiled back. "We don't need anything from him."

"It's just a few days of our time. We go, see what he wants, and leave. Perhaps he regrets his actions, or lack thereof."

"Fat chance. He's a dick, Bat." Dusti addressed Drantos once more. "He doesn't care about us. Do you understand what I'm saying? It would be a mistake if someone were to think otherwise. We're nobody to him and not worth anyone's time if they have a grudge against that bastard. I could totally relate to it if someone did. The only reason I'm here is to spend time with my sister, since she doesn't take vacations. This is the first one she's had in five years. Plus, I don't want her alone with that asshole. I never liked him as a kid and I still don't. I believe he tried to molest our mother, or something equally terrible. She told us to stay away from him, to tell her if he ever contacted us, and you don't do that with a loving grandparent."

"I'll kick his ass if he's some kind of pervert," her sister muttered. "I'm the meaner of the two of us."

Drantos silently watched Dusti. She held his gaze. In the firelight his dark blue stare had taken on golden flecks that she hadn't noticed before. He had gorgeous eyes, framed with thick, long black eyelashes. Even their shape was attractive, kind of exotic looking. He'd be extremely handsome if his bone structure wasn't so severe.

"I understand," he acknowledged softly.

Dusti relaxed slightly and turned her attention to the other passengers who had survived the crash. Most of them were sleeping but a few remained sitting upright. They huddled together in small groups, talking. A couple of them had been severely injured but were hanging in there.

Bat fiddled with her clothes, which drew Dusti's attention.

"Your suit is ruined. You can try to smooth out that skirt until your hands fall off but it's toast. Were you able to find our suitcases?"

"No. The belly of the plane ripped open so the bags were scattered all over the place. It was getting too dark to widen the search. We only brought back those few suitcases so people could use whatever clothes were in them to help keep warm tonight. I'll look again in the morning. Until then, I'm stuck wearing this. I refuse to put on some stranger's outfits." Bat tried to button her jacket.

"Give it up," Dusti urged.

"I'm trying to do something, anything. I'm not used to just sitting around, and I'm hungry."

Drantos stood. "Kraven forgot to pass out the food you salvaged from the plane before he went hunting. I'll do that now so you can eat something while we wait. Just say my name if you need anything. I have *very* good hearing." He shot Dusti another warning look before moving away.

"Weird guys, huh?" Bat watched him walk to the pile of stuff on the ground. "I'm totally getting 'future client' vibes off both of them but they don't have dead eyes, so I think we're safe."

"It scares me that you can say shit like that. Dead eyes?"

"You'd know if you saw them. Trust me."

Dusti lowered her voice. "Bat, we need to get out of here and away from them."

"Fuck that! Those guys were raised in Alaska, and look at what they've done so far. They handled setting up a camp and built a fire. There's no way I'm going to go walking into the woods to get lost searching for a cabin or a house that might have a working phone. It would be like finding a needle in a haystack. Our best hope of being rescued is to stay beside the crash site. I'm sure there're plenty of signs from above that we went down, where the plane took out those trees. It will probably resemble a path from way up there when the search planes fly over. Like it or not, we're stuck with these guys, and trust me, I'm not happy with that concept. Kraven is a lunatic." She lowered her voice to a whisper. "But he's *hot*."

Astonishment tore through Dusti. She glanced at Drantos to find him watching her from not too far away. He was close enough to overhear them. She didn't dare warn her sister of the real danger yet. "You're attracted to Kraven? Do you have a concussion? I realize you were thrown out of your seat into the aisle and hit your head. You still have a mark on the side of your temple. He's not your type, Bat. A briefcase isn't surgically attached to his hand and he doesn't have news anchor helmet-head hair."

Bat smirked. "I did hit my head but nothing is wrong with my eyesight. I see the way Biker Bear there has his eye on *you*, and how you keep watching him when you think he's not looking." Bat climbed to her feet. "I have to pee. I'll be back."

"But—"

Dusti talked to air as her sister disappeared into the tree line.

She sighed. She needed to warn her sister about the brothers but she feared Drantos would hurt them if he knew she'd tried. Her attention returned to the man, only to witness him glaring at the area her sister had disappeared into. He shoved a bottle of water at a passenger before storming in that same direction.

"Drantos!" She pushed herself up to a standing position, feeling a second of dizziness. His head snapped in her direction and he shot her a seriously pissed look as she caught up with him at the tree line. "She had to go to the bathroom. You don't want to follow her into the woods. She'll be right back."

He'd gripped her arms in a heartbeat and jerked her into the woods. In seconds, she found herself out of the firelight with her back pressed against the bark of the nearest tree.

Drantos glared down at her, his tight hold on her arms nearly bruising. She could see his features since he faced the fire behind her in the small clearing.

"What did you tell her?"

"Nothing! I swear."

His suspicious gaze narrowed. He released her arm, hesitated, and then cupped her cheek gently with his big warm hand. He lowered his face to hers, making her heart pound. She was pretty sure he planned to kiss her.

She jerked her head back when his hot breath fanned over her parted lips.

He froze. "I want some answers, and you're going to give them to me."

She swallowed the lump that formed in her throat. "Okay. Just please don't hurt us."

That response made his gaze narrow even more. "I've never harmed a woman before." He tilted his head a little, his focus lowered to roam down her body then back up. "You smell totally human. I couldn't get a good read on you before and thought it might just be your clothes. Some of us borrow already-worn clothing to fool the senses of others." Their gazes met again. "I take it your mother mated to one? You have human blood?"

Dusti stared up at him while his words sank in. "Shit. Seriously?"

He frowned. "Just answer the question. It's important."

Then it sank in that something was *really* wrong with Drantos.

She had a friend from high school who'd become paranoid and antisocial in his late twenties. He'd been diagnosed bipolar after a group of their friends had gone to check on him. They'd discovered he'd used rolls of aluminum to wrap all the walls of his apartment and screamed at them about how no one was safe. They'd called an ambulance. The meds they'd put him on helped him stay more rational, but she was familiar with how a chemical imbalance could mess with someone's sanity.

It was possible the guy in front of her had the same medical condition. He even sounded like Greg. It had all been about humans vs. aliens for her friend.

"Human? Is that what you said? It's bad enough that you're a possible kidnapper-for-ransom bad guy, but you're also off your meds, aren't you? Of *course* I'm human! So are you. You said my mother mated to one? Really? *Mated?* This is the planet Earth." She shook her head. "Could my day get any worse? What's next? A meteor shower? A forest fire? Maybe rabid squirrels will attack us."

He slowly smiled. "I enjoy your sense of humor." His smile fled. "Maybe you don't know my scent, but I'm the same as your mother was. Cut the act."

He was totally bonkers. She normally wouldn't have messed with someone like him and just backed away, but he had her pinned where she stood. "You used to be a woman?" She looked him up and down. "That's the best sex change I've ever seen. Wow. Impressive. I never would have guessed. You might want to back down on the male hormone shots. I think you've overdosed on them."

"What?" He looked angry.

"You just said you were what my mom was. She was a woman. Were you born a little girl and then had a sex change? Otherwise, I wouldn't say that." She smirked.

He studied her face and then paled a little. "Shit. You're not acting, are you? You don't know, do you?"

"Know what? That you're bipolar and went off your meds? I'm understanding that fact real quick. Didn't your doctors warn you that you'd lose your grasp on reality if you stopped taking them? Let me guess. You felt better and thought you were cured. Listen, the only way for you to be functional is to continue taking your pills. Do you have them with you? Let's find you some water, okay? You'll feel much better within a few days once you're back on them."

He stayed quiet for long seconds, studying her face again, until she shifted her body from the uncomfortable moment. His eyes closed and his head tilted back.

"Shit. You have *no* clue."

"Believe me, I do." She patted him awkwardly. "I have a friend like you. He goes off his meds sometimes too. It's going to be fine. Where are your pills? I'll help you. You've obviously stopped taking them, which has led you to think up some crazy scenario that will land your ass in prison if you end up hurting someone. Rethink it. My grandfather might be a dick but he's a human one. He's not some alien bad guy trying to attack Earth or whatever you think."

"I don't take meds."

"Of course you didn't. That's why you're like this."

He grew angry. "Shut it now. I'm not crazy."

He wasn't about to listen to reason. That was apparent. She decided to play along with his delusions. It was possible to reach him if he had any compassion. "Fine. All I'm asking is that you don't take it out on us if he doesn't do whatever you want. I'm serious about how he never lifted a finger to help us. I think he tolerates Bat, so he may give you money for her, or whatever you demand, but don't hold your breath when it comes to me. He flat-out didn't even want me to come to Alaska and was kind of a prick when Bat mentioned bringing me. He told her no, but she never listens to anyone.

"I came because I just wanted to spend time with her and—bonus—he's dying. I really hated him as a kid. He treated me like I didn't exist when he came to our house. Do you know what that does to a little girl? He made me cry at first, wondering what I'd done to make my own grandfather hate me. I finally came to the realization that he was just an asshole."

"I'm not going to ransom you. Is your illness real? Did you need that shot your sister gave you?"

She bit back a curse. He was really into his delusions. "Of course. Like any sane person would want to be jabbed with needles. I'm not a drug addict. I don't get high. I really needed it. It's for my anemia. I have a rare form of it. Iron pills don't work."

Drantos looked down at her, his gorgeous eyes seeming to study her again. "You're flawed. Decker would consider that an embarrassment to his bloodline. I assume your sister doesn't have to take any form of medications?"

"No."

"I didn't think so, if Decker wants her to come to him."

"Okay," she said slowly. "Whatever that means."

"It's all about the bloodlines sometimes." A thoughtful expression gripped his handsome features. "I believe I'm starting to figure out why he sent for your sister."

"Again with the whatever that means."

"There would have been a larger chance of birthing a weak-blooded child when your mother bred with your father. You're flawed, as far as Decker is concerned, but your sister is still useful to him. You're dependent on those shots. I take it that you've had this condition most, if not all of your life?"

"I was diagnosed as an infant. It's severe anemia, not a *flaw* or an illness. My body just doesn't produce enough iron and I have to take supplements. We have that in common. Where are your pills? You need them just like I need my shots."

"With our people, any type of need for medicine makes you flawed. It means you're weak. And you smell totally human."

He completely ignored her question about his pills. It irritated her. "What planet are you from? Mars? Saturn? I'm thinking Uranus."

He caressed her cheek. "Very funny." He didn't look amused. "Don't scream or be afraid. I need to know how human you truly are."

That so doesn't sound good for me, she thought, her body stiffening. She wanted to fight, to push him away, but instead held very still when he tilted his head to lower his face into the crook of her neck. A shiver ran down her spine and goose bumps broke out down her arms when his hot breath fanned her sensitive skin.

She had no idea what he would do but fighting him would be as effective as trying to attack a tree. The blows would only hurt her hands, and she knew she couldn't move the heavy guy away from her.

Something warm and slightly wet dragged along the top of her shoulder. She gasped when pain jolted that area for a second before his warm tongue flicked where the pain had emanated from. Her eyes widened and her hands gripped his shirt. She pushed at him when she realized he had licked her.

A deep growl sent her heart into overdrive but he didn't budge an inch. His tongue left her skin but his hot breath against her neck remained. The sound he'd made reminded her of a vicious dog. It scared her.

He stayed in that position, breathing on her neck, and kept her pinned against the tree. She stopped pushing when it was clear it didn't work.

"Not *all* human," he rasped. "I can faintly taste it on you, but it's very weak." He suddenly chuckled. "You're not ill. You're just starving for what you really need. Marvilella's bloodline is stronger in you than Decker's is. Your father's blood is also strong, and masks it."

The guy is flat-out bonkers, she realized, deciding he must be *just* like Greg. He probably saw aliens everywhere, certain they were spying on Earthlings so they could attack one day.

The smile that curved his mouth shouldn't have surprised her, but it did when he lifted his head.

"Your grandfather doesn't realize what you are. You smell completely human and he took that at face value."

"Okay." Dusti cleared her throat. "Can we go back to the fire now? I'm cold."

"You don't know what I'm talking about, do you?"

"Not a word."

"Do you know who Marvilella was?"

"No."

He shook his head and his hand returned to cup her cheek. The pad of his thumb stroked her skin lightly. "She was your grandmother."

"My mom said her mother died when she was a teenager but it was too painful to talk about. They were really close. That was her name?" Dusti wasn't sure if she could believe a word out of his mouth. His mind obviously wasn't all there but he did seem to know more about her grandfather than she did. It was possible he knew about his wife. "What kind of weird name is that? It sounds European."

"She came from my clan and married your grandfather to bring peace between us."

Dusti let that statement settle into her brain. *Nope, he's totally unreasonable and gone,* she concluded. Nothing he said made sense and it sounded as though he'd watched way too many movies. "Just stop. Let me go."

"You need to understand what you've been brought into. Decker Filmore is dangerous to you and your sister. You said yourself your mother warned you, that she disliked him. Bat said she died. Is that true?"

"Yes." She pushed at his chest again but he didn't budge. "Nobody would lie about a horrible thing like losing both of their parents."

"Decker didn't molest your mother. He killed your grandmother so she wouldn't stand in his way anymore. That's when your mother fled. We assumed she figured out it was no accidental death. He wanted to use his daughter to bargain with Aveoth. To Antina, death would have been preferable. Trust me. Now I understand why he'd want your sister to come to him. It's the only way he could force Aveoth to break our alliance. Bat is his bargaining chip to start a war."

"I'm glad one of us understands what you're saying. Did you know my mother? You seem to have."

"I know more about your family than you seem to. Aveoth's lover died a week ago. He'll be looking for another to replace her...and he wouldn't be able to resist your sister if she were offered to him."

"Offered to him? Who the hell is Aveoth? Some alien warlord in your head?"

"Stop with the aliens. I'm not insane. Aveoth is a powerful clan leader. He will be looking for a new lover and Decker will give your sister to him."

"Whatever." She was getting a headache trying to make sense of his ranting. "You're making my grandfather sound like some pimp, as if my sister is a hooker. She's not."

"I'm telling you the truth."

"Oh hell," Dusti sighed. "I'm not even going to try to follow what you're saying. There's medication out there that will help you. You really need to see your doctor. I believe Decker Filmore is a rich ol' perv, but you're saying he wants to turn Bat into some kind of hooker? No way."

"Your mother should have told you the truth."

"About what? That there are crazy people who live in their own made-up worlds? She covered that when I started noticing boys and she taught me about stranger danger."

He hesitated. "Now isn't the time to go into all of this. We're going to talk later, when we're somewhere more private."

She wasn't about to point out that he'd dragged her out of the clearing so no one could see them. She just wanted to get away from him. "Great. Let me go."

He took a deep breath. "Your mother wasn't human."

"Really?" Dusti relaxed, the bark of the tree lightly digging into her back when she leaned away from the man pinning her to it. "She was an alien?"

He smirked and his eyes seemed to crinkle at the corners. "We're from the same planet, just different worlds."

"Ah. That makes total sense." Dusti rolled her eyes, not caring if he saw her reaction. "So we're talking different dimensions? Okay. Why don't you let me go and return to yours then? Have a safe trip. Do you click your boot heels together to get there?"

The amusement left his strangely intriguing gaze. "There's the world that humans live in and the part of it that they never see."

"Ghosts then?" She couldn't resist. Her hands brushed the front of his shirt, feeling the warmth that seemed to radiate from him even through the thin cotton material. "You feel solid enough to me."

A soft growl came from deep within his throat. It disturbed Dusti, frightened her. She pressed tighter against the tree and jerked her hands away from his chest. Something in his dark gaze flashed, seeming to glow for a split second, before he leaned in closer until their noses touched.

"We'll discuss this later." He backed off, released her, and took a few steps away. "Return to camp."

Drantos watched Dusti stumble away, nearly running back to the blanket. The taste of her blood remained on his tongue. He'd only taken a few drops, but it was enough.

She didn't know what she was. It stunned and pissed him off at the same time. He thought she might have been lying at first but her responses were proof enough. She thought he was crazy and didn't believe anything he'd said.

Uranus. He snorted and turned, quickly moving into the woods. The sister was easy to find. She softly cursed, almost walking into a tree. Her night vision seemed nonexistent.

He approached her, making sounds so she wouldn't be alarmed. She froze, eyes widening.

"It's Drantos," he called out.

She turned in his direction. "I went too far. I can't find the camp."

That made his anger deepen. It was obvious *she* didn't know what she was, either, and her senses were those of a human. She was only about fifty yards from temporary camp but the thick vegetation blocked the fire from her view. She still should have been able to smell burning wood and hear the soft voices of the survivors.

He reached out and curved his fingers around her upper arm. "I'll lead you back."

"Thanks."

"I take it you can't see anything?"

"No. I hope I didn't pee in poison ivy."

"There isn't any in this area."

"That's the best news I've heard all day." She gripped his arm as they walked. "Thank you for looking after my sister."

He escorted Bat past the edge of the trees to the clearing. "Could you help me calm some of the passengers? They're still pretty upset." He wanted to keep her away from Dusti. "I think you'd do a better job of it than I would. My size seems to scare a few of them."

"Sure." She turned her head, staring at her sister. "I should check on her first."

"She's fine. I just left her to look for you. She was worried."

Bat walked away from him and toward an elderly couple. He stood there watching her, to ensure she kept far from Dusti. He needed to think.

Decker Filmore had been denied using his own daughter to bargain with Aveoth when she'd fled, but now he must be planning on doing the same thing with her daughters. *Daughter*, he corrected. *Decker believes he can only use Bat.* He mistook Dusti's scent to mean she didn't inherit any of her mother's traits.

Aveoth would never want to take Dusti as his lover with her being so human. She'd be considered too frail. She'd age faster too, if the harsh life of living with the GarLycan didn't kill her outright. He'd want Bat instead. She'd be considered more worthy because at least there were hints of some of her mother's heritage, implying she would be tougher.

The smell of a fresh kill teased his nose and so did the familiar scent of Kraven. He backed into the darkness and located his brother quickly. Kraven dumped the deer on the ground and bent, wiping his hands on the grass to clean them of blood.

He heard Drantos approach. "That was easier than I'd thought."

"I know why Decker sent for the women."

"I've been thinking about it too. Aveoth lost his lover. They're Marvilella's granddaughters. Her sister was once promised to Aveoth, so he'll be interested in her kin."

"We're both in agreement then."

"Yeah. Decker wants to break the alliance we have with Aveoth. That is, if the rumors are true that Aveoth is addicted to that family's blood. Maybe it's just a bullshit tale."

"I don't want to bet on it. Do you?" Drantos softly growled, annoyed.

"Hell no."

"It's Bat that Decker will use. We can't allow that to happen."

"Damn." Kraven sighed. "I might want to wring the mouthy one's neck when she gets going but not literally. I thought about killing them at first but it was just the shock of finding out who they were. I got past that. I'm not going to hurt a helpless woman."

"We're not going to kill them. We need to get them to safety."

"Decker isn't going to just allow them to return to wherever they've been living. Hell, he probably sent some of his men searching for the crash site as soon as he realized what happened when the plane didn't land. We might have company by morning if they can pinpoint where we went down."

"Do you recognize this area? I think we're about fifteen miles from our southern border."

"I agree. That means Decker is about thirty miles away. The darkness will slow down whoever he sends but they can cover a lot of ground when the sun rises."

"We have the advantage," Drantos whispered. "Decker doesn't know someone warned us about those women, or that we were on the plane to stop them from reaching him. And we used false names so we're covered if he gets a look at the passenger list."

"That's true."

"We have another problem."

"What's that?"

Drantos hesitated but his brother needed to know. "Dusti and Bat don't know the truth."

"You mean that Decker plans to use one of them as a pawn?"

"I mean they're unaware of *anything* about our existence. Their mother mated to a human and they were raised that way."

Kraven sucked in a sharp breath and his eyes widened. *"What?"*

"I mentioned to Dusti that she smells totally human and she had no idea what I was talking about. She thought I was crazy. They honestly believe Decker is dying of old age or illness."

"Son of a bitch." Kraven growled. "I thought that was just a bullshit story they made up, hoping to fool us. And that they're really good at masking their scents. I figured they just perfected how to do it while living with humans."

"Nope. Dusti is clueless and I'm certain Bat is too. I found her lost not far from the camp. She's never been trained to use her senses. Her mother would have done that if she had told them what they were."

"But how is that even possible? They lived in a city with Lycans and Vamps. I could pick up a hint of what Bat was right after the crash. She has a few small cuts. It's faint but there. Why haven't any Lycans or Vampires gone after her? They would have attacked her as soon as they got a whiff. You think the mom is protecting them? She might have made some kind of pact to protect her daughters with both packs and nests."

"Antina is dead."

"You sure?"

"You were gone when they discussed losing their parents. It happened when they were younger."

"None of this makes sense." Kraven softly growled. "Maybe they left Bat alone because she's a lawyer? I've heard some of the city packs have an agreement not to touch someone with an important job. Doctors, lawyers…even anyone in law enforcement can be seen as neutral and helpful to all of them, regardless of their associations. They sometimes work together to keep humans from discovering the truth. But that doesn't explain why Vamps leave her alone, unless she's got a client associated with them. Maybe she unknowingly keeps their day guards out of prison? They'd want her protected if that's the case."

"I agree."

"This just gets better and better." Kraven sighed again. "I can't believe what a mess this has become."

"I know."

"I still think maybe those sisters aren't as ignorant as they're leading us to believe. I'll buy that the younger one might not know the truth. I smelled her when Bat gave her a shot. There was nothing to indicate she's more than what she seems. I can understand how she could pass as totally human, but the older one? Not a chance. She has periods, she bleeds. At some point she'd have *had* to cross paths with someone who hates our kind enough to go after her, regardless of any city rules or her being on the payroll of some suck head. Lawyers make enemies. That means she had to know how to defend herself."

Drantos considered it. "Maybe the packs are confused by her human blood. I smelled her too when she was still bleeding. It's possible they believe she's half Lycan, since that's all I picked up off her. Not all half-breeds are taken into a pack. They get rejected for being too human and never showing any traits. She'd be deemed harmless."

"Maybe."

"It's possible none of them would even consider that one of us would live amongst them. We stay with our clans. Anyone checking into her would know she isn't just visiting the area. She has a job and a home in the city."

"I will say that Bat seems to really love her sister. Is it possible her and the mother decided not to tell the mostly human one? To keep her safe? Ignorance would have kept Dusti from doing anything to draw suspicion. Humans are oblivious to our kind unless they know what to look for."

"I'm stumped by the entire mess, Kraven. I don't think Bat was aware of me out in the woods. It would have been easy for her to find the camp if she had used her senses."

"I don't trust Bat. She's sneaky. Just keep your guard up around her. I think she knows exactly what she is."

"Why would she visit Decker? I can't see her agreeing to be handed over to Aveoth. Her mother fled to avoid that from happening. She would have warned Bat that Decker might plot to do the same thing to her one day. Do you think Bat realized he'd take her by force, so she figured it would be easier if she just came back on her own?"

"Maybe it's a revenge quest for Bat. Her mother fled Decker and had to give up her heritage to live amongst humans. That had to be tough and it left her without the safety of numbers. We should find out how Antina died. Maybe it wasn't a human who took her life. Decker might have wanted his daughter out of the way by killing her. I'd want revenge for *our* mother, if that were the case. Perhaps Bat thinks she can kill him if she gets close enough. We'll have to proceed with caution, but one thing is certain. Decker is going to come after the granddaughter he can use. He needs to force Aveoth to side with him."

"I agree. Decker murdered his own mate out of greed and from what I've guessed, he wasn't able to find his runaway daughter until after she'd mated to a human and had two daughters of her own. Aveoth already had Lane as his lover by then, so Decker had to bide his time until Aveoth needed another."

Kraven softly cursed. "Do you think Decker had Lane murdered?"

Drantos debated it but then shook his head. "No way in hell. Aveoth sent guards to keep her safe the few times she visited her parents. Decker and his enforcers wouldn't have been able to get to her."

"We're not even sure how she died, though."

"I'm certain Aveoth would have left a trail of blood if someone had murdered his lover, until he found the one responsible."

Kraven nodded. "Yeah. He's not one to fuck with."

"No. He's not. Decker wouldn't be a problem anymore if he'd ordered Lane's assassination. Aveoth would have ripped him apart to avenge her."

"Perhaps he's become as cold as we've heard."

"Regardless, it would be a pride thing. If someone took something of his, they'd pay in blood for that offense and lose their lives."

"True."

"We can't allow Decker to get his hands on either granddaughter. Dusti might smell all human but she's not. I tested a few drops of her blood."

Kraven groaned. "Fantastic. That means we'll have to take them back to our clan, where he won't be able to get to them."

"I know."

"Decker will try to get them back by force."

"I'd rather we have to fight Decker's clan than Aveoth's. We have a chance of winning."

"What if he tells Aveoth we have them? Father would have to hand over the sister to avoid a fight with him."

"Let's worry about that after we get them to the safety of our clan."

"One problem at a time." Kraven nodded. "Right." He paused. "You understand that taking them home will put us all in danger, don't you?"

Drantos reached up and rubbed the back of his neck. "Of course I do. I'd rather deal with Aveoth directly over Decker. He's not insane."

"Are you certain? It's been many years since we've spoken to him. He's changed a lot since then."

"Aveoth has honor."

"We hope he still does. Who knows what happened to make him take over his clan. I mean, he killed his own father to do it. That's pretty cold."

One of the passengers started to raise hell. Drantos cocked his head, listening to what the man was ranting about. He was starting to panic the other survivors about being attacked by wild animals or dying if the wreckage wasn't spotted by rescue teams.

"I'll go deal with that," he announced. "You work on getting them fed."

Chapter Three

Bat collapsed on a blanket near Dusti hours later. The wind had picked up, leaving a definite chill in air. Dusti had watched her sister keep busy helping Kraven pass out the food after he'd dragged the deer carcass into the clearing. It had been impressive watching him roast meat on sticks over the fire. Afterward, Drantos and Bat worked together to get everyone comfortable enough to sleep.

"I'm never going to look at venison the same way again. It's really disturbing how good that man is with a knife." Bat smirked.

Dusti glanced around looking for Drantos, and found him standing too close for her comfort, dumping more wood into a pile by the fire. She still wanted to warn her sister that he was crazy. It seemed he was never going to give her a perfect opportunity so she just needed to do it. She lowered her voice.

"Remember my friend Greg?"

Bat nodded. "The nut."

Dusti winced. "He's bipolar. So is Drantos."

Bat stared at her. "What?"

Dusti nodded. "Keep your voice down. He doesn't want me to say anything to you but he's off his meds." She glanced at Drantos and found him staring at her. She waited until one of the passengers said something to him and he broke eye contact with her. "Don't say anything, because I'm afraid it will set him off, but he thinks our grandfather is some alien or something. He hates him and plans to use us to get back at him somehow."

Bat paled. "Are you sure?"

"Yes."

"Damn." Bat frowned. "That runs in families sometimes, doesn't it? That means the brother might have the same condition."

"Did you hear what I said? We're in danger!"

"I heard. I have some clients like that. Just be cool and go along with anything he says. We'll be rescued and the paramedics can sedate him until they get him the help he needs."

Dusti nodded. It was sound advice.

"This sucks. I kinda like the brother." Bat glanced anywhere but at Dusti. "He's different. I've never met anyone like him before."

Dusti worried. "You're attracted to him?"

Bat held Dusti's gaze. "Nothing can come of it long term but he's definitely one-night-stand material. I admit I'm thinking about it."

"*No*," Dusti whispered. "Trust me for once. He went along with Drantos's crazy plan of grabbing us on that plane. What does that tell you?"

"He's probably used to dealing with the nut job and just placates him. It's what you do. How many times have you visited Greg, only to find him wearing his metal helmet so aliens can't feel his presence or some such nonsense? You actually told him you found an alien-free zone to trick him into going to see his doctor, so they could admit him to the hospital and put him back on his medication until he was stable again. You even wore one of his spare helmets to drive him so he felt secure that they couldn't read *your* mind to find *him*."

"He wouldn't get in my car otherwise."

"But you do it. That's my point. And he's just your *friend*. Kraven and Drantos are brothers. He probably just plays along when Drantos is having an episode of whatever the hell is wrong with him. At least he's still functional. He helped set up this camp and built a fire pit. I bet Greg would be screaming that aliens were going to kidnap us if he were with us right now, and trying to make another helmet out of the plane wreckage."

She couldn't deny that. "I—"

"We have enough wood to last us all night." Drantos suddenly dropped to his knees on the edge of Dusti's spread-out blanket. He shot her a warning glance before he turned his full attention on her sister. "The temperatures are going to drop lower tonight but everyone will be fine with the fire burning. What were you two talking about?"

"Dusti is worried about her friend at home. She likes to call him every day to make sure he's okay, but of course she can't since we're here. He's sickly. I was just telling her someone else would check in on him," Bat said without missing a beat. "It's so cold already. Don't tell me it'll get worse?" Bat changed the subject and wrapped her arms around her waist, hugging her middle. "The wind is already icy."

Movement had all of them glancing toward the woods in time to watch Kraven step out of the darkness. He'd gone to clean up after cooking the deer. He strode to the pile of things taken from the destroyed plane, bent, grabbed two blankets, and then approached. He spread one of them on the ground.

"The area is secure. There's nothing near us that could become a danger." He winked at his brother. "The bear didn't enjoy being chased off but he's far north now."

"Bear?" Bat's eyes widened with alarm. "Will it come back and attack? Some of these people are injured. Won't the smell of blood attract it to come investigate?"

"He won't return." Kraven shoved the other blanket under one arm. "I'm wiped out."

"It's been a long day," Drantos agreed. "We'll get up early and reevaluate the situation."

Kraven sat down on his blanket and dropped the rolled one next to his lap. He peeled off his leather jacket next. In seconds, he'd bunched it into a ball to shove behind him. He completely ignored the women while he spoke to his brother.

"The search-and-rescue teams will easily spot this mess from above. I tracked back and there's a lot of damage to the trees. They can't miss it."

"We need to make a decision then." Drantos motioned his head in the direction of the survivors. "Stay or go? You know he'll have heard the news by now and sent out his enforcers to find them."

"I was thinking the same." Kraven sighed. "We'll leave at dawn before they can find the site. We'll have to move fast. They'll be tracking us as soon as they realize some of us are missing."

Drantos nodded. "It's going to be rough."

"What are you talking about?" Bat frowned. "Are you wanted by the police? You're plotting to take off before the rescue teams arrive, aren't you?"

Both brothers turned their attention on Bat, silently regarding her. Dusti opened her mouth to tell her sister to shut up. She was afraid Bat would set them off somehow and make the situation worse. Bat spoke again before she could.

She blew out a breath. "I'm a defense attorney. I can help."

Dusti's mouth sagged open in surprise, then outrage. "You're offering to represent them? *Really*?"

"It's what I do, and while I didn't appreciate getting manhandled, they *did* get banged up in the crash trying to protect us. And the meal was good too. It beat eating those tiny cookie and nut packages we found on the plane." Bat shrugged.

"I just..." Dusti stopped talking before she blurted out that she'd *just* informed her sister that Drantos was off his meds. She worried he'd have some kind of meltdown if he realized she'd shared his secret.

Bat smoothed things over. "You know who my clients are, Dusti. It's what I do. They have the constitutional right of being represented in a court of law, even if they *are* guilty. I know the justice system is flawed but everyone deserves the best defense possible. Innocent until proven guilty. Ring any bells?" Bat lifted her chin, her gaze narrowing on her sister. "I know you hate my job but I'm damn good at it. I'd defend Greg if he hurt someone."

She shouldn't be surprised by her sister offering her services. At least she'd have a good defense for Drantos—insanity. "I know that." Dusti sighed. "I'm tired. It's been an awful day and I just want to get some sleep."

"Good idea." Drantos suddenly shifted his position and slid to his hands and knees, facing Dusti. "Move over and make room for me on the blanket."

"What?" She gaped at him.

"The temperature is going to drop more within a few hours. Take off my jacket, we'll use it for a pillow, and I'll keep you warm."

"I'm not sleeping with you!"

Those strangely beautiful eyes of his seemed to glow for a split second again. It startled Dusti and made her realize she hadn't just imagined seeing it in the woods.

"You are." His voice deepened. "Lie down on your side after you take off my jacket. My body heat will keep you warm if I spoon with you. My brother and I are going to make sure both of you make it through the night."

"Hell no," Kraven groaned. "They can keep their own body heat."

"They can't." Drantos stretched out beside Dusti and literally pushed her over a few inches to make room for him. "You know they need us."

Kraven clenched his teeth, the muscles in his jaw tensing visibly. "I'll trade you."

Drantos seemed to ignore the comment, instead arching an eyebrow at Dusti. "Take the jacket off now and lie down."

"No."

The blue of his eyes turned colder. "*Now*. You and I are going to curl up and get some rest together. You will allow me to hold you to keep you warm."

A shiver ran down her spine at his raspy, deep tone. Fear had her moving to do as he'd ordered. She removed his warm jacket. She shivered again, this time from the cold, and handed it to him.

"Wait a minute," Bat protested. She gasped in the next instant.

Dusti swung her head to stare where her sister had been, only to find her gone. She turned her head farther and spotted Bat flat on her back with Kraven stretched out next to her. He had one thigh over her sister's legs and his hand cupped her face. They seemed to be staring at each other, faces inches apart. She couldn't be sure though, since she couldn't see Kraven's eyes. But he had obviously put her sister in that position and had her pinned.

"He won't hurt her. He's just going to keep her warm and quiet until she falls asleep." Drantos gripped Dusti's arm to force her to face him. "Don't make me control you too. You wouldn't like it, and I wouldn't either."

"You're threatening to hurt me? You said you wouldn't do that." Fear shot up her spine.

He suddenly sat up and gripped her head. His long fingers curled around the back of her neck while his face drew closer. She stared into his gaze and saw the blue of his irises seem to lighten, turning a brighter shade. His hot breath fanned her lips when he leaned closer until their noses lightly touched. She couldn't look away from his incredible eyes. They stunned and frightened her at the same time. Eyes shouldn't change colors that way.

"I'm strong-blooded and you're not. I probably won't be able to take your free will but I can immobilize you. Your body will refuse to move. I'm ordering you to hold still."

Dusti attempted to lift her arm to push him back but her body didn't respond. Her limbs hung limply at her sides. Panic set in as she tried to do it again but it was as if she'd been paralyzed.

"Easy." Drantos's tone lowered, turning husky. "You're fine. I don't want to argue with you but it would be bad if you make a scene. We're going to cuddle up together nicely without you fighting me. If you resist, I'll keep you this way. Do you understand?"

She couldn't even form words to respond but a tiny whimper did manage to squeak past her parted lips. The brilliance of blue in his eyes dulled as suddenly as it had sharpened. Dusti gasped in air and was actually able to move when she jerked back. Drantos released her completely but didn't look away.

"How did you do that? Bat? Talk to me!"

Dusti leaned back, her hands clawing at the blanket, and inched farther away from Drantos. Her head turned when her sister didn't respond, only to find the other couple still frozen in the same position as before. She was suspicious that Kraven had control over her sister the same exact way Drantos had just controlled her.

Her mind refused to acknowledge that though. It was too unreal to be true. She found reasons instead. Her and Bat were tired, they'd had a rough day, and had survived a plane crash. It left them stunned and easily susceptible to wild thoughts and ideas. She latched hard onto that excuse. It sounded reasonable. People who'd survived traumatic events could be convinced of things not real or true. Their minds were messed up. Drantos had just used the power of suggestion. She'd listened subconsciously because he was crazy.

That had to be how psychopaths talked nice, sane people into following them.

His strong hand gripped her inner thigh and gave her a hard enough tug to make her fall flat onto her back. He came down on top of her. His weight pinned her but Drantos was nice enough to keep most of it off her rib cage so she could still pant from terror. His blue eyes began to lighten, brighten, and glow. She squeezed her eyes closed, twisting her head to the side to avoid him doing that to her again.

"Look at me."

She wanted to. There was something compelling about his husky voice that made her have to fight the command, but she managed to resist. She couldn't budge him when she pushed on his arms. "Get off me. Stop it!"

"Dusti? Look at me now." His voice deepened with almost inhuman gruffness.

Her eyes opened of their own accord and she turned her head enough to stare deeply into his brilliant, glowing blue gaze. Her breath caught inside her lungs and her hands stopped pushing to fall limply between them. Her entire body wilted.

"I didn't want to do this. I can smell your fear." He blinked. "You're safe and I won't harm you. Being able to use my eyes this way is one of the many gifts I inherited."

She tried to struggle but her body refused to obey, staying totally still under his heavier one. He adjusted his hips, moved one leg to push hers apart, and settled into the cradle of her thighs. Her skirt must have gotten pushed up, and her eyes widened with terror when she felt the hard press of an aroused Drantos against the vee of her panties. The rough denim of his pants brushed against bare skin.

"Easy, sweetheart. I'm not going to do anything to you. Yeah, you turn me on. It's that simple. But I won't act on it. You need to calm down and stop looking at me as if I'm going to attack you. I just want your word you'll stop fighting with me."

She couldn't speak. His eyes slowly returned to a dark blue color, the glow fading. She gasped in air the second her entire body turned ridged with alarm. Her hands lifted to fist in the material of his shirt.

"Don't make me control you again."

"What are you doing to me?" she whispered, afraid despite what he'd said. "*Stop* it."

"Your mother should have explained what she was so I don't have to. Maybe she thought there would be no reason to have to tell you about your bloodline, since you had a human father and must not have inherited any traits that would betray you to your enemies."

Dusti could deal with his crazy talk. She relaxed a little to allow her mind to calm down. With it came a sense of comfort she latched onto. "I'm not an alien."

But he might really be one…

No. That's nuts. Now he's making me lose my mind.

It was possible exhaustion and too much stress had taken their toll. That would explain it.

"I'm not either. There're regular humans but there are also other races. He took a deep breath, pressing against her chest a little while he inhaled. "I'm *other*—and so was your mom."

"Other?"

She wondered if Bat could hear them but doubted it, since they were a good five feet away from the other couple. Drantos also had lowered his voice to a soft, husky level that wouldn't travel. The voices from the survivors were just a murmur but their words weren't recognizable. Drantos didn't answer.

"Let me go. Please?"

He turned his head, reached for something, and then pulled the other blanket over their bodies. He met her gaze again but an almost sad expression softened his features. "Not until you know the truth."

Dusti hesitated. "Okay. Hit me with it. I'm dying to hear this. What was my mother?"

Sincerity softened his gaze further. "We're VampLycans."

"Sounds Russian or something."

"We're considered blooded wolves."

"You don't look red to me and you hide your tail really well in those tight jeans."

He ignored her smartass comment. "A long time ago, Lycans and Vampires banned together and had formed an alliance. The Vampires usually hired humans to protect them during the day, but they'd been betrayed too often and suffered heavy losses. They were desperate enough to turn to their enemies, the Lycans. It worked for a while. The Vampires got their protection and the Lycans enjoyed the lifestyle the Vampires could provide."

Dusti let that settle into her mind. She decided to humor him. "They had good parties, huh?"

Drantos's features tensed. "This isn't a joke. I'm attempting to inform you of your heritage."

Irritation arose inside her at having to listen to his insane garbage. "Two words for you: Take. Meds. Vampires and Werewolves *aren't real*. You've watched too many movies."

A soft growl burst from his parted lips. "Vampires have abilities that Lycans don't. They can control minds and make humans do as they wish, and can even erase some of their memories. Lycans found that really helpful since they were forced to live nomadic lives. It meant keeping their numbers low and never staying in one area to build homes. It was a dream of theirs to settle in one place. The Vampires gave them that luxury. They suddenly could live without fear of being hunted. If a human happened upon a Lycan in a compromising situation, the Vampires could make the humans forget."

"What did these Lycans do that gave them away?"

"They lose their skin if they're highly emotional. Rage. Fear. Grief. Humans panicked when they caught sight of claws, fangs, sudden hair growth…and they told others about the 'monsters'. They'd hunt and kill entire families of Lycans."

"Why not just take out the person who saw something?" Her fingers relaxed their hold on his shirt since he wasn't causing her pain. "That would protect them."

"It wasn't the way it is now. In the past, towns were smaller and they tended to be very superstitious when people just disappeared. They totally believed in monsters and they'd gather in large groups to hunt and murder anything they feared. Ever hear of the witch trials? Try a bunch of angry villagers with weapons willing to kill anyone they didn't like or didn't know well. They didn't even bother to hold a trial for someone they suspected of being a monster. They'd just lynch them."

"According to your Vampire and Werewolf tale, they would have been justified in trying to kill them."

"Exactly, if you were to see us in that light. But we're not really monsters. We're just different. You asked why Lycans didn't end the lives humans who discovered the truth. Lycans didn't want to harm innocent people, period. Vampires don't have to kill to obtain blood from their prey. I was able to control you with my eyes. I gained that ability from my Vampire ancestors. Their abilities to control human minds and wipe memories protected them but it was a constant fear they'd be discovered while they slept. They had Lycan protectors to prevent that from happening, to stand guard when they were vulnerable after the sun rose."

"You didn't burn up in the sun," she pointed out. "Your teeth aren't sharp either. Everyone knows Vampires are allergic to sunlight and have fangs."

"I said I'm *half*. The sun doesn't bother me at all. " Drantos paused to glance toward the fire, then looked back at her. "The Vampires began to gorge on blood, feasting on humans after they formed the alliance with Lycans. They grew bolder with powerful guards to protect them when they were vulnerable. It made it safer for them to feed more often. They—"

"Started killing everyone?"

"No. They just overfed on them."

"Wow. Do Vampires gain weight? Wouldn't it make it kind of hard for them to turn into bats and fly? I'm imagining a big, bloated flying rat with little tiny wings now."

He growled again. "You aren't taking this seriously."

"And you're nuts. I'm trapped under you and you seem determined to share your dementia with me so forgive me for the snarky comments."

"Stop it."

"Ditto."

He shifted his chest, pinned her tighter under his body. "No, they didn't gain weight. But all the blood fooled their bodies into believing they were more human than Vampire. No one realized the consequences—until a few of the female Lycans who had Vampire lovers ended up pregnant. It only happened with Vampire males and female Lycans. Vampires aren't able to breed with each other, but when they realized they could impregnate the Lycan women—"

She'd had enough. Dusti just wanting him to stop talking nonsense and get off her. "They threw a big ol' orgy?" she interrupted.

"Damn it," he snarled. "*Stop.*"

Fear hit her over the pure rage that darkened his features and she sealed her lips. *Don't piss off the insane linebacker-size guy on top of you,* she silently ordered herself.

"The male Vampires secretly plotted to impregnate as many Lycan women as possible. They wanted to form an army of half-breed children. Some believe it was so they no longer had to keep an alliance with the Lycans. They could be guarded by their own children. Others believe it was just because they finally had an opportunity to breed, and that appealed to them.

"Some of the Lycan men started to disappear. The Lycans quickly figured out they were being murdered by Vamps so they could gain access to the widowed mates, whether they were willing or not." Anger deepened his voice. "The Vamps were attacking Lycan women. They violated them by controlling their minds, and then their bodies. A war broke out between the two. A lot of Lycan men died but it gave the women a chance to flee. A group of them—some who were pregnant and others who had already birthed half-breeds—ended up in Alaska, since there were no major human towns here at the time. Vamps need humans to feed from. They can survive off animals but I've heard animal blood tastes like shit to them and weakens them over time.

"The Lycans and VampLycans were safer here, but we still broke into four clans in case the Vampires were able to track us. It was about survival. They wouldn't be able to take us all on at once and it would provide time for the others to flee if one clan was attacked. It helps keep our numbers in check too. It's how we stay under the radar, by monitoring the size of our population so we don't draw attention to ourselves, and what we are. Humans just see our clans as small towns, not a threat to them."

Dusti held her tongue. Drantos paused, licked his lips, and took a few breaths. The anger eased from his striking features.

"The survivors soon discovered a clan of Gargoyles in the area. They'd fled Europe to avoid being hunted by Vampires, humans, and others of their kind. They were dying out. Gargoyles tend to breed more boy children than girls. They had so few women of their own kind that they'd fight to the death at times, killing each other to gain access to one. They needed women to breed with and the survivors of the war didn't want another fight, this time with Gargoyles. They had lost a lot of their males already."

"I've heard enough." She just wanted him to stop. None of it could be true. She didn't want it to be.

"I'm telling you the truth." Drantos paused. "Imagine a bunch of frightened people in a desperate situation. Many of the Lycan women had been raped, in mind and body, and had birthed children sired by Vampires. These women had lost fathers and brothers who'd died fighting to give them time to escape. Some had lost their mates. They were vulnerable, so some of their single women offered themselves to the Gargoyles. They formed a new alliance. The Gargoyles swore to live side by side with us in peace and to help fight any Vampires who came after us, if the need arose to defend the clans. We had the common enemies of humans and Vampires."

"But according to your crazy story, the pregnant women were about to *birth* Vampires. Some had already. You said they were enemies. At least *try* to make sense."

"The Gargoyles were willing to become allies with the half-breeds because they were desperate for the full-blooded Lycan women to breed with. Our clans are linked by bloodlines, but only on the Lycan side. Gargoyles and Lycans had GarLycan children. The children born in our clans are VampLycans. Half Vampire, half Lycan. Over a hundred half-breed children made up the first generation of our new clans. They frightened the pure-blood Lycans. They were stronger than them and had inherited some Vampire abilities. A vast majority of the Lycans not mated to Gargoyles left when those children started to mature and those traits began to show.

"Your grandfather is a first-generation VampLycan, Dusti—and after he matured to adulthood and took over his clan, he didn't agree with how the clans were split into four. He's power-hungry and believes there should be one ruler, one clan. He wants the GarLycans to help him take out the other clan leaders and anyone else who opposes him. He plans to start a civil war."

"Didn't the Gargoyles take off too when these super half-breeds grew up, if they're so scary?"

"No. The Gargoyles were dwindling until they mated with the full-Lycan females. Their children born from that alliance filled their clan to a strong number. Aveoth is a half-breed who leads his own clan. They consist of a mixture of GarLycans and full blooded Gargoyles. His father was a Gargoyle, and his mother a GarLycan. Both Gargoyles and GarLycans are pretty damn tough. They fear no one. That's why we can't allow Decker to use you or your sister as leverage against Aveoth to force him into a war with us. It would be a bloodbath with few survivors."

Dusti just stared at him, trying to take in everything he'd said. It was possible he didn't believe in aliens. She almost wished he did, because she was used to Greg's world. The one Drantos had made up in his head was *way* more complicated and involved mythical paranormal creatures.

His eyes...okay, she couldn't explain that. Which unsettled her and made her nervous.

"So you're telling me I'm related to Vampires and Werewolves?" She didn't want to hear any more and felt hysteria begin to rise up. It *couldn't* be true. "Or am I part Gargoyle? I'm a little confused but it's all cool. Next full moon, I'll try to howl just to see if I sprout hair. I guess now I know why I usually get sunburned instead of tan when I lay out. I just thought it was my fair skin but now I'll know to avoid the sun and sharp wooden stakes. I don't think I'd like to be a Gargoyle statue though. It sounds boring."

The blue of his eyes darkened into near black, stopping her humor immediately as alarm spread throughout her body. It made him look evil.

"You aren't part of the GarLycan clan. And it's not something to make fun of. To be a VampLycan is an honor."

"Couldn't I be a fairy instead? They have sparkly magic dust and wings. I'd much rather you tell me I'm one of those."

He sighed. "This is how you're going to deal with what I'm telling you? Making smartass remarks?"

She nodded. "This is too messed up."

"We're trying to avoid a war, Dusti. You need to know what's really going on."

"Can you at least make your fantasy world make sense? According to you, you're already at war with Vampires."

"Vampires are no longer a threat. They've tried to come after us a few times over the years and we've slaughtered them. That war ended when they realized how strong we'd become." He hesitated. "It's a war between the clans we want to avoid right now. That's the threat. Decker's clan isn't strong enough to take on everyone else. He'd lose unless he can force the GarLycans to his side. That's why he can't get his hands on your sister to use against us. He'll hand her over to Aveoth so he'll fight us too."

"Why is Bat so important to this Aveoth? Why would he want her?"

"Aveoth was once promised your grandmother's sister. She died before that could happen. He'll want Bat because she's a direct descendant of the woman who should have been his."

"It sounds crazy. You *have* to see where I'm coming from."

His gaze lowered to the neck of her blouse. "I know, and I'm sorry I had to be the one to tell you the truth, but I can prove it. I'm dominant and you aren't."

"You mean you're stronger."

He glanced up, his intense gaze meeting hers before he focused lower once more. "You're part Lycan, even if it *is* very minimal. I can force it to the surface."

She felt really uneasy over the way he studied her throat. She pushed against his chest again, futilely, unable to move his heavy bulk. He suddenly tucked his head, burying his face against her neck. She tensed.

"What are you doing?"

"Giving you proof. I'm going to show you how you react to someone else with Lycan bloodlines." His lips brushed the skin under her earlobe and his hot breath warmed her neck. He growled low before his mouth parted. A wet tongue licked down the side and he nipped her shoulder.

Shock tore through Dusti as a jolt of awareness flashed through her body when his teeth nipped her. Oddly, it didn't hurt, but it reminded her of the time she'd accidently touched a frayed cord plugged into the wall. A current of electricity zipped from where his mouth touched, all the way down to her toes. She gasped.

He released her skin then bit her again, harder, an inch closer to her throat. The second bite made her react even stronger. He didn't break skin but she wouldn't be surprised if it left marks.

A moan tore from her lips as her body writhed under his, sexual desire firing her blood. It confused and alarmed her. Her breasts ached painfully and her stomach muscles clenched. He nibbled and bit her again, causing her back to arch until she pressed tight against him.

His muscular legs parted, spreading her thighs. His hips settled more firmly until the hard ridge of his cock nudged her clit.

Dusti clawed at his shirt, horrified but unable to control the burning need he inspired. She wanted him inside her. She hurt.

He slowly rocked his hips, rubbing against her. He bit her neck again and then did it a little harder. Her hands slid up, the desire to touch his skin overwhelming. She located the back of his neck. Her fingernails dug into hot flesh, kneading it lightly, and her legs moved of their own accord, wrapping around the back of his thighs to draw him closer.

"Drantos," Kraven interrupted softly. "Stop."

A deep, harsh growl sounded against her ear and Drantos's mouth released her. He breathed heavily and lifted his head.

Dusti was stunned and confused. Her eyes flew open to stare into his bright blue gaze again. His eyes were faintly glowing.

"Mind your own business, Kraven." Drantos didn't glance at his brother, instead holding Dusti's gaze.

"You're going to fuck her right in front of me and the humans near the fire? Think about that. There's no privacy here."

Frustration tightened Drantos's features and he snarled softly, tearing his gaze away to glower in anger at his brother. "Thanks. I may have. She...affects me."

"No kidding." Kraven chuckled. "I think you showed her enough. Hell, you've shown *me* way too much. I never want to see you in action again."

"How is her sister?"

"I ordered her to sleep. It was easy to do. She has no defenses. The Lycan is stronger in her than any Vampire traits she inherited." Kraven sat up, drawing Dusti's attention enough to make her turn her head just in time to see his grin. "Your way of dealing with yours looks more fun."

"Painful, more like." Drantos suddenly released Dusti and tried to lift his entire body off her, using his hands on the ground, but her legs were still wrapped tightly around him. It prevented him from doing little more than separating their chests. "I'm so fucking hard I could break stone."

Cold air got between their bodies, chilling Dusti instantly. She hated missing his heat and weight.

What the hell is wrong with me? How could I react to a stranger this way—and this strongly?

She didn't voice her questions but it was tough to refrain. She blushed with embarrassment at how badly her body ached to have him finish what he'd started. Her nipples were hard and she felt soaked where her panties covered her sex. Her clit throbbed painfully.

She scrambled to unhook her legs to release him. He lowered his head and studied her face. He softly groaned. "You're lucky I don't throw you over my shoulder and take you out into the woods. I'd fuck you until we both couldn't walk."

"You'd break her." Kraven chucked again. "She's so weak-blooded the human is all I smell."

Dusti stared up into Drantos's fascinating blue eyes and couldn't look away. Her heart pounded inside her chest as if it might burst through her rib cage. She wasn't sure if he was doing that thing he could do, paralyzing her with a look, but she held still.

"She'd be a snack before a hearty meal." Kraven snickered. "But you do look pretty hungry."

Drantos moved, sliding his body down hers. His hips pressed against her thighs until they halted at her knees. He lowered his head, his hands bracing his weight, and caused Dusti to gasp when he pushed his nose between her breasts. He inhaled, groaned softly once more and moved lower, to her stomach. He growled deeply, sounding more animal than human. His head lifted and he met her gaze.

"She smells so damn good to me that I could totally feast on her."

"Shit." Kraven suddenly was there, gripping his brother's forearm. "Get off."

"I don't want to." Another soft sound came from Drantos and his face buried against Dusti's stomach again, nuzzling her. He used his teeth to jerk up her shirt. He snarled when he exposed her bare navel and his tongue darted out to lick her sensitive skin. Pleasure at that mere touch had Dusti arching her back to press her stomach tighter against his face.

Kraven cursed softly—and then Drantos was torn away from her body. Dusti's eyes snapped open.

Both men ended up on their knees feet from her, nearly nose to nose, gripping each other's forearms tightly. If she didn't know better she'd think they were about to wrestle.

"Control yourself." Kraven's words were barely discernible with his snarling tone. "You're using Lycan hormones to turn her on."

"I want her!" Drantos's voice came out so deep it didn't sound human.

Kraven's tan face paled. "You aren't being rational. Drantos…you know what this means, don't you? You poor bastard."

"I do." Drantos's gaze left his brother to focus once more on Dusti.

"*No.*" Kraven shook his brother. "It's just the stress. She's weak and you've been protecting her. Your body and head are all screwed up. That's all it is. You're confused."

Dusti trembled. Her body throbbed with need unlike anything she'd ever experienced before. She could identify the source though—and what she craved was Drantos.

Half of her wanted to crawl over to him just to touch him again, while the rational, sane side wished Bat wasn't part of the equation so she could flee into the woods. She'd rather take her chances out in the wilderness with whatever unknown dangers lie in wait in the darkness, rather than continue spending time with the man who did things to her that shook her to the very core of her soul.

Drantos continued to watch her with his unsettling, intense gaze. Kraven held on to him and forever seemed to pass before they broke apart. Kraven stayed between her and Drantos, though, and studied his brother closely.

"Better? Are you under control now?"

"Yes."

"You keep mine warm and I'll hold yours for the night. The last thing you need is to touch her again."

Rage darkened Drantos's features while he glared at his brother. "Don't touch her! She's *mine*."

"You can't claim her! Not now and not here, anyway. And don't attack me."

"Don't touch her then." Drantos growled deep in a threatening tone. "I won't be able to handle it."

"Fair enough." Kraven gave a sharp nod. "Oh man. This is fucked. You just *had* to taste her, didn't you? Did you ever think that now might not have been a good time to do that? That maybe it could be dangerous if she were the one?"

"It never crossed my mind." Drantos's voice seemed to grow less deep, returning to a more normal level. "I had no inkling of it."

"Her scent didn't arouse you?"

"Any attractive woman would do that to me."

"Maybe it's the stress, as I said. And you've had to stay too close to keep an eye on her."

"No." Fury darkened Drantos's features again. "I'm sure. She's the one. As soon as I scented her arousal it became clear. I should have known when I tasted her to see what her bloodlines were. It affected me so strongly even though I only took a few drops."

"Fuck." Kraven ran his fingers through his messed-up spiky hair and turned his head to stare at the survivors around the fire. "We've drawn a little attention. Two of the humans are watching us." His voice lowered and he smiled. "Sit your big ass down and look happy."

"We need to go *now*." Drantos sat.

"I need some sleep first. We're going to have to haul them through the woods at a fast pace."

"We leave now. I can't sleep with her, and I'm going to be on you in a heartbeat if you touch her. I feel fiercely protective. I'd fight you, Kraven. They can't produce enough body heat not to freeze during the night unless we put them closer to the fire and the other crash victims. There are a few men who might set me off if they pay any attention to Dusti. Let's just move out. We'll carry them to keep them warm with our body heat."

"We need some *sleep* first, brother. Try to be rational. Think."

Drantos took a few deep breaths. "I'm in control now."

"Bullshit. You just want to touch her again, and you won't make it fifty feet without fucking her in your current condition." Kraven turned his head to shoot Dusti a glare. "Curl up with your sister. Don't try to wake her. Are we clear? You can keep each other warm and I can get some sleep before we have to hike out of here."

Dusti trembled hard. Confusion and alarm held her immobile. Her body still ached so badly it had become a deep physical pain. She tore her gaze from Kraven to stare at Drantos. She fought the desperate need she still felt to crawl to him. Her turned-on body longed to touch him and even climb onto his lap. She fought the urge hard as her nipples tightened painfully and she fisted her hands to avoid reaching out to him.

His gaze locked with hers and he softly growled.

Kraven suddenly moved between them to break their eye contact. "Damn it! Okay. Give me a minute to think."

"I want," Drantos softly rumbled. "Bad."

"No shit. You're about to bust your zipper and I'm really going to mental hell for noticing that. I can smell the damn lust; it's so thick I'm about to choke on it. Take a walk and have some private time to deal with your issue. I can't believe I'm saying this, but you and your hand need to get busy to prevent you from putting on a free porn show for everyone. That will curb some of your lust for now. You can't touch her, Drantos. You know what will happen when you do. The last thing you're going to want is to let her go once you've had her, and we need to get them to safety first. We don't have a few days for you to create a bond."

"Fuck," Drantos cursed.

Dusti watched him stand. He refused to meet her gaze before he spun around to stomp out into the woods. She whimpered the second she lost sight of him. The reaction scared her, and worse, made her certain she had lost her mind.

Maybe someone had slipped her drugs. Maybe that iron shot Bat had given her had been defective and she was experiencing some freaky hyper-aphrodisiac reaction.

Kraven turned his head to frown at her. "Lay your ass down and curl up with your sister. It will pass now that he's gone. Take some deep breaths. That will help too."

Drantos couldn't go far. His instincts demanded he keep Dusti within sight. His body hurt with the need to go to her and finish what he'd started. It became so strong he actually grabbed hold of a tree trunk to stay put.

Kraven had made a valid point. He wasn't in control and Dusti was fragile. He might accidently cause her harm by being too rough. He needed to calm.

It helped as time passed and he breathed in fresh air that didn't carry her scent. He hadn't suspected she might be his mate when he'd tested her blood. She'd tasted good and had affected him, but the truth hadn't really hit him until he'd been seducing her.

No damn way would Decker get Dusti. She was *his*.

He finally got his lust under control. Kraven's suggestion of taking care of his own needs wouldn't have fixed the problem. It was Dusti he wanted. The urge to protect her and keep her close overruled everything else. He slowly released the tree and returned to her side.

She lay facing her sister. Kraven sat behind Bat and regarded him with a frown. He glanced away from him to view the other passengers. Most of them had settled down to go to sleep or were already snoozing.

"You're still pretty tense," Kraven whispered. "You didn't jack off."

He clenched his teeth. "It won't help."

"Shit. I hope to never suffer what you are."

He gently tucked the blanket closer to Dusti. She tensed, her body rigid. He knew she hadn't fallen asleep. He pulled his hand back, too tempting to continue touching her. It wasn't the time or the place.

"We need to get them out of here. I feel as if we're sitting ducks."

"I was thinking the same thing," Kraven reluctantly agreed. "It's going to be tough traveling with them and they'll slow us down...unless we give them a ride."

He winced. Dusti didn't believe anything he'd told her. She wasn't prepared yet for the reality of how much her life had changed. He wanted to ease her into it, and seeing him in shift would terrify her. It would make her fight whatever attraction she felt toward him with more conviction. Terror tended to do that.

"No." He glanced down at Dusti and then back at his brother. "Watch your words."

"Showing is knowing," his brother muttered.

"It's too soon. It's better to reveal ourselves slowly over time."

"I understand your caution but that plan is going to hell if Decker's enforcers find us before we can reach home. Is that really how you want her to learn the truth of your words? Did you even warn her how we look?"

Kraven had a point. Dusti would know he hadn't lied if any of Decker's clan found them. She'd be confronted with evidence in the form of what her eyes could actually see. The shock of seeing a shifted VampLycan in animal form might damage her mental health, since she was so resistant to everything he'd told her so far. He bit his lip, debating what to do.

Kraven continued, "Isn't the most important thing getting them swiftly to where they'll be safe and we have backup? We're going to be outnumbered if Decker sends a dozen of his enforcers after us. You can deal with the fallout later."

Drantos wasn't so certain of that. Dusti had already suffered enough traumas in a short period of time. Humans could hear stories of other kinds of creatures and chalk it up to harmless fiction, but he'd heard of people whose minds had snapped when they were actually confronted by the world they didn't know existed.

He focused on Dusti, picking up her rapid heartbeat. He reached out again and ran his hand over the blanket covering her hip. She shifted just slightly, pulling away. He let her.

"We'll leave at first light—and *walk* it," he decided. "Decker doesn't know we're with them. He'll expect to find his granddaughters waiting here to be found by the rescue party and totally unprotected. We'll skirt any areas where we think we might run into them. They'll make a beeline for where they think the plane went down."

"Damn it, Drantos." Kraven bared his teeth. "You're not being rational."

"I'm being cautious, and I don't want to traumatize her any more than necessary." He left the rest unsaid, since Dusti could hear his every word. "She needs time to adjust to everything before it's in her face."

Kraven closed his eyes and long seconds passed before he held his gaze again. "You think she'll reject you if she sees anything before she's ready?"

"I'm certain of it. We'll walk."

"This one doesn't even have shoes." Kraven glanced at Bat. "I couldn't find anything that would fit her. All she has are those high heels. Can you imagine a hike in the woods wearing those? She'll break her ankle."

"Are you out of shape?"

"Fuck you."

"Then just deal with it. You wanted some sleep. Lie down and rest. We're out of here at first light. We'll make sure the passengers are kept warm and send them help if they haven't been found by the time we reach our people. They'll have to make it one night alone at the most. I figure we'll reach home within twenty-four hours."

"That's pretty damn slow."

"The terrain is going to be rough, and don't forget the river. We'll have to find a way to get them across it while keeping them dry at the same time. They're weak and susceptible to hypothermia or catching a cold. I'm thinking we might have to build a little raft and float them over. The water is still going to be pretty cold. I'm not taking any chances with their health."

"Shit."

"Our people will be looking for us too, so I doubt it will take that long. They could run across us by nightfall tomorrow. Best situation."

Kraven lay down, curling against Bat's back. "You owe me."

Drantos lay down and scooted closer to Dusti to keep the wind from hitting her back. He wanted to pull her into his arms but refrained. He desired her too much and it would be too tempting to do more than hold her.

Once he got her to his home, all bets were off. He'd take her. She wouldn't be able to deny there was something special between them. He'd just have to help her learn to trust him before she discovered how different he could be from anyone else she'd ever known.

He knew there were still going to be issues once he took her home. His parents wouldn't be thrilled that she was so weak-blooded. He was their firstborn. That came with responsibilities but he doubted they'd refuse to accept Dusti. They knew him too well. He'd leave before giving her up. His father would understand though. He knew the importance of a true bond.

Decker would probably try to come after Dusti and Bat, even if that meant he'd have to attack the clan to get them back. Drantos didn't have to worry about anyone wanting to hand Bat or Dusti over to prevent bloodshed. The clan would fight to the death to prevent Decker from becoming their leader. They'd stand up to him to make certain he couldn't use either woman as leverage to force Aveoth into backing his plan to merge the clans, so he could become the sole leader of all VampLycans.

Drantos inhaled Dusti's scent and couldn't resist reaching up to brush his fingers through her hair. She sucked in a sharp breath but didn't jerk away. He smiled.

He'd have to treat her like a timid animal that needed to learn how to trust. It was the best way to show her that he'd never hurt her. Patience wasn't his strongest trait but he'd learn some—for her.

Chapter Four

The sun hadn't risen yet when someone's touch drew Dusti from sleep. Bat stirred next to her where they huddled together tightly under a blanket. They both shivered from the cold air as they sat up. The fire blazed strongly in the clearing but little of the warmth from it reached them. Dusti looked at Kraven, who crouched next to them.

"We need to leave now. Get up, go to the bathroom, and eat quickly. I figure the search-and-rescue planes will take off from the airport in Anchorage in less than an hour."

"Go where?" Bat yawned. "You think the rescue teams will find us soon?"

Dusti knew that wasn't the plan. The brothers wanted them to hike away from the survivors so they wouldn't be rescued with them. Whoever they believed their grandfather would send looking for them would probably arrive before help did. Dusti wondered if Bat remembered anything from the night before, but one look at her sister's calm expression assured her she had no memory of what Kraven had done to knock her out.

Bat stood. "Damn. It's too cold." She bent, grabbed one of the blankets, and wrapped it tightly around her body as she walked in the direction of the woods. "I'll be right back if my girl parts don't freeze when I yank up my skirt."

Kraven sighed. "Hurry, and don't go far."

Dusti peered around the clearing. The survivors still slept and there wasn't a sign of Drantos. Kraven seemed to guess who she was searching for.

"He'll be back soon. He's collecting more wood for the humans in case it takes another day for help to reach them. He doesn't want them to die tonight when it gets cold. We're hoping they're found before nightfall but it's best to take precautions."

"These people are going to tell whoever finds them that you stole us. You won't get away with this. The police will be looking for Bat and I."

"Our people will contact the proper authorities to say you both are safe once we reach home. Drantos will let it slip to a few of the passengers that we're going to go search for help so they aren't worried."

"That's pretty nice, considering you're planning on kidnapping my sister and me. Criminals with a conscience? How thoughtful."

He snorted. "You have no idea what kind of danger your sister is in. If we're guessing right about Decker's plans, she'll live a life of pure hell if your grandfather gets ahold of her. Aveoth isn't the nicest person." He paused. "And my brother realized you're not as human as your scent. I'd be worried about your own ass, too, if I were you. Aveoth may settle for *you* if he can't have your sister. Your grandfather could figure out he was wrong about your bloodlines if he gets his hands on you."

She remembered the strange tale from the night before. "Are you just humoring your brother, or do you believe that story he told me about Vampires and Werewolves, too?"

"You *wish* it were just a strange tale. It's history. Your mother was a VampLycan. Your grandfather is a crazy son of a bitch who wants to start a war. Everything Drantos said is true."

"Aveoth is a GarLycan, right? Half Lycan and half Gargoyle? It sounds as if he'd be a man with a heart of stone." She smiled at her own joke.

"Cute. The heart-of-stone part would be misleading since I doubt he has one at all. His own clan is terrified of him. His viciousness is well known to our clans and it means your grandfather will gain too much power if he makes an alliance with Aveoth by using your sister as a bargaining tool."

"And that would be bad in your weird world?"

Anger narrowed Kraven's light blue eyes. "Yes. Decker isn't happy just running his own clan anymore. He wants total control. He doesn't agree with how some of the other leaders rule their people. He'd kill everyone who opposes him if given the opportunity. He can't take on three clans and win. He'd get his ass handed to him unless he gets the GarLycan leader to side with him. That's going to more than even out the odds."

"These Gargoyle-and-Werewolf things are worse than VampLycans, huh?"

He hesitated. "Yes. We're strong but they are damn near invincible. They fly and can turn their bodies into armor. The combination is deadly to anyone they go after. The GarLycans would help your grandfather's clan slaughter the rest of us if Aveoth gave them the order. With Decker pulling the strings, many VampLycans would die. That's when he'd start expanding the borders. He tried to do it with his own but the other leaders put a stop to it by threatening to attack him."

"What does that mean?"

"He seems to think humans are a threat. We got word from someone in his clan that he planned to make some of the neighboring human families have 'accidents'. Alaska's a harsh place and he could have gotten away with murdering them without raising suspicion. He's paranoid, from what we were told. Humans can be turned into Vampires, and of course they're also a food source for them. He hates full-blooded Vampires enough to want to make sure they have no reason to be anywhere near him." He paused. "He sees humans as inferior as bugs to crush under his heel. The other clans don't. We protect them."

"You know that sounds crazy, right?" She hesitated. "I don't like my grandfather. He's an asshole, but to believe he's some murdering evil bastard is kind of difficult for me to do."

"He's killed plenty of people. He's greedy and power-hungry. We get the news here about your world. How many times have you seen stories where some warlord killed innocents to gain more land or money? Decker wants more people under his control. He murdered his own mate, who he'd sworn to protect, and tried to use his own child, your *mother*, as a bargaining chip to gain an alliance with the GarLycans in order to slaughter his own kind. Now he's attempting to use his granddaughter to do it yet again. What kind of monster does that make him?"

"If he's got a dick, well…you've heard of high divorce rates, right? Men can be heartless pigs to their wives. Maybe my grandfather thought it would be easier to kill her than go through a messy divorce. I see stories about it in the news all the time. And I have no clue what happened between my grandfather and my mother. As for my sister, he doesn't know us."

"Humans divorce. Lycans mate forever. It's a bonding that is so strong, some die without the other. Filmore has to be defective in mind and heart to have been able to kill Marvilella. She was bound to him, tried to change him for the better by giving him her love, but she suffered greatly for it. She always looked sad when she visited her family in our clan."

Dusti rolled her eyes. "Now you're telling me you're old enough to have known my grandmother? She died before I was even born. You aren't much older than I am. You would have been a baby."

A chilly smile curved his lips. "You'd be surprised at how old I truly am."

"Right. Because you're half Vampire and they don't age. Sure. Okay, Grandpa. You look damn fine for a geezer."

"Your smart mouth is going to be your undoing. Fine, don't believe what you're told, but eventually you'll see the truth."

It was too much for her. It was too foreign a concept. "Whatever. If I bought into this crap, what makes my sister such a hot commodity to this Aveoth anyway? Can't he find a woman on his own? If I'm buying this chunk of swampland you're trying to sell, a lot would depend on whether or not he even wanted her. You've met my sister. Most guys spend two minutes with her and run for cover if they have a brain."

"It's the bloodline. Aveoth has a craving for it."

"Come again?" Dusti frowned.

"He was set to take Margola as his lover but she died before reaching maturity. After she was promised to him, Margola's parents gave Aveoth a bit of her blood to drink, every month for a few years. GarLycans have stronger Gargoyle genes. They don't form emotional attachments to lovers, only their mates. Margola's parents feared he'd be so callous toward her that her life would be utter misery. They'd hoped he'd become addicted to her blood enough that he'd take good care of her, and not kill her soul during the years she'd spend with him until he finally found his mate and set her free."

"Where are her parents?"

He hesitated. "That's unknown. They fled shortly after Margola's death. I think they were afraid Aveoth's father would kill them for allowing her to die."

"It sounds like they were responsible for her death or something? Were they?"

"No. Aveoth's father was a full-blooded Gargoyle and cold as ice. He *did* blame them; felt they should have watched her better since she was promised to his son. She loved to take walks in the woods, and they allowed it. She ran into a group of hunters who must have thought she was an animal, since she was in her shifted form. They opened fire on her. She escaped them but died before the clan found her. They'd gone searching when she didn't make it home. Lord Abotorus was enraged, since he'd allowed Aveoth to feed off her. He hadn't wanted to but Margola's parents had insisted. Afterward, Aveoth supposedly showed signs of withdrawal from her blood."

"Let's get back to the 'kill her soul' part, since you're just confusing me more. Why would that have happened and how?"

"Gargoyles aren't the friendliest beings you'll ever meet. VampLycan women usually crave tenderness, and a man who will see to their emotional needs. Without it, she could lose the will to live." He frowned. "Margola's parents believed drinking her blood would teach Aveoth to want more from her than just sex. It was important to our clan to cement an emotional bond between them so he'd keep her happy. His father hit the roof when his son suffered withdrawals after her death, as if he'd become addicted.

"That same blood runs in your sister's veins, and probably even in yours. Your bloodline is the taste we believe Aveoth craves the most. If it's true, he'll do anything to have that again, even go against his own beliefs. He hates Filmore, everything he stands for, but his weakness is the blood."

"Doesn't all blood taste the same?"

He shook his head. "No. Not only are we able to distinguish between types, but we can differentiate family bloodlines. Think of his addiction as a human's preference for a favorite fine wine. The others pale in comparison."

"Gross."

"You asked."

This is such a crazy story, Dusti silently sighed. *It can't be true*. "So why would Aveoth even need someone else to find him a lover to begin with? Is he really hideous looking or something? Why would any parent want to hand over their daughter to this guy?"

"I'm certain he could find one on his own, but the arrangement would have helped strengthen the alliance between VampLycans and the GarLycans. Aveoth expressed a desire to have a lover and one was found. There was no need for him to search or have to worry that she would be surprised by what he is. His Gargoyle blood might make him cold, but he's still a man. He wanted a warm, willing female to share his bed until he found his mate. Aveoth's father arranged it with Margola's parents."

"So she was whored out to him?" It left a bad taste in Dusti's mouth to even say it.

Kraven scowled. "I guess you *would* see it that way. She wasn't forced to agree to become his lover. It was considered an honor to sacrifice the years she would have spent with him to keep peace between his clan and ours."

"But she died before it happened. So who took her place?"

"Her name was Lane and she died recently. That's why Decker sent for Bat. Aveoth needs a new lover."

"Was Lane a relative of mine?"

"No, but she was willing to become Aveoth's lover."

"But you were talking about blood and how this Aveoth wants Bat because she's related to Margola. Help me out here. I'm so confused."

Kraven drew closer. "Aveoth *settled* for Lane. Once he learns about Bat, he'll want *her* more than anyone else who might volunteer to become his new lover. Is that clear enough for you?"

"Bat isn't going to volunteer for that."

"Decker won't care, and Aveoth might want her enough to overlook the fact that he has to force her to stay with him."

"Because she's a relative to Margola."

"Yes."

"Wow. So you're saying my grandfather wants to turn Bat into a sex slave and this guy might go for it. Your world is totally fucked up. My sister would castrate the bastard if he tried to force himself on her."

"You're both too weak to defend yourself."

"My sister is a shark. Never forget it. They don't call attorneys that without cause."

"Sarcasm is not an attractive trait in a woman." Kraven softly snarled the words. "Bat wouldn't stand a chance of stopping Aveoth from doing or taking whatever he wanted from her. You asked, and I have answered."

"If Decker is so bad, why didn't he just hand over his own wife to this Aveoth, if they were sisters? They might have tasted the same."

He grimaced. "I'm certain he considered it, but Aveoth would never have allowed him to live. She was already mated to Decker when her sister died. To take a woman from a mate would mean killing him."

"You gave me the impression Decker didn't care about Marvilella, if he really did kill her, so he wouldn't have fought to keep her."

"It's about pride and instincts." Kraven sighed. "Aveoth would have killed her mate just to make certain she didn't hold a bond to someone else. She was also already pregnant when her sister died. Aveoth wants a woman without offspring."

"He sounds really picky. What's wrong with being with a woman who has a kid?"

"Perhaps he doesn't want to raise another man's child. I don't know. You'd have to ask *him*. But trust me, he'll crave Bat's blood."

"You make it sound as if he's going to salt her down and serve her up for dinner."

"No, but if Aveoth is really addicted to the bloodline, it'd be a bonus if he can fuck her and drink her blood at the same time."

"That's really gross and demented."

A grin curved Kraven's features. "Remember you said that."

"What does *that* mean?"

He rose to his feet slowly while he gave her an amused look that left her feeling unsettled. "That's a discussion for you and my brother to have." He spun away, striding toward the fire.

Dusti got to her feet and shivered from the cold, missing Drantos's jacket that he'd made her remove the night before. One quick glance around revealed it was gone. She jerked up the blanket they'd slept on to wrap around her body. She nearly bumped into Bat when she stepped into the woods.

"Remind me to never visit Alaska again." Bat softly cursed. "It's so cold I didn't even want to pee. I think it froze before it hit the ground. I thought it would be warmer here this time of year. It's almost summertime."

"Always a lady." Dusti smiled to soften her words. She glanced around, still not seeing Drantos, and Kraven had his back to them while he fed kindling to the fire. "Bat," she began, staring into her sister's eyes. "We're in deep shit."

"I know."

"You really have no clue what is go—"

"There you are."

Dusti jumped. Drantos stepped out from behind a tree. She hadn't even heard him approaching but there he stood, inches from her. He wore his jacket. She stared up into his dark gaze, seeing a warning in them. She sealed her lips together.

"Did both of you empty your bladders?" He didn't look away from Dusti.

"I did, and I hope it warms up more when the sun rises." Bat shivered. "I'm going to go sit by the fire to thaw." She headed back to the clearing.

Dread gripped Dusti at being left alone with Drantos.

"You were going to warn her."

"Don't you think she's going to notice when you and your brother drag us out of here?"

"Go to the bathroom but don't go far. We're leaving when you return." His gaze narrowed. "Don't try anything, Dusti. You don't want to see me angry."

"Right. You'll suck my blood or something."

He took a step closer until they nearly touched. Dusti held her breath, fear inching up her spine at the chilly look on his face. *He may be hot but he is also*

79

huge and scary. Those were things she needed to remember.

"You love your sister and want to protect her. We have that second thing in common."

Dusti took a step back. "So let's say I believe everything I've been told. You want to keep Bat away from my grandfather but what are *you* going to do with her? Hand her over to that Aveoth yourself?"

He shook his head. "He'd probably kill her. My brother spoke the truth. Aveoth is used to getting his way. Your sister might try to attack him and it wouldn't end well for her."

She instantly knew he'd somehow been listening to the conversation she'd had with Kraven. The tree line where he'd stepped out from wasn't far from where the two of them had been.

"What are you going to do with us?"

"You are the descendants of a member of my clan." He invaded her personal space again to nearly touch her. "And I have my reasons to protect you. It would cause you pain if any harm came to your sister, so I'll protect her as well, for *you.*"

"Is that supposed to make me feel gratitude toward you? You're saving us from the big bad wolf or whatever the hell Decker Filmore is, supposedly? What do you want from us, Drantos? I don't trust you."

Anger drew his mouth into a scowl. "You should. Go to the bathroom and hurry back."

She backed away and turned. The urge to run from him gripped her but she kept up a slow pace as she moved farther away from the clearing.

She hated the great outdoors, had never been the type to go camping, and really resented not having an actual bathroom to use. If it wasn't for Bat, she'd make a run for it. She'd rather face bears than two brothers spouting off about Vampires, Werewolves and Gargoyles.

Kraven handed Dusti some of the leftover meat from the night before when she returned. The air had been so cold it had refrigerated it. Her stomach rumbled with hunger. She sat next to Bat and Kraven handed her sister a chunk of venison too.

"Eat quickly."

Kraven stayed with them to make sure Dusti couldn't speak privately to her sister. She knew both men were aware she wanted to. Her gaze drifted to study the survivors but not one of them could have taken on the two muscular brothers. Most of them were still sleeping or just too injured to be of any help. She realized she and Bat were on their own if they wanted to be saved. Even if she created a scene, that wouldn't do anything to prevent them from being taken from the clearing.

All she wanted was to get herself and Bat back home safely. She'd talk her sister out of visiting their grandfather. *Better to be safe than sorry. I've had enough of this shit.* The rescue team was the best chance they had of hitching an immediate ride back to Anchorage and catching the first flight back to L.A.

"We should get going." Kraven glanced around, looking for his brother. He wasn't within sight.

"I meant it last night when I offered to defend you and your brother if you're in some kind of legal trouble," Bat informed Kraven. "I'm not licensed to practice in Alaska but all we need to do is use your court-appointed attorney to file motions for me to be a consultant. I'll wave my fees. I can walk your attorney through every filing to help you fight whatever charges you're facing. I don't mean to toot my own horn but I'm damn good at what I do. You guys don't have to take off before the search party finds us."

"We have no legal trouble," Kraven announced. "We appreciate the offer though."

"Well, if you ever change your mind, just look me up and call my office. I'm located in Los Angeles."

Dusti opened but then closed her mouth, biting back a protest. She had to find a way for her and Bat to escape from both men. It still irritated her that Bat kept offering to represent them. Then again, her sister dealt with scary men every day in her line of work. Most of her clients were hard-core murderers, rapists, or criminal thugs.

Drantos stopped next to where they all sat minutes later. "It's time." He dropped a pair of her slip-on shoes into Dusti's lap. "Take off the ones you have and put those on. They'll be more comfortable."

She frowned. "How did you know these were mine, and where did you find them?"

"Do it," he ordered, looking angry.

She switched the shoes.

Kraven leaned forward. "Bat? Look at me."

Oh no, Dusti thought, *he's going to do that hypnotist shit on my sister again.*

Her mouth opened to distract Bat but Drantos dropped to his knees suddenly, getting her full attention. His dark gaze fixed on hers and she couldn't look away. He spoke softly to her.

"You will stand up, not say a word, and walk into the woods with me. You won't scream or fight. You will remain meek until I tell you to do otherwise."

She tried to open her mouth to tell him to fuck himself, but she couldn't. She remained silent. Shock and terror flooded her mind when he gripped her hand, pulling her to her feet. He let go as suddenly as he'd grabbed her to wrap the blanket around her shoulders, tying the ends to create a shawl. He took her hand once more and tugged, and her body allowed him to lead her into the woods. She couldn't even turn her head to make sure Kraven followed with her sister.

Her body seemed to move on autopilot when it didn't respond to her commands. She understood how a puppet had to feel when someone controlled it. Drantos's warm, large hand kept a firm hold on her smaller one while they strolled slowly away from the camp. It was tough to even move her head to look down at her feet. She tripped once, her foot bumping into something painful, but Drantos just pulled her close enough to put his arm around her waist.

"How long do you think it will take the humans to realize we aren't returning?" Kraven questioned from behind them.

"I told them we were going to take a look around to see if there's a nearby cabin. I'd give it a few hours at least, maybe mid-afternoon before they grow worried. They are injured, in shock and disorientated. I just hope none of them wander into the woods to search for us. I told them not to. I'd hate for any of them to venture so far out they get lost. If they weren't injured we could've wiped their memories of us, but it's too risky to their already fragile health."

"Yeah. I know. I feel like shit for leaving them alone, unprotected, but I cleared out all the predators as far away as I could."

"I mixed leaves with the firewood we left to make the fire smoky enough to confuse the wildlife. They should mistake the scent for a forest fire and their instincts will make them rush away from the clearing."

"Those search planes better find them today."

Drantos sighed. "I'm sure they will. Decker will be all over the rescue teams, pressing them to search, along with sending his enforcers to search the ground. He'll be frantic to find Bat."

Is Bat hearing them? Aware of what they're saying? Dusti hoped so. *She* sure was. She hated to think of the fear her sister had to be feeling at that moment if she was cognizant of their conversation, but at least now they'd be on the same "we're in deep shit" page where Drantos and Kraven were concerned.

The sun rose higher, light filtering through the thick growth of trees surrounding them. Whatever hold Drantos had on her started to fade as time passed. She turned her head to glance behind them.

Kraven wasn't holding her sister's hand but instead had her flung over one shoulder with a blanket wrapped around her body. He met her gaze with a frown.

"Yours is coming out of it, bro."

"I'm aware." Drantos stopped walking. "She's stronger than I thought she would be."

Dusti glared up at him. "Stop using that mind-control shit on me, damn it."

"I wouldn't have to if you didn't fight me at every turn."

She turned her head to glare at Kraven. "Put Bat down." She noticed he didn't seem out of breath or sweaty, despite the fact that he'd carried her sister. "Is she all right?"

"She's sleeping."

"Stop doing that to her!"

"I'm not doing anything but carrying her." He slid his hand down her sister's leg to her feet, tugging the blanket over them. "I ditched her heels. She'd have broken an ankle in those damn things and I couldn't find any flats her size in the wreckage. The ground will tear up her feet if I allow her to walk barefoot, and leave a blood trail for Filmore's men to follow easier."

Drantos tugged gently on Dusti's arm. "We need to keep moving."

"*No*. This is pure insanity. We should go back and wait with the wreckage for help to arrive." She waved a hand at the area around them. "You want Bat and I far away from here and our grandfather? Fine. I agree. Take us back and I'll have whoever finds us fly us to the airport. We can be out of the state before you know it."

"Decker will just come after you."

"I'll move in with Bat for a while. She has excellent security in her building. We'll be safe."

"Really?" Drantos growled. "Tell me about her security."

"There are a few armed guards in the lobby twenty-four seven. You need a code to enter the elevator to even reach her floor. Nobody can get to her apartment without her allowing it. One of the guards calls her when I visit and then escorts me to her door."

Drantos nodded. "*Human* guards. Ones that Decker or any of his men can mind control. They just have to walk in, look at those guards, and order them to take them right to you and your sister. Her so-called security would stand there while you were taken and never remember what happened once it was over with. Do you understand? You're not safe there. Humans *can't* protect you."

Dusti grudgingly believed him, since he'd shown her what he could do multiple times now. "We could go to a hotel or something."

"You think we don't know how to track credit cards? We might live apart from your world but we're not idiots. Decker would track you and Bat by financials. Hotels cost money. They can find your friends if you believe you could hide with one of them. Humans can't lie to a VampLycan. We can force them to tell us the truth. There's nowhere you could hide. They'd find you."

Dusti wasn't willing to give up yet. "This isn't the way either. All you're going to do is get us lost out here and we'll die from exposure or something."

"We're not going to get lost." Drantos looked annoyingly calm. "You're safer with us than you would be anywhere else."

"Bullshit." She tugged hard on her hand but couldn't break free of his hold. "And let me go. I don't want you touching me after that freaky thing you did last night. Did you slip me some kind of drug?"

He softly growled.

"Easy," Kraven urged. "Now isn't a good time to show her who's in charge. We need to keep going. Our people will be looking for us as well. They'll assume we've made better time, not knowing these two are slowing us down since you refuse to shift forms in front of your precious Dusti."

"Shut the fuck up," Drantos snapped.

"I'm just stating facts. They'll expect us to have traveled faster than what we are."

"Right." Drantos shot Dusti an angry glance that promised their argument wasn't over, just delayed. "Let's keep going. I'm hoping our clan finds us by nightfall. I don't want to spend another night out here in the open without help."

"You honestly think someone is looking for us from your..." She paused. "Clan?"

"Yes." Drantos's dark gaze narrowed in warning. "Decker wanted you to land at that small airport because all the clans live within a few hundred miles of this area. We're not that far from him or our people. The plane almost made it to the airport. Be silent and keep walking."

"How do you even know where to go? Do you recognize this area?"

"I know how long that flight takes and yes, I'm familiar with the territory. I know where we are and where we need to go. Now stop stalling and *walk*."

"Go screw yourself." She jerked on her hand harder. "I'm tired. I'm fed up. Most of all, I want this nightmare to end. I don't want anything to do with you or my grandfather. Take your crazy-weird eyes, your messed-up stories and just leave

Bat and I here."

Drantos snarled. The sound came out terrifying and animalistic. He faced her, bent, and yanked on her arm hard. She gasped when it knocked her off balance and he bent forward. He wrapped his arm around the back of her thighs while he straightened to dangle her body over his shoulder. Drantos released her wrist to grip her legs and hold her in place draped over him.

"Let's move," Drantos ordered. "We'll make better time this way."

"I think we should gag her. She's a pain in the ass when she talks."

"I don't want to hurt her. She's mine."

Dusti beat Drantos with her fists on his denim-covered ass but he didn't seem to notice the blows. He just resumed his hike through the woods. "Put me down, you jackass! And I'm *not* yours."

"You have no idea." Kraven chuckled. "I'm all for you teaching her who's in charge if we're stuck out here overnight. Maybe it will mellow her out."

"I doubt it. Mother always said we were hellions. I'm guessing this is payback for all the trouble we've gotten into."

"Oh damn. Mom is going to hate her. She wanted some sweet submissive type for you."

"I'm more worried about Dad. He's going to really be upset with her being so human."

"Shit," Kraven cursed. "You better wait and get permission first. He may forbid you the right to claim her."

"It's not up to him."

"Put me down! Do you hear me, you oversized bully?" Dusti wiggled frantically but his hold on her just tightened. "I'm going to castrate you the first chance I get."

Drantos snarled and halted so quickly her face slammed into his back. She tasted the leather of his jacket. His hand left the back of her thighs and he slapped her ass once, hard enough to make her cry out. Pain burned on her right cheek and tears filled her eyes.

"Damn it!" he roared. "I'm sorry. You just piss me off. Don't threaten me with that ever again."

He gently rubbed the area he'd struck with the palm of his hand, massaging her butt. She relaxed only slightly when the pain faded. She blinked away tears.

"You're an abusive piece of shit."

He halted the movement of his hand. "I said I'm sorry." His voice came out gruff. "I'm under a lot of stress but I didn't spank you hard. I'm trying to protect you, yet you're fighting and insulting me every step of the way."

"I almost feel sorry for you." Kraven said. "I'll never taste a woman again if this is what the future holds when I find the right one."

"I didn't mean to smack you that hard, Dusti." Drantos rubbed her ass again. He resumed his fast-paced walk. "I forget how human you are. If you were more VampLycan, that would have just been annoying rather than causing you any pain. I'll watch my strength from now on. I'm sorry, sweetheart."

Dusti clenched her teeth for a good minute but then lost her temper. She'd never been good at holding back her feelings. "Don't call me that again—and keep those bear-sized mitts away from my ass. You have to sleep sometime. Remember that, because I will."

"I believe that's a threat." Kraven laughed outright. "Damn, I almost envy you. She's got fire for being so damn clueless."

"Shut up."

"Yeah." Dusti hated to agree with Drantos about anything. "Shut up, psychopath's brother. And keep *your* bear-sized mitts off my sister's ass. If you hit Bat when she gives you hell, you can consider yourself warned too. I'll get even." She took a deep breath. "And stop playing with my ass, Drantos!"

He stopped rubbing his palm over her skirt, but he kept his fingers wrapped round the curve of her butt. She knew he did it to piss her off. She closed her eyes, her body bumping and swaying over his shoulder.

"It would serve you right if I puked on your nice leather jacket and down the back of your jeans. I bet that wouldn't be fun to have in those boots of yours either."

"You do it and I'll spank the other side."

"Asshole."

"Ready to gag her yet?" Kraven walled up next to them. "I'm willing to give up a sock for the cause."

Drantos snorted. "That would kill her. I don't even want to be in the same room with you when you take off your boots after you've worn them for a while. Keep your damn socks to yourself and stop irritating her more."

"I don't believe she needs any help with that. She doesn't seem to like you."

"She will when we're safe."

"You're dreaming, bro."

"Shut up," Drantos snarled. "Pay attention to our surroundings. I'm smelling bear."

Kraven sniffed. "Shit. It's more than one. The last thing we need is to run into some of them this time of year. They're going to be hungry."

"You better not put me and Bat in danger," she snapped. "This was your crazy plan to leave the crash site. We had fire and people there. I don't care if you two get eaten but my sister and I better not become dinner for a bear."

Drantos rubbed her ass again. "You're going to be a meal alright, but it won't be a bear putting its mouth on you, sweetheart."

What the hell does that mean?

Dusti clenched her teeth when it sank in that he was making another sexual innuendo. *What an asshole.* "That's never going to happen," she swore.

"It will," he promised. "Soon."

"Listen up, you son of a bit—"

"Enough of that, you two. We don't have time for an argument. Stop taunting her, Drantos. We should separate here," Kraven murmured. "It will double our chances of running into our clan. What do you think?"

"Good idea. You go a bit to the left and I'll go right."

Dusti panicked. "My sister and I stay together."

"You'll be rejoined with her soon." Drantos sighed loudly. "Keep just under a mile distance. We'll cover more ground that way. Whoever finds someone from our clan first, we'll know where to search for the other and still be close enough to hear if one of us runs into trouble."

"Good idea," Kraven agreed.

"We'll make camp at the river to eat and get a little break before we continue. How does that sound?"

"Bat's out still, so I'll keep going for as long as I can."

"That will put more distance between us and we need to make rafts. They might get sick otherwise."

"Right." Kraven paused. "I just want to hand this one over to someone else as soon as possible. She's annoying when she's awake."

"You can't keep her unconscious for too long."

"Got it. She'll need food. We'll both take a break when we reach the river. It shouldn't take more than a few hours to hunt up some food, cook it, and build a raft. Then we'll move out again. How about that?"

"Sounds good."

"Okay. We have a plan."

Dusti turned her head, horrified as she helplessly watched Kraven walk away with her sister tossed over his shoulder.

"Make him come back with Bat! Please?" she pleaded with Drantos.

"She'll be safe. Our chances of being found are better if we're in two places. We'll send help to them or they'll send help our way if he runs into our clan first."

Chapter Five

"Please put me down. I need to go to the bathroom and I think my head is about to explode from the blood rush." Dusti didn't expect Drantos to listen. He hadn't all morning as they'd marched through the woods. "Remember the puking threat? How do you feel about bladder issues? I can hear water and it's making it worse."

"That's because we've reached the river. We can take a short break."

Drantos stopped to bend over. Dusti had to clutch at his leather jacket when he eased her onto her feet. A dizzy spell had her swaying on shaky legs that suffered some numbness from being in the same position for too long. His big warm hands caged her hips to help keep her steady.

She lifted her chin to stare into his eyes. If she wasn't mistaken, she saw concern there.

"Are you all right?"

"No." The dizziness passed. "You've kept me upside down for hours."

"We needed to move fast to put distance between us and the plane." He frowned, studying her. "You don't look so well."

"I don't feel so hot."

He opened his jacket and reached inside, withdrawing one of her shots. "Do you need this?"

She'd forgotten about them with all the stress she'd been under. Clearly he hadn't though. "Probably."

His eyebrow arched. "You aren't certain?"

"I was in a plane crash and I've been abducted. I'm not sure if the lightheadedness is from you carrying me, the hypnotizing stuff you've done, or if my anemia is acting up."

"Sit down."

She glanced around and spotted a fist-sized rock nearby. She sat, feeling a bit better that there was a weapon within sight if she needed one. Drantos crouched in front of her. He removed the cap, frowning at the needle. "How often do you have to take these again?"

"It depends. Sometimes I can go a few days, even up to a week. At other times, every day. My doctor told me to take one every other day but I hate needles, so I avoid it when I can. I usually make sure I eat well-balanced meals. That helps a lot. Stress can also activate it and make it pretty bad. I'd say I probably need one, now that I'm thinking about it."

He offered it to her. She took it and peered at him. "Did you bring my entire case?"

"No. It wouldn't fit inside my pocket."

"Did you grab the alcohol packets?"

"No. I didn't see your sister use one on you."

"That's because Bat was freaked-out after the crash and not thinking straight." She pulled her skirt up a little, twisting her legs to keep her modesty in place by only revealing the upper part of her thigh on the side. She injected the meaty area and winced. "I hope I don't get an infection from not cleaning the skin first."

He took the syringe from her and sniffed at it.

"What are you doing?"

"Trying to figure out what it is. They aren't marked. I looked at them very closely."

"It's my medicine. It's called Bord-orallis."

"I've never heard of it."

"I'm not surprised. It's a rare disorder."

He capped it, and shoved it back inside his pocket. He pulled out another syringe. "I think you take after your grandmother. You know that anemia you suffer from? While you smell pure human, you aren't. Your grandmother inherited more Vampire traits than Lycan. Your body is starved for a blood source."

That wasn't funny in the least to Dusti. "A lot of people have anemia."

"I'm sure they do, but yours is easily cured if you start drinking fresh blood. I can prove what I'm telling you."

"How? I'm not drinking blood."

"We could test it."

"Forget it."

Drantos removed a syringe from his pocket. He snapped it in half and Dusti gasped, watching the drug spill out on the ground between his spread thighs where he crouched. He sniffed at the contents of the two pieces he held.

"What is *wrong* with you? I don't have many of those!"

"We can get you more once we reach my clan. I'll personally send someone to fill your prescription in one of the larger cities."

"You can't just pick that up at a pharmacy!"

"What does that mean?"

"Only one company produces the drug and it's sent straight to my doctor's office, because there aren't too many people who need it. Pharmacies don't stock it."

His eyes narrowed and he lifted the broken vial to his mouth. He stuck out his tongue and allowed some of the drug to drip onto the tip of it. Dusti grabbed his hand, attempting to make him stop.

"Are you *nuts*? Don't do that. It could make you sick!"

He pulled his tongue back into his mouth and sealed his lips. He closed his eyes. They opened almost immediately and he looked really angry.

"It tastes bad, doesn't it? It serves you right. Can you *not* destroy the rest of my medicine, please?"

He suddenly stood. "I don't suppose this doctor you see knew your mother?"

"Of course he did. I've seen Dr. Brent my entire life. He's our family doctor."

"Son of a bitch." He spun away. "I was right."

She stood, already feeling much better. "About what?"

He kept his back to her. "We'll discuss this later."

"I hate when you do that."

"Do what?" He turned around.

"Make some strange statement that makes no sense and then drop it. Either explain what you mean or don't talk at all."

"Fine."

She waited for him to say something else but he just watched her. Her temper flared. "Leave my shots alone. Don't break any more." She peered around. "Where is my sister?"

"Close by. Don't worry. She's safe. We'd have heard if they were in trouble."

"There you go again. It's annoying. What does that mean? How would we know? We can't see them."

"We'd hear it if there was trouble." Then he walked down to the edge of the river.

She glanced around again, just seeing a lot of woods. It was tempting to go search for Bat herself but there were bears somewhere out there. She wasn't about to forget that anytime soon, and she edged closer to Drantos's side, going down on her hands and knees. "Do you think this is safe to drink? I don't want to get some parasitic disease."

"Go ahead. You won't."

She cupped both her hands into the icy water, flinching at how cold it was, but brought it to her lips. It dripped onto her clothes but she didn't care as she swallowed big gulps of the fresh-tasting water.

"Easy," Drantos ordered softly. "You don't want to make yourself sick by drinking it too fast."

He dropped to his knees next to her, mimicked her position, and sipped from the river. She turned her head to watch him drink until he'd had his fill. He cocked his head to meet her gaze.

The beauty of his eyes struck her hard. They were so dark blue they edged on black. The sunshine reflected off the water, hitting his irises enough to reveal those golden flecks she'd noticed before, seeming to highlight them. His black, long eyelashes were so thick that she felt a bit envious, and they only made him more appealing.

Memories of him touching her the previous night suddenly flooded through her mind. The urge to stroke his skin almost overwhelmed her but she fought it down. It made no sense to be so attracted to him. Sure, he was looking better every second but he'd kidnapped her and told her crazy stories about mythical creatures that she didn't want to believe existed. That thing he did with his eyes couldn't be dismissed either.

"I have a few questions and I want answers. What did you do to me last night?"

"Now is not the time to have that discussion."

She clenched her teeth. "You're the one who forced me to leave the crash site with you. The least you can do is tell me what I want to know. Did you drug me or something?"

His expression softened. "No."

"You're attractive. I'll give you that, but that was..." She wasn't sure how to describe it.

"Powerful," he rasped. "Intense."

She hesitated. "What did you do to me last night to make me want you so much?"

"Drink more water. I don't want you to be dehydrated." He broke eye contact and stared up at the sky. "We need to eat and get moving again soon."

He wasn't going to discuss it. It irritated her. "Right. Shut up and don't slow you down. Got it. You don't care if I'm confused or freaked-out."

He stared at her and frowned. "I do care."

Those three words he spoke in a near whisper unsettled Dusti. She could almost swear he meant them, considering the intense look he gave her. Drantos was one handsome man, in that super-masculine way that would draw any woman. She hated noticing that but she couldn't help it. Her gaze dropped to his chest and arms. He was also really fit and muscled.

"Stop looking at me like that, sweetheart. Otherwise I'm going to forget the fish and just eat *you*. This isn't the time or the place for that. You're going to have to wait until we reach my home. This is just a short break."

His words stunned her and they seemed like a verbal slap. She jerked her gaze up, holding his. "Excuse me?"

"You were looking at me like you wished I was on the menu." He grinned. "Hold that thought until we're somewhere with a bed."

"No, I wasn't. I was just thinking how sad it is that for such a good-looking guy, you're a few crayons short of a rainbow."

His amusement faded fast. "What the hell does that mean?"

"It means you look really good at first glance but then as you take in the whole picture, you notice something is missing. Like your sanity. You're crazy if you think I want to have sex with you."

Drantos shook his head and his gaze softened while he continued to watch her. "I expect an apology for all the insults you keep giving me when you realize the truth about what we are to each other." Amusement suddenly flashed in his gaze, which matched the wide grin that spread across his face, a reminder of how handsome he could be. "You can give it to me on your knees."

Her gaze lowered down his body to the front of his jeans. She couldn't miss the outline of his aroused cock. She frowned in response, refusing to allow him to intimidate her.

"The day I blow you is the day you turn into a eunuch. Do we understand each other?" She snapped her teeth at him to make her meaning clear.

"Don't threaten to bite someone unless you want to be bitten back—and sweetheart, I have sharper teeth."

"Stop calling me that. I don't like it *or* you."

He glared. "Go to the bathroom."

She carefully stood and headed deeper into the woods to find a safe spot to empty her bladder. The fear of bears and other animals made her do her business fast before returning to the small clearing next to the water to wash her hands in the river.

Drantos wasn't where she'd left him, and one sweeping glance around didn't show any sign of him. Her heart accelerated from the jolt of fear that he might have abandoned her. He had seemed mad when she'd stomped away.

A noise made her jump and she faced the splashing sound. Drantos's head popped out of the water as he stood up about ten feet from the bank. Dusti gawked outright at the sight of his wide, tan back. He'd removed his shirt to expose his muscular upper body. The guy obviously belonged to a gym that he worked out in *a lot* to have gained those thick biceps. She'd seen bodybuilders at her own gym with less muscle mass. She had to close her mouth that had dropped open.

He turned his head, seeming to sense her there. His gaze met hers.

"Now is the time to do it if you want to strip down and use the water to get clean. Just splash yourself with water. I'm about to build a fire to cook our meal."

"No thanks." No way would she remove any of her clothes for a sponge bath in front of him.

He shrugged those impressive broad shoulders of his before wading deeper into the water, up to his armpits. He took a sharp breath before he pushed up with his legs. His sleek, wet skin showed as he rose to dive into the river. Dusti gasped when she saw his bare, beefy ass flash before he disappeared under the water completely.

She spun away, refusing to see that sight again. That's when she spotted his neatly folded clothes. He'd left them near a small bush she'd walked right past when she'd left the tree line. A pair of black briefs was on top of the pile.

Water splashed behind her and she tensed. He was probably showing off his body again. Cold water hit her and she gasped, spinning around. Drantos stood in waist-high water and grinned. He shook his hair again, more drops of the river striking her skin.

"Knock that off."

He grinned wider. "Did I get you wet? It wouldn't be the first time, would it?"

The words sank in. He was referring to the night before when she'd lost her mind. "You're so rude, and that was uncalled for."

"Was it? That was for the crayons remark. Be happy I don't walk over there, strip you bare, and remind you how much you want me. Kraven isn't here to stop me this time from finishing what I start."

She wanted to smack him. He was purposely being an ass. Two could play at that game. "Keep being a dick and I might toss your clothes in the river with you."

His amusement died. "I wouldn't recommend it. Don't piss me off any more than I already am, sweetheart. You already insulted me. Get my clothes wet and all bets are off on what I'd do in revenge."

His tone implied a threat. "Fine. You're not crazy. Everything you've told me is true. Prove it to me then. Turn into a dog. Don't Werewolves do that? Your brother said something about shifting forms. Show me."

"You'd be terrified and run from me. That's the last thing I want."

"Right. Like I'm currently here because I volunteered to be. What are you going to do if I *do* toss your stuff in the river? Suck my blood? I'm not forgetting that you said you're also a Vampire."

"Damn it, Dusti."

"Damn *you!*" She was tired of living in fear and her life had turned to hell since the moment she'd laid eyes on Drantos. He'd appeared next to her seat, and then the plane had crashed, and now she was in the middle of the wilderness worried about her sister. "I want my sister and I want to go home!"

His expression softened. "I'm sure you do. I'll catch a few fish and we'll eat. You'll feel better with a full belly. Let's call a truce for now. I could use your help."

"I'll feel better when I see Bat and we're on our way back to California." She glanced at his bared chest. His nipples were hard pebbles. "I'm not coming in there. It looks cold."

"It is. I just meant I'm going to catch some fish and I want you to prevent them from flopping back into the river once I toss them on the bank. That's all." He paused. "You'll see your sister soon. I promise that Kraven is keeping her safe. They're probably down river already eating."

She hoped so. "Fine. Let's see you catch fish. Where's your pole?"

He grinned and took a few steps closer to her, revealing more of his body. "I'll show you."

She spun around to give him her back when she saw his hipbones. "You're naked. I'm not looking."

He chuckled. "I thought you wanted to see my pole."

She clenched her hands into fists at her sides. "That's not what I meant and you know it."

"I was hoping," he muttered.

She turned back around. He hadn't exposed more than just his upper body and his lower stomach. He had the best body she'd ever seen. It irritated her to notice that. He stared at her for a moment but then turned, walking deeper into the river. She watched the way he moved, his muscles flexing as he lifted his arms and then dived back in. His lower body surfaced, flashing his nice ass again. He disappeared under the water completely.

Primal and beautiful. Those were the two words that popped into her head to describe how he looked. *Sexy*, she added. Her heart rate increased suddenly at the memory of the night before, and she clenched her teeth. *Thank God Kraven pulled us apart.*

She had to admit that she'd wanted Drantos so bad, she'd hurt for him for hours. *I've lost my mind. I snapped when the plane crashed.* That had to account for why she was attracted to him.

"Ready?"

His voice made her start, aware her mind had drifted off with her thoughts. She met his gaze where he stood in waist-high river water. He held up a big wiggling fish to show her. Somehow he'd caught a monster-size one with his bare hands. It shouldn't have surprised her but it did; he had a way of doing that to her often.

"I'm going to toss it to the shore. Make sure it doesn't flop back into the water. I figure five more and we're good. If you let one get away," he grinned, "that one was yours."

He pitched the fish right at her.

The fish hit the ground in front of her, lay stunned for a few seconds, and then started to flop around on the grass. She bit back a curse and lunged to prevent it from getting close to the water's edge. Sympathy rose inside her for the poor thing but hunger won out.

"Sorry, pal. You're dinner."

"What?"

She turned her head to glance at Drantos. "I was talking to the fish."

"And you think I'm the crazy one." He dived back under the surface.

"Asshole."

He caught all six fish in a quick amount of time, throwing her each one, and then started walking to shore. Dusti presented him with her back again when he came out of the water, to give him privacy while he dressed. She resisted the temptation to glance over her shoulder to sneak a glimpse of that amazing body he had, and he remained quiet until he approached her, fully dressed, to hover at her side.

"We'll have to set up a temporary camp. It will be risky to light a fire long enough to cook these but we need to move on soon anyway."

She looked up at him. "You know it's freaky that you can fish with your bare hands, right? Is that an Alaskan thing?"

"No but you don't believe me when I tell you what I am."

"I asked you to turn into a dog to prove what you've said but you wouldn't do it." She figured that would shut him up about his delusions.

"You're not ready for that yet."

"Right. I was only kidding. Like you actually could." She rolled her eyes. "How did I know you'd have an excuse?"

"You're already fearful of me. You'd be terrified and fight me even harder if I showed you what I look like in 'dog' form, as you call it. I actually don't look like one. I'm a lot bigger and scarier."

"I'd have run away from you when you were in the water if I'd thought I had half a chance of surviving without you. I'm stuck."

"You'd run. Trust me. It would probably get you killed. I'll wait until it's safe to give you proof. Let's go." He bent, picking up the fish. "See those rocks a little down the way? Let's head there. It's far enough from the woods not to risk the fire spreading and I can use them to build a small fire pit."

"Do you need help carrying them?"

"Nope."

"Good. I don't like big wet things." She wanted to groan the second the words were out of her mouth, the memory of Drantos's naked body flashing in her mind.

"Really?" He bent over, easily scooping up the half-dozen fish into his big hands. "I like small wet things, myself." He looked directly at her when he straightened.

"Okay," she sighed. "We're going to stop right there on that statement. I totally didn't mean it in a sexual innuendo way when I said it." She strode away from him in the direction of where he wanted to go.

"I did," he called out.

"I got that."

He made her mad. He was lucky she was the one stuck with him and not her sister. Bat would have probably killed him by now.

Worry surfaced. She hoped Bat hadn't killed Kraven, or vice versa, wherever they were. She slowed her pace, waiting for Drantos to catch up. He placed the fish on a patch of moss and set to work building a fire. His skills impressed her when he made a small pit with rocks and twigs.

"How do you plan to start a fire? Were you a Boy Scout?"

He reached inside his jacket, withdrawing a lighter. A grin spread his lips. "I could start one without this but it's easier."

"Nice." She had to admit she was hungry. Fish wasn't her favorite but she wouldn't complain. "I hope you know how to clean them. I don't."

The fire blazed as he added some larger pieces twigs. "I can. I have a knife in my boot."

She had almost forgotten about that, and she still wondered how he'd gotten through security to get onto the smaller plane. His mysterious-eye hypnotic trick was probably the reason. He fed the fire more until it was large and set to work on cleaning the fish by using a semi-flat stone as a table. There were plenty of them littering the ground.

"Will your brother feed my sister?"

"He'll take care of her."

She could only hope that was true. "What are you going to do to us once we get out of here?" *If we ever do*. She glanced around the thickly wooded area, hoping they didn't die. Animals could kill them or they could get lost, eventually succumbing to the elements.

"You'll be safe at our village. Decker wouldn't dare invade it to try to grab either of you."

"If we *find* this village." *If it even exists anywhere outside of your head.* "My grandfather won't want to find me. I wasn't kidding about how much we didn't get along the few times I met him. He gave Bat hell when she mentioned bringing me on this trip with her." Memories surfaced of being a young girl and feeling rejected. It still hurt a little but as she'd grown, it had turned to anger. "He's a jerk."

Drantos paused in cutting the fish to glance at her with a frown. "Don't take it personal. He's cold inside. He couldn't even muster feelings for his own mate."

"Your brother told me more about how he's got some evil plan to kill a bunch of VampLycans and rule the survivors."

"He is dangerous and greedy. He won't be happy until he's destroyed many lives and controls everything around him."

"I don't like him one bit but he just seemed like a creep. I think you're giving him too much credit."

"He rules his clan with brutality and fear."

"Why would they stand for it? What is a clan, exactly? And you live in a village? As in, a fishing one?" It would explain how he was so good at catching dinner if he'd been raised by fishermen.

"Our clan consists of a group of VampLycans and a very small number of Lycans. Some of us are related, most of us are not. We live together because there is safety in numbers. It's not a fishing village. It looks a lot like this wooded area." He shrugged, his focus back on preparing their dinner. "Village or town, same thing. I thought you didn't believe anything I had to say?"

"I don't but I'm bored. Tell me more."

He arched one eyebrow as he paused in cutting the fish again. He finally looked down, going back to work. "Laws are important in a clan. It's not a democracy. Each clan has a leader and a group of his trusted enforcers to carry out those laws. Enforcers are the strongest fighters. Decker keeps his people in line with fear and by murdering any who dare defy or questions his orders."

"So he's a dictator with a vicious army at his disposal?"

"A small but lethal one. It's also about traditions. Everyone in a clan swore alliance to obey the clan leader and his rules. It would be dishonorable to break an oath."

"Even if he's wrong?"

Drantos sighed. "Even so."

"That sounds stupid."

"I agree up to a certain point." He looked at her again. "You have your ways and we have ours. We follow our clan leaders and the laws they set forth. It's just the way it's done."

"It still sounds stupid."

"I'm certain there are some laws or rules in your world that you don't like or agree with. You still follow them. Why?"

"I don't want my sister to have to bail me out of jail and then ask her to defend me in court. I never want to go to prison."

"Jail or prison would be the least of their worries if anyone in a clan went against their leader. His enforcers would kill them as punishment."

"Fantastic." She hoped her sarcasm was clear. "Why isn't he in prison if he has people murdered?"

"We don't live according to your laws."

"Everyone has to. You live in this reality, right? Or are we back to that another-dimension scenario?"

"Humans don't live in our village. We keep separate from them as much as possible. They aren't aware of what goes on with our people. Your law enforcement has no way of knowing who is killed or why."

"I'm trying to imagine this world you're telling me about but it's hard," she admitted. "Why don't they just stop voting for Decker to lead them if they aren't happy having him in control?"

"He wasn't voted in. He took over from his father when he reached maturity and no one fought him to the death to take his position. Decker has loyalty from his enforcers. Think of it like one of your drug lords with a bunch of thugs who take out any people in town who want the tyranny to stop. His clan members aren't even allowed to leave. He'd kill them first or punish the family they left behind. They're trapped, and they send us warnings when they can to stop him from starting a clan war. We were at the airport searching for you after we heard two women had been sent for by Decker, and you'd help him accomplish that war. Our spies informed us of your travel route but couldn't get your names or why he needed you. We only became certain you were the right ones after you boarded the second plane."

"You have spies?"

"All four of our clans are mixed together by some bloodlines. Not everyone who is in Decker's clan agrees with what he does. They send word to their families if they hear of anything that could threaten them. They don't want to go to war with siblings, parents, or cousins."

Dusti mulled that over, deciding to let that part of his story go. "There were other women on that plane. Why didn't you pick them?"

"You and your sister were the only women traveling together. It made sense to us that you had to be the ones."

"I still don't understand why he wants Bat so badly."

"I told you."

"Tell me again."

"Decker grew greedy as he aged. Now he wants to rule all four of the clans. He probably got fed up with our interference, like when he wanted to kill the humans who lived by his borders. The three clans let him know they wouldn't allow it to happen. He can't win a fight against us without the GarLycans fighting on his side."

"Why haven't the other three clans just attacked him and ended the threat?"

Drantos paused, staring at her. "Don't think it hasn't been discussed. It has. No one wants to fight their family though. And as I said, some of us are connected by bloodlines to his clan. The lives lost would be many. We try to avoid war." He stabbed the raw fish onto sticks, dangling it over the fire to cook.

The smell had her stomach rumbling. She let his words sink in. It was tempting to keep arguing with him in hopes he'd see how illogical it all sounded but the smell of food distracted her. She'd rather eat. "I am so hungry."

He finally passed her a stick. "Careful. It's hot. Don't burn your mouth."

She almost drooled as she blew on the fish, taking a tiny bite. It wasn't seasoned or the best she'd ever tasted, but it was still good. "Thank you."

He turned his back to her to cook more. "Tell me about *your* life."

She debated on answering but felt a little generous, what with warm food in her belly that *he'd* provided. "There's not much to say. I work a regular nine-to-five job in an office as a secretary. I live alone. I don't get to see my sister that much so I jumped at the chance to come with her when she said she was taking time off work."

He glanced back. "Even though you hated who she was planning to visit?"

"Especially because of him. No way did I want her to be alone with that jack off. Bat comes off as tough as hell but she's really not. I didn't want him to get past her defenses just because he's family. She expects him to be grandfatherly and I think it would hurt her deeply when she sees him for what he is. It would really mess up her head. I wanted to be there for her."

"Weren't you worried he'd hurt your feelings if he was still cold to you?"

"My expectations of him are as low as they can be. Nothing he could do or say would surprise me unless he turns out to be a nice guy. He wasn't there when we needed him. Bat hired a private detective to get his phone number after our parents died, thinking he'd help us. She called him, sure he'd send us money. He didn't. He offered to send her a plane ticket. Just one. He told her to hand me over to foster care; as if she would ever just abandon me. My sister would never do that. It made her mad but she thought he might be broke or something. But the detective said he was rich. That blew her best excuse."

"He didn't come after her?"

"Bat had been accepted to college and had planned to live in a dorm. All that changed when our parents died. The state tried to come in and take me. They didn't feel Bat was mature enough to be my guardian. She'd just turned eighteen and graduated from high school. We listed the house for a lower price to get it sold within days and moved out of state. She switched colleges so we'd be a little harder to track if social services looked for me. We lived in some really crappy places but they didn't ask for background checks. Most of the money went to her books, her classes, and I worked part time to help pay our bills."

"That sounds difficult."

"It was but we were together. That's all that mattered."

"How did your parents die?"

Dusti hated the pain that surfaced when she thought about the evening the police had knocked on their door. "My parents had a date night. They'd go out to dinner and a movie once a week." She swallowed hard. "A semi-truck ran a red light and slammed into their car on their way home. They were both killed instantly. It had been raining and the cops said the driver had hit the brakes but skidded into the intersection."

"I'm sorry, sweetheart."

She looked up at him. "Thanks. Bat was my rock. I completely fell apart but she held it together for the both of us. We were terrified when social services showed up after the funeral. As I said, they wanted to take me away but Bat knew what to do. She always does. She told them about our grandfather and lied by saying he was coming to live with us. It bought us enough time to disappear. At least he was useful to us in that way, having a blood relative who was alive."

"Was she angry that he only offered to take her in?"

"Furious, but she said he was old. Like that excused what he did. She felt he might be afraid to take on a teenager with two years of school left, which means he'd be stuck helping to raise me."

"She probably wanted to try to make you feel better," Drantos guessed.

"No. She really wanted to think he was just an old man set in his ways, albeit a selfish one. It pisses me off too. She had the detective run his criminal history but he didn't have one. That seemed to make him a decent guy to her. She believes we should make peace with him because he's technically family since we're related by blood. It helps that he's rich, and she hopes he might leave us something in his will. Money is important to her."

"But not to you?"

"It doesn't buy happiness. My sister should know that. She gets the big bucks for doing her job but she's miserable. She'll deny that but she can't lie to *me*. I know her too well. It's as if she thinks if she makes enough money, it will make up for the past. And it represents security to her in case anything tragic ever happens again."

"Was the loss of your parents what made her that way?"

Dusti sighed. "It was a combination of things. It was really tough after our parents died. Bat would have had to fight social services to get me back if they'd taken me away. It would have eaten up all the money from the sale of the house to take them to court. I know she would have done it though. And then living like we did until I hit eighteen was rough. There were cockroaches and the neighbors were less than stellar. The cops were hauling them off on a daily basis. They were either drug dealers, hookers, or addicts who wouldn't hesitate to slit your throat if they thought you had money to steal to get their next fix. That's putting it lightly.

"It made her feel guilty because we had to live that way until she could finish getting her law degree, but that wasn't the most important reason. It was because those places made it tougher for us to be found. We moved back to California and into a nice place when she got her first job. *Then* she met someone who ripped her up."

"She was attacked?" Drantos frowned. "By what?"

"*Who*. She fell in love with this pretty-boy type who was too charming, if you get my drift. She gave him her heart and he really screwed her over. He stole her credit cards to rack up a shitload of debt. The jerk was buying other women jewelry, taking them out to fancy dinners, and fucking them in hotel rooms she ended up paying for. She really thought he loved her and never realized he was a leach until it was too late. It was how he lived. He'd pretend to love one woman, all the while stealing from her while looking for another with more money. Like she was just a stepping stone to something better. He was gone by the time the collection agencies began calling. He'd stolen her identity, racked up a bunch of credit cards she knew nothing about until the bill collectors began to call. He'd had the statements sent somewhere else."

Dusti still got pissed, remembering what had happened to her sister. "She felt like a fool and utterly devastated. He's the man she believed she'd spend the rest of her life with. It took her a year to clear up that financial mess and it deeply embarrassed her. She changed after that."

"She grew less trusting."

"It was more than that. It turned her mean. She began going on the offense. She never allowed anyone to get close to her again. She keeps everyone at arm's length by being a total bitch. It's pissed some people off enough to want to lash out at her. Her law firm employs bodyguards to protect her."

He arched an eyebrow. "Bodyguards?"

She nodded. "Yeah. Her bosses wouldn't pay for protection while she was on vacation or they'd still be with us."

"She really has bodyguards?"

"She defends bad guys for a living who people love to hate. It makes her a target for a lot of nut jobs. Maybe they think if she dies, whoever she's defending at the time might end up in prison. It's not as if she's some sweetheart of a person who apologizes for what she does, either. She tells them to kiss her ass."

Drantos chuckled.

"It's not funny. Bat is too good at her job. Once trials have ended, some of her own *clients* have made death threats. That's not a surprise, though. They're assholes and thugs with the mentality that nobody should stand up to them, especially a woman. But you've met her. I think the shock of the crash has actually mellowed her out a bit. Imagine how angry my sister can make people when she's normal."

A smile played at his lips. "Kraven probably can."

She didn't smile back. "Please tell me he's got the patience of a saint."

"He won't hurt her, Dusti. I give you my word."

What is his word really worth? She could only hope Bat was safe.

Drantos watched Dusti eat. She looked miserable and worried. "Your sister is safe," he swore. "Kraven will protect her and make sure she's cared for. He won't let anything happen to her."

She still didn't look convinced. He ate quickly, studying the area. There had been no sign of trouble so far. That didn't mean things couldn't change. Decker's men might have already located the crash site and begun to hunt for their trail. They would be able to move faster without two women slowing them down but he hoped they still had hours before they could catch up. It would help when they crossed the large body of water.

He needed to get Dusti across the river without getting her drenched. She would become cold once night fell. He scanned the sky. They had some daylight left but only a few hours. He needed to put out the fire and build some kind of raft. She could hold his clothes while he paddled her across to the other side. A few logs tied together should work.

He glanced at Dusti, wondering how she'd react when he got her home and proved that everything he'd told her was true. He'd need to shift forms and hope she didn't see him as a monster. It might kill every ounce of attraction she felt for him if all he inspired was terror.

He stifled a groan. He wanted to get her naked in the worst way. Memories of the evening before flashed through his mind. Her responses to his touch had driven him out of his mind. Pure lust and animal instincts had taken control. His dick hardened just thinking about how she'd felt under him and how hot she'd gotten when he'd been touching her.

He couldn't wait to get her home so he could stop fighting his desire to make love to her. He'd have plenty of time to seduce Dusti then and teach her exactly what was between them. She'd learn they were meant to be together and exactly how different from human men he really was. He wouldn't have to hold back anything.

He just hated that he'd frightened her the night before. She had no idea how much passion their Lycan blood could inspire.

Why in the hell didn't her mother tell her the truth? It still pissed him off. Everything would have been so much easier if Dusti had known about VampLycans and the kind of real danger Decker posed. He wouldn't be taking verbal abuse about his state of sanity or worried that she'd refuse to give a relationship between them a chance once she saw him shift forms.

She would fight him every step of the way until she realized everything he'd told her was the truth. Maybe shifting for her wasn't such a bad idea. He debated it but quickly came to the conclusion he was right before; it would terrify her even more. Long term, it wasn't worth it. She'd already endured enough trauma. It was best to allow her to think he was a little crazy, rather than her seeing him as some kind of horrific monster. She'd resist harder against her attraction to him. That was the last thing he wanted.

Time spent together would help. She'd get to know him better and he'd be able to earn her trust. He just needed to be more patient and not lose his temper when he became frustrated. He regretted swatting her ass, never meaning to cause her pain. It was a reminder that he needed to be gentler when he touched her. He never imagined his mate would be half human. It didn't bother him but it did change things. Her skin was more delicate and sensitive than the women he had become accustomed to.

I'll get her home and we'll work this out. She'll have to accept me.

He studied the moving river. That was the obstacle he needed to face next. He'd just take one problem at a time.

"Stay here and finish eating that fish, Dusti. I need to find a few fallen logs."

"For what?"

He jerked his thumb toward the water. "To cross that."

"You're determined to get me killed, aren't you?"

He closed the distance between them and crouched. She flinched when he reached out and brushed his fingers down her cheek but didn't totally pull away. She grimly held his gaze.

"I'm determined to keep you safe. We will lose anyone who finds our trail by crossing it. It's just a little water."

"It's a freakin' river, and I've been watching branches floating by near the center. That current is really moving. I'm not totally dumb. That water's probably coming from the mountaintops that are melting from the winter ending. It means that ice chunks are also mixed in there and I know how cold it got last night. The day is almost over, which means we're going to get hypothermia tonight, if we don't drown first."

He decided to try a new tactic. "I plan to get you naked in my bed, Dusti. That wouldn't happen if I got you killed. I'm very motivated. Think about that. I am."

He stood and walked toward the woods. Her shocked expression had him grinning. He'd rather face a flustered or angry woman than a terrified one.

It didn't take long to find a few dead trees. Some of them hadn't survived the winter, and the wind and snow felled many. He allowed his claws to slide out, hacking at the excess branches to remove them from the small tree trunks. He'd use his belt to bundle some of them together and it would hopefully keep Dusti dry and out of the water.

I'll get her wet later. He grinned, imagining stripping her out of her clothes and spreading her out naked on his bed. Images filled his head of making love to her but he pushed them back. Daydreaming about claiming her would have to wait.

One thing at a time. Raft first. Sex later.

He dragged the trunks one by one into the camp he'd made. Dusti watched but didn't question him as he made a few trips back and forth, and then began to build his makeshift raft.

Chapter Six

Dusti found herself staring at Drantos. It irritated her that she was so attracted to him. Since he had stripped out of his jacket, she could see the thick muscles in his arms flexing as he worked on his project. She'd never met anyone like him. He looked so utterly masculine building a raft.

He wasn't like men she knew in Los Angeles. They would be lost in the woods, helpless and probably as freaked-out as she felt. He reached up and shoved his unruly hair back. The thick, dark tresses were a bit out of control. He could use a trim in the worst way but she doubted he ever went into one of the fancy barbershops most men used to cut their hair. She figured he probably used a knife to hack at the strands or something equally as barbaric if he wanted it shorter. She bit her lip as he leaned forward, his ass in the air as he weaved his belt around two branches. He had a muscular ass that his pants molded to.

Damn it, stop ogling him. She forced her gaze to shift to the river. He wanted her to cross that. It was an insanely dangerous concept. A large log floated near the center, moving at a rapid pace. She mentally pictured it slamming into the raft Drantos built and sending her into that bubbling water. She cringed and focused on him again.

He had blatantly admitted he planned to have sex with her. What happened between them the night before resurfaced in her thoughts. It was probably going to haunt her forever. The way he'd touched her and made her feel had been downright animalistic. He'd growled and bitten her with his teeth. Worse, she'd really enjoyed it.

Her abdominal muscles clenched and her nipples throbbed at the vivid memories, desire resurfacing.

Drantos scared her. She had to concede that fact. He could make her forget everything around them except him. She'd have let him fuck her on the ground, in front of anyone present, if his brother hadn't pulled him away. He caused her to lose all common sense and willpower.

He suddenly leaned back and rolled his shoulders. She bit her lip, the urge to go massage them rising. It frightened her more and also pissed her off. She turned her back so she didn't have to see him any longer.

I need to get away from him so I can regain my sanity. I've lost my mind. He's no good for you, Dusti. Don't make this mistake again.

She flashed back to the one and only time she'd fallen in love. Reed had been handsome in his business suits. She'd met him right after she'd started working for a mortgage company as their receptionist. He was one of the loan officers.

They'd dated for two months before they'd taken a trip to Las Vegas. Reed had talked her into a quickie marriage after they'd arrived. He'd had big dreams and she'd been on board with all of them. He thought he'd make a bunch of money and she could quit her job. He'd wanted the picket fence and children. So had Dusti. Bat had flipped her lid when she'd found out her baby sister had gotten married, but Dusti hadn't cared.

Within six months, their marriage turned into a nightmare. The housing market started to fall and Reed turned really moody. He'd start arguments with her and storm out of their apartment, disappearing for hours. That's when he'd decided to switch careers. Dusti had been supportive. He was her husband and she wanted him to be happy. She'd taken a second job to help him pay for night school. It had been difficult on them both. They barely saw each other but she'd sworn to stick with the marriage for better or worse.

Drantos drew her attention once more as he kept working on the raft. Her ex-husband never would have done something like that. He hadn't even been able to fix their leaking sink. She'd had to do it. Her ex-husband wouldn't have wanted to mess up his manicure. Drantos was nothing like Reed.

She bit her lip, rehashing the past. Her taste in men couldn't be trusted. It's why she'd avoided dating after her divorce. There had been the occasional boyfriend over the years but she'd safeguarded her heart. She left at the first sign of trouble. Drantos was exactly that. It was a really bad idea to get involved with him. He made her feel too much and she never wanted to hurt again like she had while suffering through her divorce. It was painful to admit she'd given her heart to someone who'd smashed it to bits.

Just lie down and try to get some sleep while he finishes building that thing.

It sounded like a good plan to her. She slid off the rock she sat on and put her back to it, closing her eyes. She tried to blank her mind.

"Tired?"

She startled, opening her eyes. Drantos had stopped working on the raft and was crouched by the still burning fire in front of her. She hadn't heard him walk over. "A bit. I didn't get much sleep last night." She didn't mention he'd been the reason. The night before she'd slept poorly because her body had ached for his, and she hadn't slept while dangling over his back.

Knowledge flared in his eyes and a smile hinted at his lips. "Let's go to the river. You can splash some water on your face." He glanced at the sky as he shoved dirt over the fire to put it out. "We have about half an hour before we must leave. I want to cross the river about the same time Kraven should be. It's imperative to keep moving for as long as we can while we have daylight left, and stick close to them."

"Plus the smell of cooked fish will have bears and additional predators heading this way," Dusti guessed. "We don't want to still be here when they arrive for the bones, right?"

Drantos stood, brushing dirt off his fingers. "Good guess. Come on." He held out his hand.

She put hers in his, allowing him to help her up. "We have nature shows on cable."

He grinned, releasing her hand. "Do you watch them often?"

"No."

Dusti followed him and she crouched near the water's edge. She cupped icy water in her hands and splashed her face, then leaned farther over the edge to avoid dripping water onto her clothes. The shock of how cold it was had her gasping and she felt her knees slide a little on the grass. Her eyes flew open to see the water coming at her. She'd bent over too far and was about to fall in.

Drantos's big hands gripped her hips and jerked her back. She ended up leaning against his wide chest. His arms slid from her hips and around her rib cage. He bent forward enough to press his lips next to her ear.

"Be careful. As much as I fantasize about making you wet, it's not in that way."

She took a deep breath to calm her racing heart and turned her head. Their lips almost brushed as she gazed into his eyes. "Why do you say things like that? Is it to shock me?"

"Because I mean it."

Her heart pounded. He had beautiful eyes. His big body braced hers and his arm wrapped around her tighter, holding her close. It was impossible to ignore that he was an attractive man. She decided to try humor to cool down the situation. "Thanks for saving me. Turning into a human popsicle when the sun goes down isn't my idea of fun."

No luck. She became even more aware of how he held her. He was on his knees, legs spread, and her ass was firmly pressed against his groin. She wiggled her hips a little and couldn't miss the hard ridge of arousal she felt. She froze.

He softly growled at her, the golden highlights in his blue eyes seeming to flare brighter so she could see them better, and he breathed in her scent through nostrils that flared.

"Let go." Her voice came out shaky.

"Do you know what you do to me?"

"I can feel it."

His gaze lowered to her mouth. "At least allow me a kiss. I did prevent you from falling into the river. Don't I deserve something for that?"

He adjusted his arm and brushed his palm over one mound of her breast, cupping it. He gently squeezed.

Dusti closed her eyes and bit down on her bottom lip. It felt good and a jolt of pleasure hit. He squeezed again, the sensation turning her on in a rapid flash of desire until she arched her back a little to press more firmly against his palm. He slid to the ground from his crouched position and his other hand gripped her skirt. She didn't protest when his hot fingers curled around her inner leg and slid up her thigh.

"Kiss me." It was a harsh command.

"No," she whispered. He was making it difficult to think. It frightened her how he affected her. She couldn't remember anyone else ever being able to turn her on so fast and make it so impossible to think. She tried to resist. "That would be a dumb thing to do."

He paused, and then moved the hand on her inner thigh to just inches from her panties. "You think I'm insane, so you should expect me to do rash things." He slid his hand higher and cupped her through her panties. Dusti tensed before shivering as he rubbed his fingers over the soft material there, brushing against her clit and pressing tight against the lips of her sex.

He softly growled. "You smell so good that I want to have you for dessert. Would you let me do that? Let me remove your thong and spread these silky thighs around my face if I stretch out on my back? Could I nibble on you until you're about to come, and then fuck you with my tongue until you scream out my name when you do?"

It shocked her that he'd say something so crude. She opened her eyes to stare at him. Her heart beat erratically inside her chest. No one had ever spoken that graphically to her before. The visual of him doing exactly what he said made her unconsciously grind her ass against his jeans. The thick bulge trapped inside the denim became more noticeable.

He used his finger to shove her panties to the side. He traced the seam of her sex, found her wetness, and used that moisture while pressing the tip of his finger against her clit. He drew tight, small circles around the bundle of nerves until she couldn't pretend it didn't affect her. Dusti moaned, unable to hold back the sound of pleasure. He continued to taunt and play with her until she couldn't think. It was just desire and longing. Aching.

"You're so hot and smell so damn good, I have to taste."

She didn't protest when he lifted her, forcing her to stand. He remained on his knees while he yanked her panties down. She actually lifted each foot to help him free them from her ankles. His hands gripped her hips, turning her to face him. Dusti stared down into his sexy eyes, mute, clueless about what to say at that moment.

He brought his knees together and pulled her forward, so she had to step on each side of his hips when he shifted position until he was sitting on his ass in the grass. He used his hold on her to keep her close. He slowly started to lay back until he was stretched out flat, bringing her down with him. She ended up straddling his chest. She silently stared at him.

"Climb forward." His gaze shifted to the grass next to his face. "Put your knees right there on each side." He looked up at her with sexy dark blue eyes that flared with yearning. "Now." He pulled on her hips, urging her to move.

This is insane, she admitted, even as she bent forward. Bracing her hands on the grass over his head, she crawled up his body. She put her knees where he'd indicated, her lower legs bent up over the curves of his shoulders since they were too wide for her to avoid.

Drantos released her hips and grabbed her skirt, shoving it up and out of the way. The material bunched on her lower back and fell over the top of his head, blocking her view of what he was about to do. She just closed her eyes, since she couldn't see him anyway. His hot breath fanned over her sex right before his hands gripped her inner thighs. She gasped when he forced them wider apart to lower her body, adjusting her—and then she felt the vee of her thighs pressed against his mouth.

Her fingers clawed the grass, her nails digging into the dirt below when he sealed his hot mouth over her clit. His tongue traced over the sensitive bud. He started to suckle, the strong tugs making her cry out in ecstasy.

She'd had guys go down on her before but none of them had ever had her in that position, and they sure hadn't been aggressive about it. Drantos wasn't just teasing her with light little licks. He seemed to want to devour her. His strong mouth and tongue conquered her, overtook her ability to think, until all she could feel was raw sexual desire clawing inside her to find release.

He suddenly stopped when she knew she was about to climax. She wanted to protest, to beg him not to stop doing what he was doing to her clit. Her mouth actually parted to say the words...

Then his tongue breached her pussy, entering her fast. He had to have a long, thick tongue for her to feel that wonderful stretching sensation. She threw her head back and cried out his name.

He snarled in response and pulled her even tighter against his face. He'd said he wanted to fuck her with his tongue and that's exactly what he did. He withdrew and then plunged back inside, over and over. He pressed the tip of his nose against her clit and rubbed it while he moved his head. The up and down motion set a rapid pace that drove Dusti insane. He snarled deeper, causing slight vibrations. His hands kept her hips in place in a near-bruising hold to prevent her from getting away when she started to rock her hips against his driving tongue. It was too much, felt too good; she swore she couldn't withstand it.

"Drantos," she pleaded, just wanting to come.

He pressed tighter against her pussy and slid his tongue out of her completely. His mouth latched around her clit again and this time he used his teeth to lightly rasp over her swollen clit that ached to the point of pain. The new sensation sent her over the edge.

The climax tore through Dusti, shocking her with its intensity. She opened her mouth to scream but the power of the climax gripped her too strongly to draw in that much air. She panted and moaned, shivering hard, and nearly collapsed over him when her entire body started to turn lax.

He rolled them both over in a heartbeat. Dusti didn't even care that she now lay sprawled on her back, the transition a little rough. Her bared ass against the soft grass. She stared up at Drantos when he climbed upward to settle over her body. She watched him tear at the front of his jeans, shoving them down just far enough to free his cock. He looked huge, rock hard, and it was proof of how much he wanted her. She lifted her gaze, wanting to look at his face when he entered her.

His eyes had turned so blue they appeared surreal. They were too bright. It startled and confused her. He breathed heavily, panting, and seemed to sense her distress. He closed his eyes and turned his head slightly. Long seconds passed before he opened them again. They still held some of that neon look but not as much.

"Don't be afraid of me, sweetheart. I'd never hurt you."

The gruffness of his voice made her shiver. It wasn't fear though. She reached up and touched his face. The urge to kiss him was strong but she held still. He lowered over her until she was pinned under him, though he kept most of his weight off her chest so she could breathe fine. She gripped his biceps with her other hand, liking the strength she felt there.

"I'll be gentle. You're so fucking tight I'm afraid I'll injure you if I go too fast."

He didn't look away from her when he adjusted his body to free one of his hands then reached between them to guide his cock to her. The rounded, generous-sized crown of his shaft slid into the soft folds at the opening of her pussy. He gently pushed forward when he found the right spot that would welcome him.

Dusti moaned and slid her fingers from his cheek to the back of his neck. She tightened her hold on him, needing to cling to something. The sensation of the thick girth of his rigid cock penetrating her pussy felt amazing and a little scary at the same time. No pain came but she could feel her body struggling to stretch and accommodate his size. He was gentle though and kept his word, going very slowly. She stared into his eyes.

"It's okay, sweetheart." His voice deepened. "This is going to feel amazing. Just relax and I'll ma—"

A roar tore through the woods suddenly.

The terrifying noise wasn't one Dusti had ever heard before and she couldn't identify what would have made it. It sounded really close though, judging by how loud it had been.

Drantos snapped his head up to glare into the dense trees near the edge of the clearing. An inhuman snarl tore from his lips when they parted—and then his teeth seemed to lengthen into sharp fangs that dented his bottom lip.

Dusti watched them grow even longer. She stopped breathing, her mind stunned. He lifted off her fast, withdrawing from her body.

She lay there dumbfounded, legs still spread, as he shot to his feet with a speed that astonished her.

"Get up," he ordered.

Dusti couldn't respond. She was still in shock as Drantos glanced down at her. Those terrifying fangs were still protruding from his mouth when he bent and wrapped his hands around her upper arms. He just jerked her upward into a standing position. Her knees miraculously locked to hold her weight when he released her.

His eyes were bright blue. They were glowing.

"Run," he hissed. "Cross the river and just keep moving. I'll find you."

She gaped at his face. Those fangs sticking out of his mouth were real and his features had changed just enough to terrify her. His cheekbones looked denser, the shape of his eyes now appearing sunken in a little under a forehead that seemed to have thickened. A fine coat of black hairs darkened his temples, the sides of his face, and his chin.

"Run now!" he snarled, shoving her. "Get across the river. Forget the raft. There's no time."

The push broke her from her stupor. She stumbled but made it to the river's edge. It was a long way across and the current appeared strong. It reminded her that she wasn't the best swimmer. She hesitated and turned slightly, staring at Drantos. His back was to her as he faced the line of trees. She peered past him when movement caught her attention.

A big creature crept out of the thick forest and paused on all fours.

Dusti whimpered. It was huge and looked like some kind of screwed-up dog. *Hell hound*, popped into her mind. The fur that covered it wasn't thick, so she could make out the muscular, meaty arms and legs. It had to weigh hundreds of pounds, far bigger than any normal dog she'd ever seen. Its shape was odd, too, maybe part human and dog. It was the limbs that reminded her of a human but it lifted one front leg and she couldn't miss the claws protruding from its fingers. They looked razor sharp and inches long.

It growled, raising the hairs along the back of her neck.

Dusti was frozen, horrified. The horrendous-looking dog-beast turned his head a little and pure black eyes met her fearful ones. It looked evil and she had flashes of horror movies running through her mind. It *did* remind her of a hell beast.

Drantos moved between them, using his body to block her view of the thing right out of a nightmare. She didn't miss seeing Drantos's hands spread open at his sides or the long, sharp, pointed claws that somehow had grown from his fingertips.

"Do what I said," Drantos demanded in a voice way too deep to ever be confused with something human. He didn't turn to glance at her, instead kept focused on the thing that he faced off against. "Swim for your life. I'll find you."

She spun around, finally able to tear her gaze away from the clearing. The briskly moving water ran across a wide stretch of distance, with random logs floating near the center. It moved at a fast enough speed that she paused again.

Fear of drowning was strong but there was a hellish creature behind her.

I'm fucked.

Another ear-piercing roar sounded and a second one answered it. *Don't look*, she chanted inside her panicked mind. *God, don't look. I'm going to have to swim. He said swim.*

Drantos had ordered her to get to the other side of the river but it just looked too dangerous. She hadn't even learned how to swim until her eleventh birthday, when her mother had signed her up for an after-school program. She couldn't even remember the last time she'd been in a pool. It had to have been at least ten years.

Vicious sounds of a fight began and terror motivated her to rethink her fear of going into the river. Those animalistic snarls and growls were scarier than the possibility of drowning.

Guilt ate at her, too, because she'd accused Drantos of being insane. Multiple times. But that thing she'd seen in front of him wasn't a typical animal. It was some really fucked-up looking monster.

A horrific pained scream erupted from behind her. It was the final straw. Her terror over what was happening next to the river overrode her fear of drowning. She waded into the icy water.

Her feet instantly sank into muddy earth, slowing her speed, but she trudged forward, motivated to live. Her shoes got stuck but she didn't have time to bend and try to find them when the mud held them prisoner. She just stepped out of them and kept going.

The current pulled her in deeper once it was at her thighs. She lost her balance and pitched forward, completely going under the freezing water. She desperately kicked her legs, finally remembering she needed to, and used her arms in her fight to reach the surface to draw air into her lungs.

Her head broke the surface and she opened her eyes. The current pushed her along but she caught sight of the trees on the other side to help her know which direction to go. She struggled to swim toward them. The loud river drowned out any more sounds from the fight.

Is Drantos still alive? She didn't know, and that weighed as heavily on her as her soaking clothing did. She panted, urging herself to keep swimming. Her survival depended on crossing the river. She battled on, ignoring the way her limbs didn't want to respond as easily as before. The temperature was so cold it was swiftly numbing her body.

Finally, after what seemed like forever, her foot touched something and she realized her toes dug into wet earth. She bounced up, got better footing, kept wading through water until she was able to crawl out. The urge to collapse was strong but she kept going, knowing she needed to get into the thicker trees to get out of sight. One quick turn of her head assured her the current had swept her far enough downstream that she might escape that beast thing if it got past Drantos.

The cover of the woods was welcome when she finally stopped crawling, just collapsing onto her side. She panted, trying to catch her breath. Chills racked her soaked body. Her clothes were stuck to her and icy cold. She listened but only heard the moving river. No more terrifying animal sounds penetrated the woods. *Is that good or bad?*

Drantos's face flashed through her mind when she closed her eyes. He'd stood up to that horrible beast instead of running away with her. The sight of those fierce claws shooting out of his fingertips hadn't been a trick of the light.

He's really a VampLycan. They exist.

Her grasp on reality might be skewed by fear but she didn't think so. Everything Drantos had said taunted her. She'd thought he needed medication but *she* was the one wishing for drugs at that second. It also made sense now why he'd refused to shift forms in front of her, if he looked anything similar to that hellish beast she'd seen. He'd predicted it would terrify her, and he'd been right.

She finally caught her breath and pushed up to her knees, stumbling to her feet. The loss of her shoes became clear immediately as she felt the loose dirt stick to her feet. She'd also forgotten to grab her discarded panties before she'd run. That was the least of her worries. The biggest would be freezing to death or being found by that horrible creature. There were also other predators out in the woods. She wasn't about to forget their near run-in with a bear.

She hugged her body, shivering. A hiding place would be good but she had no idea where it would be safe.

Dusti glanced up at the sky, dreading the coming night. The bears suddenly seemed tame in comparison to that hell beast she'd seen. It'd had an almost humanoid form except for the hair and wolf like features. It almost made her wish someone had dumped illegal chemicals in the area that had affected the wildlife, turning them into some kind of radiated freaks. She'd read stories of things like that happening. That sure hadn't been some two-headed turtle though, nor caused by anything so simply explainable. The beast had been huge, a monstrosity.

A VampLycan. Vampires and Werewolves were real.

She stopped and leaned against a tree, breathing deeply, fighting hysteria.

She suddenly wished Drantos were with her. As much as she had hoped to get away from him, wandering around in the woods while wet and terrified was turning out to be so much worse. She was torn on how far to go from the river's edge, too. How would he be able to find her? It was probably for the best if she stayed in the same area, to help him locate her. She had to have faith that he'd be okay and come looking. The alternatives were too much for her to consider. Drantos couldn't die.

She bumped into a tree, distracted. A soft curse left her mouth as she paused, taking in her surroundings. The large, intimidating shapes of more trees spread out as far as the eye could see. The ground wasn't level, plenty of large stones were littered around the area, and a few fallen logs blocked her path.

"I hate the outdoors," she whispered, coming to the conclusion that she'd likely die on her own. Either the exposure would kill her or the animals would. Her gaze lifted to the tree branches as she wondered how she'd fare if she climbed one to get off the ground. The sun would go down at some point and she needed to make a decision.

She walked to one of the trees and wrapped her fingers around the lowest branch. It was a sad attempt, trying to pull her weight up. She was too exhausted. Frustrated tears blinded her until she blinked them back. Climbing was out of the question. She just didn't have the strength.

Think, she ordered her mind. She took some deep breaths and slowly stripped with trembling hands. There was no way to dry what she had worn but she squeezed out as much water as possible. It was chilly being naked but worse when she redressed. She hoped the clothes would help her avoid cuts and scratches, at least. Her bare feet would be a problem but it was pointless to grieve the loss of her shoes.

She huddled next to a fallen log, trying to get warm. It was impossible to do but she was low to the ground and partially hidden. Chills shook her so hard that the fish in her belly threatened to come up but she resisted the urge. There was no certainty she'd see another meal. It would also probably draw predators.

"Drantos," she whispered, wishing once more that he was at her side.

She turned more into the mossy tree. The smell of decaying wood was faint but the log blocked her from the worst of the chilly breeze. She only could hope that Bat fared better with Kraven. One of them needed to survive.

She decided to rest for a little while to regain her strength and then try to climb the tree again. *Just a little break and I'll be able to do it...*

* * * * *

Drantos wanted to kick his own ass almost as much as the VampLycan he faced off against. He never should have touched Dusti until they'd reached the safety of the clan but she was just too damn tempting. They might have been across the river already if he hadn't gotten distracted by his need to claim her body.

He snarled at the idiot who thought he could take her away from him.

"Don't even think about running after her," Drantos softly warned. "I'm going to shift and we'll battle it out—unless you have no honor. Then I'll just rip through my clothes. You know I'll catch you if you get a few seconds' head start, and the woman could get hurt if she gets between us. Decker doesn't want that, does he?"

The VampLycan crouched, his intent to launch an attack again clear, but he hesitated. The enforcer's side was already torn up from when he'd tried to dodge around Drantos to go after Dusti once already. It was possible he was buying minutes so he could recover from the wound a little. Either way, it gave Drantos the precious time he needed to strip.

He quickly did it in record time. He could shift in clothes but they would be torn up in the process. The enforcer eyed him, moving a little to the left, tearing his gaze away from Drantos to look toward where Dusti had gone.

Drantos shoved at his already open pants and they fell to his ankles. *Good enough. At least the bastard has some regard for fair fighting. Apparently not all of Decker's enforcers are totally like him.*

He'd tried to get Dusti to believe everything he'd told her but to be attacked by a VampLycan enforcer wasn't how he'd wanted her to realize his world truly existed. He snarled again to draw his enemy's attention. The male crept forward, trying to skirt around him, clearly his patience at an end.

Drantos attacked, shifting as he slammed into the enforcer.

His claws tore into meaty flesh and the male screamed in agony. Blood sprayed his own body. The fight was on.

The male rolled when he hit the ground hard and tried to slash at Drantos's throat. He ducked his head and savagely bit into the arm that had swung his way. Bone snapped under his powerful jaws. He was fighting for Dusti. It made him lethal and furious.

She is mine!

The taste of her on his tongue was replaced by rich, fresh blood. He viciously jerked his head, his fangs still embedded in the enforcer's arm. The male roared in agony. Drantos released him and jumped back. He snarled a warning. *Stop or die.*

The male stood and his front limb hung uselessly as he backed up. He flashed fangs and snarled his own warning. He wasn't willing to concede. He was willing to die following Decker's orders.

The bastard glanced toward the river and quickly tried to take off that way, but with his injured leg, Drantos was on him before he could make it ten feet. He did glance at the water for a precious few seconds himself as his body landed on the enemy's back. Dusti had gone into the river but she wasn't within sight. He only prayed she had safely swum to the other side and hadn't drowned. He'd been too occupied keeping the enforcer from getting past him to watch her progress.

He and his opponent rolled together on the ground. The enforcer roared in rage and twisted, trying to get Drantos onto his back. He made another attempt with his good arm to slash open his neck. Drantos jerked out of the way but it was close. He actually felt claws brush against his skin. He thrust one arm back before stabbing his own claws into the male's chest.

His opponent's eyes widened in disbelief as he realized it was a killing blow.

Drantos felt no sympathy. Any enforcer of Decker's who would attack other VampLycans to steal a woman deserved death—especially one who had come to kidnap Dusti and Bat.

They knew why their clan leader wanted the women, and the outcome if Aveoth accepted a trade. They'd be helping the war begin. It would mean families fighting members from different clans. Cousins killing cousins. Brothers battling each other, in some cases, if they'd mated women from other clans and joined them to keep her with her family. Decker would probably have killed any of his enforcers who refused his orders but death would be preferable than starting a civil war.

This man under him bought into his clan leader's craziness.

The male screamed when Drantos dug his claws in deeper, piercing his heart. It was a sickening feeling, finding the beating source of the male under him and tearing into it. He watched the enforcer's eyes as death took him. It was fast in reality but time seemed to stand still until the tense body under his grew limp. The male exhaled his last breath and his head slightly turned. Sightless eyes peered up at the darkening sky.

Drantos yanked his claws out and slowly pushed himself off the male. Then he turned his head, frantically searching for Dusti in the water. The river turned out of sight a few hundred yards up. She wasn't anywhere to be seen. He sniffed the wind but could only pick up the scent of blood from the enforcer he'd just killed. He studied the surrounding area and crept toward the woods. There could be more of them out there, and he'd kill them all to prevent them from following Dusti.

It alarmed him that Kraven hadn't arrived on the scene. It was possible his brother had already crossed the river with Bat. The wide flow of water might muffle sounds of the attack from the other side.

The other alternative could be that they'd taken his brother by surprise.

Rage surfaced fast but then he calmed. Decker's enforcer wouldn't have attacked him if they already had what they wanted. Kraven also wasn't one to allow anyone to sneak up on him. He was an excellent fighter.

He scanned the area again, still wondering if more enforcers would arrive. Long seconds passed. No one else came at him.

Drantos entered the woods to peer around but didn't find any immediate threat. He returned to the clearing and stared down at the dead enforcer. He couldn't leave him there. A hunter could come across the body. Not too many humans lived in the area but there were a few. It was also too close to the river. Some humans traveled along it. They might spot the downed man. It left him feeling torn between desire and duty. He wanted to go after Dusti but law demanded he take care of the evidence. Humans couldn't learn of their existence.

He used his claws, digging into the earth. He'd bury Decker's enforcer and send others back later to return the fallen man to his surviving family members. It was the best he could do. Even an enemy deserved a decent burial given by his loved ones, even if he had made a bad decision that had gotten him killed. He was part of the clans.

It took Drantos time but he finally shoved the male inside the shallow grave, covered him up with dirt and heavy rocks so wildlife wouldn't dig him up to eat.

He walked into the river and submerged his entire body, scrubbing the blood and dirt from his skin. He returned to the embankment and retrieved his clothing. That's when he realized his jacket had been destroyed. Claws had torn through the material during the fight. And another problem became known—Dusti's shots hadn't survived. They had probably rolled over them in battle, breaking the thin syringes. The liquid from them had seeped into the material of his jacket and the ground under it.

"Fuck." He blew out a frustrated breath. He'd find her and make sure she was okay, then worry about the rest later.

He bundled his remaining clothing and boots, hooking them onto the highest point of a branch on his makeshift raft. He'd hopefully at least keep his things dry by pushing the damn thing across the river. He just wished Dusti were on it, too, warm, dry, and safe.

A snarl built up inside his throat. He needed to find her, and was outraged that she wasn't at his side where she belonged. He'd kill Decker Filmore with his bare hands if Dusti died because that jackass wanted to use his own flesh and blood to start a war.

Chapter Seven

"I'm so screwed," Dusti whispered, staring at pure blackness around her. The sun had gone down while she'd slept. The woods were unusually quiet with the exception of the breeze stirring leaves.

A soft crunch noise made Dusti blindly snap her head in the direction of the sound. She hugged her waist hard, pressing tighter against the log, praying it wasn't some animal on the hunt for an easy meal. She silently swore to fight if anything tried to eat her.

Exhaustion had caught up with her while she'd tried to get warm and she'd dozed off. That little nap had turned out to be a mistake, one she only realized now. It was impossible to even see her hand in front of her face. The treetops above entirely blocked the moon, if it was even out. Her plan of climbing a tree wouldn't happen until morning. She'd even debated on stumbling around in the dark but fear had kept her in place.

She imagined falling into a hole or worse, off a cliff. All the unseen dangers filled her thoughts. She could stumble right into a nest of sleeping snakes. *Or a bear.* She shuddered, hugging her waist a little tighter. Animals wouldn't have to hunt for her if she found them first. It was best to just stay still and quiet.

No other sounds scared her so she started to relax. Her head lowered to rest on the tops of her drawn-up knees, her breath the only source of warmth against her chest where she trapped it there with her bent body. She was cold but she doubted she'd freeze to death overnight. Things could be worse.

"I should have climbed a tree," she muttered aloud, the sound of her voice her only comfort.

"That would have been a good plan," a deep voice stated from behind her.

Dusti cried out, startled, and nearly toppled over.

Firm hands suddenly curled around her shoulders and a big body eased down along her back, his thighs caging her body. "Easy. It's Drantos."

"Damn it! You scared the shit out of me." She twisted though, grabbing hold of him. "I'm so glad you're here. You're alive!" She latched onto one of his arms. The warmth of his skin made her shiver again. "Are you okay?"

"I'm fine. I'm sorry I couldn't find you faster. You stayed in the river longer than I anticipated so it took time to track you."

She managed to wiggle enough to get to her knees, leaning heavily against his chest. Warmth radiated off him as if he were a living heater.

"You're freezing cold."

"Why aren't your clothes wet?" She touched his chest to assure she hadn't imagined the dry feel of his shirt.

"One of us got to use that raft I built. Strip down now, take it all off. I'll give you my shirt. I had to unfortunately leave the jacket behind."

"Why?"

"Remove your wet clothes, Dusti. They're just making you colder."

She only hesitated for a second. The lure of something dry against her skin was too much of a temptation to resist. It took effort to back away from him and rise to her feet. She instantly missed being against him. His big hands helped her tug the still very damp clothing from her body. The chilly wind seemed a bit colder without the thin barrier when she stood naked. Drantos tugged his warm shirt over her head.

"Can you see anything?"

"Yes," he admitted softly. "Don't worry. You're just an outline and I'm not enjoying it as much as I wish I could. Are you okay? I don't smell blood."

"I'm frozen and terrified but fine. What happened? Is that thing still out there? Is it coming after us?"

"He's no longer a threat. I handled it."

She allowed him to pull her into his very warm arms as his words sank in. His bare chest radiated wonderful heat that had her hugging him as tightly as she could. His big body felt heavenly while he cradled her against his front.

"Handled it?"

"Yes."

"You got away from that thing?"

"You could say that. That particular enforcer of your grandfather's won't be a problem to us again."

"How? You grew claws, didn't you?" Her mind was fraught with questions and her sanity depended on getting answers she could understand. "Drantos, is that what you look like when you shift?"

"Yes. I told you what my people are." He rubbed her back. "That really was one of your grandfather's enforcers. It's what we look like in our other form."

She shivered again but it had nothing to do with being cold anymore. "That didn't look like a wolf." She clutched at him tighter. "You don't look that scary, do you? That thing looked like some kind of hell beast. It's because he's evil, right? I totally want to believe that."

"Damn it, Dusti. Don't make things up to account for what you don't want to believe. We're half-breeds. Part Vampire and Lycan. It's why we don't look like wolves. We're more." He sighed, sounding frustrated. "Let's talk about this later. I'm just glad you're safe. Right now we need to find shelter and get you warm. We're in no immediate danger."

"How?" She wasn't really sure she wanted to hear the answer.

"How am I going to find shelter?"

"How did you deal with that creature?"

He said nothing.

"What happened?" Dusti wasn't about to let the subject go. "How did you get away from that thing?"

He took a deep breath. "Do you really want to know?"

"No. I'm just talking because I love the sound of my voice." She rubbed her face on his warm chest. "Answer the question."

"Let's find somewhere more comfortable to get you warm. We're too in the open here. We'll talk then."

"Fine."

He lifted her without warning. "Wrap around me and hold on, sweetheart."

She didn't chastise him for the endearment. Her arms wound around his neck and her legs hugged his waist. She should have been embarrassed that her bare pussy pressed against his lower stomach but she was too cold and tired to care. His shirt hung low enough that it covered her ass when his arms shifted their hold to shelf her butt. He started to walk.

Dusti dozed in his arms until sometime later, when he adjusted both their bodies to sit down. She had to release her hold around his hips. He cradled her on top of his lap and kept her firmly against his chest, with his arms around her in a hug.

"This is the best I can do. We can't have a fire."

She tensed. "Are there more of my grandfather's things looking for us?"

"They are *men*, Dusti. Not things. And probably, but that's not the only reason we can't have a fire. I forgot to grab the lighter I used when I had to abandon my jacket. I had other, more serious things on my mind at the time. I'd borrow one from Kraven but he seemed to have lost his jacket too."

"You saw your brother? Is Bat okay?"

"She's fine. Kraven ran into trouble, too, and I found him first while I was searching for you. We took care of Decker's men but more could be close by."

"Are you sure she's okay?"

"Your sister and my brother are fine. They're nearby. They had to cross the river as well, and I just brought us closer to them."

"Where are they?" She stirred in his arms, blindly looking around. "I need to see Bat. I want to talk to her."

"She can't hear you unless you yell out, which I don't suggest. More enforcers could be out there."

"Why didn't you take us right to them? I don't think splitting up was such a good idea." She worried about her sister far too much, especially if Bat had seen one of those creatures.

"We're sitting in a small dent in the ground space next to a tree that will shield us from the wind. There isn't enough room for all four of us. Kraven found a hole not too far away. He'll keep your sister warm and safe until the sun rises."

"Did she see what I did?"

He hesitated. "I'm not certain what she saw or didn't."

"She'll be freaked-out and scared. I should check on her, Drantos. It's not every day you see some creature that looks like it came right out of one of those hell-dog movies. She doesn't even like horror flicks."

His arms tightened around her more and his head lowered to rest against the top of her head. "Kraven will deal with her if she saw one of us shifted. He'll explain to her the same thing I am to you. We lost the ability to resemble wolves when we inherited our Vampire genes." He drew in a deep breath. "Hell isn't involved. It's just genetic mutations from being half-breeds. Decker's men could track us faster in animal form than they could if they'd remained in their skin."

An image of that terrifying beast flashed in Dusti's memory. It had been huge and vicious looking. *The claws...* She trembled.

"Easy," Drantos urged. "I'd never hurt you. Feel my warm skin?" He brushed his fingertips over her arm. "No claws or fur, sweetheart."

"Stop calling me that. You're doing it on purpose."

"I am. There's no reason for you to ever wonder if I'd hurt you. That's why I didn't want to show you proof of what we are so soon. The last thing I want is for you to be afraid of me."

"I'm not one of those beast things."

"No. Your father was pure human. Your blood is diluted enough that you're unable to change forms. You took more after him than your mother."

Her mind wanted to resist believing what he said but she'd seen that thing as clear as day. She'd never forget it either. And Drantos could turn into one of them. She'd been intimate with him.

"I told Bat that you were nuts," she admitted. "I know you didn't want me to say anything to her but I did. I'm sorry."

"Don't worry about that now, Dusti."

"I thought you were like my friend Greg. He thinks aliens are after him when he doesn't take his meds."

Drantos rubbed her back. "I'm not crazy and I don't need medication."

"I think I'm going to lose my mind. Maybe *I'm* the one who needs meds."

"Please don't fall apart on me. Call me names, insult me, but damn it, don't cry. I can't handle that. If it helps, remember that your mother was pure VampLycan. She could shift."

"You're *not* helping."

"Sorry. I just wanted to remind you that we're all not monsters. I got the impression you loved your mother and she was good to you."

"She was the best."

"She loved you and cared for you. Not all of us are bad."

"If that's true, if she had to run away from her father, why didn't she go to her own people to protect her from being given to some bad guy?"

He shrugged against her. "Maybe she feared it would cause deaths in whatever clan that took her in, if her father tried to get her back. I don't know, Dusti. No one could answer that but her. We would have tried to protect Antina and welcomed her if she'd sought sanctuary. Maybe she believed everything bad her father ever said about us. He feels we're too soft and weak because we're not as bloodthirsty as he is. That's why he wants to rule all the clans. It's possible she felt we couldn't protect her. We like to live in peace but that doesn't mean we're not deadly when we're on the defense. We are. Was she happy in the human world?"

"Yes." She fought tears. "My parents were really in love. You could see how much they meant to each other every time they touched. That was often. We were a happy family. She used to say meeting my father had been the best moment of her life, besides having her daughters. We had a lot of great times." Memories of her childhood surfaced in her thoughts. "We laughed a lot."

"Didn't you ever notice anything strange about her?"

Dusti racked her brain. "She looked pretty young for her age. Everyone used to comment on it. Of course, it's just in the genes. Bat and I get mistaken all the time for being in our early twenties."

"How old are you?"

"Thirty-one, and Bat is thirty-three."

"You don't look it." He paused. "You may have inherited the very slow aging process we possess."

"What does that mean?"

"Vampires don't age at all from the time they are turned. Lycans have a lifespan of about five hundred years."

She couldn't imagine. "Are you kidding me? How is that possible?"

"Vampires use blood to heal and survive. As long as they feed, it repairs most damage, including any from aging. Lycans heal much faster than humans. The same applies but they don't need fresh blood. They just have to keep in good health by eating regularly and allowing the shift to happen from time to time. It would be as if a human refused to use their legs to stand and just sat around nonstop instead. Over time, it would make their bodies weaken."

She let that sink in. "What about what you are? How long do you live?"

"We're not sure."

"How is that possible?"

"We've only been in existence for about two hundred years. We age slower than Lycans. "

"How do you know that?"

"Just meet a Lycan and a VampLycan born the same year. The Lycan will look a few years older than one of ours. It's the best measure we've found so far. It's estimated that we might live eight hundred years or so but that's a guess. It would also depend on what traits are more dominant of the two. A mostly Vampire-blooded VampLycan will probably live longer than a mostly Lycan-blooded one."

"My grandfather had gray hair when he visited us."

"He probably dyed it and put on makeup to look aged before going into your world. He was playing a role for you and your sister. Some of us do that if we have dealings with the same humans long enough. We try to blend in and not raise suspicion."

"What kind of dealings?"

He hesitated.

"Is it a secret or something?"

"No, I was thinking of a good example to use. There was a family who used to own some land by one of our borders. My father met them thirty years ago. They ended up moving away but kept ownership of the land. Two years ago they wanted to sell it, so they contacted my father and wanted him to meet them. He always makes it clear to surrounding human families that he's interested if they're ever willing to sell. He hasn't aged in that time and they would have noticed. He had to pretend to be his own son." Drantos chuckled lightly. "He didn't want to wear makeup or dye his hair to appear older."

"Did it work?"

"Yes. They sold the land to him and weren't suspicious."

She let that sink in. "I'd ask you how old you are but I'm afraid to know the answer. I don't want to be grossed out if you're super old, considering where your mouth happened to be earlier. Just tell me you weren't born in the year eighteen hundred and something."

He chuckled again. "I wasn't."

"I'm glad you think this is funny." She swallowed the lump in her throat. "Are you just saying that to make me feel better?"

"No. Do you want to know how old I am?"

She shook her head. "I've had enough shocks for one day. You only appear to be about thirty."

"We grow a bit faster than humans do as children but then it slows once we hit adolescence. Lycans tend to hit between the mid-twenties to low-thirties range and then the aging just seems to halt there for a few hundred years. We might be the same way. I'm older than the number you said I look but I was born in the nineteen hundreds. Are you warmer? You're trembling less and your skin doesn't feel as chilled."

"You put off a lot of heat."

"We run hotter. I wish you had gained that trait from your mother. I knew you hadn't though when I saw how cold you became when the sun went down last night. In that regard, you're totally human and need to be kept warm."

The silence stretched between them. Dusti wasn't sure what to say. She knew so little about Drantos except he certainly wasn't at all similar to any guy she'd ever been interested in. She needed answers though to the questions relevant at the moment. The future seemed bleak.

"Are more of those...men going to come after us?"

"Not the ones who attacked Kraven and I."

The tone of his voice, the sureness of it, made her heart stutter. "What does that mean? How can you be so sure?"

He adjusted his body into a more comfortable position and pulled her firmer against him, and continued to hedge. "We did what we had to."

"What is that?"

"They won't be coming after you again. At least not those three."

Her eyes opened to pitch darkness. The grim tone of his voice finally gave her a hint. "You killed them?"

"Two died. One conceded. We had no choice, Dusti. They would have killed my brother and me if we hadn't won in battle. That would have left you captured, taken to Decker, and he would have handed Bat over to Aveoth."

She'd known deep inside that's exactly what he'd meant. He'd killed to protect her.

A laugh burst from her, totally unexpected. Random, silly thoughts followed. She pictured trying to put that beast she'd seen into a coffin. It wouldn't fit. That seemed funny to her, despite knowing it shouldn't. It happened when she was under too much stress. It was as if twisted humor helped her cope.

"You find it funny that I had to take a life?" He sounded surprised.

"No. I think I'm having a breakdown of sorts. And I was just thinking that I couldn't even get a guy to buy me flowers, and you *killed* for me. We haven't even been out on a date yet."

He pulled her tighter against his body. "I'll cut down a field of flowers to give you when we reach the safety of home. We don't have any restaurants in the village but I'll cook you dinner."

"That's so sweet of you to say. Its total bullshit but I appreciate it."

"You'd be surprised over what I'd do for you, Dusti." Sincerity rang in his tone.

"You just want to finish what we started today."

"I won't deny that."

"You can't hide what you want from me in that regard. I can feel you digging into my stomach. My, what a big bulge you have."

He tensed. "I can't help it. You're touching me and in my arms. I know you need rest though. You're exhausted."

She nodded again, enjoyed rubbing her cheek against his hot skin. She loved the way he smelled too. Masculine and woodsy. *The woods part may be coming from the tree we're next to,* she acknowledged, but it didn't matter.

She focused, pushing away lightheaded sensations that threatened to make her giggle. Her head swam again and she felt as though she might float away. Her fingers and toes tingled...

The symptoms sank in. She wasn't having an emotional breakdown. It was more of a physical one.

"We have another problem."

"I know you're hungry. I can hear your stomach rumbling. We'll catch something at first light, and I hope you enjoy sushi since we can't start a fire."

"It's not my favorite but I can eat it. That's not it. You said you had to leave your jacket behind. My shots were inside it. I'm feeling lightheaded and dizzy again. My thoughts are a mess and my emotions are all over the place. It's going to get worse. I'll start to ramble, as if I'm drunk, if I don't pass out soon. I'll go into shock next, then lapse into a coma. It happened once when I was fourteen. I hated taking the shots so I'd lied to my mom about giving myself one. I blacked out and next thing I knew, my mom was staring down at me with that look on her face that said I was in big trouble. She yelled at me for an hour about how dangerous it was not to take my shots and how I could have slipped into a deep coma."

"I told you that you don't need shots. You take after your grandmother."

"Right. What are you going to do? Kill a rabbit and make me drink its blood? Big ewww. I'd throw it up before I could even get it down. I know you said I'm part Vampire but I can't stand the sight of blood. I tried volunteering at a hospital in my teens for extra credit during high school and fainted the first time I was in the emergency room, when they brought in some guy with a head wound. That makes me a shitty Vampire, doesn't it?"

"Dusti." He sounded irritated.

"I need a shot, Drantos. That's what I'm saying. I think the cold water was too much of a strain or something on my body. I'm exhibiting all the symptoms of when I've gone without a shot for too long. Only worse. The stress probably didn't help matters." She fought to calm her thoughts and keep in control of her emotions. Tears filled her eyes but she managed to resist bursting into sobs. "It's going to get worse. It always does."

"Do you trust me at all?"

She paused to feel out her emotions. "Yes. You're not a lunatic. You saved me on the plane, protected me again from that beast by the river, and you found me tonight to keep me from dying in the woods."

He chuckled. "You don't have to sound so irritated about it."

"I just don't feel well. I get kind of bitchy when I'm dizzy and scared. It beats the giggles. Trust me."

"Straddle me."

"You're going to hit on me *now*? Really?"

"Straddle my lap," he repeated. "Do it."

"I thought you said you knew I was too tired for sex."

"That was before I knew what you needed."

"I need sex? I hate to break this to you but it's only going to wear me down more and make me sicker if I do physical activity. I think the swim across the river exhausted me or sent me into shock."

"Please trust me."

She hesitated but when his arms released her, she moved. She didn't have a lot of room to maneuver. She could feel the chilled vegetation brush against her legs when she faced Drantos and put her knees on either side of his hips. His thighs shifted together and she adjusted until she wasn't touching cold Earth anymore except for under her knees. The rest of her sat on his lap. The bulge in his jeans pressed against her pussy and her hands flattened on his chest.

"Now what?"

"I'm going to supply you with blood. Lean in until your face is at my throat."

It took her seconds to understand his meaning. "You want me to bite you?" The absurdity of it caused her to laugh. It wasn't funny but she couldn't help herself. "You *are* nuts. I don't have fangs."

"No, but I have claws. I'll scratch my skin to bleed for you."

All humor left. She wished she could see his face. "No. That's insane. I'm starting to get a bit woozy but I'm not that far gone."

"You need the iron, Dusti. You're part VampLycan."

"You drink blood?" She reached up to examine her neck on both sides where he'd bitten her the night before. She didn't find any scabs or flaws on her smooth skin. "You drank *my* blood?"

"I nicked your throat with a fang, then I licked it closed. My saliva heals wounds.

It's one of the Vampire traits passed down to us. It hides the bite marks quickly on someone we've fed from to help us survive without detection. The more saliva, the faster the healing."

Dusti leaned back away from him. "Are you serious?" She searched her skin again with both hands but couldn't find any healing injuries on her neck where he'd been kissing her.

"Calm down. I smell your fear. We don't need blood the way a Vampire does."

"Then why did you take some of mine?"

His arms wrapped around her waist and he sat up enough to press against her chest, pinning her to him. She didn't resist. He was warm.

"Easy, Dusti. We get our blood through eating meat. You'll never find a vegetarian VampLycan. I told you that you take after Marvilella, your grandmother. She needed to drink fresh blood about once a week or she'd suffer some symptoms of illness. You obviously need it as well. I needed to test your blood to determine exactly what you are."

"And what am I?"

"Mostly human, but more Vampire than Lycan."

"You could taste all that with just a little blood?"

"Yes."

"How do Lycans, Vampires, and humans taste?"

"You really want to know?"

"I'm trying to be rational. Work with me or watch me flip out."

He chuckled. "It's impossible to explain. Can you tell the difference between chicken, pork, and beef? I can tell the difference between species."

"That disturbs me on so many levels."

"I'm sorry." He rubbed her hips with his hands. "You still need blood."

"Maybe my body will recover if I just rest. It happens sometimes. I've had to go without my shots for a few days when I didn't have time to go see my doctor."

"Who is this doctor? You said he knew your mother?"

"He was an old friend of hers and she only trusted him. My mom was really protective of us. She didn't want her daughters to be treated by some careless doctor who might mess up. She read the news a lot and would point out malpractice lawsuits as reasons why we needed to go to Dr. Brent for everything, so he's always taken care of me. He kept seeing me even though I couldn't afford to pay him after our parents died, for the visits to refill my prescriptions. Bat and I would drive to see him once a month until we moved back to California after she got her law degree. He said we were like family to him."

"Your mother knew of your Vampire needs, and this doctor knows what you really are too. That's why you can't get your prescriptions filled by a pharmacy. Your doctor gets it from the Vampires. It's not iron you've been dosed with. I tasted what I suspect is blood, mixed with a little bit of a sedative, plus a light chemical…something that probably keeps it from clotting."

It put a new spin on things. "Are you sure? You just said you know the taste of blood, but you don't seem sure."

"It's almost like a synthetic of blood, or maybe mixed. It was odd but had the same metallic taste. The sedative was probably added to prevent you from feeling a blood high. You would have felt that otherwise."

"A blood high?"

"It can range from feeling aroused to experiencing a sense of being intoxicated. Dr. Brent isn't human. I'd bet on that. He either makes up your shots himself or, as I said, he gets it from Vampires."

"You expect me to believe Dr. Brent steals blood from different people to put in my shots?" She scoffed. "No. He's a nice man."

"He could have taken the blood from other patients he has, or some Vampires own blood banks. They pay money to those who donate."

"Why? Can't they just grab someone and take it?"

"They can but some Vampires have been known to inject blood when they travel or need to go into hiding. I'm not sure what they add to it so it doesn't coagulate but we've been aware of the practice for some years."

"But Dr. Brent seems so normal."

"Most of the non-humans do in the cities. They've had to learn to hide what they are. I'm guessing your doctor is a sympathetic Lycan or Vampire who helped your mother out when she had children."

"You mean a VampLycan."

"No. It's extremely rare for one of us to move to a city. Your mother is the only exception I've ever heard of. You've seen one of us changed. There's no way anyone could mistake us for a wolf or a coyote in a park if they ever caught sight of us shifted. Lycans live in wooded areas if possible, or near big parks so they can shift and run from time to time. They need to shift or, as I said, they can get sick after a while. Vampires prefer big cities. Tons of feeding options, it's easy to blend in, and they are a lot more social with humans than Lycans are. Your doctor has to live in the city if he's been treating you all of your life. VampLycans can visit cities, even stay there for a few months if they have business to attend to, but never more than that."

"I've seen Dr. Brent during the day." She paused. "But none of the rooms have windows. I never realized that until now. His offices are set up in a basement of a large building." She wondered suddenly if the man she'd always known could really be a Vampire or a werewolf. "Is it true that Vampires sleep during the day? I've been to his office plenty of times during daylight hours."

"He's probably a sympathetic Lycan. Old Vampires can move around whenever they want but younger ones lapse into comas when the sun rises, until it sets."

"Do you transform every full moon?"

He snorted. "That's bullshit movie stuff. I admit it calls to us but we don't have to shift. It's more a case of better hunting, since most animals tend to let their guard down when the lighting is better." He took a deep breath. "You need blood, Dusti. Face it. We lost your shots. I'm going to have to bleed so you get better."

"Tag, huh? You're it?" She winced. "I don't think I can do it. Even if I were willing—and I'm so glad I'm blind with how dark it is because I'd faint at seeing blood—that's just so gross."

"I'll distract you."

"I don't think—"

His lips closed over hers. The kiss stunned her but when his tongue invaded her mouth, it quickly snapped her out of it. She kissed him back. Just the taste of him, the feel of his tongue exploring hers, sent desire shooting throughout her body. Her hands clutched at his shoulders, pulled him closer, and he unwound his arms from behind her. He reached between them.

She heard his zipper moving, knew when he lifted them both that he'd tugged down his jeans enough to free his cock, but she wanted him to. Her hand slid lower over his chest to explore his tight abs until her fingers curled around hot, aroused flesh. His cock felt thick, velvety, but also reminded her of steel from how hard it was.

He growled into their kiss, tearing his mouth away from hers. Dusti protested.

"Don't stop."

"Lean back for me. Arch your hips so I can reach you." His voice came out harsh, deep, and sexy as hell.

She released his cock to lean away from him a bit. Her hands reached back to curve around the tops of his thighs just below the knee to brace her body. She raised her hips a little off his lap until a few inches of space separated them. He delved his hand between her parted thighs, found her clit and massaged it. He used his other hand to shove the material of the shirt she wore out of his way. His calloused palm surfed up her stomach until he teased her nipple with his fingers.

Dusti threw her head back and moaned. She wiggled against his talented fingers, knowing it wouldn't take long for her to come. Drantos's touch made her hotter than hell. Everything he did seemed amplified a hundred times from what lesser men had made her feel when they put their hands or mouths on her.

"You're getting so damn wet," he rasped in that harsh tone. "You smell so incredibly good that I want you over my face again but now isn't the time."

She disagreed but only managed to moan instead of getting the words out. Her hips rocked against his fingers. He pinched her nipple, jolting her passion to a higher level, and made her ache painfully to come.

He released her nipple with one hand and pulled the other away from her pussy. "Lift up and take me."

She didn't know what he meant until he took over. He gripped her hips, lifted them with his strong hands, and she had no choice but to sit up. She blindly found his shoulders, clutched the tops of them to keep her balance, while he slowly eased her down on top of his cock. The broad head of it pressed against her pussy, slid a little in the slickness of her need, and then he eased her weight down.

Dusti's nails bit into his skin as she moaned. Her face fell forward until her forehead rested on the curve of his shoulder. He tortured her with the unhurried way he eased inside her. The thickness of his cock stretched her vaginal walls until he was all she could feel.

A soft snarl tore from Drantos. His grip on her made her entire body shake slightly when he seemed to tremble too. He froze there to keep her suspended over him.

"Wrap your arms around me," he ordered.

His deep, passion-rough voice made her hotter. He didn't even sound human but she sure hoped he wouldn't change into a beast under her. She ran her hands over hot skin, not feeling any hair. She relaxed from the tension the thought of him shifting had caused.

She wound her arms around his shoulders and hugged him. He lowered her more, until her ass rested on his bared thighs. He was all the way inside her. She moaned, adjusted her knees to brace on the moss next to his hips, and lifted her weight up. She sank down, moaning again at the wonderful sensation of him inside her. She started to slowly ride him.

Ecstasy had her crying out against his skin with her parted mouth. Every nerve ending seemed focused on the slide of his cock while she moved. Drantos growled softly, his hands cupping and squeezing her ass. It helped her glide up and down on him until he tightened his hold, halting her.

"Don't stop," she pleaded. "I'm so close."

"You need blood. Trust me. I don't want to stop either but you need to take from me. I'm going to reach up to scratch my skin." He took a ragged breath. "Then I'm going to fuck you until you come, sweetheart. Trust me on that. Just take my blood while I do it."

"I don't know if—"

He lowered her fast on his cock, making her cry out in rapture. He held her still with his strength.

"You'll do it for me—for *us*. I'm not going to allow you to stop me from caring for you. You're mine."

His words didn't make sense but the flames of burning desire inside her body could only make her concentrate on her lust. He released her ass with one hand, reaching up. His entire body stiffened for a second, and then he gasped.

"Drink, Dusti. Do it for me."

The irony scent of his blood filled her nose. She felt wetness against the side of her lip, a little to her left on his neck. His hand returned to grip her ass and he lifted her, nearly withdrew totally from her body, and pulled her down again. She cried out in pleasure.

He froze. "*Drink.*"

She turned her head, opened her mouth, and tasted the coppery wetness found there. She hesitated but Drantos started to move, his hips bucking under her thighs, driving in and out of her pussy in deep strokes that stole her breath from the raw intensity of sexual hunger. She licked at him, not caring anymore that she was drinking blood, as long as he didn't stop. The climax built, her vaginal walls gripping him tighter and upping her pleasure. She sucked on his neck as frantically as she wanted to come.

Drantos snarled. "That's it, sweetheart. Damn, you're perfect."

His hands lifted her hips and slammed her on his pumping hips faster. She cried out, released his skin, and started to climax hard. Her entire body jerked from the blinding pleasure. She seized, shook violently, and clung to him for dear life.

Drantos suddenly turned his head, nudged her, and she felt a sharp bite of pain where shoulder met neck. She cried out as another climax tore through her, the second time as violent as the first. Drantos shook with her, his hips bucking under her, and she felt it when he came. Hot jets of his semen warmed her insides.

They stilled, both panting, until Drantos released her neck. His tongue lapped at where he'd bitten her. The pain eased until she only felt the rasp of his tongue on her skin. She lay against him limply, her body too tired to even attempt to move.

He softly growled. "You're mine, Dusti."

"I felt you."

"I bit your neck. I'm sorry. I didn't mean to but I couldn't resist. I just needed to taste you again."

"I meant when you got off too. I've never felt a guy come inside me before."

He nuzzled her neck again. "There are going to be a lot of new things we'll experience together."

He tipped his head back and Dusti startled when he licked her along her jawline. She pulled back.

"What are you doing?"

"Cleaning my blood off you."

She grimaced, realizing she'd actually taken his blood. "Seriously?"

"Do you want to scare your sister when she sees you in the morning? There's no doubt she heard us." He chuckled, his voice not as deep as when they'd had sex. "You've got blood all over your face. Turn toward me. You know you like my tongue."

She hesitated. "I guess some handy wet wipes would be great to have right now."

"Yeah, but they aren't here. I am. Allow me to clean you."

She squeezed her eyes closed and held still while he slowly licked the blood away. It felt weird but not unpleasant, especially when he sealed his lips over hers to brush a tender kiss there. She parted her mouth to deepen it but he pulled back.

"If I kiss you, I'm going to fuck you again. You're exhausted."

She realized his cock remained rock hard inside her. "I know you came so why aren't you softening?"

"I'm not human."

"Right." She rested her cheek against the curve of his shoulder. "I don't feel weak or dizzy anymore. I guess taking your blood worked. I don't want to believe this but I can't dispute the fact that the blood is affecting me the way the shots do." She actually felt better faster than she normally did. "Thank you."

"Never thank me for giving you what you need. It's my privilege and honor to care for you."

She chewed on her lip. He sounded sincere. Part of her felt uncomfortable with the situation. She hadn't known him that long but they'd just had sex. It was a first for her. She normally dated someone for months before taking that step. Drantos was different. It wasn't just because of how they'd met or the fact that they'd gone through so much together in such a short time. There was a strong attraction Dusti hoped they shared. She wondered if he felt the same way.

"Was this just sex to you?"

"No." He held her tighter.

"Okay." She relaxed a little.

"I've never felt this way about someone else."

She liked hearing that. "Me either." She was warm now, no longer cold, and felt comfortable in his arms. They were still physically joined since he kept her on his lap. It was the most intimate after-sex time she'd spent with a man. The silence bothered her, though; made her feel like the emotional connection was missing. She just wanted to hear his voice so she said the first thing that came to mind.

"Talk about firsts. I've never jumped into bed with someone this fast—and I drank some of your blood. Are you a little freaked-out too because you bit me during sex?"

He didn't say anything.

"Did you fall asleep already? I know guys conk out after sex but I thought you were different."

"What do you mean by freaked-out?"

"You know, the whole being bitten and having sex thing."

He cleared his throat. "You'll get used to it."

He spoke so quietly she barely heard the words, but she had. Uneasiness slowly sank into her. "You've done this before then? You bite women during sex?" *Does he do this often?*

She'd thought what they did was special. She was feeling things for him. Did that mean he'd just walk away in the end? What they'd shared had felt so exceptional to her.

He cleared his throat again and he massaged her with his hands. She thought he would lift her off him but instead he settled her more firmly against him. "Neither of us were virgins."

"What does one have to do with the other?"

He held her just a little tighter. "You know how you don't want to know my actual age? I believe this is another subject you don't want to discuss tonight."

Confusion had her lifting her head away from him. She wished she could see his face. "What are you not saying? Now I'm going to imagine all kinds of bad stuff. Just tell me. Do you drink blood from all the women you have sex with? Is what we just did together your normal?"

He took a deep breath. "Fine. Sometimes during sex, VampLycans draw blood. It's foreplay if they are into rough sex, or if they want to test to see if the woman could be their mate. One will bite, but we don't bite each other at the same time."

She let that sink in. The image of Drantos with other women, allowing them to fuck and suck on him, wasn't one she enjoyed at all. She forced her body to relax and rested her head against his shoulder again. *It's not as if we're engaged or even dating*, she reasoned, trying not to feel jealous but failing. Pain surfaced too. What they'd done was way out of her comfort zone and she'd mistaken it for a lot more than he seemed to.

"Dusti? I can feel your heart pounding. I told you that you didn't want to know."

"It's no biggie," she lied.

He remained silent. She held still for a full minute.

"I should get off you. I can't sleep with you inside me."

He softly cursed. "I shouldn't have told you. You're angry."

"No. I just don't sleep straddling a guy's lap with his dick buried inside me."

He growled. "You will with me."

"I still plan to curl up on your lap. You're keeping me warm."

"You'll stay where you belong."

That had her eyebrows lifting. "What does that mean?"

"Sleep. You need to rest. You're comfortable and warm where you are. You're right where I want you."

"Just because I fucked you doesn't mean you can order me around."

His body tensed. "Sleep, Dusti. We'll finish this argument in the morning if you want to have one. We need to rest. It's been a long day."

She relaxed. "Fine. We'll fight in the morning. If I wasn't exhausted, you'd be in a world of shit though for acting all caveman with me."

His hands roamed her body, massaging where he touched. "None of them mattered, sweetheart. You're special to me. You and I exchanged blood together during sex. That's a first for me."

Some of her anger eased. He probably said that to all the women he had sex with but she wanted to believe it. She allowed the exhaustion to take hold. She didn't want to deal with the fact that she might be falling in love with someone who wasn't human and that her entire world had turned upside down.

I'm not totally human either. Tears filled her eyes but his massaging hands on her body soothed her into a dreamless sleep.

Chapter Eight

Drantos woke before dawn. He knew he'd messed up the night before. He never wanted to lie to Dusti but admitting that some biting during sex wasn't rare with VampLycans had angered her. It was possible it even hurt her feelings.

Her slow breathing assured him that she still slept. His own anger stirred when he remembered the shape she'd been in when he'd found her curled into a ball, near death.

His pure hatred for Decker burned inside his chest. The clan leader had forced his only daughter to flee into the human world to escape a horrible fate of being sent to the cliffs to live with a GarLycan. Dusti's mother, Antina, had either told the human she'd lived with the truth about her being a VampLycan, to actually form a mating bond with him, or she'd bypassed her instincts. It would have been difficult to get pregnant but not impossible if she snuck his blood, taking hold of his mind to make him forget afterward. It was a depressing thought to have to live with someone that way.

There wouldn't have been a safe place for Antina to shift, even inside her home, if she'd hidden her nature from everyone living with her. He still couldn't imagine how she'd survived without being attacked by Vampires and Lycans, but learning about Dr. Brent meant she'd had some kind of an alliance with one of the two. Vampires were stronger so he would bet the doctor was a master Vampire. Those bastards couldn't withstand direct sunlight but they didn't have to sleep during the day.

Antina had birthed two daughters with a human. It had been her responsibility to warn them of the truth of their heritage and to have prepared them for her father attempting to use them in the future. Decker's reason for wanting Bat in Alaska couldn't be mistaken.

He couldn't blame Antina for avoiding Aveoth. It would have doomed her to never having a family or being loved. Aveoth had once been a good man. Things had changed in his late teens. He'd become a heartless, vicious leader who'd instilled wariness in VampLycans after his father's death. He wasn't as bad as Decker though. The GarLycans didn't want war. They just believed in segregation of the clans.

He closed his eyes and tried to slow his breathing. He'd listened closely to the details he'd learned of Dusti's mother. She'd died before Dusti had reached maturity but Bat had been eighteen. *The age of consent. Why didn't she at least warn Bat?*

It left a bunch of unanswered questions. He believed Bat was as naive as her younger sister, despite Kraven's reservations. He didn't think Bat would have willingly boarded that plane to walk into Decker's world otherwise, especially with Dusti at her side. She wasn't submissive or the type to take orders without question. Drantos had to assume their mother hadn't said a word to either daughter.

He adjusted his hold on Dusti to make sure she slept comfortably. She could have died when they'd had to separate. Her human blood made her weak and vulnerable. He slid his fingertips down her arm and grasped her limp hand. It felt small in his. He ran his thumb over one of her fingernails. They were thin and delicate. She had no way to defend herself. No claws were sheathed below the surface. He just wanted to protect Dusti and would do whatever it took to keep her safe.

Maybe that's what Antina thought too.

He sighed. It was possible the female VampLycan believed she'd be there to deal with her father if he ever tried to take Bat. She would have been a fool, though, to assume she'd be able to prevent her daughter from being kidnapped. Decker never did his own dirty work. He always sent his enforcers to do it for him. She would have been outnumbered.

Maybe she had a spy within her clan who'd assured her Aveoth already had a lover. It's possible she didn't want to tell them unless she absolutely had to. Then she'd died before that happened, which left them in danger.

Word of Aveoth losing his lover had spread fast right after Lane's death. The beautiful VampLycan from another clan had actually volunteered to share his bed. No one knew how Lane had died, but rumors spread that the GarLycan leader must have killed her in a fit of rage. Drantos didn't believe it. He didn't want to.

Lord Abotorus, Aveoth's father, had been a full-blooded Gargoyle, and he never would have willingly allowed his son's friendship to bloom with any VampLycans. Their clans might have had to forge an alliance but he hadn't been happy about it. It was acceptable to take one as a lover but the old bastard had seemed to view them as servants. He tolerated Lycans since they needed them to have children. It was part of the deal though that they had to live in peace near the VampLycans. Old thinking made some of the Gargoyles wary of anyone with Vampire blood running in their veins.

The son had defied his father's wishes by hanging out with Drantos and his brother. Aveoth would meet him and Kraven near the river that divided their clan lands. He smiled as memories of those times flashed. Aveoth could fly and it had fascinated them, seeing his large wings when he landed. He'd shown them what he looked like transformed into his solid Gargoyle shape and had even taken them for a few flights.

In return, they'd taught him how to use the Lycan traits his father demanded he ignore. They hunted in the woods, fished in the river, and shared their fighting skills. They'd mused about a future where Aveoth would strengthen the bonds between their clans once his father stepped down and he took his place. They wouldn't have to meet in secret anymore, worried about Aveoth being punished if Lord Abotorus discovered who his son spent his time with. He and Kraven had grown to look upon Aveoth as if he were another brother. They'd been that close.

The warmth inside Drantos faded. Lord Abotorus hadn't stepped down but instead had been challenged to the death by his own son. Aveoth had won. All those years they'd spent together seemed to have been a mockery when Aveoth cut all ties to the brothers. It had left him and Kraven confused and, worse, hurt. The boy they'd bonded with had grown into a man who'd turned his back on them. They hadn't seen that coming.

Over sixty years had passed, and not a single word from Aveoth. No explanation or apology for just walking away from them. Kraven had wanted to travel to the cliffs the GarLycans called home to speak to him but Drantos had too much pride. He'd always talked him out of it. Aveoth obviously wanted nothing to do with them. They shouldn't have to ask for his audience and admit he'd caused them grief. He was just another clan leader who shunned others.

Drantos hated to admit it, but in his mind, Aveoth had become somewhat like Decker.

Not that bad, he amended. Aveoth had never attacked any of the clans. He'd kept the alliances in place, his people sticking to their territory. He'd send one of his enforcers to share information if they knew of a threat in the area, and they did the same.

Decker, on the other hand, never gave warnings. They wouldn't have known Decker had sent for two women from California if it weren't for a few trusted spies in the VampLycan's clan. The spy who'd told them about the women hadn't had many details to share, not even their names, but he'd said Decker bragged to all that their arrival meant big changes were coming. That was never good.

Drantos and Kraven had volunteered to seek out and eliminate the threat. They hadn't been sure what to expect. All that was certain was they weren't Vampires. Decker hated Vamps and the flight was scheduled for daylight hours. Drantos had thought the women might be Lycan representatives, and Decker had planned to form an alliance with their packs, in order to attack the clans.

Kraven hadn't cared who they were. He'd just wanted the threat to end. It had been confusing when they'd boarded the plane full of humans. They'd gone to Anchorage to scope out the passengers and figure out how to deal with the threat before the smaller plane landed. They'd grabbed a few drinks, then boarded the flight.

Kraven had leaned into him, whispering, "Shit. Do you think he's going to form an alliance with humans? Maybe the military? Would he nuke our clans to just wipe us out completely?"

Drantos had disagreed. "He'd destroy the land he wants. And he can't take over the clans if no one survives. It would also cause issues with Vampires and Lycans. They'd all be terrified the humans would target them when the truth of their existence is revealed. Decker hates humans more than he does us. He's insane but not stupid." He'd scanned the passengers. "There're two young women traveling together. They might be the ones. He can control their minds and force them to his will." He'd glanced at the two blondes a few rows up and over.

"Them?" Kraven scowled. "They look about as dangerous as baby bunnies. What in the hell could he use them for?"

"The one in the business dress kind of looks like a scientist. Maybe he plans to poison all the other leaders and their enforcers. It would leave our women and the weaker males at his mercy. Someone with knowledge about chemicals could figure out what kills one of us."

"Shit." Kraven winced. "That's all kinds of fucked-up."

"We need to question them. We'll grab them as soon as we land. We should have about twenty minutes to get out of there before Decker's enforcers arrive since we have the plan in place to state the plane was delayed taking off. Decker knows to call and check the status of that since these smaller flights are notorious for that."

"Okay."

It had gone to hell when the pilots announced they were going to crash. Drantos had needed to know what Decker planned, and that meant making sure the women survived. It had come as quite a shock to learn they were Decker's granddaughters, since no one had known Antina had children.

Everything had suddenly made sense. The crazy clan leader wasn't trying to use humans or Lycans to wage a war. He didn't need to bring in forces from the outside. He had a clan of GarLycans already in place and the leverage to make an alliance of his own with Aveoth. Decker could offer him a new lover.

Drantos caressed Dusti, pulling away from his grim thoughts. She was too sweet to be a descendant of that devious monster. He silently swore not to allow Decker to win. He needed to protect his family and his clan. He nuzzled his cheek against Dusti. That included her, since she was now his. She wasn't ever going to end up being sent to Aveoth.

A slight noise drew his attention and he tensed, sniffing the air. The sky had lightened but the sun hadn't risen above the mountains yet. It could be more enforcers sent by Decker. He'd fight them to the death if they tried to take the woman in his arms.

He gently shifted Dusti and laid her on the ground next to him. She shivered in her sleep but promptly curled into a tight ball, not waking. He rose and fixed the front of his pants, closing them. He tensed, his claws sliding out of his fingertips.

A twig snapped to his left. He curled his lip up and his fangs sprang forth. He didn't growl a warning in case it was Kraven. He wanted Dusti to sleep for as long as possible. He sniffed again and caught a familiar scent.

His rigid muscles relaxed and he bent, tugging his shirt over Dusti's exposed bottom. He straightened and placed his body in front of hers.

A shape strode from between the trees and he advanced a few more steps to meet his cousin halfway. "It's good to see you, Red."

"So the plane went down. Did you make that happen?" The slightly taller man tilted his head, sniffing—then his narrowed gaze honed in on Dusti. "Is that one of them? You *fucked* her?"

"She's Decker's granddaughter. There are two of them."

"What?" His cousin appeared shocked.

"It seems Antina had two daughters."

A growl burst forth from Red. "Why didn't you kill them?"

"They're innocents. Their father was human and Antina never told them about their heritage. They didn't have a clue that they were different, since they take after their father's bloodline so much. They boarded the plane believing their long-lost grandfather was dying. The bastard planned to use their ignorance to have them come right to him." He explained what he assumed Decker's plan had been.

"You should have taken out the threat. Decker can't hand either one over to Aveoth if they're dead."

"No." Drantos shifted his stance to keep Dusti out of Red's view. "She's *mine*."

"Shit!" Red took a step back. "Are you certain?"

"No doubt. I've spent time with her and the bond is there."

"Your father isn't going to be happy about who she is, and I'm certain your mother will be less so. You know this is going to cause a ton of problems for our clan. Decker won't just let this go. He finally has some leverage to use against Aveoth."

"I can't help biology. Decker will die if he comes after Dusti. Aveoth too. I'm not letting either of them have her."

Red was silent for long moments. "How are you dealing with discovering she's your mate?"

Drantos assessed his emotions. "It came as a surprise."

"How human is she?"

He debated on answering but he trusted Red. They were almost as close as brothers. "Very. She does have some Vampire traits."

"Fangs and bloodlust?"

"No. She just gets weak every few days without blood, from what I've been able to ascertain. The desire rises more when she's under a lot of physical stress. Injuries weaken her if she isn't given blood."

"Is she sensitive to the sun?"

"Thankfully, no."

"Her mother didn't tell them *anything* about us?"

Anger stirred again. "Not a damn word. Dusti thought I was insane when I tried to tell her about VampLycans, until we ran into someone from Decker's clan. She got to see a shifted enforcer."

"Shit." Red tensed, going on alert. "He has clan in the area? We haven't come across any of them."

"I took on one, and two of them found Kraven. I take it more of our people are nearby?"

"Yeah. We split up to cover more ground to search for you."

Drantos reached out his hand. "Can I borrow your jacket? She had to flee across the river and only has my shirt to wear. She can't keep her own body heat worth a damn."

Red shrugged it off and passed it over. "You know this is going to cause a stir when we get back home. Not only are these women mostly human, but they're Decker's blood. That isn't exactly going to endear them to anyone."

"Marvilella was from our clan. They carry her blood too."

"I'd forgotten about that."

"Let's hope everyone else hasn't—or I'll remind them."

Drantos spun away and approached Dusti. She shivered in her sleep and he couldn't miss the gooseflesh that covered her arms and legs. He dropped to his knees and crouched over her.

"Dusti? Wake up. My clan has found us."

She was slow to wake and it worried him. He opened the jacket. "Dusti. Wake up." He used a sterner tone and her eyes parted. Confusion was easy to read while she peered up at him. He showed her the jacket. "Put this on."

That got her moving. She sat up and allowed him to wrap her in the jacket. It didn't sit well with him, smelling Red on Dusti, but keeping her warm was more important. He helped her to her feet and then scooped her into his arms, careful to keep her modesty.

"Curl into me, sweetheart. You're barefoot and we're going to be moving fast."

"Thank you for not tossing me over your shoulder."

It would be easier on him to transport her that way, but he didn't want to possibly expose her ass to his cousin or anyone else if the shirt and jacket rode up past her mid-thighs. He advanced until he stood before Red. His cousin forced a smile that didn't reach his eyes. He was glad he didn't have to snarl at him to be polite.

Dusti clutched at his shoulders when she first got a glimpse of Red. Her arms slid around his neck and hugged him tight. Her body tensed in his arms. Protective instincts pounded at him when he identified her fear.

"It's okay," he assured her. "I want you to meet Redson, Dusti. He's my cousin. You can just call him Red."

"Hello." Red inclined his head.

"Hi," she whispered.

Drantos stepped back, putting more distance between him and Red. "Kraven is close, with her sister. I could lead you to them."

Red glanced at Dusti then held his gaze. "I'll find them. Just head north and you can't miss the rest of our group. They'll find you if you can't find them."

He appreciated his cousin's offer to look for the other couple alone. He wanted to get Dusti to safety but he didn't want her afraid at the same time. "Thanks."

Red sniffed the air and Drantos jerked his head. "They're in that direction."

"I'll see you soon." Red took off.

Drantos adjusted Dusti into a more comfortable position. "No one is going to hurt you."

"All I can think about is what I saw yesterday. Does everyone change into one of those…creatures?"

He realized it might take a while for her to become accustomed to VampLycans without feeling fear. It didn't bode well for their future if she couldn't accept what he was, or the rest of the clan. She'd have to though, since she'd never be safe if she returned to her old life. Decker would just send more of his enforcers after her and Bat. Drantos wouldn't be there to protect her.

He also wasn't letting her go.

"Yes." He wouldn't soften the truth. "We're people, Dusti. You don't fear *me*."

She tucked her head against his throat. He noticed she didn't say anything. He bit back a frustrated growl.

"Just hold on and try to hide your fear."

Dusti just wanted to talk to her sister. Bat needed to know everything she did and her older sibling was much better at evaluating facts to form a plan of action. Drantos's words sank in. "Why would I need to hide my fear?"

"They can smell it and it would be considered a weakness."

"Right." She was still a little groggy but that helped snap her out of it. "I saw on Animal Planet that sometimes it will attract predators. Am I going to smell like dinner to them or something?"

He snorted. "The things you say. No. It's just that weakness is perceived as a bad thing. I'd like for my clan to respect you. That means you need to be brave. I would never allow anyone to hurt you. Trust *me*, if no one else. Does that make you feel safer?"

"That guy was pretty big."

"Red?"

"Yes. And he was scary. He didn't like me."

"He didn't say that."

"He didn't have to. It was the way he looked at me."

"You're Decker's granddaughter. That shocked him but he'll get over it. Anything associated with your grandfather is met with distrust and dislike."

"Great. You know how I feel about Decker Filmore. He's an asshole."

"They'll realize that and understand you're nothing like him."

"I hope so."

"Me too," he muttered. "Don't be alarmed when you spot them and remember you're totally safe."

"Don't show fear." It sounded easy. She locked her fingers together behind his neck. She did trust Drantos to keep her safe. He'd faced off against that hell beast to protect her. People in skin, no matter how big they were, had to be tame in comparison. She took a few deep breaths. "Got it."

"Good." He lowered his voice more. "They're approaching us. I smell them."

She scanned the thick woods until she spotted movement at the base of a tree. One of those large, terrifying beasty creatures stalked forward. Drantos halted and squeezed her, as if reminded her that he would keep her safe.

"It's someone from my clan," he whispered. "Not the enemy."

Dusti tried not to stare but it was impossible. The creature was big, vicious-looking, and had sharp fangs. The claws on the toes could probably tear through flesh as easily as if skin were butter. She sucked in a deep breath and tried hard to manage her hammering heart. The creature growled, sounding unfriendly.

Dusti tensed, praying it wouldn't attack.

"They were raised in the human world and didn't know about us," Drantos announced, speaking to the creature. "Their mother was VampLycan but their father was a human."

The creature sat on its haunches, staring directly at her. It didn't snarl or lunge forward to attack. The dark eyes freaked her out though. They did look evil. It also had a long black mane. The one she'd seen the day before hadn't had one that nearly touched the ground.

It growled again, paused, and made some whining noises. Drantos shook his head. "She was never told the truth since she doesn't exhibit enough traits that would have betrayed what she was. She's not afraid. It's just that she's seen only one other, and he tried to take her away from me. That's why she's leery."

It sunk in that they were having a conversation. It stunned her. "You speak growl?"

"Not exactly but we use tones. I can guess what the questions would be according those, or guess moods by sounds, and also by imagining what I'd be thinking and feeling."

Drantos gently bent and placed her on her feet. He clasped her hand though and held on tight. She wondered if he did it to assure her or keep her from bolting into the woods when she caught sight of more people. They were in skin, at least.

The beast growled again and Drantos shook his head. "Don't change. She'll adjust to how you look."

The thing ignored him by lifting up to all fours and tucking its head down—then it started to shift.

The hair receded as Dusti stared in horrified fascination. It made disgusting noises that she guessed were bones popping as the shape started to shrink in a little. The skin tone lightened slightly as it became more humanoid. Finally a woman stood before them, stretching as she rose to her feet, seeming to work out kinks in her shoulders and arms.

The woman was tall and lanky, and when she threw back her hair to get it out of her face, it flowed to her ass. Her nakedness didn't seem to bother her, but it did Dusti. The woman's perky breasts were displayed and she seemed chilly in the early dawn morning.

"Who is her mother?" She had a husky voice.

Drantos paused. "Do you remember Decker's daughter who disappeared? Her name was Antina."

The woman stepped closer and her dark brown eyes widened. "I thought he killed her or she committed suicide to avoid her fate."

"She was hiding amongst the humans. She mated with one and had two daughters. This is one of them. Kraven is with the other."

The woman had a graceful, almost catlike way of moving as she advanced. Her nostrils flared and she jerked to a halt. Her eyes narrowed and fixed on Drantos. Anger was an easy emotion to read.

"You *fucked* it? I smell you all over her."

"She's mine, Yonda."

"No." She shook her head, some of her long hair falling forward and hiding one breast. "That can't be."

"It is."

Yonda paled considerably. "She reeks of human. This can't be! You can't accept a *human*. You're the first son. She's not good enough for you!"

"She carries VampLycan blood. It's faint but there. And you know it's not a requirement."

The scary woman snarled and lowered her chin, glaring at Dusti. *If looks could kill...I'd be dying right now*. She inched closer to Drantos and even took a step back, putting part of her body behind his. It was impossible to look away from that much rage, all of it directed at her. She just didn't know why Yonda hated her enough to look as if she wanted to tear her apart.

"Enough," Drantos ordered. "Don't even think about it. She belongs to me and I'll defend her. I'd hate to hit you but I would."

Dusti usually resented when he spoke possessively of her but at that moment, she was glad. The woman took a step back but she didn't appear happy about it.

Pure anger seemed to radiate off her. It confused Dusti but it was also scary. She'd witnessed that woman changing from a hellish beast. She could revert back.

"Yonda," Drantos snapped. "Go cool down."

Yonda didn't budge. She turned her anger on him. "Does she know how important your place is with our clan? She's *weak*, Drantos. You can't do this! Did you explain your duties to her as first son?"

"It's none of your business. Butt out, Yonda."

"You've always been my business! I can't allow you to make such a huge mistake."

Dusti glanced between the pair, a sick feeling settling in her stomach. She suspected Yonda had been one of the women Drantos had slept with. She studied her—and then a worse suspicion clawed at her. She had to ask the question that she wanted to know most.

"Are you his girlfriend?"

Yonda didn't spare her a glance, her gaze locked on Drantos. "We don't use those terms. What do you call it when he sleeps in *my* bed more than he does his own?"

Dusti tried to extricate her hand from his. Drantos had a girlfriend but he'd slept with *her*.

She felt betrayed and her fears became reality. She thought he might break her heart and but hadn't expected their budding romance to come to a screeching halt so soon. It hurt far worse than she thought it would. She'd come to care about him deeper than she'd realized until that minute. The tearing pain in her chest proved that.

He turned his head and frowned at her. "I can explain."

"Let me go."

He refused. "Dusti, you don't understand."

"Were you sleeping with her before you met me? Do you live at her house?"

"I slept there sometimes. I don't live with her. It's not how you think."

"Let me go," she repeated, louder. She wasn't afraid anymore. She was hurt and angry. "I don't want you touching me. You're a cheating bastard and you made me a part of it." She glanced at Yonda. "I didn't know. I'm so sorry."

"He's too good for you," Yonda spat.

Now the woman was just being rude and bitchy. Dusti twisted on her hand and shoved against Drantos with her other one. "Let go."

"You call it a 'fuck buddy' in your world." He sounded and looked furious. "We had no commitment." He snapped his head in Yonda's direction. "Tell her!"

"You think that helps your case?" Dusti punched his arm, still trying to get him to free her hand. He held it tight enough it almost hurt. "We have another term in my world that applies too. You're a man-whore. No thanks. I'm so done. *Let go.*"

"What is going on here?"

The deep voice of a man startled Dusti and she twisted her head, staring at the mid-thirty-something big guy storming out of the woods. He was dressed at least, not a creature. He wore a shirt, faded jeans, and running shoes. His hair was a little long and she took note of the resemblance to Drantos. It was probably another cousin of his.

"Dad." Drantos released her and lowered his head.

Dusti gaped. She glanced between both men, rubbing her freed hand to return blood circulation to her fingers. They only looked a few years apart. Drantos had said VampLycans aged slowly but it still came as a shock.

"I asked what was going on." The man halted a few feet away and sniffed. "Is this one of Decker's associates?"

"She's his granddaughter." Drantos lifted his head. "She and her sister—"

The slightly older man snarled and lunged, attempting to grab Dusti.

She gasped and jerked back but Drantos was faster. He put his body between them. A loud, terrifying snarl came from him. Their bodies clashed and Drantos used his chest to shove the other man back.

"Don't!"

"You're protecting Decker's kin? Get out of my way, son. That's an order."

"No! Listen to me, Dad. She isn't aligned with Decker. She hates him as much as we do."

"Lies," the other man growled. "She's his blood and I know what that means. She's to be offered to Aveoth in exchange for the GarLycans' help to slaughter the other clans. I'll kill her before I allow that to happen. Is the sister dead?"

Drantos widened his stance and lifted his arms, his claws sliding out. Dusti backed up until a tree blocked her escape. She was tempted to make a run for it but Yonda took the opportunity to creep up on the left, glaring at her. Dusti held still, afraid to move farther away from Drantos's protection.

"*No*. She's with Kraven. I know you're furious but listen to me," Drantos demanded. "They had no idea about us or what was going on here. Decker lured them to Alaska by letting them think he was dying. You know his daughter fled. Antina mated with a human and never told her daughters about their heritage. They had no real contact with Decker."

"They still pose a danger. I can't allow a war to begin. Their deaths will end it here and now."

"Don't make me do this, Dad." Drantos didn't budge. "You're being unreasonable."

"I'm protecting the lives of many VampLycans. Two deaths are better than dozens or hundreds. It must be done. Get out of the way right now."

"No!" Drantos snarled.

His father snarled back.

Dusti gawked, horrified that it seemed son and father were about to fight. More clothed people arrived, watching both men. She glanced at the strangers, seeing shock and dismay on many faces.

"You're going to challenge me?" Velder hissed the words. "I gave you a direct order, Drantos. Two lives are not worth many more. We both know it."

"I'm not challenging you." Drantos spoke loud and clear. "They are the granddaughters of Marvilella. Don't forget that. She was clan. They need sanctuary."

Velder seemed to consider that briefly. "We'll give them to Aveoth ourselves then, without strings. He can pick one of them. That is the best option I'm willing to afford."

"This one is *mine*." Drantos growled low. "Aveoth doesn't get her—and Kraven will fight for her sister. The bonds won't be denied. Don't ask that of us."

The other man stumbled back a few steps until Dusti could see his face. He appeared completely horrified. "No!"

"It's the truth. You're not turning them over to the GarLycan. I'll fight Aveoth to the death before he touches what belongs to me, and Kraven feels the same. You can ask him when he arrives, which should be soon."

"Tell him you forbid it!" Yonda shouted. "She's *human*. Smell her. Weak!" The woman turned her head and spat on the ground. She glared at Dusti. "Not worthy of one of your sons. She's already causing dissension in our clan. Your son is openly defying you. Kill her!"

The older man snapped his head in her direction and his features twisted into a mask of rage. "Stay out of this."

Yonda dropped her head and backed away. "I'm sorry, Velder."

"This is a family issue. Tell the others to prepare for our journey home and keep your mouth shut about what you've heard. I won't abide gossip." He spun around, addressing the rest of the people who'd approached. "My son isn't challenging me for leadership. This is a family disagreement. We're leaving. Go now!"

Yonda spun and fled, running fast. She was buck naked but didn't seem to care. Dusti watched her until she was out of sight and saw the others follow. She turned her focus back to Drantos's father. He seemed to be having a glaring match with his son.

"Don't even think about hurting either one of them," Drantos warned. "Kraven and I will leave the clan if you make us."

"You just defied me in front of the others."

"I'm not going to let you kill Dusti or her sister. She's innocent in this mess. Decker Filmore might be their blood relation but that's the only tie they have. Plenty of our people have blood ties to others in his clan. It doesn't make them our enemies."

"Decker will target our clan to get them back."

"I'm aware but that doesn't mean I'm willing to hand Dusti over. I'll leave with her and go somewhere else if you don't want to fight him."

"I'd rip out Decker's heart and feed it to him if he ever dares step into our territory. It's the GarLycans I don't want to fight with." Velder paused, glanced at Dusti, then back at his son. "We have kept the peace since settling in this area. We have too many women and children, Drantos. I have to protect them at any cost. They are yours to protect as well, your responsibility as my son."

"Dusti is my one," Drantos stated firmly. "I'm certain."

"We're done talking right now. This is not over though. No one is going to forget what they witnessed here but we'll face the consequences later. I don't want to leave our clan unprotected, now that I know what Decker plans. He could have already contacted Aveoth to launch an attack." Velder spun around and raised his voice. "Move out. We're returning home."

Drantos turned and frowned at Dusti. He glanced at her feet. "I'll carry you. Come here." He reached for her.

"Forget it." She inched around him and avoided touching his hands. The ground was cold against her bare feet but she didn't want him touching her again. "I can walk."

"Dusti." Frustration sounded in his voice.

She avoided his gaze. "Save it. Don't you have a girlfriend to go apologize to?"

"Damn it," he snarled. "It isn't like that."

"Spare me." Despite the fact he'd protected her again, she was still mad and hurt. His girlfriend or ex situation, whatever, didn't sit well with her. She hurried her pace, following his father. The man wasn't friendly and he'd wanted to attack her but it beat arguing with Drantos. There was no excuse for him being involved with one woman and then having sex with her. He hadn't mentioned anything about Yonda, and he should have.

More people were ahead of them once they cleared a thick area of trees. A dirt road curved out of sight and two pickup trucks carefully drove along them, stopping where the group assembled. They were a rough, fit-looking bunch. Yonda walked to one of the cabs and jerked the door open. She withdrew folded clothing from inside and dressed. It stunned Dusti that she seemed unaware of all the men around her. Some of them were glancing at the bent woman putting on sweats, obviously checking out her ass.

What kind of world does Drantos live in? It unsettled her and made her even more leery of VampLycans. Her mother had been one of them and had fled. She was starting to understand why. They just weren't...human enough. Their modesty was nonexistent and they seemed like a brutal race.

The sight of Bat and Kraven across the clearing, along with Red, made her feel relief. Her sister looked worse for wear but alive. She seemed to be arguing with Kraven. Velder switched directions and advanced on them. She went to follow but Drantos suddenly gripped her arm, gaining her attention.

"We keep some sarongs in the trucks for when we shift. Come with me and let's get one wrapped around your legs. They're cold."

"My legs aren't your concern." She jerked out of his grasp. "I'm going to go check on my sister."

He planted his body in her way. "Cover your legs first." He glanced around and seemed mad. His voice lowered. "They are staring at them."

She glanced at a few of the men nearest them and noticed they were appraising her. She didn't like it. "Fine. I'll wear a sarong."

He pointed at the truck that Yonda wasn't near. "Over there."

She spun and advanced on it. Drantos was the one to open the passenger door. The floor had piles of folded material. He grabbed a black one on top and turned, opening it. He even started to bend, as if he planned to help her put it on. Dusti just yanked it out of his hands.

"I can do it myself."

"Dusti," he whispered. "You need to trust me."

"Fat chance," she muttered, figuring out a sarong was a lot like a thinner version of a big towel. She wrapped it around her waist and tied it in a knot so it formed a skirt that reached her ankles. "You were dating that woman before we met. That's all kinds of messed up, Drantos."

"Look at me."

She released the soft material and threw her head back, glaring at him. "What?"

"I told you it wasn't like that. We were having sex."

"She wanted your father to kill me. She said I wasn't good enough for you. She acts like a jealous girlfriend."

"It's because you're human. It's difficult to explain." He frowned. "We'll discuss this at length once I take you to my home. Now isn't the time. You're still in danger and so is the clan. Just stick close to me and do as I ask."

She just wanted to hug her sister and go home. She was done with Alaska, her insane grandfather, the whole VampLycan thing, and especially Drantos. Her life had turned to shit ever since she and Bat had boarded that flight. She was hungry, sore, and felt miserable. They'd survived a plane slamming into the ground and then had been kidnapped from the crash site. To make things worse, she'd almost been attacked by some hell beast. The near drowning in the river and almost turning into a human Popsicle hadn't been fun, either. Last but not least, she'd learned that her mother had been keeping big secrets from her daughters and she wasn't what she'd appeared to be.

All those things had lowered her guard enough to trust the man in front of her. Who was a cheating bastard.

Tears filled her eyes. It was too much. It just all slammed into her at once. They weren't alone in the woods anymore and people were around them. *Maybe not people. Creatures in skin.* She darted a frightened look around, really understanding that she wasn't anything like them. Her and Bat were surrounded by the things they probably would have paid money to see featured in some horror movie.

I'm having a breakdown, she acknowledged, but didn't try to reign in her emotions. *I'm entitled to one after all this shit has happened.*

It wasn't actually Drantos's fault that her grandfather was some kind of evil mastermind or that Vampires and Werewolves were real. But he'd been the one to tell her the truth and take her away from the other survivors from the plane. Maybe a rescue team would have found them and she'd be back in her apartment if he hadn't done that. She'd still be clueless—and happier for it.

"Dusti?" Drantos inched closer and tried to take her hand.

"Don't!" She stumbled back.

He growled. "Keep your voice down."

"Fine," she whispered. "I know you saved my life a few times but stop touching me." His earlier words replayed through her mind. "I just need you to back off me right now, okay? Just leave me alone."

He blanched, his expression paling.

"I mean it. Don't keep grabbing me." She fought tears by blinking them back. "I just want to go home. Do you get that? I want the hell out of here. I'm so done with all of this shit!"

Movement from the corner of her eye made her startle and she jerked her focus off Drantos. Yonda, now dressed in sweatpants and a tank top. The woman grinned slyly. "You heard her. I know *I* did—and I'll repeat it to anyone who asks. She just renounced you, Drantos."

"Fuck," he growled. "She didn't. She doesn't know anything about our culture. Knock your shit off."

Yonda proceeded to murder her with a ferocious glower. Dusti wasn't about to forget that she could transform from a woman into a hell beast and tear her to shreds with her claws. Pure hatred seemed to radiate off the dark-haired beauty, directed solely at her.

Velder's sudden appearance almost right behind Dusti had her jumping again, twisting to stare up at him. He hadn't made a sound when he'd snuck up on her.

"Dad," Drantos argued. "She's been raised by humans. She's just upset because she misunderstood about Yonda and I. Yonda's manipulating the situation because she's pissed that Dusti isn't a full VampLycan. It's none of her business."

"It doesn't matter." Velder looked angry as he spoke low. "Some of them overheard it and I have to follow the laws, despite you being my son. She made it clear that she doesn't want you touching her. You must keep away from her at all times. Shift and run back to the clan. You'll make it there before we arrive and can tell them we're coming. We'll find her lodging somewhere safe." He paused. "Don't cause another scene. We'd have to fight for certain, son. I'm your clan leader. You must heed my words or be punished more severely. One of us would die." His voice deepened and grew loud. "You're to return to our clan now. Go!"

Drantos threw back his head and let out an enraged bellow.

Dusti's knees almost collapsed under her at the horrifying sound and the shock of seeing him like that. He spun away the second it ended, taking off toward the thick trees. He began to shift, his clothes just tearing apart as his body transformed. He disappeared behind trees before the shift was even complete.

What the hell just happened?

She had no idea…and was afraid to find out.

Chapter Nine

Velder gripped Dusti's arm in a bruising hold. She didn't try to pull away when she saw his enraged features, too afraid of him to protest. He jerked her forward toward the nearest truck and then spoke to one of the men.

"Protect her." He let go and glared down at Dusti. "Give him trouble and he'll knock you out. Don't give us any more problems." He spun away and turned his anger on Yonda. "You and I are going to speak later."

Yonda's smug expression morphed into one of fear.

"Dad." Kraven approached with Bat.

Dusti tried to go to her but the man assigned as guard grabbed her arm. He didn't hurt her but it was clear he wasn't allowing it. She froze, afraid of the way the situation had turned.

"Don't," Velder hissed. "Just take that sister and get in the other truck. We'll sort this out when we reach the clan. Right now we have bigger problems to deal with. I wouldn't put it past Decker to lie to Aveoth and say we stole his granddaughters. We both know what that means." He glanced up, seeming to search the sky. "We need to get home."

"Fuck." Kraven just scooped Bat up into his arms, carrying her to the other truck.

"Come on," the tall, muscled blond still holding Dusti whispered. "Climb into the back of the truck."

She let him assist her since the tailgate hadn't been lowered. Both sides of the bed had a bench and she took a seat where he pointed. He sat on the right of her. Red climbed in next, taking up the space to her left. She stared at him. He wasn't a fan of hers but he was Drantos's cousin.

"What just happened?" She needed answers.

"You renounced Drantos and caused him to openly disagree with his father." He sounded pissed and it showed in his eyes when he turned his head to peer at her. "You're unfit to become a member of this clan."

"I never asked to be."

"Good. You're nothing but trouble for Drantos. Everyone will be talking about what happened between him and Velder. Fathers and sons shouldn't argue."

"In what world do you live in?"

Red growled low. "*This* one, and you don't belong here."

"I'm just trying to get my sister and I home."

"It will happen eventually since you renounced Drantos. He'll have to stay away from you. It's law."

Dusti felt confused about what had just happened. Drantos had been ordered to leave her and she was surrounded by a bunch of strangers who could shift into beasts. She hadn't wanted him being all grabby, but she also hadn't meant to trigger some weird law, either. *Renounce? What the hell does that mean to these people? I need to get Bat and I away from here.*

She gripped the seat when the truck moved, bouncing as they drove over uneven ground to turn both vehicles around. She glimpsed Bat and even managed to catch her eye. Her sister was talking and lifted a hand to wave. She even flashed a tired smile, as if to say it was all going to be okay.

Dusti wasn't so sure of that. Maybe she and Bat could talk someone into taking them to an airport. Drantos's dad might agree to let them go since he seemed less than thrilled to have them there. Though it was possible that their bat-shit crazy grandfather would send some of his minions after them.

She glanced at the faces around her and shivered. They'd at least be surrounded by humans in California.

Or maybe not. A quick image of one of her neighbors flashed. Tim wasn't the friendliest guy when she ran into him at the mailbox. He'd even growled at her once but she'd figured he was just in a bad mood since she'd overheard that his girlfriend had dumped him. It was possible he could be a Werewolf. She'd never seen anyone with that much body hair before. It covered his arms in mats, probably his chest worse, and the sight of him sporting a pair of shorts had left her horrified. She couldn't even see skin for all the hair. It even covered the tops of his feet, which she'd seen in flip-flops.

Shit!

With the vehicles turned around in the grass and back on the narrow dirt road, the other truck was within sight ahead of her. Dusti gripped the edges of the truck bed and leaned back, trying to catch glimpses of her sister. It was a rough ride when the drivers accelerated. The wheels hit deep ruts and drove right over rocks.

"Stop leaning over the side," Red ordered. "You're going to fall over the edge."

"I just want to make sure they're taking Bat to the same place we're going." She didn't want to be separated from her again.

"They are." Red gripped her by the knee. "Just sit up straight."

She straightened and followed his order, then pointedly stared at him.

He frowned in response, seeming unhappy with her still. "What?"

"Why are you holding on to me?"

"Because Drantos would be angry if I let you fall out of the truck. He's not here to do it, thanks to you."

They hit another dip and it did help having his big hand pressing down on her leg. "I didn't know that was going to happen." Dusti sighed. "You don't like me."

"Nope."

"I hate Decker Filmore. It's not my fault I'm related to him. I wish I weren't."

"That's what I was told." He leaned in closer, lowering his voice. "How could you do that to Drantos?"

"Do what?"

His eyes turned a weird color. It might have been a reflection of the sun that made them appear blue with golden streaks. "He'd die for you, yet you sent him away. How could you?"

"I just said I didn't want to go home with him."

"You renounced him."

She grew frustrated. "I'm not even sure what that means here. One second we were having a little private argument and the next his dad ordered him away from me. Don't you people have disagreements?"

"You really *don't* understand, do you?"

"That's what I said. Explain it to me."

"He—"

All hell broke loose around them. Howls came from different directions, almost deafening Dusti, and something slammed into Red. One second he sat next to her, his hand on top of her leg. The next instant he was just gone. Then she saw one of those hell beasts slam into the ground behind the truck, Red beneath it.

She was pitched sideways as the driver hit the brakes. The blond kept her from being flung into the back windows of the cab as she hit his body instead. He was solid. He swiftly grabbed her and twisted, dumping her on her back on the metal bed of the truck, and then rose up, standing. Another hell beast landed in the back of the truck with them. Dusti gasped, seeing his sharp front paws just inches from her face. The blond tackled it and they both tumbled out of the back.

Dusti was in shock. The few other men still left in the back of the truck with her had bailed out. She lifted up, peering over the edge of the bed.

She wished she hadn't. It looked like a war. Men from Velder's side were wrestling and fighting with beasts. There had to be at least a dozen of them.

Bat! She pulled her body up to a crouch, keeping close to the cab. She spotted the other truck but it had been tipped on its side. A big dent had collapsed the upright side panel, as if something had T-boned it. Bodies were sprawled on the grass where the passengers in the back had been thrown clear.

A few of them moved, seeming stunned but alive. Two beasts suddenly leapt up on the side of the tipped truck and then launched at them. Their claws tore into the victims before they could even get to their feet. She watched in terror as two men tried to fight back.

Kraven's body was sprawled flat in a bloody heap near the carnage. It looked as if something had already torn up his back, his skin shredded and stained red. Her sister lay trapped under his big body, just part of her thigh showing. It had to be

Bat. She looked so pale against the green grass and all that bright red blood.

Dusti almost fell out of the back of the truck and frantically glanced around as she crouched next to the passenger door of the cab. The men who belonged to Drantos's clan were shifting into beasts too. She watched Redson toss the beast he fought and rip at his own clothes to get free of them as hair sprouted along his arms and chest. His fangs looked huge, his mouth and nose elongating. Soon she wouldn't be able to tell Decker's men from Velder's.

I need to get to Bat. She looked back at where Kraven lay so still. That was definitely Bat under him. She wasn't even sure if her sister was alive or dead. Kraven didn't look as if he'd survive with all that blood soaking him.

She took a few sharp breaths and prepared to sprint toward Bat. She refused to believe her sister was dead. She had to try to save her since all the men seemed occupied with fighting for their own lives. It would mean leaving the safety of the little cover she had but that was her sister. *Bat would do it for me.*

The sound of metal creaking caught her attention and she saw the driver's side door of the tipped truck being pushed open from the inside. The hinges protested loudly but it finally gave way. A man tried to climb up and out of the cab. It was Velder. She recognized him despite the fact that blood covered the side of his face. He almost made it out but then another beast leapt up on the side of the truck, using one swipe of his claws to strike the struggling man. He fell out of sight, back inside the cab of the truck. The beast used those same claws to tear into the door and shove it closed, placing both front paws on top of it, as if it were purposely trapping Drantos's father. But the creature didn't stay there long, leaping off to attack someone else.

Dusti tensed, placing her hand on the truck to brace herself as she prepared to run like she'd never run before. She just needed to shove Kraven off Bat and pray she was alive. If she could move, they'd run like hell and hope none of those beast things followed them.

After a few ragged breaths, Dusti sprinted the distance to the other truck. She pressed her body against the back of it then slowly eased around, so close to her sister and Kraven that only about eight feet separated them.

A hairy beast suddenly stepped out from in front of the truck, just a feet away. Dusti waited for it to turn its head and see her. She held her breath, praying that didn't happen. It stepped out more, blocking her path to Bat.

"Batnna?" it snarled in an inhuman, horrible voice. "Batnna?"

Terror held Dusti immobile. The creature advanced and seemed totally focused on Kraven and Bat.

It sunk in that it might have been saying Batina. It was looking for her sister.

That thing was one of her grandfather's people and it had come to take her sister to him.

It prowled closer to Kraven and Bat. They weren't moving, unaware of the danger. Dusti shook all over but moved. Her voice wouldn't work, the creature too terrifying for her to get words out. She struggled to even swallow but finally managed. She had to draw it away from Bat.

"I'm Batina," she whispered.

The thing turned its head so fast that Dusti lost her footing, falling back against the truck. It was the only thing that kept her from landing on her ass.

The beast had pitch-black pupils and scary teeth. It stared at her and came closer.

"Batnnna?"

It sounded worse when it hissed than when it made the rougher, louder snarling sound. She nodded. "I'm Batina," she repeated.

It moved to her side, inches away, and paused next to her. It crouched down. "Grrrr onnnn."

She didn't understand.

A naked, bloodied man strode forward, gripping something that appeared similar to a girdle. Hope flared that he'd attack the beast but instead he grabbed Dusti by the back of the jacket she wore and yanked hard. She ended sprawled over the back of the shifted VampLycan. The man released her and twisted her body until her legs fell on both sides of the creature, as if she were about to ride a horse. He shoved her flat so her stomach and breasts pressed tight against fur. Something snapped over her back and squeezed her sides. She cried out in pain as it was tightened until she felt as if she might break in two.

The guy straightened. "You've got her, Craig. She's secure." He hit the beast's ass. "Go! We'll put down a false trail for them to follow."

The creature under her bolted forward and Dusti realized exactly what that man had done. He'd effectively tied her onto the enforcer's back. The girdle thing belted her to the creature from her hips to just under her ribs. It ran, picking up speed. The fur covering the beast's body did little to cushion her from the rough ride.

He jumped, a sick feeling going through Dusti when they were in the air, but he landed hard enough to make her scream if she'd been able to draw breath. It was just too painful being slammed around.

Decker Filmore was going to end up with her instead of Bat but she doubted she'd still be alive by the time she reached him. The hell beast under her leapt again and when he landed, the tight material around her felt as if it might snap her spine from the jostling. She blacked out.

* * * * *

Fury gripped Drantos. He roared into the woods over not being close enough to protect Dusti. His father carefully lifted Kraven off Bat, evaluating her limp body with a shrewd assessment. He ran his hands carefully over her ribs.

"Is she alive?" Drantos couldn't retract his claws to touch her himself. His rage had his animal side too close to the surface.

His father nodded. "Yes. She's breathing fine and I don't detect any broken bones. Kraven used his body to cushion her but the force of him landing on her appears to have knocked her out." Velder turned, checking on Kraven. "He's badly injured. He's lost a lot of blood and we need to get them home."

"I'm going after my mate." Drantos clenched his teeth.

His father frowned as he straightened to his full height. "No. I need you here. Our trackers will find her. They're going after her now."

"I'll do it," Drantos snarled. He didn't give a damn what his father ordered. She had been taken. He had to get her back before she was killed by Decker for being the granddaughter he believed useless to his cause—or it was discovered she wasn't as human as he believed. He'd send her to Aveoth. It would be hell trying to recover her from the cliffs and the GarLycan clan, if not impossible.

It drove him insane thinking about losing her forever, either way.

Kraven opened his eyes, drawing Drantos's attention. "Bat?" His fear showed on his features. "Is she breathing? I don't hear her."

"She lives but she's unconscious." Velder crouched again and caressed his son's face. "You acted quickly enough when they leapt out of the trees. You took the brunt of the attack with your back and seemed to have cradled her when you were thrown clear of the truck. Don't try to talk."

Relief etched across Kraven's pained features. "We must protect her." He turned his head to meet Drantos furious stare. "I heard Dusti claim she was Bat. I couldn't move but I was conscious. She allowed them to take her to save her sister. She should be safe until Decker realizes she lied to his men to dupe them into taking the wrong woman."

Drantos threw back his head to roar out in rage again. It made it worse that Dusti had purposely put herself in danger and lied to be the one taken. He paced, unable to keep control of his beast. Not only were his claws extended but his fangs elongated. More hair sprouted down his body. "I'm going after my mate!"

His father stood to confront him. "No, you're not. The clan comes first."

"She needs me."

"She renounced you. It is forbidden for you to go near her."

"She doesn't understand our ways!"

"It is still the law. It's up to our trackers to find her and bring her back."

"No," Drantos snarled. "She's *mine*."

"We've been attacked and some of our people are injured. Your own brother is hurt. You need to calm and allow our men to find Decker's granddaughter. They will bring her to safety. *Our* people are your priority right now."

"Let him go, Dad." Kraven coughed up blood, rolled to his side, and reached for Bat. His hand rubbed her leg where he could reach her. "They took what they want. They won't be back. He needs to go after his mate."

"She's not his mate." Velder shook his head.

"I exchanged blood with her during sex but I didn't tell her we had begun the mating process. I planned to explain everything once I had her safely inside my home." Drantos forced his mind to work. "She's wearing Red's jacket. It masks her scent." He glared at his father. "Do the trackers know that?"

Velder hesitated. "Take a walk with me."

Drantos spun, marching a good ten feet away. He glared at his father. "What?"

"You need to pull yourself together. The woman will be found. I sent two good trackers after her."

"That's not good enough." Drantos dared his father to tell him otherwise. "You can't talk me out of it."

His father grabbed his arm. "I forbid it! Our clan is in danger and I have one son down. I need you, Drantos. The men I sent will find her. Your place is *here*."

"You're wrong." Drantos glared into his father's stunned gaze. "Ban me from the clan if you must but I'm going after her. Decker might realize she's not completely human if she's injured and bleeding. I won't allow Aveoth to have her. She's mine to protect and I will *die* to do so if that's what it takes."

"You can't risk your life for a woman who has shunned you."

Drantos jerked out of his father's hold. "And *you* can't take what she said seriously."

"Laws are still laws, son. Several of us heard her say she doesn't want to live with you."

"Dusti is my mate regardless of what she claimed."

"And I'm your clan leader, and I'm *ordering* you to help me escort our injured home."

Drantos was furious. "No!"

His father snarled. "Do what you're told!"

People around them turned their heads.

Velder lowered his voice. "My orders are clear. Follow them."

"You're being unreasonable. You'd go after Mother."

"She's my mate and birthed my children."

"Dusti is my mate will birth my children one day."

"You're disobeying your clan leader. We are keepers of the laws. You can't just ignore protocol because you're obsessed with this woman. Our family needs to stay united. The other clan leaders won't tolerate family squabbles. You know this. It's a bad reflection on me as a leader. They'll demand I punish you for defying me if you go after her, like any other clan member would be."

"Fine. Punish me when I get back. I'm still going." Drantos met his father's grim stare. "You need to understand that she's already mine."

His father growled. "Don't do this, Drantos," Velder warned. "I raised you not to break the law."

"You also taught me to do the right thing and to follow my heart. That's Dusti." Drantos held his father's gaze. "Don't give me orders where my mate is concerned. I'm going after her."

Drantos turned, shifted into his beast form, and sniffed the ground. His father tried to grab his tail but he shot forward in the direction he knew they'd taken Dusti.

He'd committed his life to living in accordance with the laws of the VampLycan, but none of that mattered if he lost his mate.

He had to slow when the trail of the attackers broke apart into different directions. He studied the ground instead of following the scents. One set of tracks dug into the Earth deeper than the rest. His nose told him to follow another trail but he chose the deeper prints. One of the males carried Dusti's weight. They would have no choice. She couldn't shift and in skin, she'd be too slow for them to have a real chance of escape.

Decker's men were good but Drantos knew he was better. His father's trackers had veered off after the other four sets of prints, following the wrong ones. A soft snarl tore from his throat. When he caught up to the enforcer carrying Dusti, he would kill him. No one touched his mate and lived.

The enforcer had eventually slowed to a walk. They'd chosen a smaller male to abduct Dusti in an attempt to mask the heavier tread his paws left with a passenger, but it also appeared the added weight made him somewhat weaker. A quick glance at the sky assured Drantos time wasn't on his side. His eyesight was good at night but tracks were harder to spot.

The tracks changed direction again and pure rage poured through Drantos.

The enforcer wasn't taking her to Decker's clan anymore—but instead headed toward the GarLycan cliffs.

Decker had probably ordered her delivered directly to Aveoth. He followed the trail a little longer until he was certain it wasn't just a ploy to mislead him. Drantos burst into a run to cut them off. He needed to rescue Dusti before Aveoth got his hands on her. That meant stopping the enforcer before they reached GarLycan territory.

* * * * *

Pain pulled Dusti from her unconscious state. Disorientation had her rubbing her face on the hairy, soft pillow.

Hairy?

Reality and memory instantly clashed together when she lifted her head. The thing under her panted heavily. It wasn't running anymore but instead lay on the ground. Her legs were pinned under a soft, warm belly, where the VampLycan had settled to rest. It turned its head, sharp teeth nearly brushing her jaw. A set of dark eyes met her stricken ones.

He was a man, despite looking exactly like something out of a horror movie. The bloody guy had called him Craig. She tried hard to remember that as they stared at each other. It might help combat some of her fear. *He's Craig. Not hell beast.*

"Ssssilll," he gasped.

The word came out messed up, his voice too throaty and guttural to really understand. She took a guess at what he'd tried to convey, that perhaps he didn't want her to fight him. She didn't even know how to do that. As a beast, he had claws, fangs, and a body twice the size of hers. All she had were fingernails and a determination to escape. The odds weren't in her favor.

Their staring contest seemed to end when he twisted his muzzle away to drop his jaw back on the ground. His labored breathing continued.

Think, she ordered her mind. *Come up with a plan.* She wiggled a little, tested the thick band that kept her secured on his broad back. It didn't allow for much movement. She reached back and touched the leather-like material. It felt pretty thick and not like something she could tear with her fingers. Craig had obviously run until he had dropped. She guessed his exhaustion would be the only advantage she had.

She let her fingers trail lower along the girdle, trying to figure out how it was secured. The restraint limited her reach. Craig didn't seem to notice or care what she did. She discovered the metal line in the material that probably held the girdle-like binding in place. It was tough to blindly try to figure out how to release the tension on it. There were no ties or holes to indicate it had locks. It was frustrating.

She tried to assess her injuries at the same time. Her jaw hurt just under her chin but she wasn't sure why. Maybe her head had flopped around when he'd been running. Her ribs and lower back ached from being crushed between his hairy body and the thick binding but the fact that she could feel her legs made her think her spine hadn't really snapped.

She watched Craig's head, ready to freeze her motions at the mere sign that he might look at her again. He didn't. A little chunk of metal on the side of the girdle jabbed her thumb. She tested it, feeling it out. It might be some kind of release.

She ignored the pain and dug her thumb against it, trying to force it to move.

It did—the tight pull around her back eased when the two sides of the belt came apart.

Craig didn't seem to notice what she'd done. She assumed he must have fallen asleep. Dusti frantically glanced around to study her surroundings. She held still, knowing the second she tried to climb off his back that he'd awaken. She needed a plan before she tried it.

A dirt path, if it could be called such, sat a little to her left. It probably led to

Decker Filmore. She turned her head, quickly spotting a very tight cluster of trees with a few large boulders behind it. The spaces between the trunks were so narrow they might not even allow her to ease through, but Craig was bigger than her. It meant he *definitely* wouldn't fit. Two gigantic boulders resting next to each at an angle had created a slight curved space, where trees had grown in close proximity. The limbs had tangled in a lot of places, probably from being confined in such a shallow area. Each of the massive rocks were over thirty feet in height. She looked for a gap between them that she might be able to escape through but the trees blocked her view.

Maybe I can climb it, if there's not enough space to get between the boulders. It seemed a daunting undertaking but her only other choice was to run along the path. Craig would be on her in seconds flat if she tried to make a run for it. The trees and rocks might keep him away from her long enough to give her a chance of escape. It was the only option.

She slowly lifted up with care. Craig didn't stir. She took a breath and tried to ease her leg out from under him but it was pinned. She closed her eyes and silently cursed. She tested her other leg and it slid out easily from under his belly. It was just her right foot that was the problem. She leaned back down, resting against his hairy back. She pulled her left leg out more, away from her.

She wiggled those trapped toes, trying to pull her foot free. He rolled a tiny bit, to her surprise. She must have tickled him a little with that slight movement. Whatever the reason, her foot wasn't trapped any longer.

Dusti pushed up fast and lurched to her feet. She sprinted toward the trees and the huge boulders. A loud snarl assured her that Craig was wake and not happy. The ground bit into her tender feet but she ignored the pain as she ran. She twisted sideways, tossing her body between a gap in the trunks.

Her skin scraped across rough bark in a few places but she managed to squeeze through. She tripped on something just a few feet past the trunks and a sharp jab of pain stabbed at her lower leg. It sent her sprawling on her side in a bed of dirt and dry leaves. Her shoulder hurt too from the impact with the ground. A second later, she didn't have time worry about any of that.

Craig was attempting to push between the trees to reach her but his broad shoulders hung him up. He reached in with one clawed arm to swipe at her but only caught air since she was already using her legs to put more space between them. She sat up when she felt safe, instantly spotting blood on the ground.

A snarl jerked her attention up. Craig twisted, trying to fit his chest through the gaps in the trunks. Wood creaked a little but he still couldn't get through. He was too broad. He glared at her, snarling. There was a promise of pain and punishment in the malevolent look he gave.

She glanced around, seeing her new predicament. The two boulders turned out to be one massive one. There wasn't a gap to be found, and the wall of rock was too sheer. It looked impossible to climb without gear. At least the trees would shield her from Craig until he either broke through or found a way to get over the boulder, maybe by climbing the trees to reach her.

Dusti got to her feet, prepared to use that time to her advantage. She'd make a run for it if he did start climbing. She put weight on her leg and cried out in pain, almost falling over. She looked down and twisted her leg a little, finally spotting the source of the blood she'd seen. Her calf was torn up, with blood all down the back of her leg and covering her heel. She stared at the wounds. It took her a second to understand.

He'd nailed her with his claws before she'd totally been out of his reach. He'd probably tried to grab her leg to haul her back but gravity and momentum had torn her out of his grasp. She glared at him.

"You asshole. You ripped open my leg."

He snarled back and tried a new place to try to squeeze through. The trunks creaked a little, making soft popping sounds. It scared her enough to limp backward, putting more space between them. She pressed against the rock wall and glanced around, not seeing anywhere that he could fit through without a lot of effort and muscle.

The space wasn't large, where she was enclosed by rock and trees, and her new predicament sank in. *Shit! I trapped myself.*

Craig disappeared from her sight and that made things worse. *Where is he?* It was possible he was circling the boulder to find a way to climb it. She jerked her head up, frantically searching for any sign that he might drop down on top of her.

A loud roar tore through the woods. The sound sent her heart into a frenzied beat. She didn't need a translator. The sound of Craig's rage told her plenty. She doubted he'd kill her since her grandfather needed "Bat", but she wasn't sure how sane or in control his men were in shifted form. For all she knew, the shift could totally turn them animalistic inside, incapable of having human thoughts. And she couldn't even make a run for it with her leg so injured.

A sob tore through her chest when she saw movement through the trees to her left. The man in hell-beast form was back, pacing now. He still hadn't found a way to reach her through the little alcove nature had made, but she knew it would only be a matter of time before he breached the space.

He couldn't fit between the trees with his immense body unless he used his claws to hack at the tree trunks. That would take time. He might even have to shift into a man again to catch her. It would make his body slightly less bulky. Her gaze lowered to search for a weapon. It would be easier to hurt his bare skin than fur.

She bent, pretending to examine her leg. It was bleeding pretty badly and she couldn't do anything about it. She scooped up a handful of tiny rocks and dirt, fisting them in her hand. Craig screamed his rage, still pacing the trees in front of her. He glared at her every few seconds.

"What's wrong?" She tried to hold back the tears the pain in her leg caused. "Too hairy to squeeze in here to get me? So lose the hair, asshole."

He stopped pacing and watched her. She had a sinking feeling he planned to pass time until the sun disappeared. She'd be in the dark, blind, and wouldn't see him coming after her then. Would she pass out from blood loss? She couldn't afford for either of those things to happen.

"Are you scared of a puny human chick? What's your name? Ball-less?" she goaded. "No wonder my grandfather chose you to be his pack mule. You probably don't even know how to fight."

He lay down, watching her with those evil eyes. It became obvious that he *did* plan to wait until she couldn't see or had passed out. She looked away from him, not able to keep staring into that horrific black gaze. She glanced around at the ground, saw a sharp-looking rock the size of her palm, and knew she'd found an effective weapon if she could just use it on the jerk. She needed to draw him to her first, surprise him with it, and hope she could take him out.

What would Bat do? Her sister had a serious talent for driving men into rages when she opened her mouth. It made her a very effective attorney. She could send prosecutors or witnesses against her clients into full-blown rants inside a courtroom that discredited them in front of both judges and juries. Bat had made so many enemies with that winning stunt it was yet another reason why she needed the around-the-clock security her law firm provided.

Dusti took a deep breath and lifted her gaze to the asshole still staring at her. A plan formed. Bat always said the best tactic to anger a man would be to accuse him of something he wouldn't do. They had the urge to defend themselves every time. The more outrageous the accusation, the stronger the response.

A forced smile curved her lips while she watched his eyes carefully to gauge for any kind of response. "Wow, are you going to be in seriously deep shit." She twisted her injured leg to show him the damaged he'd caused. "Do you know why my grandfather wants you to bring me to him? He's going to give me to Aveoth. Take a good look at what you did to me. That's going to leave a scar—and make the GarLycan leader very unhappy. I mean, what guy wants to see *that* on his woman?"

The beast's entire body tensed and his eyes flickered with something akin to fear.

Got you, asshole, she thought.

"He's *really* going to flip when I tell him how you tried to touch me in bad places." She batted her eyelashes at him. "I'm going to assure Aveoth that I only ran from you because you tried to get under my skirt. Sarong. Whatever." She lifted her hand and shook a finger at him. "Tsk! Tsk! Shame on you. From what I hear, GarLycans are pretty vicious guys and Aveoth is the worst. Do you think he'll just beat you or tear your limbs off one at a time?"

The beast lifted to his feet and snarled.

"What was that? I don't speak growl."

He crept closer and the threat of retribution showed clearly in his furious black gaze.

"I'm going to cry and cling to this Aveoth." She inwardly winced at that image. "And as his future lover, I'll ask him nicely to please hurt you really bad before he kills you."

He pushed against two trees hard but his broad, hairy chest still wouldn't fit. He squeezed until some of his body became trapped and he had to jerk back when he realized the pointlessness of it. Another snarl tore from him.

"What was that? I still can't understand a thing you say. If you want to talk me out of my brilliant payback plan for tearing up my leg then you better change into skin so you have a voice, asshole. I'm willing to make a deal," she lied. "I don't want to be taken and you don't want Aveoth to tear you apart."

He just watched her.

"I'm going to lie my ass off to make sure this Aveoth guy wants you dead," she promised softly. "Understand? Change into a person and let's make a deal."

His black glaze seemed to glisten with pure rage before he started to change. Hair receded and the squishy noises they made as they transformed was sickening. *The good news is*, she thought, *the planned worked. The bad news is, now those trees probably won't prevent him from reaching me.*

The second his head lowered, she bent and grabbed the rock in her palm, hiding it behind her sarong skirt. She straightened and maneuvered it in her hand, cupping it until the sharpest part ended up in the open space between fingers and wrist. Her heart hammered from terror and uncertainty.

She may have to kill someone, beast guy or not. Anxiety had her stomach rolling with nausea as she realized it had come down to survival.

Chapter Ten

Craig rose to his feet to glare at her with dark brown eyes. He didn't appear very friendly with the sneer plastered across his thin lips. In skin, he stood about five feet nine, had a wiry but average-sized body. She put his age in his early twenties.

"I'll kill you before I allow you to tell those lies about me." He had a rough voice, deep and raspy. "I didn't try to fuck you."

"You wouldn't survive if you killed me," she bluffed. "My grandfather is an asshole. He assigned you to complete a task and he won't be a happy camper if you fail to bring me back breathing. We both know he doesn't tolerate that kind of shit. I'm worth too much to him."

He took a step forward.

"Freeze. Don't come any closer."

The guy glared at her but stopped advancing. "You don't tell me what to do, you little bitch."

"I can't shift to gain a tail so I'm assuming you don't mean that term in a doggy way. My feelings are hurt by that insult, really." She hoped he could pick up on her sarcasm.

He snarled. It only sounded a smidgen less frightening when he made that noise looking human. "What do you want? I can't free you. You know your grandfather will kill me if I don't follow his orders. The team he sent knows I have possession of you."

"Fine," she lied. "You're right. I'm reasonable. I'm not opposed to going with you but I don't want to be strapped across your back as though I'm a side of beef. I'll walk."

His focus lowered to her legs. "You are injured and barefoot."

"I'll be fine right after I wrap this up to stop the bleeding and I can use part of this sarong to wrap my feet." It sounded so good, she hoped she'd be able to really do that part of the plan. "Riding on your back doesn't agree with my stomach."

She noticed when some of the stiffness eased from his frame. He bought her bullshit. His gaze lifted. "And you won't lie about me if I take you there your way?"

"Nope." She had no intention of going anywhere with him. "I give you my word as a Filmore." Her grandfather was a lying bastard who'd told Bat he was dying to get them to Alaska. She wasn't a Filmore. She was a Dawson. Her father had been a good man. Decker Filmore could never claim that honor. "I'll behave, and look on the bright side. Carrying me probably wasn't fun for you either. That belt was cutting me in half and it was against your stomach."

"True." The anger faded from his features. "You may come out of there. I won't attack you."

I don't feel the same, she silently warned him. "Sure. I don't suppose you could turn your back though so I can pee in private? That motion of you running and the squeezing from that contraption holding me against you didn't do my bladder any favors." She inched closer, overstated her limp to make him think he'd hurt her more than he had.

The guy nodded. "Do it there. You will not leave my sight."

Ignoring him, she squeezed between the trees. "It's too cramped in there."

She flung the dirt when mere feet separated them.

It hit his face before he could react, totally unprepared for the attack. He jerked his head back to claw at his eyes with his hands.

She took advantage of his blindness in those critical seconds. She swung her other arm as hard as she could manage with her remaining strength.

It hurt her wrist when the rock connected with the side of his head but it must have been effective, considering he dropped to his knees with a cry of pain.

She drew her arm back and hit him again. This time he slumped to the ground.

Dusti hesitated, watching him. He seemed lifeless except for the rise and fall of his chest. Her gaze avoided the bloody gash to the side of his head. She'd puke if she looked at it too closely or acknowledged her hand was wet from his blood.

Seconds ticked by. He was breathing but seemed knocked out. She kept hold of the rock and turned, moving as fast as her injured leg would allow in the direction he must have carried her. The dirt path was the only thing she knew to follow. She hoped that someone from Drantos's clan was looking for her and found her before the guy woke up with a headache from hell.

The pain in her leg grew worse with each step but she kept going. She didn't have time to really bind her leg until she felt safe. That wasn't going to be anytime soon. A little blood loss was a lot better than being recaptured. Craig would be furious and he'd strap her to his body again.

She ran when she was able to find flatter ground. The sun would go down at some point. It was scary, since she'd eventually lose sight of the path, but every step took her farther away from Craig and everyone associated with him. She'd already been lost at night in the woods once but she wasn't soaking wet this time. It would have to be better than before.

A roar tore through the woods a short time later. She turned her head, her gaze searching for any sign of pursuit. Nothing moved except the trees from the wind. Her labored breathing hindered her, along with her limp. She strained to hear a river or perhaps vehicle traffic. If she could stumble into a highway, if one existed in this remote area, it may save her. The icy river water would even be a welcome sight. Its strong current would wash her downstream and perhaps lose the asshole who she knew had to have already started tracking her. He'd obviously recovered from the blows to his head if that was him screaming out his rage.

A howl tore through the woods next, much closer, and she came to a stop when she realized she wouldn't be able to outrun him. She turned to wait for Craig to come after her again. He wouldn't dare kill her but that didn't mean he wouldn't want to put some serious hurt on her for what she'd done to him with the surprise attack. She swept the ground with her gaze in a desperate search for anything she could use as a more effective weapon than her rock.

A thump behind her left her heart in her throat. The distinctive sound of something falling hard onto dirt couldn't be mistaken. She could sense eyes on the back of her head as though something physically touched her.

He'd found her, somehow had dropped from above, had probably used the trees to sneak up on her.

She started to turn around, even though it was the last thing she wanted to do. She had to confront him.

"I know you're angry but if you hurt me, my grandfa—"

Shock silenced her.

It wasn't the guy she'd struck with a rock standing mere feet from her. This one stood much taller, maybe six feet five or six, had short black hair cropped close to his head, from the little of she could see peeking out under his black hood. Her eyes widened as they examined his bare, expansive chest made of deeply tanned skin, and finally reached the handsome face of a man with intense eyes that were an unusually bright blue.

They mesmerized her—until a loud roar coming from close behind jerked her from her stupor.

The guy opened his mouth, revealing white, perfect teeth with elongated fangs on both sides. He glared at something over her head. "Back away from the woman."

His voice sent chills down her spine. It rumbled with each word as if he spoke from the bottom of a pit. The tone of his command terrified her. This wasn't a guy anyone sane would argue with.

She turned her head in time to see the guy she'd bashed with the rock instantly backing up about ten feet. Blood coated the side of Craig's face, running down his neck and chest from the injuries he'd suffered. He lowered his head in submission and his body followed when he dropped to his knees.

"Of course."

Dusti turned her focus back on the very tall man who wore a strange hooded black duster that was open in front. It had short sleeves, revealing muscular biceps. She raked her gaze up and down him. He wore black leather pants with silver bands over muscular thighs. His heavy-duty boots reminded her of military-issue ones. Leather encased his skin from wrist to just under the elbow, with more silver strips attached to the armguards, each sporting small, sharp-looking spikes. If she wasn't mistaken, they were a form of weapon that looked as if they could do serious damage if he struck someone.

She finally met his compelling bright blue gaze again.

"Who are you?" His voice sent chills down her spine again but his tone had softened just slightly.

"I..." She swallowed the lump in her throat; perhaps her heart, still there from all the fear. She wasn't sure what to say. "Who are *you*?"

"You're in my territory without permission." His nostrils flared when he inhaled, took in her scent, and generous lips curved downward. "Your scent confuses me. You smell male but you obviously are not. Is that your blood?" He glanced down her body.

"Blame him." She hooked a thumb in her kidnapper's direction. "I'm only here because he forced me to be. I'm just trying to get home."

"I smell him even from this distance. That's not his blood on you." He crouched suddenly, his attention straying to her leg, and he inhaled again.

She watched his eyes change color. It made her gasp when the blue suddenly flashed sparks of silver. It looked like little lightning bolts were exploding inside his irises. He sniffed again and suddenly gripped her leg, his hand moving too fast for her to follow. He inhaled deeply.

He didn't look away from her. "Human." His expression became grim when he rose to his full height. He finally looked away from her to make his obviously unhappy discovery known to her kidnapper. "You attacked and brought one of them into my territory to kill? Do you want us blamed for her death?" Rage dripped from every word he spoke. "We don't sanction hunting them on our lands. You offend me."

"No!" Her kidnapper raised his terrified gaze to the stranger. "I was under orders from Decker to bring her to you, Lord Aveoth."

I'm in such deep shit, Dusti thought. She gawked at the warrior before her. Using that term described how he appeared in the getup he wore and the danger that seemed to radiate off him in waves of anger.

I'm so screwed. This is Aveoth, the one everyone is so afraid of. I so get why now. He looks meaner than hell.

"To me?" Aveoth actually appeared confused for a split second before his face hardened to an unreadable mask again. "Why would he gift me with a human?"

"She's his granddaughter."

His masculine features slackened in astonishment to reveal his emotions once more before his gaze shifted to pin her where she stood. "Is that true?"

Fear rendered her speechless. Aveoth made a rumbling sound from deep in his throat. It reminded her of something she'd once heard watching a documentary about volcanoes. He, like those volcanoes, made that noise right before he seemed to explode. The raw fury on his handsome face made her back up a step on legs that threatened to turn to rubber.

"*Is it true?*" he roared.

Her mouth opened but nothing came out. She locked her knees together to remain on her feet. Falling on her ass in front of the scary GarLycan didn't seem a smart thing to do. His coloring started to slightly change. He turned from a deep copper tone to more of a gray shade.

"It's true! Her name is Batina and she is the eldest child of Decker's daughter," the jerk on his knees supplied. "He planned to offer her to you as a lover. She carries his dead mate's bloodline."

Aveoth's skin had definitely transformed into a slate gray in color. His flesh lost some of its human facade to harden and smooth out. Dusti had a sinking fear his Gargoyle traits were showing.

"She smells human."

"Her father was one of them. Her mother was pure VampLycan, as you know."

"Batina?"

Her sister's name coming from Aveoth's lips had her taking another step back to put more distance between them. Even those inches made her feel a little better.

"Is that your name?"

She still couldn't speak. She shook her head no.

"She lies!" Craig rose to his feet. "She is—"

"DOWN!"

The loud order from Aveoth hurt Dusti's ears as if thunder had torn through the woods. She nearly dropped to her own knees even though he apparently spoke to Craig. Out of her peripheral vision, she didn't miss her kidnapper collapsing back to the ground, lowering his head and trembling violently, as though he were having a mini seizure. She could relate. Her instincts screamed at her to curl into the fetal position.

Aveoth seemed to suddenly appear right before her. The guy moved too fast to track with her eyes. A cool, smooth hand that definitely didn't feel fleshy gripped her face. He didn't hurt her but he used a good hold that kept her immobile. She whimpered when she saw his eyes. They glowed silver now, the color seeming to swirl around his irises, as if they had a life of their own.

"Are you Batina, granddaughter of Marvilella and Decker? Don't lie to me."

"No," she whispered.

"She lies," her kidnapper quaked. "I took her myself. She acknowledged her identity when I did."

The handsome man lowered his face to stare into her eyes. "I see no lie."

"There were only two of... *Shit!* You conniving bitch! You allowed me to take you instead of your sister, didn't you?" Craig tried to get to his feet again.

Aveoth turned his head to give him a warning look and rumbled again inside his massive chest. The VampLycan dropped back to his knees.

"She lied to me. She's the younger granddaughter," he hurriedly explained. "The more human one who didn't inherit the strong bloodline."

Aveoth's color started to return to a normal shade as he took deep breaths. His hand on her face seemed to warm while he calmed down, the texture of it softening to flesh again. His silvery eyes cooled to blue. Dusti couldn't look away from his gaze when he gave her his full attention again.

"What is your name?"

"Dusti."

"Your full name."

"Dustina Ann Dawson."

"Are you also the granddaughter of Marvilella?"

"I...that's what I've been told. I never met her. My mother's name was Antina."

His hand slid down her throat, his thumb pausing on the area just above her collarbone, before inching forward until she knew he could feel her rapid pulse over her carotid artery. She prayed he wouldn't slice it open to just kill her where she stood.

"Feel no fear." He lowered the volume of his voice to a husky rasp. "I would never hurt a descendant of Margola. She was Marvilella's sister. We'd intended to become lovers but she died before reaching maturity."

"I don't want to be your lover," she blurted. "No offense." She couldn't seem to shut up once she got words to pass her lips. "You're a good-looking guy for someone who makes me want to run away from you screaming. But I met someone. He might be a cheater. I'm not sure. But I fell in love with him. I didn't even know Vampires, Werewolves and what you are existed until a few days ago. You wouldn't like me anyway. I'm a shitty cook. I'd end up killing you with food poisoning. And I drool when I'm asleep if I'm really tired." She sucked in air. "Also, I think my grandfather is a piece of shit who doesn't have the right to give me to someone as a gift. He's a cheap bastard who never lifted a finger to help my sister and me. I hate him." She sealed her lips together to stop babbling.

One of his black eyebrows arched upward. "Are you done?"

She managed a small nod.

He watched her silently but his thumb moved slightly to caress her throat. The soft touch distracted her from her terror a tiny bit. He didn't seem angry over anything she'd said. He actually appeared to be a little amused, if she were to judge the softening of his features and the way one side of his full lips lifted as if he tried to hide a smile.

A deep growl came from Dusti's left. She tried to turn her head but Aveoth prevented it when he wrapped his fingers around her throat. He didn't cut off her air but he had a secure hold on her. He lifted his other hand and held it up, almost a signal for something to stop.

"Hello, Drantos. What are you doing in my territory without calling first to inform me you wanted to visit? I knew someone approached from half a mile away. You attempted to stay upwind but my senses are too keen not to hear that lumbering body of yours, no matter how skilled you've become at sneaking up on a target. And the wind shifted once to reveal your identity."

Dusti strained against the hand still wrapped around her throat, just enough to see a sight that left her trembling on shaky legs.

A huge, black, hairy beast crept out of the edge of the woods and onto the path they stood in.

That's what he looks like when he's a hell beast, her mind acknowledged. The trembling grew worse since Drantos was a terrifying sight. Aveoth released her throat and gripped her hips to steady her. It helped.

She couldn't stop gaping at Drantos. He looked similar to the scary beasts she'd already seen, only bigger, with those same evil-looking black eyes. He lowered his head so they weren't staring at each other anymore. Bone popping noises began and she squeezed her eyes shut, not wanting to see him transform. It sounded painful and very uncomfortable.

"That woman belongs to me." Drantos had his voice once he'd turned back into human form. "That asshole is mine too. I'm going to kill him for stealing her away from my family."

"No." Aveoth smiled coldly. "You may kill the male but you won't touch her."

"She's *mine*." Drantos stalked forward, snarled viciously, but halted. "Don't do this, Aveoth."

"Do what? Not allow you to harm Margola's descendant?" The GarLycan's voice deepened into a rumble that threatened violence.

"She's my mate. I'd never hurt Dusti. I'd kill to protect her."

"She doesn't smell like you."

"She's wearing my cousin's coat. That's *his* scent you're picking up. She was cold and it was the only thing available."

He narrowed his gaze on Dusti. "He's the one you spoke of? The cheater?"

Drantos snarled again. "Yonda *wasn't* my girlfriend."

Aveoth glanced between them but he cocked his head finally, arching one eyebrow at her in question.

She was too afraid not to answer. "He was seeing someone before we met. I didn't know and I got upset when I found out."

"She doesn't understand," Drantos rasped. "Dusti thinks like a human. I was trying to ease her into our world before I told her too much."

Aveoth turned his head, watching Drantos. "You haven't completely bonded to her yet. She doesn't carry your scent."

Drantos paled. "Please, Aveoth. I've bedded her and we've exchanged blood. We've begun the mating bond."

A calculated glint flared inside Aveoth's dark gaze. "You have the sister who is not human? I will trade your mate for her."

"No!" Dusti blurted.

Drantos growled softly. "Silence, sweetheart."

"*No.*" She glared up at Aveoth. "My sister is not a bargaining chip, nor will she agree to be your lover. Bat would castrate you the first time you fell asleep if you forced yourself on her."

"Damn it, Dusti. Shut up," Drantos ordered.

"You don't speak for my sister." She didn't glance his way to see Drantos's reaction. She wouldn't deny being his mate if it got her away from the big GarLycan. "My sister is a person, not a thing to be traded."

"I want her."

That statement from Aveoth chilled her blood. "Too bad."

"Dusti," Drantos warned. "Please trust me and stop talking. You are only going to make the situation worse."

"How is that even possible?" She gripped the strange leather arm guards Aveoth wore, avoiding the sharp silver spikes. "Please let me go. I can stand now."

"No."

"I said please." Her temper flared. It wasn't her life on the line at that moment. It had become about Bat's. She'd face the devil himself to protect her sister. She pointed at Craig. "That asshole over there thought he could claw my leg open and get away with it. See that blood on him? *I* did that. Now please let me go. I am *fed up* with being manhandled."

"Dusti," Drantos pleaded. "Don't, sweetheart. He's not someone you want to get mouthy with. Just be quiet and allow me speak."

Aveoth surprised Dusti by chuckling. Amusement sparked in his gaze that started to turn bright blue again. His hands on her loosened but he didn't remove them from her body. "This is becoming entertaining."

"I'm glad you think so. She's been raised human." Drantos kept his tone soft. "Dusti has no understanding of others, our laws, or how to show respect to any type of authority. She and her sister have a distinct talent for saying anything that comes to mind."

"Is the sister similar to her?"

Drantos hesitated to answer.

"She's way worse," Dusti informed him. "She's a defense attorney from Los Angeles. Her law firm had to hire Bat her own personal security team because she's pissed off so many people she gets death threats on a daily basis." She took a breath. "I am not kidding about that castration if you were to force her into going to bed with you. She'd actually do it, and probably buy a case to carry your balls around in her purse just for the meanness of it."

"Dusti," Drantos rasped, "stop."

Aveoth laughed again and released her, backing up. He studied Drantos. "She's got spirit." His gaze lowered down his body. "I see you still have your balls."

Drantos sighed. "Yes. Dusti's the sweet one."

All humor disappeared from Aveoth's features. "I want to meet Batina."

"She already has a mate." Drantos kept his voice very low. "He'll never allow you to have her."

Dusti turned her head to gape at Drantos. "Who?"

He met her gaze. "Kraven."

Her mouth fell open. "No."

He gave a sharp nod. "He hasn't informed her yet but it's true."

"Oh, that poor bastard." Dusti winced. If it *was* true, her sister would hurt the guy. Bat had obviously liked Kraven enough to consider fooling around with him but her sister didn't do long-term relationships.

"Your Kraven?" Anger tinged Aveoth's voice.

Wariness tightened Drantos's features. "Yes. My brother." He shot a glare at Craig, still on his knees. "That one and several others attacked my family to steal my mate, and my brother was injured protecting Batina."

"How bad was he hurt?" Aveoth's skin seemed to darken to that dusky gray again and his flesh appeared to harden.

Drantos cautiously inched closer until he reached Dusti's side. He wrapped an arm around her waist, hoisted her against his naked body, and backed away from the GarLycan.

"He'll live but it was pretty serious. They tried to rip out his spine and almost succeeded. He couldn't defend himself because he was holding on to Bat to protect her."

Aveoth's head snapped in Craig's direction. "You attacked VampLycans from another clan? I forbid fighting amongst the clans."

"Decker ordered us to retrieve his granddaughter Batina at any cost. Those were his words. He said to bring Batina to you, regardless of who we had to kill to do it." The guy's voice shook with fear. "He specifically stated even if we had to kill VampLycans."

In the blink of an eye, Aveoth was gone. He moved so fast that it just seemed to Dusti as if he'd teleported. He appeared in front of Craig for a second then suddenly turned around. Dusti choked back a scream when she realized what she was witnessing.

Craig's head rolled in the dirt, his body slumping in another direction.

Aveoth had avoided the blood spray by taking one step to the side. He'd beheaded the guy.

Drantos snarled and transferred her from his arms to behind his back. She knew he did it to protect her, just as surely as she knew he didn't stand a chance against a GarLycan. Aveoth could move too fast. An image of Drantos ending up that same way flashed through her mind, his head removed from his neck...

She didn't think. She just reacted by lunging around him and throwing her arms up, putting herself between him and the threat.

What am I doing?

She wasn't sure, but Aveoth hadn't killed her when he'd had the chance. He'd said he wouldn't hurt a descendant of Margola. She prayed he'd meant that.

Drantos gripped her hips but she just pressed back against his front tightly and clutched at his bare hips to keep him from moving her. She didn't want Drantos to die. Even if that meant using her body as a shield. She stared at Aveoth, praying he wouldn't come at them next. He was a terrifying sight with his slate-gray skin, appearing more stone than flesh.

"Please don't hurt him," she pleaded softly.

Drantos growled and tried to lift her. "Release me and be quiet."

"No." Her nails dug into his skin and she shoved her back against him harder. "*You* shut up."

Aveoth didn't move but he did watch Dusti closely. "She protects you? Interesting."

"She is unique," Drantos said, sighing again. "Are we going to fight?"

Aveoth's gaze lifted to Drantos. He waved a hand at what used to be Craig. "He deserved it. He attacked another clan against my orders, stole a woman, and his scent is on her leg. He drew her blood. I hate anyone who would abuse a woman. The fact that she's so human and helpless to defend against him really riles my sense of vengeance."

"Understood. I would have liked to kill him myself, though you were kinder than I would have been for drawing my mate's blood. I wanted to make him suffer first."

Dusti wondered if either of them realized how cold they sounded discussing the dead corpse on the ground. She refused to glance at what used to be Craig. Throwing up would ruin the image she wanted to display of being tougher than she really felt.

"*You* killing him may have caused tension. I do it and it's justice. These are my lands and my laws were broken." Aveoth took a deep breath. "Speaking of laws, what does your father think of you mating to someone who smells so human? You're the eldest son and it's your duty to produce strong offspring. You risk failing with her."

"It doesn't matter what he thinks. She's mine."

"He could reject her."

Drantos softly growled. "I don't care."

Aveoth studied Drantos with a frown. "I believe you."

"I wouldn't lie to you."

"Are you still close to your father?"

"Yes."

"But you'd defy him if he rejects her as your mate and you'd leave your own clan?"

"I'm not giving up Dusti."

"So possessive." Aveoth smiled. "Go. Take her and leave."

"Thank you." Drantos wrapped his arms around Dusti's middle. "Did you know Decker planned to use Batina to blackmail you, to help him start a war between our clans?"

Aveoth's skin seemed to harden more, darkening to a dull gray. "No. You believe he still plots a war?"

"I'm certain of it." Drantos hesitated. "We still get a few families every so often seeking asylum from Decker. He murders his own clan members who show stronger Vampire traits. He also deems any younger siblings a loss, assuming they will mature and become the same. He's beheaded toddlers and babies."

Aveoth narrowed his eyes. "You're certain this is true?"

"Yes. We'll give you access to speak to the survivors and witnesses if you find it as horrifying as we do."

Aveoth said nothing. Dusti felt horrified too, even if the man turning to stone in front of her didn't. Her grandfather was way worse than anything she'd ever imagined.

Dusti was in his arms but Drantos didn't feel as if she were safe yet. Aveoth was a danger to her. The GarLycan leader had changed a lot over the years. He'd grown bigger, stronger, and fierce. Traces of the young man he'd once been where there too, faint as they may be.

"What happened to you?" Drantos stared at Aveoth, hoping for an answer. "Why?" He didn't need to say more. They both knew what he asked. They'd been best friends once, close as brothers. Then Aveoth had shut him out of his life.

Aveoth regarded him for a long moment, only his eyes revealing any emotion. The silver in his gaze turned blue. "Our childhood ended and my responsibilities began. It was best if we didn't speak any longer. I have earned enemies. It would have put you in danger, being my friend."

"From who? I heard about your father. I know he wouldn't have approved of us spending time together."

Aveoth's gaze grew brighter blue. "You mean you learned that I challenged and killed him." He inclined his head.

Drantos couldn't comprehend how anyone could do that. He and his father had plenty of disagreements but he'd never attack him or take his life. Especially to take control of the clan.

Aveoth's eyes lightened, the silver bleeding through. "Don't look at me like that, Drantos. Lord Abotorus and Decker Filmore are of the same ruling mindset. Cruelty and fear are what kept or keeps them in power." He glanced at Dusti, then back at him. "They both believed their children were acceptable pawns to use in a political game. I no longer wished to be a part of my father's."

"I'm sorry." The meaning behind the words Aveoth had spoken was grim. There had clearly been no love between father and son.

"I have the same problem with some of the full-blooded Gargoyles that I had with Lord Abotorus. They feel the mixing of bloodlines has weakened our clan. They fear I'll be too lenient with VampLycans because of our shared Lycan blood."

"I think Craig would disagree if he still had a head to talk with," Dusti muttered.

"Quiet," Drantos whispered.

"Now Decker wishes to try to use me for his own political gain." Aveoth's irises turned almost white. "And I still don't want to be used. I have no desire to go to war with VampLycans, Drantos. I like the peace." His tone deepened, his anger clear. "You are not my enemy."

"I do miss my friend," he admitted.

Aveoth broke eye contact and turned, putting some space between them. Drantos thought he'd leave but the other man paused, glancing over his shoulder at him. "I wish you and Kraven well. I have fond memories but times have changed. A close association with you would be seen as a weakness. I can't permit that." He slowly turned his body to face them once more. "Tell Kraven I have no interest in Batina."

Drantos relaxed. "Thank you." His relief upon realizing Aveoth wouldn't go after Bat, that Kraven wouldn't have to fight to the death to save his mate, was immeasurable.

Aveoth inclined his head and actually smiled. "I'd like to keep my balls exactly where they are and not inside a box in some woman's purse." He glanced at Dusti, then back at Drantos. "Protect your mate better."

"It's been a bad few days."

"We were in a plane crash," Dusti added.

Aveoth looked surprised, staring at Drantos for confirmation. "A plane crash?"

He nodded. "I don't have your wings. I wished I did when we were about to slam into the ground. All Kraven and I could do was wrap our bodies around them and hope it would be enough. We've been trying to get them to our territory ever since but Decker sent enforcers to attack us while we were vulnerable."

"I'll handle Decker." Aveoth's tone took on an icy edge. "He's attempted to blackmail me for the last time. I know you have your own reasons to go after him but again, it will be considered justice when I kill him."

Drantos had no argument with that. "I just want the threat to end."

"I agree." Aveoth glanced at Dusti again and his smile returned. "I like her."

Drantos tensed, prepared once more to fight to keep Dusti.

Aveoth didn't attack, but said instead, "Listen to me well, Drantos."

He expected a threat.

"I'm giving you the gift of knowledge. Old Vampire masters keep their made children in the dark in more ways than one. They don't share their secrets, believing the fear of the unknown will help them stay in power over their nests." He paused. "Lycans tend to send their young and females of breeding age to safety when they face a battle. That means their elderly are often killed when they remain behind to fight, so much of their history is lost." He paused. "Gargoyles, however, are record keepers—and we have thousands of years of knowledge written down, everything we've learned from both races."

Drantos frowned, not sure how this was relevant to him.

Aveoth chuckled, seeming to sense his confusion. "VampLycans are children compared to some of my ancestors. I spent many a year in our libraries reading." His expression turned grim. "I didn't have a happy childhood, but my time spent amongst the records was helpful." He paused again and glanced at Dusti, then Drantos. "All the reasons your father might fear you mating to her wouldn't be a problem...if you were to share your blood with her generously while she carries your line. Do you understand?"

"You're saying my blood will—"

"Yes," Aveoth cut him off. "Exactly. I would hate to see you leave your clan and venture into the human world. You belong here. So do your offspring. They'll be as strong as you are."

"You're sure?" If Aveoth was right, his children could still be born with the ability to shift if he fed Dusti blood on a regular basis while she was pregnant.

"I'm certain. It's been done for generations with Gargoyles. It's why all of us retain our bloodlines so strongly, regardless of the race of women we breed with. That information is for you and your family only. Do you understand? Never repeat where you learned it."

"Thank you."

Aveoth stared at Dusti. "She is tempting. I miss the blood so much." He looked at Drantos. "Take her and go now. I have a corpse to dispose of and a few more to make."

Drantos shifted Dusti in his arms, gently draping her over his shoulder, then sprinted off into the woods.

Aveoth had practically admitted that the blood-addiction rumors were true. It made him afraid for his mate. She carried the bloodline Aveoth craved in her veins. She was already bleeding. Drantos could smell it, felt the sticky blood under his hand even now, and had glimpsed the damage to her leg. He just wanted to get her far away in case Aveoth reconsidered letting her go.

Motivation to protect his mate made him push his limits. It would have been faster if he'd shifted to all fours to run but he didn't believe Dusti was up for another shock.

He'd never forget the way she'd looked when she'd first seen him coming out of those woods. He'd been enraged to find Aveoth touching her. That probably hadn't helped. He just hoped that one day she could accept both sides of him without fear or revulsion. Otherwise their future might be tough...but it wouldn't matter. They'd have to find a way to make it work. He wasn't ever letting her go, even if he had to fight her every step of the way.

Chapter Eleven

Drantos stopped at the river. He gently repositioned Dusti to lower her to her feet. She didn't miss the sweat that sheeted his skin—every inch of it, as she could see, since he stood before her naked, but she raised her attention above his waist after a quick peek at his lower half.

"Thank you for coming after me."

"Did you honestly think I wouldn't?" Anger darkened his gaze. "I will always come for you."

"Are Bat and Kraven really okay?"

"She was fine when I left her to go in search of you. No broken bones or severe injuries. She is safely with Kraven. He'll recover. We're strong and heal quickly."

Dusti relaxed. "Thank God. I was worried."

"Kraven told me what you did, why it was you who was taken." Drantos scowled. "What were you thinking?"

"You mean because I said I was Bat?"

"Yes."

"Kraven was really hurt and on top of her. She wasn't moving. That thing…" She paused. "Craig was heading right for her. I had to stop him. You would have done the same. I didn't know how badly she was hurt or if moving her would kill her. I just wanted to protect my sister. "

Some of the anger eased out of his features. "I might have done the same thing in your place. I don't like it but I understand."

"You called Aveoth your friend."

"We spent a lot of time together in our youth."

"You made him out to be some terrifying badass."

"He is. He grew hard." He paused. "Gargoyle jokes aside, I wouldn't ever count on our past to prevent him from killing me. The winters are very harsh here and

VampLycans tend to remain close to home. One summer he was the Aveoth I knew, winter came, and I never spoke to him again. He wanted nothing to do with us. I don't know exactly what caused him to change so much but our friendship died along with any softness inside him."

"Margolia's death maybe?"

"He'd already lost her. No. I think it was having to challenge his father. He avoided us after that. It was..." He grimaced. "Many years ago. He's grown a reputation for viciousness. You saw how easily he took a life."

"You wanted to kill that guy too." She lifted her chin and hugged her chest. "Don't even deny it. You would have taken out Craig, right?"

"I'd never deny the truth to you. Yes, I would have ended his life. He kidnapped you, helped injure Kraven severely, and harmed you. Turn around and let me see your leg."

She hesitated but turned. "I wouldn't have minded you beating on him but can I admit I never want to see you kill someone?"

He crouched behind her but she refused to look back to glance at his naked body. The sight of all that raw male muscle left her a little tongue tied and she wanted to talk to him without her mind straying from the things they needed to discuss.

His gentle touch on her calf didn't startle her. She'd expected it. He used one of his hands to cup icy river water to pour over the wound. She gasped but held still. "You could have warned me. That water is really cold."

"I'm going to lick the injury closed. Don't pull away."

Her body tensed. "You can do that?"

"Yes." Hot breath warmed her icy wet skin. "I don't want you to scar, sweetheart."

She closed her eyes and tried not to tense. The first touch of his raspy, hot tongue made her heart race. Something about him always did funny things to her body. He instantly made her react sexually, and even with the tension between them, she had to admit to being severely attracted.

Talk to him, she ordered. *You need to find out about him and Yonda.* Her mouth parted. "Is she your girlfriend? Did you cheat on her with me? I want the truth."

The warm tongue paused in licking the back of her leg. "Are you willing to listen now?"

"I asked. Duh."

He chuckled. "Hang on. I'm almost done."

Her leg tingled slightly as he swiped her with his tongue. She wondered what else he could do besides change into a fury, terrifying beast, lick wounds closed with a few strokes of his tongue, and hypnotize people with his beautiful eyes. It unsettled her that she knew so little about him yet they'd had sex.

He finished with her leg and released her. She knew when he rose behind her, could sense it when he stepped closer, even though he didn't touch her.

"Do you mind if I dive into the river first? We'll sit and talk while I dry. I itch from the sweat."

"Go ahead."

"Move away from the edge. I don't want you falling in. I won't be long. I just need to rinse off."

She took a few steps forward and heard water splashing behind her. Her gaze drifted around her surroundings until she found a warm patch of grass in the setting sun. Darkness would come soon. She hoped Drantos wouldn't freeze when it became dark and colder. He didn't have any clothes with him.

She fingered her skirt. She could give it to him. She still had his shirt and the jacket

that fell to her mid-thigh. It kept her covered. It would be preferable talking to a guy in a skirt over a sexy, tempting, naked one. *Focus*, she demanded. *You need answers before you drool over his bod.*

He'd won serious honor points by risking his life and facing Aveoth to get her away from him. Drantos didn't have to come after her, yet he had. She'd insulted him by renouncing him in front of some of his people, whatever that meant in his world. It boiled down to her embarrassing him. She'd figured that much out. Most guys would sulk or just have nothing to do with a woman after that.

She couldn't prevent her gaze from seeking him out when she heard him get out of the water.

He shook his entire body, his hair sending water in all directions, and her gaze lingered on the drops coating his tan, muscular chest. *Drool worthy*, she silently admitted. *Best damn bod…ever.* His entire form appeared sculpted to perfection, from his masculine facial features, to his broad shoulders, to that muscled flat belly.

Her attention halted on his slightly hardened cock. It amazed her that he could have so much blood in that area despite the freezing water he'd just been in. A human guy would be cursing the cold, his parts shriveled, and definitely not be looking so tempting. She forced her focus to the grass in front of her so he didn't catch her studying him when he stopped trying to dry his body as best as he could.

"Do you want my sarong?"

"No. I'd just get it wet. Perhaps I'll accept it when I'm dry." He closed the distance between them until he sat just feet in front of her.

She noticed he positioned his body in a way that hid his lap, his knees drawn up, but it did nothing to hide the curve of his beefy ass when he turned slightly. His gaze met hers when she stopped gawking at him again. He had a slight grin on his lips that told her he'd noticed her interest.

"Um, yeah. Yonda. Talk."

He drew in a deep breath, didn't look away from her, and spoke. "I've had sex with her over the years but we weren't in a committed relationship. I've also had sex with other women. We're not human, Dusti. We don't have attachments to sexual partners in the way you'd identify with or label them. It wasn't cheating when I touched you. It would imply Yonda and I had an understanding of monogamy, which we did not."

It hurt to imagine him with the tall long-haired woman. She didn't want to know how many other women he'd slept with. "So you really don't have feelings for her?"

"No. We have had sex without emotional ties."

"I would say *she* had feelings. You saw how she reacted to me. I'd have died if looks could kill. She was upset."

"That surprised me, but I think mainly her objection is because you are so human." He blew out a breath. "She's more of a friend than anything. I mentioned we have harsh winters. I've spent weeks at a time at her home, but again, we weren't in a relationship as you'd understand it. It's about sex and survival."

"You have to have sex or you'll die?" She hoped he heard the mockery laced in her voice. "Gee, I've never heard a guy say that before."

"No. It was about not freezing to death during a blizzard by being stupid enough to travel from her home to mine." He looked annoyed. "I am sorry you believed she was important to me. She isn't. It was just sex. I was single, she lost her mate to death, and we hooked up from time to time. Does that clarify it enough for you? There wasn't a woman in my life that I had any emotional attachments to until I met you."

Dusti let all he'd said sink in. It really helped her understand, even though she knew she'd never want Yonda anywhere near Drantos ever again.

"I should have told you that you were my mate."

"What does that mean?"

His beautiful eyes softened as he watched her. "It means there's a very strong bond between us. I'd like to make it permanent."

"What the hell does *that* mean?"

"Mates are for life. It means I'm offering to care for you, share everything that I have with you, and will protect you. I'd even die for you."

He meant it. The sincerity in his gaze left no question.

"You don't love me."

An eyebrow arched. "Don't I?"

"We just met."

"Do you feel bonded to me?"

She did. The guy always made her *feel*. He pissed her off, made her so turned-on she actually hurt with a need to touch him, and when she had thought he'd cheated it had nearly ripped her guts out. "But love? I'm not sure about that."

"I am."

He always surprised her. "You love me?"

His jaw clenched. "I do."

"But we just—"

"It's a VampLycan trait, sweetheart. We fall hard and fast. I liked your spirit and the way you stood up to me. I had a taste of your blood and I knew the first time I scented your arousal that you were mine."

"What does that have to do with it?"

"It's difficult to explain. Finding a mate doesn't easily happen. You don't want to know my actual age but I've looked for a long time for mine. You are *it*. We know after tasting the blood. If a woman is mate compatible it changes things inside our bodies. The first scent of arousal from that female affects us so greatly, it's undeniable. My body knew you belonged to me. It's as if for the first time in my life, I truly became alive."

She had no words. Her mind tried to understand what he'd said but she had to admit she just couldn't grasp the concept. He loved her. That part hadn't gone unnoticed, but she couldn't really believe it. They'd been together for such a short time. A lot had happened…but love?

"Have you ever felt instant attraction to someone the moment you met them?"

She thought about it. "Sure."

"Humans learn to ignore their instincts. VampLycans rely on them to survive. We hone them. I didn't need to date you for months or years to realize you were the right one for me, Dusti. My body, mind, and instincts told me what you meant to me. Feelings have to be involved, if that matters to you. If I weren't so drawn to your personality, I wouldn't want to be your mate."

"I guess that's good to know. Not that I'm saying I accept this but what does mating detail? Give me the mechanics."

"You make it sound so cold." His tone told her it saddened him.

"I don't mean to."

"You've been raised human. I try to remember that. I wish you hadn't been or you would rejoice in finding your mate, as I do."

"Sorry."

"What do your instincts tell you about me? You've lived your life ignoring them, haven't you?"

Dusti closed her eyes, trying to "feel" what her body might tell her. She had the urge to climb onto his lap and have him hold her. She missed being in his arms. She wanted the closeness and the feelings of warmth he gave her just by being near. She looked at him.

"My head screams run but my heart wants to stay with you."

His expression softened. "Always listen to your heart."

"I'd have to give up my life in Los Angeles, wouldn't I?"

"Yes. It would be too dangerous otherwise. VampLycans can't exist inside a city. I'm not sure how your mother was able to do it, to be honest. I could never change forms and run free. I'd do it for you but my spirit would wither. I don't want to lie to you. I won't stop you if you wish to return to your home but I will follow you there. You're my mate. Where you go, I go. Every Lycan and Vampire would target us as well. They fear VampLycans and you'll smell like me. Do you understand why it wouldn't be safe? I'm an excellent fighter but we'd have entire packs and nests coming after us. I will gladly face that every day and night, though, if it keeps me close to you. My life is wherever you are, Dusti."

She fought the desire to cry but tears filled her eyes anyway. She blinked them back. No man had ever said such wonderful things to her or expressed his feelings in a way that left no doubt she meant everything to him. He was pretty much saying he was willing to battle every day just to be by her side. "You'd still try to live there for me?"

"I'd wither without you faster. I've touched you and know how you make me feel. I can't walk away from that. It would kill me for sure if you weren't in my life. I wouldn't want to go on."

She stared deeply into his beautiful eyes. "You really mean that."

"You sense the truth. I will never lie to you."

Maybe falling in love this fast is possible, she admitted silently. *I love him. How can I not? The guy is telling me he'd rather suffer untold hell just to be with me if I want to live in Los Angeles and he'll die if I leave him.*

"What are you thinking?"

"What about other women? I won't tolerate cheating, and I mean *my* definition of that, not some weird VampLycan one. It means you aren't allowed to touch another woman and they aren't allowed to touch you. I'd leave you so damn fast your head would spin if you did that to me. I'd never forgive you."

Hope etched onto his features so clearly it was easy to read. "I give you my word. Once we cement the bond, my body will only respond to yours."

"What does that mean?"

He turned to face her, spread his thighs, and revealed how hard he'd become. His cock jutted up thick and proud. "You're the only woman who will do *this* to me. We'll bond and no one else will be able to compare to you. I don't want anyone else, Dusti."

She couldn't look away from his cock. Her nipples hardened just at the sight of him in all his glory and that urge to climb in his lap grew stronger. Only now she didn't just want him to hold her. She wanted to ride him, feel him inside her, and she knew dampness spread between her legs. Just thinking about having sex with him made her ache to do it.

"What are you doing to me?"

"We're mates. Your body knows it, even if your mind doesn't. It's why you crave my touch and react so strongly to me. You're not completely human, Dusti. This is how VampLycans react to their mates."

That made sense, in a weird way.

"I'm only going to get hard for *you*, sweetheart. That's what I'm saying. If we complete the bond, you become a part of me and my body will only react to yours this way. Another woman could rub all over me but to put it in terms you'd understand, it would be like someone dragged their claws along a chalkboard. It would just irritate me and make me angry. I'd have the reverse reaction. I'd soften and remain that way, regardless of any stimulation she tried."

"Seriously? That's tough to believe."

"Believe it." He frowned. "I wouldn't lie about that. We are true mates. Only matings that aren't strong fail to get that kind of physical loyalty from the couple."

"What if she blew you?"

"I wouldn't enjoy it. I wouldn't harden. Have you ever had a man touch you and it revolted you? It would be like that."

She studied him closely but saw honesty reflected back at her. "Damn. You're saying you're pretty much dependent on me for sex then, right?"

"Yes. You don't need to look so pleased about that."

"Have you ever trusted someone completely, only to find out the person cheated on you?"

"I've never been in that kind of relationship."

"It devastates you. When a man cheats it makes you feel as though you weren't enough for him, and even though you know its bullshit, it just crushes you inside. Every aspect of what you had with them suddenly is all fucked-up. You love someone and they betray you in the worst possible way. It rips your guts out."

Anger darkened his features. "You loved a man before?"

"I was married. I mentioned that."

A snarl tore from his throat and he moved quickly, rising to his knees and pressing her back until he'd caged her under his body.

Fear of him struck Dusti instantly while she stared up into his face inches above her own. His parted mouth showed sharp fangs.

"No, you didn't. *I'm* your mate."

"Oh. I thought I'd told you about that. I was married when I was much younger but it didn't last long. He was a cheating piece of shit."

Drantos snarled again.

"Stop that. You're scaring me."

"I'd never harm you. It just enrages me that you loved before. He was important to you if you made a commitment to him."

"You're jealous?"

"Yes."

Her hands trembled slightly as she reached up to cup his face. He didn't flinch away but instead pressed tighter to her palms, rubbing against her slightly to encourage her touch. Her fear melted away.

"I don't love him anymore, Drantos. It's in the past. I was younger and came to the conclusion that he wasn't the man I thought. We ended up being strangers. I think I wanted to love an image he represented, instead of the person he really was. He wasn't ready to settle down to be with one woman. Do you understand?"

His anger left as quickly as it had come. His fangs retracted. "You're my mate. *Mine*, Dusti. Love me. I won't ever hurt you."

All reservations she had evaporated with his heartfelt plea. *Love him*? *I do*, she acknowledged. She nodded and knew she'd made the right choice when he smiled tenderly at her.

"What does completing a mating take?"

He lowered down on top of her, pressing her gently between the grass and his firm, warm body. He braced his elbows next to her ribs to keep enough weight off her chest for her to be able to breathe easily. She only hesitated a moment before spreading her thighs to give him access. He sank his hips between them and she wrapped her legs around the back of his thighs to entwine their bodies. The sarong easily parted to allow for close contact.

"It's a process. We share blood, have sex, and open ourselves to each other to help the bond lock into place."

"That sounds kind of hot except for the blood part. How do we open up to each other?"

"Don't hold back from me. Open up to me. Your heart, your mind, and your body."

"Okay. I can do that. What about the blood?"

"You take from me and I take from you during sex. We do that to help become a part of each other. Your VampLycan genes will respond to my blood, as mine will to yours."

"You've traded blood with different women." She hated to remember that bit of information she'd gotten out of him.

"It's not the same. Please don't look at me that way. If I'd known it would cause you pain, I never would have done it. It's how we test to see if we're mates. It really couldn't be avoided. Their blood was only a taste in my mouth. Yours is life to me that spreads through my entire body. Do you understand?"

"You're really good at knowing what to say to a woman to make her feel special." She smiled and let his past go; it helped that he wouldn't taste any more women in his future. "Charmer."

"You *are* special to me. You have no idea."

"I was a little confused about what Aveoth was saying when he started talking about history and records but I understood some of it. Is that why your father doesn't like me? And what does being generous with your blood mean?"

"He was informing me that if I shared my blood with you while you're pregnant, that our children will be born strong. I'm the firstborn of my father's children. It's my responsibility to give my father strong grandchildren to keep our line intact for future generations. Your being so human could result in our children having more human traits than VampLycan. Aveoth was telling me how to avoid that to get my father to accept you and our future children into the clan."

She let that sink in. "You want kids?"

"Don't you?"

"Yes. Just not right away."

"Fair enough. We have plenty of time."

"Okay, Drantos. Let's do this."

He smiled at her again. "Now?"

"You're on top of me and I'm so totally turned-on, I ache. I'll hurt you if you try to leave me this way."

"We can make love without cementing the bond. It's not a one-shot deal, sweetheart. It can take days. I'd rather we start the process when we reach my cabin. I don't want any interruptions once we start."

"Cabin?" She made a face. "Oh, please tell me it's got electricity and a computer with internet connection. Satellite or cable television would be a must too. Have I mentioned I'm a city girl? I suck at camping and roughing it."

"I have all the modern-day amenities," he chuckled. "Just because I love to roam the wilderness doesn't mean I don't enjoy all the comforts life has to offer. I even have a Jacuzzi tub inside the bathroom in our master bedroom."

"You're perfect."

"So are you." He grinned. "I need to get you home soon. Wouldn't you prefer us to be on a bed, rather than on the ground?"

Her legs lifted to hook across his ass. "No. I'm impatient. I guess I should warn you about that. Kiss me."

His mouth lowered without hesitation and Dusti lifted her chin to meet him halfway. The instant his tongue swiped hers, the desire inside her changed from an ache into a raging inferno of need. She moaned and arched against his chest. She wished she were naked to feel him skin to skin. The material between their upper bodies nearly hurt. She whimpered.

He tore his mouth away, concern in his gaze. She released his face to frantically claw at the waist of the shirt she wore. He had to lift up slightly for her to be able to free it from between their bodies. She wiggled and squirmed but eventually tossed the shirt over her head. Her fingers gripped his shoulders to yank him down on top of her again, mouth going for his, and she ground her hips against his pelvis to urge him to enter her. The material of her bunched sarong didn't bother her so much, since it was high on her hips between their lower bellies. The sensation of her breasts smashed against his hot chest was pure heaven.

"Slow down."

She shook her head, gazing up into his eyes with desperation. "I want you so bad. I've never had much patience."

"Taking my blood last night started the mating process already." He looked a little stunned but then adjusted his hips. "It's rough in the beginning. Passion can flare up suddenly."

"I like rough sex. Just fuck me."

He chuckled. "I mean the need for sex. It's near uncontrollable for the first few days."

"Don't talk me to death."

She used her hold around his waist to grind her hips, seeking him, and moaned when his hard cock nudged at the seam of her sex. He closed his eyes when she rubbed her pussy against him. A soft growl came from deep in his throat.

"Slow down or I'll lose control, sweetheart. You're too human. You don't want that. If you think you've ever had rough sex before, you haven't."

"I don't care! Just fuck me," she demanded. She moved suggestively against the hard ridge of his shaft until she got him to slide across her clit. She bit her lip hard enough to draw blood and threw her head back from the intense pleasure. Her eyes closed. Raw ecstasy tore through her.

Drantos drove into her fast and deep. The sensation of his thick cock stretching her, filling her, made her cry out again. He froze, buried inside her, and snarled.

"Did I hurt you?"

She shook her head. "Felt good. Move, baby. Please? Will you do that bite thing on my neck? You have no idea what that feels like."

He growled, buried his face against her neck, and bit down hard enough to send that wonderful jolt of electricity throughout her body. Her vaginal walls clenched around his cock and he snarled against her skin.

Maybe he does know, she guessed, when he bit again while he started to move inside her.

Passion roared through her veins to a height she'd never been before. He'd mentioned his blood must have triggered the beginning of their mating process. If this was just the start, she doubted she'd survive when it hit full force. She bucked frantically against him, used her legs wrapped around his ass for leverage, and lifted her face to blindly find his skin. She bit *him* instead of her lip.

He snarled, his hips slamming into her harder and faster.

The slide of his cock against all those nerve endings inside her body seemed to amplify the fervor to come. Pleasure and pain blurred in her mind. She felt as if she'd die if she didn't climax. It hovered just out of her reach but every time Drantos clamped down on her skin with his teeth, the electric jolt shooting through her from head to toe drew her closer to that goal.

Sweat slicked their bodies, helping them glide against each other smoother; her nails dug into him and she didn't care if she drew blood. She doubted he would either, with the way he snarled, moaned, and growled against her skin. The sounds he made turned her on more. He wasn't just a man but part animal at that moment. They both were. She acknowledged it with acceptance.

His mouth released her but his hips didn't slow the rapid pace he'd set. "Bite harder," Drantos demanded. He bit her again on her throat and pain registered. That bite didn't jolt her but the pain faded quickly.

She bit him as hard as she could, tasted blood, and an overwhelming desire gripped her. She fastened her mouth on that spot and sucked, her tongue frantically lapping at his taste that filled her mouth. She realized he was taking her blood as well. His knees spread wider as he drove his cock into her a little deeper.

Dusti blew apart inside. It started at her pussy and spread to her brain in an instant. She screamed against his skin when the pleasure became too intense, too devastating, and so strong her body tensed until she thought her bones would snap. She became too wrapped up in the climax to care if they did.

Drantos tore his mouth from her skin to nearly deafen her when he roared out his pleasure. She gasped softly from pressure she felt inside her pussy when his cock seemed to swell a little against her vaginal walls clamped tightly around him. When he started to come, she felt the heat spreading inside her. The warm blasts made him shake on top of her with every drop he emptied inside her body, and they drew out her glorious quakes of pleasure until they finally receded. Their bodies slowly relaxed together, their panted breaths mingling, and Dusti smiled.

"Oh, wow."

Drantos nudged her throat, made her turn her head away from him more, and his tongue lapped at the areas he'd bitten. The taste of his coppery blood remained on her tongue. He licked the bites closed. The slight pain the bites had inflicted faded away completely.

"Look at me."

She opened her eyes, turned her head, and smiled at Drantos. He smiled back.

"You're my mate. I love you, Dusti. Please love me and don't leave."

The look in his eyes nearly broke her heart. He was still afraid she'd refuse him. It leveled her that she could make someone as fierce as Drantos feel real fear. Her hands slid from his shoulders. She caressed the column of his throat and winced a little at the sight of the ragged wound she'd inflicted with her teeth. She didn't have fangs so the bite mark resembled two big half-moon shapes with blood welling out of them.

"I'm sorry. I didn't mean to do that."

"It doesn't hurt. It will heal."

She forced her attention from what she'd done to him. "I can't lick you to seal your wounds, can I? I want to."

"You can lick me, but no. Those traits weren't passed down to you. Your human blood likely blocked it." He held her gaze. "Will you stay with me as my mate?"

She nodded. "I will, Drantos. I'm your mate." Her fingertips moved to trace his jawline on both sides of his face. "I do love you."

The grin he gave her revealed his pure joy. "You won't regret it."

"I believe you."

"I need to get you home."

"That means we have to move, right? I'm kind of comfy right where we are."

"We can't remain here. Decker may send more men hunting for you and I won't risk your safety." He paused. "There's a faster way to get home than to walk there."

"You want to sling me over your shoulder again? I'm not loving that idea. I know you had to run with me to get away from Aveoth but I really don't want a repeat."

"No." He hesitated. "I could shift and you could ride on my back."

Dusti grimaced. "Shit."

"It's still me."

"I know but I like you this way so much more." She knew he worried about her safety and, as a beast, he could move faster with four legs instead of just two. "Damn. I'm going to need a drink later."

He chuckled. "I have a fully stocked bar at the cabin."

"You really are perfect. Okay." She forced a nod. "I can do this. I can."

"It's like riding a horse."

"I lived in L.A. I never had access to one. I don't count being strapped to that asshole when he kidnapped me as a fun experience either."

"It will be a fun adventure with me."

"Right." She sighed. "Let's do this. The faster, the better, before I chicken out."

"You're being very brave for me and I appreciate it. I know you'd prefer not to see me that way."

"It's not really bravery motivating me. It's the fact you told me you have a Jacuzzi tub that urges me to deal with you in fur a lot faster. Plus, I really am starving. I'm assuming you have food at home." She hesitated. "Your eyes turning pure black scare me more than the hair or the deadly looking claws do. I also feel a little sick when I hear the transformation. It's kind of a yucky sound. I don't want to offend you, don't mean to, but I want to be honest. I think I'm doing good though, considering a few days ago before the crash I would have just run screaming if I saw you in fur."

Drantos lifted up a little and gently withdrew from her body. She hated the feeling of him separating from her but didn't protest.

"I can't help any of that. I know my eyes turn black. It's me though. Just remember that, and yes, I have food at home. While you enjoy the tub, I'll make you a wonderful dinner. This won't be so bad. Just wrap your legs around me and hug my neck. Hold on tight."

"Okay but don't ever ask me to do you in fur because *ewwww*. You're damn hot in skin but not the other way."

He laughed, lifted totally off her to his knees, and then held out his hand. "You have my word."

She put her hand in his. "Good because yeah, that's just too freaky for me."

"I swear." He chuckled. "It doesn't do it for me either. Some VampLycans have sex in their animal form but I never have. Not a turn on." His heated gaze darted down her body. "I love creamy, soft flesh."

"Well, I have that in abundance."

"I'm happy about that." He easily pulled her to her feet and then rose to his.

Chapter Twelve

Dusti walked into the woods to use the bathroom and when she returned, she faced Drantos in fur. His massive beast body stood perfectly still while he watched her silently with those black eyes that still made her shiver. No sign of the man she loved lurked in their dark depths.

She realized she'd jerked to a halt. She took a deep breath, moved to the discarded shirt, and bent to shake it out before slipping it over her head.

"Give me a minute." She glanced at him. "I need to do something about this sarong thing. I think I came up with a way to make a kind of diaper shape with it, which would be good because I'd like something between my pussy and your fur. No offense but that's why I trim down there."

He sat on his haunches and she swore he grinned when his mouth parted to reveal those wicked-sharp teeth. She smiled at him.

"You still look terrifying. I don't suppose you'd consider wearing a collar one day? I can't tell you apart from the others when you're like that but you do look bigger."

He softly growled.

"I guess not." She untied the two ends of the sarong to put it between her legs, and then she tied both sides of the ends tightly at her waist. Her thighs were exposed high on each side but it functioned the way she wanted it to. She focused back on Drantos. "Okay."

He eased up to stand on all four of his muscular legs. She held still as he slowly stalked forward. When he reached her, his head lowered near her hand and nudged her palm. She hesitated before running her fingers through the soft black fur behind his head. She refrained from making any jokes, even if she was tempted to call him a "nice doggy". He didn't appear to resemble one, besides the shape of his head and the pointed ears. His muzzle turned to bump against her thigh.

"Got it. Climb on. Okay." She studied his broad back. "Like a horse. Right."

She moved to his side. He wasn't as tall as a horse on all four legs but his back was still as high as her stomach. She gripped him with both hands and threw her leg over. He lowered just enough to help her straddle him and then he rose up until her toes left the ground. She lunged forward to press her chest against his back.

"Can we go slow at first?"

He turned his head to peer at her. The sight of his pitch-black eyes didn't scare her as much as before. His fur was soft and comfortable. She knew he wouldn't bite into her or claw her. *This is Drantos*, she silently reminded herself. He straightened to face forward.

When he took the first few steps, she realized she needed to wrap her arms around his neck. She hugged him tightly. He paused, and one of his front clawed hands gently pushed on her shin just enough to clue her in that he wanted her to hook her legs under his belly. She hoped she didn't accidently kick his genitals but his torso seemed longer in this form than in his human skin. His hand dropped away and that quickly, they were moving.

* * * * *

Drantos couldn't deny how proud he felt that Dusti rode his back without fear. She hadn't exactly accepted all of him yet but it had gone far better than he'd imagined when she saw him in his animal form the second time.

He slowed, sniffed the air, and avoided the main body of town when he approached his village.

Worry rose but he had no time to consider what sort of punishment might be dealt to him. He had rescued his mate, carried her safely to clan lands, and soon he'd have her secured inside his home. She needed a warm bath to remove the chill from her skin and a full belly of food to alleviate her hunger. He would inform his family he'd returned after she was cared for.

Dusti shivered once again, her arms slack around his neck now. He knew exhaustion had set in. He paused, waited for a sentry to pass without detecting them since he kept downwind, and then crept forward. He relaxed when he stepped onto his own property where his cabin rested. He crouched down by the front door and started to transform without giving his mate a warning.

She softly started to curse when the hair receded and his bones shifted but she didn't try to fling her body away. He grinned in amusement while he listened to her list of foul words expand. His mate could make a trucker blush with the things she muttered. He reached back, gripped her thighs, and straightened.

"Just hold on. I'll give you a piggyback ride straight to that tub I promised. Do you mind opening the door?" He turned her toward the handle, bent his knees, and she released him with one hand to turn the knob.

"Don't you people lock your doors?"

"No. There is no need. We don't steal from each other."

"That wouldn't happen where I come from. You leave your door unlocked and you come home to an empty house that's been stripped."

"You're totally safe here." He didn't bother to turn on lights. His eyes were already accustomed to the darkness outside. "We're almost there. I'll settle you in warm water and bring you a meal. How are you doing?"

"I'm tired." She yawned to make her point. "Maybe I could skip the bath and food for a nap first."

"No. You haven't eaten all day. It's my job to care for you."

"Do you do dishes and laundry too? If you do, I'll love you more."

He snorted back a laugh. "I've been a bachelor for a very long time. I even clean my home."

"I wouldn't know. I'm assuming you haven't turned on lights because you don't want me to see wall-to-wall beer cans and dirty clothes piled everywhere."

"I don't need lights. Sorry."

"You can see in the dark without the moon to help you out?"

"Yes." He turned to gently ease her down on the edge of the bathroom counter. "Hold on and close your eyes. I'll flip on the lights. I don't want to startle you."

"Okay." She released him to sit back.

He flipped on the light and turned to face his mate. He watched her wince and lift a hand to shield her eyes from the bright lights. She blinked a few times before gawking at his bathroom.

"Wow. This is nice. Double sinks, that shower is huge, and you didn't lie about the Jacuzzi tub." She gave him a smile that tugged at his heart when he saw how happy it made her. "I could live in here."

"Lucky for you, we have an entire cabin. It has three bedrooms and two bathrooms."

"I think my bedroom at home would fit in here. I can't wait to see the rest of the place if this is any indication. It's huge, isn't it?"

"We've been on these lands for a long time. I started building my home…" He stopped talking. She didn't want to know his age. "Some years ago. I wanted it to be comfortable when I found my mate."

He spun away and turned on the water in the deep tub to draw her bath. He kept his back to her until the water rose to where he wanted it. He glanced over his shoulder.

"Do you need help in?"

She scooted off the counter edge. "I can manage. Thanks."

He didn't want to leave her but she needed to eat. "Relax. Make yourself at home. This is yours now too. I'll cook you food."

She reached for the ties on the sarong. "Thank you, Drantos."

"Never thank me for caring for you. It's my privilege." He quickly left her before he saw too much of her naked skin. The hunger for his mate boiled inside his blood, already laced with hers.

He started to prepare a meal and then reached for the phone. He hesitated briefly but knew someone might see the lights on inside his house if they were patrolling the area and report it to his father. He knew he couldn't put off the call. He dialed.

"When did you get home, Drantos?" His father answered on the second ring. "My caller ID said it was you."

"Does it matter? I recovered my mate and she's home with me."

"Do you need a doctor for her?"

"No. She was slightly injured but I licked her wounds. They are almost healed. The bastard who stole her had clawed the back of her leg."

"I take it that he's dead?"

"Yes. I wasn't the one to kill him. Aveoth found them first. He—"

Velder snarled. "Lord Aveoth was there? What happened?"

"I'm trying to tell you. He located Dusti and Decker's enforcer before I reached them. I told Aveoth how she had been taken and that we'd been attacked."

"Did you tell him why? Did he know of Decker's plan?"

"He wasn't aware of what Decker was up to but he is now. He said he'd handle it and it doesn't bode well for Decker. He also said he doesn't want a war with us. He likes the peace."

"That's excellent news. I'll share it with the other clans. I've kept them apprised of what is going on. We've all been worried."

"I know. Aveoth is aware of Dusti and Bat now but he made it clear he isn't going to come after them or make a trade with Decker. I told him Dusti is my mate and he accepted it."

"She's so human."

He knew where the conversation was headed. "She's still part VampLycan, and she's mine. I won't give her up. I know what you're worried about, but our children will be strong-blooded if I feed her my blood while she's pregnant. There's no reason for you to reject her as my mate. I'll be able to fulfill my duties as first son."

"Who told you that?"

"I gave my word I wouldn't share that information but it's a reliable source. Someone with old knowledge told me."

"Did someone hear that from one of the Lycan elders and pass it on?"

He hesitated. Aveoth's clan *had* probably gotten the information from an old

Lycan. Someone had to have shared that information to enable the GarLycans to put it in a book. "You could say that."

His father remained silent for long seconds. "I'm glad the GarLycans aren't a threat to us but we still have to address the issue of what you did today. Your mate rejected you in front of others and you went against the law to go after her. You must face punishment. There's no way around it. People are talking."

"I figured."

"I can't protect you, Drantos. It would look bad."

"I know."

"The last thing we need is dissension in the clan by my playing favorites. I must always be fair."

"I don't regret what I've done," he admitted. "I'd do it again. You were wrong for making me chose between you and Dusti."

"It shocked me when I learned who the sisters were. My hatred of Decker runs deep. I've had time to cool down and think it through, and I agree with you. Your mother and I spoke. I can't publically apologize without it making me appear weak but I do, son. I'm sorry. I should have ordered you to go after her instead of remaining with the injured."

"Thanks, Dad."

"I wish I could take it back."

"It's done. Let's just get this over with."

His father sighed. "Sometimes the bullshit gets to me. This is one of those times."

"You've changed a lot of the laws but this is an important one. You can't have our people arguing with your every decision."

"I know, but there should be an exception between fathers and sons."

"I'll take my punishment."

"Be at my home in twenty minutes. I consulted with the clans so everyone is satisfied with the outcome. I had to explain everything that happened and your state of mind when you defied me. They were generous. We were lucky. They took into account that your Dusti doesn't know our laws and that it was stressful to find out she's so human. They were sympathetic, considering she's a relation to Decker on top of it and he had his clan attack us."

"How severely will I be punished?"

"Nothing you can't handle. Tell your mate you will return in the morning. You probably want to avoid her until you've had time to heal."

Drantos winced. "You're right. I don't want her to see me when they're done. It would terrify her. I'll be there in twenty minutes. I won't be late."

"I'll double the sentries to make sure your mate is safe. I wouldn't put anything past Decker. He's insane."

"Aveoth is after him."

"It could take time for Aveoth to find him and Decker might still try to come after his granddaughters. It's better to be safe than sorry. We'll stay on alert until we hear he's been captured or killed."

"Thank you, Father. How is Kraven doing?"

"He's almost totally healed."

"And Bat?"

"She's fine and with him."

"Good." He ended the call.

*****

Dusti backed away when Drantos hung up the phone. She'd overheard enough of the one-sided conversation to know he'd gotten into trouble for going after her. She turned in the hallway and tiptoed back into the bathroom. She'd been on her way to ask him if he had new razors, not wanting to use his personal one. If she hadn't, she'd have never known about the punishment.

She stripped out of his shirt to climb into the large tub. She had no clue how to turn on the jets but it didn't matter. She washed quickly, used his shampoo and conditioner in her hair, and readied to climb out of the tub when Drantos entered the bathroom carrying a tray. The smell of soup and toast made her stomach rumble.

He smiled. "I need to go tell my family that you're safe. You'll find clothing in the dresser, and just leave the tray in here when you're done eating. Go to sleep afterward. Don't wait up for me."

"How long will you be?" She was upset that he wasn't mentioning his conversation with his father but she tried to hide it by forcing her own smile. She hoped hers looked less fake than his did. "Do they live far away?"

His gaze shifted from hers when he set the tray on the corner shelf of the tub. "I thought I'd go by and check on Kraven. While I'm out, I'll also make sure your sister is settled in. And I'm sure my father will want to discuss what happened." He backed away, still avoided looking at her, and then paused. "I'll be back by the time you wake in the morning."

Liar, liar, pants on fire, she thought. "Okay. I'd like to see Bat in the morning."

"That's fine. I'm sure she'll be happy to see you as well." He met her gaze. "I hate to leave you."

He wouldn't meet her eyes when he fibbed. She caught on to that quickly but decided to test it. "Can't you stay? You haven't even shown me around the house and you need to eat too."

"I snacked while I warmed your soup."

Truth, she surmised, since he didn't look away. "Okay. Are you leaving right now?"

"I'm going to use the second bathroom to shower real quick and put on some pants." His attention shifted away. He met her gaze again. "I'll be thinking of you, and will hurry back as quickly as I'm able."

"Okay." *You suck at lying*, she added silently.

He hesitated and then backed toward the door. "Eat all that food. You need it."

"I will," she lied. She wanted to eat so bad she wouldn't even need silverware. She'd happily just tip the bowl and drink the contents. "See you in the morning, baby." She purposely added the nickname, hoping he understood that she cared about him. He was facing some kind of punishment thanks to her—and he probably believed he was protecting her by keeping it a secret.

He spun and left her but not before she saw regret flash in his beautiful eyes.

Dusti waited until she heard a dresser drawer slam closed before she rose out of the tub. Her hungry gaze landed on the tray of food and she softly groaned, but grabbed a towel instead. She didn't even bother to dry off before entering his large bedroom.

She glanced around. He had a massive room with a king-size bed, a big-screen television, and a soft-gray stone fireplace in one corner. It was the kind of bedroom she'd always dreamed of having. Her focus locked on the dresser. She advanced quickly to find something to wear.

Drantos had a lot of clothes but they were all huge on her smaller frame. She settled on a thick black sweater with a hood that she rolled the sleeves on to free her hands of the extra material, and a pair of black drawstring pants. She hoped the dark color would help her sneak around. She was tugging on two pairs of black socks to protect her feet when she heard a door slam.

"Damn, he showers fast," she muttered. She ran to find the front door.

She glimpsed him disappearing into the woods when she peeked out the window. He didn't have curtains covering them. The cabin had to sit above the rest of the homes, since she could see lights down in what appeared to be a valley. She eased the door open and moved outside into the chilly night. She made sure to close it softly before she sprinted after Drantos.

He didn't seem to notice when she followed from a distance. She figured he had to be pretty distracted not to pick up her scent. It probably helped that she wore his clothes, and the socks were nearly silent on the forest floor. She nearly lost sight of him a few times before catching glimpses of his bare back gleaming in the moonlight. She tried to stay behind trees, there were plenty of those, and hoped she wouldn't run into any.

"I've lost my damn mind for doing this," she muttered under her breath, jogging from one tree to the next, and grateful he didn't seem to be in much of a hurry to get to his destination. She wondered where that would be.

He walked into a well-lit backyard where she recognized one of the men who stood waiting by the back door of another cabin. Velder looked grim when he faced his son. Dusti hid behind the thick trunk of a tree, peering around it, wondering if she should just step out there to find out what kind of trouble Drantos faced. She should be included in the punishment, since she felt responsible.

She held back for now. When they went inside, she'd go sneak a peek into one of the many windows. She frowned. They didn't appear to own drapes, either, since she could see inside the back of the house.

Irritation flared when she saw their lips move but she couldn't hear the words spoken. Velder did most of the talking but another older man also had words for Drantos, whose back remained to her. He nodded a few times. The older guy moved for a bag on the back steps while Drantos walked toward a swing set in the yard. It looked old, rusted, and the seats had been removed, only the frame of it looming there in the floodlights.

What the hell?

She tensed when Drantos reached up to grip the top of the frame with both hands, spread far apart above his head. Her gaze traveled to the old man, who carried something close to his chest that she couldn't see as he followed Drantos. He stopped about eight feet behind him.

"Ready?" the older guy called out. "It's twenty-five."

"Do it," Drantos said. He lowered his chin to his chest.

Do what?

The thought had barely crossed her mind when the older man's arm flew back.

In horror, she saw something black, long, and thin sail through the air, and then his arm arched, flying forward, and so did the thing gripped in his hand.

The sound when the whip hit Drantos's back nearly crumpled her to her knees.

A silent scream froze inside her throat when the older man threw his arm back again and lashed down hard. A red line tore open down Drantos's back when the whip struck him once more. The sound cracked loudly in her ears. It took this second time before what she was seeing totally sank in and she found her legs.

"NO!" That one word flew from her mouth.

She ran into the clearing before she realized she could even move.

Drantos snapped his head around and released the bar but she barely saw the movement out of the corner of her eye. Rage had her fixed on the asshole with the whip, who turned to gape at her. He just stood there slack-jawed, obviously stunned, and watched her barrel toward him.

She turned her shoulder, tucked her head, and slammed hard into the man. He gasped and they both went down.

"Dusti!" Drantos roared her name. "No!"

She landed on the guy, who'd cushioned her fall nicely, then pushed up quickly. He lay on his side, his green eyes wide, shocked, and locked with hers. She sat up to straddle his legs, pinning one arm between their bodies, and yanked the whip out of his loose fingers from his other arm sprawled on the grass near her knee.

"What the fuck is wrong with you people?" She fisted the thick handle of the whip to shake it at the guy under her, wanting to hit him so badly she knew she probably would. "How would you like this shoved up your—"

A big, warm hand clamped over her mouth while another arm wrapped around her waist. Drantos yanked her off the guy, lifted her high in his arms, and backed away.

"I'm sorry." He snarled the words. "She didn't know, Carlos. She doesn't understand our laws. I didn't realize she'd followed me."

Velder was suddenly there, helping the older man—in his fifties, Dusti guessed—up from the ground, and he gaped at Dusti as well. Drantos clutched her against his chest, kept his palm over her mouth, and backed up farther. He took ragged breaths before he spoke again.

"She meant no harm."

"Bullshit," Dusti muttered against his skin but it came out muffled.

"Silence," Drantos hissed in her ear. "You just tackled an elder Lycan from our clan who volunteered to punish me so my father didn't have to do it."

Carlos brushed off dirt as he frowned at Dusti. His green eyes started to take on a scary look and she realized she probably shouldn't have tackled him. "Was she going to threaten to shove that whip up my *ass*?"

"No," Drantos denied, though he didn't sound convinced.

Velder sighed. "She's been raised human. We apologize, Carlos. Did she harm you?"

The older guy snorted. "As if she could." He brushed off more grass and dirt from his pants. He didn't turn his disturbing gaze from Dusti. "Is that what you were going to say, young lady? Don't lie to me."

She nodded against Drantos's hand.

Drantos groaned. "Sweetheart, just be quiet."

Carlos crossed his arms over his chest, his focus lifting to Drantos. "Your mate, I assume?"

"Yes."

"Put her down."

Drantos hesitated. "I will take her punishment if you want someone to pay for what she's done to you. I state my right as her mate to protect her from all harm."

"I said put her down," Carlos demanded.

Drantos removed his hand, and then his arm around her waist eased to slide her down the front of him until her feet touched grass. She didn't move away from him though. Fear made her press back against his chest.

Carlos focused on her again, his eyes still glowing, and he pointed to the area in front of him. "Come here, human-raised female."

A growl tore from Drantos. "I will take her punishment."

"Stay out of this. I won't harm your mate." Carlos pointed again. "Where is your courage now, female?"

Dusti trembled but she lifted her chin and stalked forward. She wanted to run, to hide behind Drantos, but she'd be damned if she'd cower in front of the asshole who'd struck him with a whip. She stopped a feet away from him, where he'd indicated. She stared into his eyes.

"It's right here," she got out. "This is my fault."

"Damn it, Dusti," Drantos said. "Seal your mouth, for *me*."

Carlos cocked his gray head to peer down at her. "You're afraid, yet you still came to me."

She shrugged.

"If your mate hadn't pulled you off me, would you have attempted to follow through with your threat?"

"To shove the whip up your ass? Probably. You hit Drantos. That's fucked-up. He rescued me and shouldn't be punished for that."

Velder stepped forward. "I plead with you, Carlos. She's difficult but she's my son's mate. She comes from a world totally different. She has—"

Carlos lifted his hand and Velder stopped talking. The Lycan studied Dusti closely as his glowing gaze cooled to a soft green. "She has courage and a mouth on her but I respect that she'd attack despite knowing she had no chance. She is aware of what you are, correct?"

"Yes."

Drantos startled Dusti when she realized he'd moved up behind her without her knowledge. She turned her head to glance up at him. She looked back at Carlos.

"You realize I could shred you in seconds with my claws? I'm a full-blooded Lycan, one of the few who remained with the clans when we settled here."

Her heart pounded in her chest. "I figured you were one of them."

"Us," Drantos sighed. "You're part VampLycan."

A sniff came from Carlos. "She smells totally human."

"It's there but very faint. Her mother bred with a human." Drantos put his hand on her hip to tug her against his body. "I apologize. Her intentions were honorable."

Carlos turned his head. "Hold her, Velder. I won't punish her for the attack but your son's punishment isn't negotiable. It has been decreed. He still must take twenty-three more lashes."

"No!" Dusti cried. "I don't think that's fair. I didn't know your stupid laws. Drantos and his father were arguing about me."

"This isn't about you," Drantos whispered. "I disobeyed my father in front of clan members on more than one occasion. It's difficult to explain, but this needs to be done so no one else dares to do the same."

"The laws are in place for reasons you couldn't understand, human-raised Dusti." Carlos sighed. "The punishment could have been far worse. Trust me, young lady. He's getting off easy." He jerked his head. "Hold her, Velder. I'll add ten lashes to his punishment if she attacks me again. I'm amused it happened once, impressed by her fearless act to defend her mate, but enough is enough. I have a football game on that I wish to catch some of this evening."

"Are you serious?" Dusti yelled. "A football game? You—"

Drantos clamped his hand back over her mouth and pushed her gently toward his father. "Hold her damn mouth, Dad."

Velder grabbed Dusti around her waist and hoisted her off her feet. The second Drantos released her mouth, Velder put his own hand over her lips. He spun and strode toward cabin.

"Be silent," he hissed at her. "He'll take an extra ten lashes if you aren't. Be a strong mate and control your temper for my son."

Hot tears filled her eyes when she watched helplessly as Drantos returned to the old swing set frame, presented his bloodied back with two jagged lines already marring his skin, and reached up to grip the top of it. Carlos picked up the whip she'd dropped when Drantos had jerked her off the older man. She watched him pull his arm back, poised to strike, and closed her eyes.

The noise wasn't something she could avoid. She whimpered when the first crack of the whip striking Drantos sounded and turned her face into Velder's shirt. He nuzzled her with his head, shielded her view, and whispered in her ear.

"My son is respectful of our laws. He'll heal by tomorrow night. Just hang on. It will be over soon."

I hate these people, Dusti's mind screamed, since she couldn't say it aloud with a hand pressed firmly over her mouth. *They are nothing more than barbarians.*

She flinched with every strike Drantos took from the whip.

Chapter Thirteen

Dusti glared at Velder while standing in Drantos's living room.

His father had carried him home, slumped nearly unconscious over his shoulder. He'd washed Drantos's bloody, damaged back, before helping him to lie flat on his stomach across the bed. Velder had asked her to wait in a different room to prevent her from getting sick at the sight of the vivid marks covering his son's back.

"You people are animals," she spat after he'd entered the room and they were alone.

He arched one eyebrow. "Partly."

"How could you allow that asshole to do that to your own son?"

"He will heal. The punishment wasn't severe and he's a grown man. He made his own choices. I can only support him and care for him when he needs me to. Carlos offered to whip my son so I wouldn't have to. That was a kindness."

"A kindness? Are you high? Drantos was in so much pain he passed out when that son of a bitch was done beating on him."

"Carlos is a Lycan, not a VampLycan."

"And that means what?"

"He's not as strong as we are. The blows were less severe."

"Did you see Drantos's back?"

"Trust me. It could have been far worse. He'll heal from that faster than if the lashes had gone deeper. Only his skin was sliced. No deep muscle or bone was harmed."

"I don't understand you, nor do I want to. No way in hell would I ever just stand there while someone took a whip to Bat. I'd have killed that son of a bitch for striking her, and I know how easily she pisses people off. I wouldn't care *what* she did."

"Your world has laws you must follow. They punish your criminals. No one is locking my son up inside a cage. That would be cruel. He'll heal, and I doubt he'll even carry a scar since I tended to him well. This will just be a painful memory to hopefully prevent him from breaking another law."

"He's not a criminal. From what I understand, he just had an argument with you."

"I'm the leader of this clan. Disobedience of any kind is met with punishment. It's hard to explain to someone like you, but it's how we live. It is for the harmony and peace of all. Otherwise there would be chaos and deadly fights amongst our people. My son took his punishment and it will dissuade others from making the same mistake."

"Unbelievable. You people are nuts. Violence isn't always the solution, you know."

"It is in this world." His mouth hardened. "You're no longer living with humans. You're my son's mate and you need to toughen up to do him proud."

She hugged her chest hard. Arguing with the man wouldn't do any good. He was the biggest barbarian of all. "I want to see my sister."

"She's not here."

"What does that mean?" Fear rose. "Drantos told me she and Kraven were fine after the attack and had been brought here."

"Decker Filmore broke the law when he attacked us to take you. He drew blood and caused the deaths of his own men in his quest for power. The clans' meeting earlier not only discussed Drantos's punishment, but also your grandfather's. We were unaware at that time that Lord Aveoth is seeking him as well. A joint team from the three clans breached his land to bring him to task. He'd already fled though.

"His only recourse is to get his hands on your sister to attempt to use her against us. Now we know it won't work, but *he* probably doesn't. He'll continue to believe she would be the one thing he could use to force the GarLycan leader to form an alliance with him. Kraven took your sister away for her safety. He didn't want more of our people attacked or to risk your grandfather obtaining possession of her."

"I didn't even get to talk to Bat. How could Kraven just take her away?"

"He was determined to get your sister far from here. He wouldn't be swayed to stay overnight."

"Where did he take her?" Fear turned to alarm. "Where are they?"

"I do not know. He refused to say. My son is very cunning. She's his mate and he'll do whatever is necessary to protect her."

"I want to talk to my sister I'm worried about her. Do you *get* that? Does Kraven have a cell phone?"

Velder sighed. "He'll contact us when he feels it's safe to do so. You both have been too softened by the human world, too spoiled. The first thing you need to learn is to not always question my words."

Her arms dropped to her side and she fisted her hands. The guy made her so *angry*. "We're not spoiled. Bat worked her ass off to get where she is and we both know about survival. We had to go through a lot after our parents died."

"The hardships of the human world are nothing compared to ours. Your life there didn't depend on your ability to fight and kill."

His answer irritated her. "You have no idea what it's like out there. People die every single day. When was the last time you lived in my world?"

He cocked his head and smiled slightly while his gaze focused toward the front of the house. "Crayla comes."

She noticed he ignored her question but before she could point it out, the front door opened and a tall black-haired beauty stormed through. She wore only a sarong wrapped around her middle that barely concealed the tops of her breasts, and with her long frame, the lower hem of it just reached her upper thighs. She had blood smeared on one cheekbone and down both arms.

"I take it she apologized?" Velder chuckled. "Do you feel better?"

Crayla moved right to the man and smiled, her arms wrapping around his waist when she pressed tightly against the front of his body. "You know it. She'll never do that again." She turned her head and her bright blue gaze fixed on Dusti.

Dusti tried not to stare but knew she failed. The woman looked about thirty years old, had to be at least six feet two, and definitely didn't appear to be anyone's mother with her lithe body. Certainly not Drantos's or Kraven's. Her beauty stunned Dusti as well.

"She's so small," Crayla sighed. "Cute though. Not exactly what I had in mind for my baby but her coloring is attractive." She released her mate and stalked over to Dusti. Her hand hesitated before she fingered Dusti's blonde hair, met her gaze, and smiled again. "Is this your true color? I know humans dye their hair often."

Dusti resisted the urge to jerk away from the hand touching her. Dried blood made her feel a little ill and the fact that it covered the hand in her hair made her shiver.

Crayla released her to step back while her smile faded. "You have no reason to fear me."

"It's not you." She glanced at the woman's hand. "I don't like the sight of blood. What happened to you? Are you okay?"

Crayla's mouth opened and she seemed stunned for a second. "Of course I'm alright. There was a small disagreement I had to settle between myself and one of the women."

Velder moved next to his mate, wrapped an arm around her, and sighed loudly. "Scent her. She smells totally human, though Drantos claims she tastes slightly other. She believes we're barbarians and animalistic for our punishments and aggressive natures."

The woman's features showed amusement. "I see. I suppose that's how we would appear to you. We also love and have a lot of human traits you will identify with. You need to care for your mate. I had planned to stay but I believe it will be good for you to do this. Just clean his wounds, feed him when he wakes, and stay near him. Touch will make him feel better." She glanced down Dusti's body. "Skin to skin. I'm sure you prefer clothing but when you're alone with my son, you won't wear them."

Dusti was outraged. Her new mother-in-law spoke to her as if she had the right to dictate. "You can't tell me what—"

"I can." The woman cut her off and her blue gaze turned decidedly chilly. "My son has claimed you as his mate and he'll want to die if you leave him. While *he'd* never harm you, regardless of what you do, I am his mother. You and I *will* fight if you break his heart or make him suffer sadness with a lack of concern for his wellbeing. I won't unleash my claws since you don't have them, but you sure don't want to get into a fist fight with me. Are we clear?"

"Crystal," Dusti murmured, anger turning to fear.

"Good." Crayla smiled. "We'll get you adjusted to life with a clan. Rule number one, never fight with me. I'm in charge of all the women. You do as you're told. Treat my son well and we'll get along great." She turned to her mate. "Take me home. You know how fighting makes me want to fuck. I need you."

Velder lifted her and the woman wrapped her arms and legs tightly around the guy. He strode toward the door with her in his arms. Dusti gawked at her in-laws until the door slammed behind them.

"I'm going to need therapy," she whispered. "Yeah. I hope they have shrinks in this clan."

She slowly turned and walked to the bedroom. She really didn't want to get a good look at the horror of Drantos's back but he needed to be cared for. She knew he'd do it for her if she were hurt. He already had when she'd needed his blood, and he'd licked her wounds. Her leg didn't even hurt anymore.

The bathroom light had been left on, the only source of light in the bedroom, and she paused at the open doorway. The sight of a naked Drantos stretched across the big bed on his stomach froze her. His ass and arms had been spared the whip but from shoulders to waist, the horrific cuts haunted her. They no longer bled and actually appeared a lot better than they had when he'd hung over his father's shoulder on the walk to the cabin."

"I'm okay," he rasped.

She inched closer. "You're awake. I thought you were sleeping."

"Come here. Don't look at my back. It doesn't hurt near as bad as you'd think."

"What can I do?"

"Just lie beside me and let me feel you."

Dusti hesitated at the side of the bed but stripped off the sweater. She bent, tugged off both sets of socks, and removed the sweats last. She hoped no one entered the cabin to find her stark naked. She tried not to make the bed move when she climbed onto it to stretch out on her side inches from him. Her gaze met his.

"My mother will never touch you. I heard her threat. She just tried to intimidate you. It's her job."

"It worked. She's scary."

He grinned. "I would never allow anyone to strike you. That includes my family."

She reached out to brush her fingertips along his arm. The warmth of his skin under her touch made her relax while she breathed in his masculine, woodsy scent combined with soap from his father cleaning his wounds.

"I don't know if I can live in your world, Drantos." She knew tears welled in her eyes. "What they did to you wasn't fair and I don't know how you could just stand there, taking that asshole whipping you."

He slid his hand on the bed to touch her leg. He gripped her firmly. "You just don't understand our ways, but laws are important. We're the keepers of them. They could have banned me from all the clans. It would have been a death sentence in the long run. I would have become the hunted for everyone we've ever had to punish for breaking our laws."

"You mean like other banned people?"

"Them, and we've had to deal with some Vampires and Lycans who made trouble in the area."

"They whipped you because you didn't agree with your dad or some such shit. How fair is that?"

"Life isn't fair. The laws were set into place for reasons. There can only be one leader in a clan. Our lives depend on fast decisions. We don't have time to vote on everything. I've seen your political debates on television. It's confusing and gets messy with so many people wanting different things for their people, until it seems nothing ever really gets accomplished. We're not humans. We respect strength in a leader, structure, and laws. There's no crime in clans, no insubordination. We follow our clan leaders' orders or punishment is swift. Any sign of weakness makes that leader appear unable to do his job." He paused. "I took that whipping so they'd know no one is above following the law. He couldn't spare me, Dusti. It could cause someone to challenge him to take his place. That means the winner rules the clan and the loser dies."

"That's horrible."

"It's life here. It works. I know it's very different from what you're used to but it's necessary."

She contemplated that. "I'm going to end up getting whipped at some point." A shudder ran through her.

"Never," Drantos rasped. "I wouldn't allow it."

"You couldn't even stop them from whipping *you*."

"I chose to take the punishment, and I'd do the same for you."

"That makes it worse. So I mess up and you get your back torn up again?"

He reached out and curled his fingers around hers. "I'd do it in a heartbeat."

"I don't even know when I'm breaking laws."

"You'll learn, Dusti. Just don't fight with anyone and listen to me when I tell you to. It will be fine."

"Am I allowed to fight with *you*? Because couples do that."

"We won't. We're true mates."

"What's a true mate mean?"

"What we are. It's when two people come together who are so compatible that they begin to feel and think what the other does. Does that make sense?"

"I guess."

"For the ones who mate when it isn't true, we call that settling. It's when they take a mate without the true bonding. It usually only happens when they can't find the right person or their true mate has died. They don't want to be alone for the rest of their lives. They can love each other but it's a shadow of what they could have. It would be as if two humans joined together in a relationship."

"You make that sound insulting or something."

"I don't mean to but human relationships are different. You'll understand once our bond strengthens. We'll be able to sense what the other is feeling. It's as if we'll become one person in two bodies. Do you understand?"

"You said my grandfather killed his mate. How is that possible if they were bonded?"

"He's a cold bastard. Maybe he settled for her. I don't know. I wasn't around them enough to judge what kind of bond they had. He has no heart. He kills without mercy."

She held his hand, playing with his fingers. "How much pain are you in? Can I do anything?"

"Just stay close to me. I'll recover soon." He turned just a little, tried to hide a wince from the pain but failed. "Something has been on my mind. I didn't mean to hurt you in the woods. It bothers me."

"I like rough sex. I said that."

"Not that. It hurt you when you realized I've bitten other women. You're the only woman I love, Dusti. I had sex with women, and it's considered polite in some cases to test a mating. There wasn't an emotional attachment involved and we weren't monogamous."

She hated the idea of him ever being with anyone else. "So have you been with a lot of women I'm going to be running into around here?"

"No. I hoped one day I'd find my mate. I learned from my father's mistake."

"What does that mean?"

He hesitated before explaining. "He slept with just about every unmated female in our clan. When he found my mother and brought her home...well, let's just say it wasn't easy for her to be around a lot of jealous females who seemed happy to hurt her feelings. It's considered an honor, and the most powerful position a woman can obtain, to be with the leader of a clan. They tormented her with the details of his past sexual exploits to get even with her for being his mate. I remember her crying when I was a child, and my father's regret. He suffered, watching what she went through. You can't hurt without it hurting me too.

"No one dares bring it up now. Mom started to beat on anyone who even looked at her wrong. Yonda is the only female in this clan I've ever touched. I didn't want my mate to face that. Though I never thought she'd be a problem. We were friends."

"Past tense, right? I have to tell you the idea of you hanging out with her is not going to sit well with me. I'll trust you because you said you can't get hard for another woman but I still don't want her anywhere near you."

"It won't happen. She ended that friendship when she insulted you." He paused. "She's never been inside my cabin either. If you were VampLycan, you'd be able to pick up scents inside my home. I purposely never brought any woman here except my mother so if I were lucky enough to find my mate, she wouldn't smell any lingering traces of past sex partners."

Dusti smiled. "Seriously?" She had to admit she found it touching that he'd be that thoughtful, and again, it set him apart from any of the men she'd ever known in her life.

"Yes. I built all this with my mate in mind. I'd never dishonor you by allowing another woman into our bed."

She glanced at the black comforter. "You've never had sex in this bed?"

He grinned. "Not with someone else present."

It took her a second to understand his meaning. Her eyes widened. "You admit you jack off?"

"Of course I do."

She grinned. "Human guys usually don't admit to that."

"They lie if they have a sex drive and deny it."

"Women do it too."

"Do you?" His hand slid a little higher up her thigh. "I'd really like watching you touch yourself." He moved to turn on his side to face her more but then groaned. "In a few hours I'll be healed enough to enjoy it more, when I can take you afterward. I want you but will open my wounds if I fuck you. I know you don't like the sight of blood."

His hand so close to her pussy affected her. His touch did that to her body. It turned her on until she ached. Her nipples hardened and she glanced down his body, where he'd lifted enough on his side for her to see just a hint of his aroused cock.

"Can you turn just a little more?"

He nodded, a slightly confused expression on his handsome features. He released her thigh. "I want you to curl into me."

She winced a little with him when he eased onto his side. It still prevented him from touching the wounds on his back to the comforter while also giving her access to the front of him. He expected her to burrow into him but instead she released his arm to wiggle down the bed. His dark blue eyes widened slightly but he groaned when she wrapped her hand around the base of his hard shaft.

"I bet I can distract you from the pain."

"Dusti." He growled her name.

She met his passion-filled gaze, licked her lips, and lowered her attention to the tempting sight in front of her. Her tongue darted out to swipe across the tip of the crown. Drantos groaned softly in response and his cock twitched in her hand.

She took him slowly inside her mouth, tested his thickness to make sure he cleared her teeth before wrapping her lips around him. A hand tangled in her hair but he kept a loose grip. She moved cautiously at first, taking a little and sucking him in deeper until he threatened to choke her. She backed off to set a steady pace of using her mouth to suckle him. With every caress of her tongue, he growled.

Men who growl are hot, she thought, her entire body responding to the animalistic sounds she drew from him. She knew he'd hardened even more, the texture of his arousal undeniably stiffer, and his hand tugged gently on her hair in an attempt to make her stop.

She pulled back and released him. Her gaze lifted. "What? Don't you like this?"

His eyes glowed light blue. "Flip, sweetheart. If you stop I'll die, but I want access to you. I need your taste on my tongue."

She hesitated. "Your back…"

"Trust me. Sixty-nine position on our sides. I've been hurt far worse than this in the past. I can take a little discomfort."

"Are you sure? This is about you."

"I smell you," he snarled. "I want and need your taste. Give it to me."

She eased up and then readjusted her body until she faced his lap, with hers in front of him. She paused, unsure what to do.

Drantos gripped her thigh and tugged her closer, until she ended up pressed flat against his body, her lower belly high against his upper chest. "Spread your thighs for me."

She did, and watched as he tucked his head, used her inner thigh to pillow his cheek, and then bent her upper leg until he'd trapped her foot under his arm along his side, where her limb rested against his ribs. His hand spread her vaginal lips and she gasped when his mouth found her clit. He didn't warn her before he sealed his lips around the sensitive bud. When he started to use his tongue and the suction of his mouth, she cried out in pleasure.

His hips thrust a little, his cock bumping her cheek.

She got the message and would have laughed, if what he did to her didn't feel too intense to allow anything but another moan. She opened her mouth, took him back inside her, and adjusted to the new angle. He slowly moved, not thrusting deep enough to choke her, but setting the pace.

His mouth on her clit and the drive of his hips while he fucked her mouth in shallow strokes threatened to make Dusti lose her mind. She moaned against his flesh, sucked him hard trying to hasten her own climax, which had her pressing her pussy tighter against his wonderful mouth. He growled deeper, creating vibrations against her clit with his tongue, and she gripped his thigh with her hand while bracing her body further by clutching the bedding.

Pleasure gripped her when his tongue rubbed faster, his hips bucking to force her to take him deeper inside the wet, tight seal of her mouth, and she swore he seemed to thicken in size just a little more. A snarl tore from Drantos and the first burst of his release started to fill the back of her throat.

She swallowed, loving his heady taste, his cock pulsing against her tongue, and then she screamed around him when pure rapture gripped her. She started to come hard, her own hips jerking in a frantic motion. His hand released the leg pinned to his side to grab her ass, holding her in place pressed tightly against his mouth, while he licked at her to draw out her pleasure.

Drantos jerked out of her mouth and released her clit. They both were out of breath, their labored breathing the only sound in the room, until a chuckle came from him.

"I love your taste, sweetheart. I can't get enough. Next time you're going to be sprawled over me when we do this position. You're stronger than you look."

She rolled onto her back but made sure she didn't pull her thigh out from under his cheek, and lifted her head with a grin. "What does that mean?"

"Holding your leg down to keep you spread open for me became difficult. You totally would have used your thighs to pin my face if I'd allowed it."

She laughed. "I really liked you there."

"Come here." He lifted his head to free her thigh.

She turned around on the bed, burrowed into his chest. His arm pillowed her head while his other one curved tightly around her back to draw her even closer.

"I love you, Dusti."

"I love you too."

"In the morning we'll share blood, unless you need it now. Promise me you'll tell me if you feel dizzy or weak."

"I feel okay." She rubbed her cheek against his skin. "You're so warm."

"It's been a long day. We're both exhausted." He paused. "Take from me. I won't risk your health. You have to remember your Vampire traits." His finger rose and she managed not to gasp when his fingernail lengthened as she watched. He scratched his neck, drew blood, and cocked his head a little more. "My blood is yours."

Dusti leaned forward after only a slight hesitation. He'd already cut himself, she knew it had to hurt him, and she wasn't about to have his pain be for nothing.

She closed her mouth over the wound, half surprised the sight and taste of his blood didn't make her feel disgusted. The first taste of him had her moaning with pleasure. It disturbed her on a small level that his blood had that effect on her but she didn't stop. His hand curled into the back of her head to hold her in place.

"That's it." His lips brushed her shoulder. "My blood to yours."

His mouth closed over her skin but she didn't flinch away when a sharp point dragged over her. The slight pinch didn't hurt so much as send a jolt of desire through her. She knew he had bitten into her enough to draw blood. He suckled gently at her shoulder.

Her mouth left his throat. "I want you again."

He released her, licked the small wound he'd inflicted with the point of one of his fangs to heal it, and then pulled his face back to gaze at her with a grin.

"We both need rest. I want you too but that was a goodnight kiss."

She nodded. "You suck." She flushed. "I didn't mean that literally. I'm just turned-on now."

He pulled her closer. "It's my duty to care for your needs but right now you need sleep more."

Dusti tried to ignore her urge to reach down and stroke his cock until he couldn't resist her, but the mental image of his damaged back kept her still. She decided to think about something else besides sex.

"Do you think Bat and Kraven are okay together? He looked really hurt when I saw him after we were attacked in the trucks."

He rubbed her back. "He won't allow anything to happen to her. He'll protect her. I'm sure he's mostly healed by now."

"I'm more worried about who is going to protect *him* when he tells my sister he wants to mate with her."

Drantos chuckled. "He's tough and she's small."

"Have you met my sister? She's going to try to hurt him."

"It will work out."

She lay in silence listening to his strong heartbeat. It soothed her and she couldn't deny the feeling of rightness being in his arms created. The cabin remained totally quiet otherwise. She had to admit she didn't miss the sound of traffic she always heard in her apartment.

"What are you thinking about?"

"My old life."

His body tensed a little but relaxed again. With her ear pressed against his chest, she didn't miss the change in his heart rate. It accelerated as if he were afraid. She lifted her head and peered up at him. His beautiful dark blue gaze met hers.

"Don't leave me."

His plea nearly broke her heart. He didn't try to mask his emotions from her or hide the way his raspy voice hitched a little when he'd spoken. The idea of losing her definitely tore him up.

"I won't. I didn't really have that great of a life in Los Angeles. I'm just uncertain about this new one."

"I promise we'll be happy together. I won't travel anymore on missions. Mated males stay near home. The responsibility will go to someone else to hunt down lawbreakers. I'll be assigned duties here within the clan to keep me close to you."

"I hadn't even thought about that but I'm glad to hear it. I really wouldn't want to be left here alone while you're out of town. I don't know anyone and I feel kind of like a sore thumb"

"You're part of this clan. You'll make friends and they'll accept you. We'll be happy, Dusti. I'll make certain of it."

"I believe you. I'm not uncertain about you and me. For the first time in my life, I know what home feels like. It's here in your arms. It's just that I don't know about the rest of your people."

Drantos smiled. It melted her heart.

"It's this whole VampLycan thing," she admitted.

"You'll adjust. We're not monsters. Sleep now. You're tired. We'll deal with all this tomorrow."

She nodded and tucked her head against his chest again. Drantos brushed a gentle kiss on the top of her head, then snuggled her closer. She closed her eyes but worry for Bat still bothered her. Drantos rubbed her back, the caresses eventually lulling her to sleep.

Chapter Fourteen

Nightmares woke Dusti a few times during the night. It wasn't a mystery what caused them. It was tough to wrap her mind around her new mate being punished and the barbaric method used. But Drantos healed at a phenomenal rate every time she checked on his injured back. It just emphasized the fact that he wasn't human. No normal person could recover that fast.

First his skin no longer appeared split where the whip had struck. Then scabs formed but were gone within a few hours, just leaving angry red lines. Around dawn, those marks were so faint she felt the need to trace her fingertip over them just to be certain her eyes weren't playing tricks on her.

Drantos slept heavily and she still felt anger that he'd been punished for something stupid. VampLycan laws were too foreign to her. It made her worry about what she could accidentally do or say that might get him into trouble. She eased out of bed finally and decided to give herself a tour of his house. She put on one of Drantos's oversized shirts. It fell to mid thigh on her.

It was a nice place and well built. She liked the wood beams along the ceiling in the living room and the fireplace was beautiful. It looked as if he'd used river rocks, which ran from the hardwood floor all the way up to the ceiling.

She ended up in his kitchen. It was modern but she was more interested in finding something to eat than exploring the rest of his home. She settled on a bowl of microwavable oatmeal and sat at the counter. Two barstools made a nice eating area that separated the kitchen from the living room.

As she ate, she thought about her new circumstances. Her life would never be the same. She'd agreed to be Drantos's mate and that meant having to adjust to life in Alaska with a bunch of VampLycans. It was tough to wrap her mind around the reality of them even existing.

Mom, why didn't you tell us what you were?

There had been no reason for Drantos to lie to her about that. Decker Filmore was a VampLycan and way worse than just a shitty grandfather. He was some kind of supernatural villain. She didn't blame her mother for running away but she should have told her daughters the truth. It stung and left Dusti feeling hurt.

Had her dad known? How could her mom hide it from the man she loved and lived with? It made her feel as if her entire childhood had been a lie.

The pain settled in deep and she wished her sister were with her to discuss it. What did Bat think about Aveoth wanting to take her as his lover? How was she adjusting? Did she finally understand that Decker Filmore was a complete asshole? Were they okay? Was Bat scared? Angry?

Frustration rose at the lack of answers. She worried about Bat. She just hoped they were safe, wherever they were.

She finished the oatmeal and washed the bowl. Her gaze traveled around the kitchen. It was her new home. She bit her lip and had to admit the roomy log home was way nicer than her crappy apartment back in California.

"Dusti?"

She turned to face Drantos. He was awake, just wearing a pair of low-hipped silky boxer shorts. His hair was mussed from sleep and the expression on his face uncertain.

"Morning."

"You look so sad." He closed the distance between them, studying her eyes. "What's wrong? Tell me."

"I was just thinking about things."

He reached out and put his hands on her hips. "Do you regret becoming my mate?"

She didn't have to think about it. Her feelings for him left her no doubt. "No. Never."

"What is it then?"

"I was thinking about Bat, my parents, just everything."

He pulled her closer until she was gently resting against his body. "Kraven will take care of your sister. He'll send word when he feels it's safe. We have a strong sibling bond, and he knows Bat has one with you. He won't wish us to be concerned."

"As if getting a message to us will be enough. I just want this mess to be over."

"Aveoth is a skilled hunter and you heard him say he will go after Decker. He always keeps his word."

"I almost feel sorry for the old bastard but not quite."

Drantos arched his eyebrows.

"That Aveoth guy is pretty scary."

"Yes, he is."

"Can you move as fast as he did? I swear I blinked and he was somewhere else."

"It's a Gargoyle trait."

"His skin changed color and texture, too. Another Gargoyle trait?"

"Yes."

"And he flies? I heard you mention that when we were talking about the plane crash. How does that work? He's huge."

"It's hard to explain."

"I'm not going anywhere. We have time. This is my new world, I should learn about it. Those GarLycan things are our neighbors, right?"

Drantos took her hands and backed up, leading her into the living room. He had her take a seat on the couch and he lit the fireplace. She liked the way it made the room feel cozy as he sat next to her.

"Gargoyles can blend into their surroundings by camouflaging their bodies to appear rock-like, and they can harden their skins into rigid outer shells. It makes fighting them really tough when you can't pierce their skins easily. They also become denser when they do that. I don't know how it really works but when Aveoth sprouts his wings, his skin takes on a kind of less dense structure."

"He sprouts wings?"

"Yes. I've seen him do it when we were younger. They are concealed near his shoulder blades. In human form you can't see them. The skin seals to look perfectly normal on his back, but these flaps open and his wings elongate and expand outward."

"That's so strange." She took his hands, needing that connection. "And you change forms."

"Yes."

"It sounds painful when you do it."

"We adjust. It's not the most comfortable experience at first but with time it becomes much easier. It doesn't hurt me."

"Are you totally you when you have hair and a tail?"

"I'm always me."

"You know what I mean."

He grinned. "Yes. I was attempting to tease you into laughter. You look so serious. I'm still the same person, regardless of my shape. I admit I feel a little closer to nature when I have claws. I'd never hurt you if that's your concern. I'm able to rationally think."

"I believe that. You seemed like you when you gave me a ride here on your back."

"Good."

Dusti hesitated. "What about your Vampire side? What do you get from that? I know your saliva can heal your bites, and the sun doesn't bother you. You're really tan."

"Slower aging. I don't need blood to survive and the sun isn't a weakness. I'm mostly Lycan. That bloodline runs stronger in our family."

"But I'm the opposite."

"You need some blood to keep you healthy."

"That's still gross."

He chuckled. "I don't think so. Do you need me to show you how sexy it can be again?"

Just remembering what they'd done together when he fed her his blood had her adjusting her position on the couch, inching closer to him. Drantos turned her on so much. "It's going to take some time before I stop hating the sight of blood but I guess it's something I'd better get over."

"You've been very brave about this."

"And a pain in the ass." She felt regret. "I thought you were insane."

"It was annoying but understandable. I put myself in your shoes and it had to sound as if I had lost my mind when I told you about things you've only seen in movies and books. The information they give isn't accurate in most cases."

"Right. You don't shift into a hell beast and go all bat-shit homicidal."

He laughed again. "No. I don't."

She envied him his light mood. "I keep trying to figure out how I'm going to fit in here. I need some kind of job to help pay the bills and a way to retrieve all my stuff from my apartment."

"You don't need a job. You're my mate. It's my duty to take care of you. I'll hire someone to go clean out your apartment and drive your belongings here. We have a few Lycan packs who work with us from time to time. They are related by blood to some of us."

"I take it that I won't be able to go do that myself?"

"No. It's too dangerous with Decker still loose."

"Fantastic. Werewolves are going to be packing my underwear." She grimaced. "Okay."

"I'm sure they'll be professional about it. It's the only way to get your things here."

"I wasn't bitching. It was more like me saying it aloud because I never thought those words would come out of my mouth."

He laughed. "I love that you're keeping your sense of humor."

"I'm trying." She paused. "I'm a housewife now? I have to warn you that my cooking skills aren't the best and I'm not a huge fan of cleaning."

"We'll share the housework and I can teach you how to prepare meals. It will be fun cooking together."

"What do you do for a living?"

"I'm an enforcer for my father."

"Does that pay enough to keep the lights on?"

He looked highly amused. "Yes."

"Is it like a nine-to-five job?"

"No. We're assigned shifts to patrol and sometimes I was sent on missions, like finding you and your sister."

"Is it dangerous living here or something? Do bears and rabid squirrels attack?"

He chuckled again.

"I'm not trying to be funny." She shrugged. "I'm just clueless."

"We don't have an issue with rabid squirrels. Bears wandering into our territory are persuaded to move on. We live in harmony with nature but we can't exactly have them trying to get inside our homes to go after food. We keep all the dangerous predators distanced from us."

"So that's what you do? You scare away mean animals?"

"We also make certain no one trespasses in our territory. Humans like to do that sometimes to hunt. Nobody enjoys being shot at when a poacher mistakes us for a wolf."

"That happens?"

"Rarely. We patrol so it doesn't."

"What do you do with them?"

"We scare them off. They're told this is protected land, a sanctuary, and private property. VampLycans always try to keep the peace."

"What if they aren't easy to scare and refuse to leave?"

"We use our ability to control their minds and implant that they never wish to return."

"Does that always work?"

"Yes, so far."

"Is it a dangerous job?"

"It can be, but I'm damn hard to kill, Dusti. I don't want you to worry when I go out on patrol."

"You heal really fast."

"Yes. It would be very difficult for something to sneak up on me too."

The memory of him confronting the hell beast that had found them near the river flashed in her mind. "You're also obviously a good fighter."

"I am. I've been trained how to defend myself since I could walk."

"Speaking of, you said VampLycans age slowly. Does that mean if we ever have kids that they'll take forever to grow up?"

"We age the same way humans do when we're very young, growth accelerates for a few years, then slows again once we are through puberty."

"So we could have a baby and it's going to want to move out when it's ten years old?"

He laughed. "Not quite that fast. Most of our children begin building their own homes when they're nearing their eighteenth birthdays. That's the age of consent to take a mate. We want to make certain they are trained well enough to survive on their own. It's just that we learn things faster than a human would."

"Like what?"

He sobered. "I could walk at six months. Human children usually don't do that until they're a year old."

"Wow." She was stunned. Then she had a horrible thought. "Shit."

"What's wrong?"

"I'm going to grow old faster than you are."

He shook his head. "I'm going to share my blood with you, and you already look younger than your actual age. You do have some VampLycan traits, even though they are faint. We tend to live so much longer than humans because of our ability to heal so quickly. By giving you blood, it will help slow your aging process."

She sighed. "That's good. I was picturing me looking ninety and you still being hot. That's something I really wasn't looking forward to for either of us."

"You think I'm hot?" he asked, grinning.

She glanced at his chest. "Scorching hot." She met his gaze again. "And you know it."

He leaned in closer. "Show me."

Arousal coursed through her body. She moved, straddling his lap. He leaned back and his big hands cupped her ass through the shirt she wore. Total awareness of Drantos was an exhilarating experience. Her heart raced, her skin felt as if it were super-sensitized, and the need to be skin to skin with him became almost overpowering.

The front door opened and Dusti gasped, twisting her head.

Drantos stood, lifting her with him so fast it made her head spin. He turned slightly, putting his body between her and the man who entered. The sudden appearance of bright sunlight blinded her for a second until she blinked a few times, then was able to identify their guest.

"Father, what's wrong?"

Velder closed the door and strode to a chair, taking a seat. "I came to check on you."

Drantos grumbled low under his breath and gently lowered Dusti until she stood at his side. "I'm fine, but you knew I would be. What is the *real* reason you've come? There's no need to be polite."

Dusti bit her lip to prevent herself from pointing out it was extremely rude to just walk into someone's house unannounced. The memory of what could happen if she offended the clan leader, and how it could cost Drantos in some way, helped her remain silent.

"Fine. We're spread thin with this current threat. Kraven is gone and I need you back on patrol. I realize you just mated and need time to bond, but it's a priority that we keep our women and children safe until things are stable." He glanced at Dusti. "It's also important to send a strong message that your mating her isn't going to weaken your position in this clan. There are some rumblings."

"Did you mention to them that her grandmother came from our clan?"

"It's not her bloodlines that are in question. It's her strength. Some also heard about what happened last night and word spread. They don't feel as if she'll be able to accept our ways and it will affect you. She *is* your mate."

Drantos snorted. "She attacked a Lycan. I wouldn't call that weak. She believed he was a *VampLycan*, yet still came to my defense."

Velder scowled. "An elder Lycan who is respected by all. That didn't earn her favor. No one doubts her bravery, it's her sanity they question, and they wonder if you'll act more human to please her. You know that would be a problem. You're my first son. One day you'll lead this clan."

"Maybe in a hundred years or so if you decide to step aside. I'm sure as hell not going to challenge you."

Velder shrugged. "It makes them nervous. Anxiety amongst our people is the last thing we need right now. They are already worried about Decker and how that will play out."

"Fine. When do you want me to take a shift?"

"This evening. Get your mate settled today, and perhaps it would be a good idea if she was seen."

"I'll take her to get clothing."

"There's also the problem that she rejected you at first. It's causing talk."

Drantos snarled. "Don't they have better things to do than gossip?"

"Apparently not."

"She didn't understand how mating works."

"Your mother pointed that out to the women this morning when she met up with them at dawn. She's hoping it will ease some of the tension." Velder glanced at Dusti. "Outings with the women would be good for her."

Drantos laughed.

"I'm serious," Velder stated.

"Should I be insulted?" Dusti stared up at Drantos. "What's funny?"

He held her gaze. "Our women bond by hunting a couple of times a week when it's summer. They shift forms and go take down a few large animals. They bring their kills back to the village to cook for feasts that bring the clan together. Humans would consider it a BBQ for the community."

She wasn't amused. "Great. I see the problem."

"I didn't mean to make light of it but you don't like the sight of blood. Hunting is grisly. They use their fangs to rip out the throats of their prey."

"I got it."

Velder sighed, drawing their attention. "She could take a rifle and guard the downed kill while they hunt for others. We've seen a lot of wolves in the area where they hunt. It would make her a useful part of their outing."

"There's one problem with that," Dusti volunteered. "I don't know how to shoot a gun. I take it that I'd have to fire the thing to scare them off?"

"Perfect. So she could shoot one of our people by accident," Velder muttered. "I shouldn't have brought up that option. Maybe she could gather firewood for their cooking pits while they're out hunting."

"I can tell the difference between one of you guys in shift and a wolf. Give me a little credit." VampLycans were bigger and way scarier looking. But she didn't point that out.

"She's not a youth. That's their job." Drantos looked pissed. "You want her status set in this clan but giving her firewood duty would undermine it."

Velder stood. "This is the problem with mating with someone so human. How is she going to fit into our society? Everyone has a duty, but what can she do?"

"Be my mate."

"And what of your clan? She will make you antisocial. We're a community that depends on each other for our survival. That includes her, now that you've brought her home."

Dusti had her own doubts about how she'd live with VampLycans but a sense of sadness filled her. She stared up at Drantos, watching him regard his father with a stern expression—and it sunk in that it wasn't all about her.

She felt a little selfish in that moment. She'd been fixated on how *her* life would be affected but not really about the consequences *he'd* face for taking her as a mate. She loved Drantos. His people, not so much, but they needed to live with the clan.

"I'll think of something," Dusti swore.

Velder frowned. "Excuse me?"

"I'll learn more about your people and figure it out. I get that it's important that everyone accepts me. I'll think of something," she repeated.

"It's not important." Drantos put his arm around her. "You're my mate. They will have no choice but to accept you. No one can possibly expect you to be a VampLycan. You're not blooded enough to shift."

"It *is* important," Velder argued. "You're going to lead this clan one day and she's your mate. I couldn't do my job effectively without your mother's support. We're a team. It brings balance to our people."

And I don't have claws or fangs, Dusti silently acknowledged. She wouldn't be beating up women like Drantos's mother had admitting to doing the night before. She saw the problem. Velder had made it very clear.

"I can fit in," she stated with a firmer tone. "I just need to figure out how to make it work."

Velder sighed. "I hope so. For your sake and for his."

"Father, enough." Drantos shook his head. "It's not Dusti's problem how others react to her. I'm not taking over the clan for a long time. They'll get to know her as I do and she'll make friends. You're making too much out of this."

"It's my job to always think of the clan first." Velder paused. "You're thinking of your mate first."

"Mother is always your priority. Don't deny it."

"I took a mate who was easily accepted by the clan."

"You would have taken her even if she'd been a GarLycan. I know you were with one before you met Mother. What if *she'd* been your mate? You would have claimed her, consequences be damned."

"True."

Dusti was stunned. She couldn't imagine a female version of Aveoth—or Velder dating her. She assumed "with one" meant they'd been an item. "Would a GarLycan be accepted easier than I would be, with my mostly human blood?" She was curious.

Velder shook his head. "No. They are known to be more difficult to bond with and they are fiercely loyal to their own clan. Trust would always be an issue. Our clan would also have had doubts about the ability of any children I'd had with a GarLycan to lead the clan in the future. GarLycans can make cold decisions that don't involve their hearts. It's more about logic with them."

"Everyone in that clan is military minded," Drantos explained. "We're geared more toward protecting our family and friends."

"Well, there's a bright side. I'm not a GarLycan. Score one for me."

Drantos chuckled.

Velder scowled. "I don't see the humor."

"I'm all about making decisions with my heart. I mated to Drantos. I also pointed out I don't even know how to shoot a gun. I'm obviously not military minded. See where I'm going with this?" Dusti forced a smile.

Velder closed his eyes.

"Ease up, Father," Drantos rasped.

Velder opened his eyes, glowering at his son. "You need to take this more seriously and so does she."

"It's her first day in the clan. Cut her some slack."

"Second day," Velder corrected. "She attacked a Lycan elder on her first and made it clear she holds no respect for our laws or how they're carried out. I cringe thinking about how day two will go once you take her from your home. Perhaps you should just keep her hidden. Out of sight, out of mind might be the best plan of action."

The front door opened and Crayla entered. She wore a blue sarong wrapped around her body that started just above her breasts and fell to mid-thigh. She sniffed the air, closing the door behind her. "The tension is so thick in here I can smell it. What's going on?"

Great, now I get to deal with Drantos's scary mom. It was annoying how his parents just walked into their home as if they owned the place. They really needed to start locking the door. She made a mental note to bring up that subject with Drantos later.

"Father is being rude to my mate."

Crayla looked amused. "I see." She walked up to Velder and leaned against his chest, rubbing her cheek with his. She turned her head, staring at Dusti. "We're not sure what to do with you."

"You'll do nothing," Drantos growled.

Crayla chuckled. "Calm down. Your mate is safe. We're worried about how the clan will accept her."

"She doesn't like the sight of blood and doesn't know how to use a weapon," Velder muttered. "I am out of ideas."

"Well, that's why this is a problem for *me* to sort out. She's a female and they are mine to take under my wing." Crayla grinned at her mate. "Stop being grumpy and annoying our son. Don't you remember how it was when I first arrived? Be nice to his mate. We'll figure this out. They can mingle at the roast and then I'll come here tonight while Drantos is on patrol. I'll talk to her and see where we stand then. She's got to be useful in some way."

"Fantastic." Dusti hoped the sarcasm didn't sound in her voice when that word popped out.

Crayla laughed again. "She has potential. She's not cowering behind our son. Let's leave them alone for now. I know you wanted him to take her out today to show her off to the clan. They can't do that while we're still here."

The couple strolled out holding hands, closing the door behind them.

Dusti sighed, peering up at Drantos. "This isn't going to be easy, is it?"

"Nothing worthwhile ever is. It will be fine."

She wanted to believe him.

***

Drantos wanted to pull Dusti into his arms and carry her to bed. The instinct to protect her was strong. The clan could go to hell, but he knew that kind of thinking was what his father feared most. Dusti would have an easier time if she were accepted by everyone.

"It doesn't matter what anyone thinks." He wanted her to know she was his main concern.

"These are the people you care about."

"I love you. You're my mate. You are always my priority."

She smiled. "Thank you. I know you mean that. We'll make this work. I wasn't just blowing smoke up your father's ass. I get that we're in your world so I need to play nice with the natives."

He laughed. She always amused him with the way she spoke. "They'll get to know you and see how wonderful you are."

She nodded. "I guess that means we should get ready and leave the house if I'm to be put on display."

"Don't look at it that way." He could sense she was worried. "It's just a new place. Deep down we're basically the same as you."

"Okay."

"We are, Dusti. Don't let the fact that we're not human convince you otherwise. We have bad days and good. Dreams and disappointments. You love your sister the way we love our siblings."

"I understand. It's just going to take some time for me to adjust to the idea of living with a bunch of people who grow claws and fangs, but I will. I'm going to shower. Do you want to join me?"

He would make love to her and they'd never leave the house. He admitted as much. "I'll go eat since you already did. It will be a quick trip out and then we'll have the rest of the day to bond. We'll go to the gathering later this afternoon. My shift won't start until about ten tonight."

"Got it. Horse and pony show first, then the good stuff. I like that plan. It's like being rewarded after doing something that I know is going to be tough. Then we'll face off against your entire clan at this dinner."

Her words made his chest hurt. "I'm sorry this is difficult for you." He meant it. He tried to put himself in her shoes. It would be drastically different for him if he attempted to join her world. He at least knew how hers worked. She hadn't known his existed before he'd come into her life. "You're very brave."

She flashed him a grin that brightened her eyes. "It's a good thing you're seriously hot."

He laughed. "I'll make it up to you."

"I'm counting on it. On that note, I'm going to shower."

He watched her disappear into his room and his mood darkened. His parents were going to be a pain the ass. It would be simpler if Kraven were home. His brother had a way of finding solutions and dealing with their parents better than he ever could. He also was mating to Dusti's sister. It would give their parents two targets to focus on instead of just him.

He strode over to the front door and twisted the bolts. That was one thing that would change, regardless of how anyone felt about it. He didn't want everyone just walking into their home. A few minutes more and they would have been caught having sex on the couch. Father or not, he would have wanted to rip out the throat of any man who saw that much of Dusti.

He fixed a quick bowl of cereal, more than aware of the sound of running water down the hallway. He wanted to go to her. His dick throbbed. It wasn't natural to refrain from sex while their mating bond still formed. Then again, the clan was on high alert thanks to Decker's bullshit.

He might understand that he was needed, but that didn't mean he didn't regret it.

Chapter Fifteen

Dusti knew the people in the town of Howl would be curious about her, and she had to admit she wasn't immune to the feeling either. She peered at every face they passed and noticed how closely they studied her. Drantos clutched her hand tighter. She lifted her chin to give him a worried glance.

"Are they all VampLycans? The whole town?"

"At night, yes, with a few Lycans thrown in. During the day like now, not always. There's a main highway just a few miles away. There's a sign that leads people here but not a lot of them come. Tourists visit but we refused to build a motel. We want to keep humans from staying too long."

"Why allow them at all?"

He brought her to a brief halt. "A lot of travelers need food and fuel in this remote area, and that earns us a little income. It also makes humans less suspicious of us. We're just a boring, isolated place to them. We even have an auto repair shop for the unfortunate ones who break down. We do keep an apartment above the shop for the occasional overnight customer. There's a guard posted to make certain they don't wander too far. We can't allow them to roam freely and possibly see one of us when it isn't a good time."

Transformed into beast-looking creatures, she thought, translating his meaning regarding what they didn't want a human to see. "Are they going to be worried about me walking around?"

"No. Word has spread that you're my mate. There's no reason to fear anyone. This is your clan."

"Maybe we shouldn't have come into town so soon. Your dad might have been wrong."

"You need clothing and shoes. While we don't have much to offer here from our small store, it could take a week or two for your stuff to arrive from California; and the same for any packages to arrive from online orders. They don't even deliver them this far out. We have to drive to another town to pick up mail. That's how we mainly buy things in this remote area of Alaska."

"Wow. You don't even get mail here?"

"Nope. We won't allow a post office to be set up in our territory. Mail is federally regulated. That means scrutiny we don't welcome. Post offices are run by humans and we don't wish for any to live in our town. It's just easier if another town handles mail, and for us to send some of our men to go pick it up."

"I see. " She wiggled her toes in the three pairs of socks he'd made her wear to protect her feet from the ground. "I'm okay though. I don't want you blowing a lot of money on me. It's not as if I'm going to be outside much. I won't be very popular around here. It's probably better if I stay indoors."

"Don't think that way. Now, you need shoes, and my clothes practically tent you." A grin flashed when his gaze lowered to her breasts. "Although I wouldn't complain if you remained naked."

She grinned. "As tempting as that is, your family tends to drop in announced. Lead on. Just don't leave me alone."

He started to walk again, keeping her hand inside his, and they entered a small tourist shop. The woman behind the counter smiled until her gaze lowered to Dusti. The twenty-something-looking woman frowned at that point.

"Drantos." The woman inclined her head; her silky, short black hair brushed her tan shoulders revealed by a tank top. "It is good you have returned."

"Peva, this is my mate, Dusti. She needs some temporary clothing and shoes."

"Of course."

"Drantos?"

Dusti turned to gawk at the six-foot-four guy with shaggy dark brown hair down to his broad shoulders who'd somehow managed to sneak up without a sound. His piercing brown gaze trained on Drantos. She guessed this had to be the guy who ran the auto shop, when she noticed engine grease smeared over his metal band T-shirt, the front of his faded jeans, and down both of his bared, muscular arms.

"What is it?" Drantos released her to address the tall man.

"We need to speak privately for a second." He ignored everyone else. "I got a phone call. Can you step outside?"

"Yeah." Drantos forced a smile at Dusti. "Go find shoes and some clothes. Don't worry about the price and get enough to last you a few days. I'll be right back." He strode out of the store.

"So you are the human causing so much talk in the clan."

Dusti turned to face the woman behind the counter. A little fear inched up her spine at the unhappy expression on Peva's features. "My father was one. I've been told my mother was a VampLycan."

"Drantos deserves to have a strong mate. That isn't you."

Shock held Dusti silent until her temper flared to life. "I take it you're attracted to him? Too bad. *I'm* his mate."

"That's not true. He's like family and I already have a mate. From what I hear, you rejected Drantos." The woman moved around the counter but kept her distance. "You will make him appear weak to the clan." She pointed to the back of the shop. "There are shoes and clothing over there. I even carry underclothes. Get them and get out. Drantos can pay up later. I hope you make his home life a happy one since he's giving up so much for you."

Dusti hesitated. "What does that mean?"

Anger burned in Peva's glare. "He's the first son of our clan leader. That means he's expected to breed strong children to ensure our future. To take a weak mate is the equivalent of shirking his responsibilities to the clan. The men will lose respect for him. That's a big deal. Do you have any idea how many women turn mating age and travel here in an attempt to get him to taste them, to see if they're his mate? It devastated every female he turned down, and they came from strong families with good bloodlines. Their fathers were enforcers. He's probably the most desired male in our clan, hell, in *any* of them. The men envied him—until *you* came along. Now they will pity him. They can be assholes. He'll ignore it but it will make life hard on Drantos."

She let that information sink in. Drantos had lost respect? That bothered her a lot. "I don't know how to fix this. It's not my fault my father was human. What do you expect me to do? I love him."

"I see." Peva's anger seemed to drain somewhat. "I'm glad to hear that, at least."

"Do you have any advice to help us with this mess or would you rather just try to make me feel worse?" Dusti edged closer to the clothes rack in the shop.

"Do you really care?"

Anger burned. "He's my *mate*. I deeply love him," Dusti ground out. "You could give me advice if you're truly his friend, since I know so little about your ways."

The woman appraised her. "You need to show the clan that you are worthy to be his mate. If you truly care about him, you try hard to fit in and make people like you. They might be willing to overlook your bloodlines."

"Do you want to share some suggestions? I'm not a mind reader."

Peva took a deep breath. "Be respectful to him at all times, especially publicly. Relationships work differently with VampLycans. You never contradict him in front of others. Do that at home, in private. You're allowed to argue with your mate as much as you wish behind closed doors. Men like a woman with spirit and he'll encourage that. Rumors are circulating that he had to plead with you to be his mate. "

"He didn't beg me to come home with him."

She shrugged. "It doesn't matter. That's what everyone believes. You need to fix that immediately before the rumors spread to other clans."

"Fine." Dusti spun around and quickly found things in her size. She got an armload of clothing, picked out a pair of canvas slip-ons, and then turned. "Do you need to add this up?"

"I see what you've taken." Peva held out a bag.

Dusti put all the things into it. "Thank you."

"Make him happy. That is all I want. We grew up together. He's been as close to a brother as I have after my own died."

"I'll do my best," she promised, before stepping out into the sunshine.

Drantos and the taller guy stood ten feet away whispering but they noticed her immediately. She paused until Drantos motioned her over. The big man ignored her still as if she didn't exist. He didn't glance at her once.

"Thank you," Drantos said.

"Not a problem. Let me know if you need anything." The guy disappeared down an alley next to the store.

"What was that about?"

Drantos took her burden from her then cradled her against his chest with one arm. "We'll discuss it later. Do you want to put on the shoes now?"

"Not really. I'd just like to go home."

He offered his hand. "Are you okay? You appear a little irritated."

"I'm fine."

He didn't seem convinced but he tugged her toward the walkway. "We'll be home soon."

She noticed a group of five couples heading toward them on the sidewalk. Dusti bit her lip and then released it. "Are those your clan people ahead of us in that group?"

"Yes."

Now is my chance, she thought, mustering up her courage when the group drew closer. She jerked on Drantos's hand to bring him to a halt. He turned to peer at her with a questioning gaze. Dusti took a deep breath, her heart racing, and she made sure she spoke loudly.

"Thank you for allowing me to be your mate, Drantos. I mean it. You're the best thing that's ever happened to me."

She rushed on, ignoring his shocked expression and the fact that the couples had stopped to gawk. "I don't deserve you. I've been so unworthy. But I swear I'll make it up to you every day."

His jaw clenched and his gaze lifted over her head. Understanding dawned, quickly followed by amusement. His lips twitched. "You'll show the clan that you're more than worthy of being mine. They just need to see how courageous and strong you are, as I have."

She winked at him subtly. "You're the best. I love you."

He lifted her hand to his lips, pressed a kiss on her knuckles, and then started to move down the sidewalk as he lowered it. "I love you too, sweetheart."

She couldn't resist glancing at the VampLycans when they passed them. All ten of them appeared openly stunned and she resisted the grin that threatened to curve her lips. She hoped that little display of them as a couple dispelled any gossip about Drantos having to talk her into being with him.

"You didn't have to do that," he said softly, once they'd cleared the town and reached the path to his cabin.

She opened her mouth to tell him she'd done it because she cared about him.

"But I appreciate it."

Dusti understood. "I'd do anything for you."

"My friend I spoke to heard from Kraven. He didn't want to risk reaching out to me on the phone in case your grandfather tapped the lines to trace the call. He and Bat are somewhere safe. He knew we'd be worried."

Tears filled Dusti's eyes. "Thank you. When are they coming back? When will I see Bat again?"

"They will return as soon as Decker is caught and brought to justice. She'll be safe once he's no longer a threat."

"Where are they?"

"He didn't pass along that information."

"Did Kraven mention to your friend if he'd told her yet that he wants Bat to be his mate?"

"He didn't mention Kraven sounded in pain, so I assume not."

Dusti chuckled. "Yeah. I almost feel sorry for your brother." Her humor faded as quickly as it surfaced. "I don't see how that can work out between them, to be honest."

Drantos paused to gaze down at her with his beautiful eyes. "Love is the most important thing of all. He'll love her."

"She has her career that she's suffered a lot for. It's everything to her."

"That's not true. She loves you, and *you* matter more than anything to her. I saw that in her eyes every time she looked at you."

"I've never tried to step in the way of her career. She just reached her ultimate goal. The law firm is considering making her a partner. She'd have to give it all up to be with him, wouldn't she? You said VampLycans can't stand living in cities. Her entire life is in Los Angeles."

"Let's go home. We can't do anything for them but be here when they return." He started to move again.

Dusti worried. She knew Kraven would do his best to protect her sister and that Bat wasn't a slouch at watching her own back. But she really couldn't see how their relationship could work out. Bat would fight Kraven every step of the way and have a major meltdown when he explained everything she'd have to give up to be with him. That was if her sister even allowed him to get that close to her. She'd sworn off ever loving a man again after having her heart broken.

Please don't ever leave me. I couldn't live without you, sweetheart.

Her heart melted when she glanced up at Drantos. "I don't plan on going anywhere."

He jerked to halt in front of their cabin, his dark blue eyes widening.

"What?"

"You heard me?"

"I'm not deaf. I'm not going to leave. I love you. I'm not as hung up on my old life as Bat is."

A grin curved his lips, reminding her how handsome he was. "I didn't say that aloud. I thought it. You've picked up my thoughts. You can hear me." He closed his mouth. *Tell me you love me again.*

Shock tore through her. He hadn't spoken that last part but she'd heard it as if he had. His voice had been that loud and clear.

Drantos lowered to his knees in front of her. "The bond is in place! We're officially mated."

Can you hear me? She tried to think toward him, carefully attempting to project each word without moving her own lips.

A deep rumble of a laugh answered her before his thoughts did. *Yes, I can.*

Oh shit, he can hear everything I think? I'm so going to be in a world of trouble the next time I get mad at him.

"No, Dusti. Only the things you project will come through the bond. If you're mad, I *will* hear your thoughts unless you shield them. You'll learn. I won't invade your privacy."

"But just a few minutes ago we couldn't do this."

"The bond just snaps into place. We've been sharing sex and blood. Our emotions are involved. My blood and yours have started to take hold in each other. This is a true mating."

Her gaze lowered to the front of his jeans. "So that means you can't get it up for other women now?"

"That's the first thing you think about?" He shook his head, looking amused, and rose back up to his feet. "Yes, that's what it means."

"What else is going to change?"

He released her hand to open the cabin door, pausing long enough for her to enter first. He threw her new clothes onto the table just inside the entry, used his boot to slam the door closed, and grabbed her before she could do more than gasp. He nearly ran with her toward their bedroom.

"What are you doing?"

He dropped her on the bed. Her body bounced once on the soft mattress and she gaped at Drantos while he tore at his clothes. He nearly fell over when he bent to tear off his boots. She laughed and lifted up on her elbows to watch him. The amusement left when his gaze met hers as he straightened. His eyes glowed.

"Don't do that hypnosis shit on me."

He shook his head. "I can't anymore. You're my mate. It wouldn't work. I'm just not hiding my desire for you any longer. You know what I am, Dusti. My eyes turn this way when I'm extremely horny."

"Why would you try to keep that a secret?"

"I wanted your feelings for me to build and I thought that might be easier for you if I wasn't constantly reminding you how different we are. We're compatible in all the ways that matter."

It was kind of sweet and she understood why he'd think that way. "I see."

She lowered her gaze down his incredibly sexy, muscular body until she paused at the sight of his rigid cock straining straight out toward her. Her body instantly responded. Her nipples beaded and between her thighs, she felt moisture dampen the sweats she'd borrowed from him.

"Open your mind to me." He bent over to reach for the waist of the sweats, tugged them down her body, and tore off all three layers of socks from her feet. "You're going to love this part of being mates. At least I think we both are. I've heard enough about it to always envy the idea of being able to link with someone else."

Dusti sat up and tore the shirt over her head. She met his gaze and took a deep breath, blew it out, and nodded. She wasn't sure how to do it but she mentally pushed toward him with her thoughts.

Is this what you mean?

Yes! His knee made the bed dip.

"What..." Her mouth closed and she tried to think her words again. *What were you talking about?*

Open your thighs wide for me and keep your mind open.

Okay. She nodded. Her heart raced but she spread her thighs. *I wish you'd tell me what we're doing.*

Drantos flattened onto his stomach on the bed, his hands slid under her ass, and he jerked her hips closer to his mouth. His eyes seemed to glow more, turning a neon-blue that entranced her. *You're so beautiful. God, I love you. You smell so hot, so good, and your taste is addictive. Stay open to me.* His face dipped, his thumbs spreading her sex lips open, and his tongue traced her clit.

Pleasure shot through Dusti—but it wasn't just from him teasing her clit. Confusion struck her for an instant as she licked her lips. A hunger gripped her; a wonderful flavor filled her senses, as if she'd just eaten something fantastic. Her passion amplified until her elbows supporting her upper weight gave way. She fell flat on the bed, crying out when her sex seemed to throb as if it had a heartbeat.

"Oh my God," she moaned. "We're connected, aren't we? I'm feeling what you do."

He growled against her clit, the vibrations of rapture on her sensitive nerve endings heightening her desire, and her vaginal walls clenched hard. The pounding in her sex seemed to rush to her ears, her body writhed under his mouth, and her fingers clawed the bedding just to hold on to something.

Drantos tore his mouth away from her clit, climbed up her body, and her eyes opened. She knew how desperately he wanted inside her, how much he hurt, and even how tight his balls had drawn up with pure need to fuck her. His cock filled with blood until the skin seemed ready to burst from the pressure. She spread her thighs wider to help him ease inside her. She nearly drowned in the strong emotions of his need and her own. He wasn't thinking words anymore but she understood.

The second the crown of his cock brushed her slick pussy, they both groaned again. She knew how hot she felt to him, how the scent of her arousal filled his nose, and how it made him ache more to feel the tight sheath of her body wrap around his.

Mine. Home. My everything.

Dusti nodded frantically and her hands released the comforter to grab him instead. She could feel her nails sinking into his shoulders as if they were digging into her own. Pleasure at the slight bite of pain had her back arching and her legs wrapping around the back of his thighs. She could feel her heels sliding against him.

He hesitated and she knew he worried that the sensations would overwhelm her. He didn't want to rush things, to make her feel too much, too fast.

Fuck me, she demanded. *I need you and I'm okay.*

I love you so much, Dusti. He pressed forward and she cried out loudly at the sensation of warm, slick flesh parting for his throbbing cock. It was amazing, how it felt for both of them as he stretched her, her muscles clenched tight around every inch of his cock while he pressed deeper.

He moved, fucking her fast and furious, out of control. And Dusti wanted him to be. Their bodies moved together, her bucking under him frantically while he pounded into her, and rapture gripped them both. Every throb of his cock, every twitch of her pussy around his swelling cock made her spin higher out of control. The ecstasy became a living thing between them that locked them together.

She gasped when the first tinges of her climax started and he roared out above her. She screamed as his semen started to shoot from the tip of his shaft. She not only felt it deep inside her womb, but also felt it from his prospective, flooding into her. Her mind blew from the intensity of his release coupled with her own. A white haze of delight drowned her until she eventually surfaced and realized they lay slumped together, panting hard on the bed.

Drantos had collapsed on top of her but just enough to the side not to crush her under his heavier weight. Her eyes opened and a grin spread across her face. She could feel each little pulse of his cock and how he softened just slightly, easing some of the pressure inside her.

That was so cool!

Drantos chuckled and lifted his head. She knew he wanted to groan when he forced his limbs to support more of his weight, that he'd have been content to remain sprawled on top of his mate until he caught his breath enough to take her again, but he wanted to see her face. He thought she was the most beautiful sight he'd ever seen and looking into her eyes made him believe he gazed into heaven. She had become his life, his entire world, and he loved her with his very soul.

"I know," he whispered. "You feel the same way about me. We're mates."

"I'm so happy you came into my life."

Tears blinded them both and Drantos laughed. "Damn. You're going to make me cry too. I just found a down side to this."

She laughed with him. "Good thing I think sensitive men are hot."

"I'm relieved to know that." His lips lowered to brush across her mouth.

Dusti moaned. *Again? Really? So soon?* Desire flared through them both.

I'm not human.

I love VampLycans now.

Drantos chuckled against her lips. *I love you, Dusti.*

"This is going to work out."

"We'll make certain of it."

Dusti wasn't really sure how she'd fit into his clan but didn't want to share that with him. Drantos brushed another kiss over her lips. "You're projecting. I don't mean to overhear your thoughts but it's going to be fine."

"It's just such an unfamiliar way to live. Your rules and world are so different from mine."

"They will become yours. You are VampLycan, Dusti. You were just denied the knowledge of your heritage."

She felt anger come through their bond. "It pisses you off?"

"I would have found you so much sooner if you'd been raised in the clans."

"I would have lived with Decker's if my mother had stayed, or she would have been forced to mate with Aveoth." She shivered a little, remembering the fierce and intense warrior. "He could have been my father. How scary is that? Imagine having to face him at every holiday get-together. Talk about a nightmare in-law."

"He wouldn't have been able to have children with her."

"Why?"

"Gargoyles hate Vampires to a level that is extreme. We're half Vampire but even we're not fond of the full-bloods. GarLycans tend to avoid mating with us half-breeds because we carry Vampire blood. Even a drop is too much."

"But he was addicted to the bloodline. I don't understand."

"I don't either but it would be an affront to his clan if he had children with any Vampire blood running in their veins. It's acceptable in his culture for him to take her as a lover but nothing more. He would have either had to dump her to take a mate or found a GarLycan willing to breed his children without the bond mate."

"That's so weird and messed up. What about the woman he took as a lover? She'd just have to turn a blind eye to him screwing someone else to have a baby?"

"Yes."

"That's so wrong."

"I agree but that's how they live."

"What if he wanted to mate his lover?"

"He'd have a hell of a fight on his hands to stay in control of his clan if she had any Vampire blood in her veins. They'd want him to step down. They don't always mate the mother of their children. It's not a requirement, but a VampLycan would be offensive to his clan if he bonded to her. It would give her status that none of them would wish her to have."

"That's so confusing. They're like friends to VampLycans, right?"

"It's complicated."

"Uncomplicate it for me."

"They *are* willing to join forces with us but we're not considered totally equal."

"No wonder my mom took off to avoid that kind of fate. I just wish she'd told us the truth."

"So do I."

"I keep thinking about Decker. Where is he, and will Bat and Kraven be safe from him?"

"Aveoth is now aware of what his plans were. Decker no longer holds the advantage and the GarLycan leader knows Bat already has a mate. Your sister is going to be fine. Decker wants her alive, so he wouldn't hurt her if he's able to find them. Worst case, he'd turn her over to Aveoth and he'd just send her to us. He knows she has a mate and he's got honor. It's Kraven I'm more concerned about. He'd never allow her to be taken without forfeiting his life first."

"I just wish we could help them."

"Kraven is more than capable of surviving and staying under the radar. He'll return when he feels it's safe to bring his mate home. Have some faith. I do." He caressed her skin. "Let me distract you from your worrying."

She smiled. "I love you touching me."

"I love everything about you."

Chapter Sixteen

Dusti could relate to being a tourist who'd lost her luggage. She looked the part in her ill-fitting clothes she'd bought at Peva's shop.

Nothing about that afternoon's event held a familiar feel. They were in a clearing with thick woods surrounding it and three large fire pits burning. A bunch of strangers milled around. The men were all muscled and big, most sporting jeans and tank tops. The women were tall and seemed to have a "dress for less" fashion sense going on. They mostly wore summer dresses with open backs or sarongs.

"Yeah. I'm totally fitting in," Dusti muttered.

"Everyone knows you had to buy temporary clothing."

"As if I'd walk around in nothing but a thin towel wrapped around my torso."

His eyebrows rose.

"Sarongs. It's basically what they are."

A smile curved his lips. "You'd look sexy in one."

"With my luck, it would come untied and I'd drop it."

"I'd like that."

"I meant in front of everyone."

Drantos put his arm around her. "Just be yourself and relax. You're nervous."

"Thanks for not saying no one is going to be judging me. They totally are."

"We can leave."

"Yeah. Right. Talk about getting off on the wrong foot with the new mother-in-law. No thanks. She kind of frightens me. Just make sure I don't end up roasting in one of those pits. What does elk taste like, anyway?"

"You'll like it."

"I hope so. Your clan can really eat two of them? I thought they weighed a ton."

"VampLycans can eat about six times what a human can, and we *really* gorge at a feast. Think of it like your Thanksgiving holiday, only we do it more often."

"No wonder you're all so big."

"It takes a lot of fuel to shift. We're also naturally toned."

"You mean mega-muscled."

He grinned. "Yes. Relax. You're really talkative."

She sealed her lips. He was right. She had a tendency to babble when anxious. He just had a nicer way of putting it. She clutched at his hand as they strolled deeper into the clearing. People stared at her and some even stopped talking. She resisted the urge to drop her chin and lean against Drantos. It might make her appear weak. She lifted her head a little higher and clenched her teeth together.

Relax, Drantos thought at her.

I'm trying.

Velder came up to them first. It was his way of letting the clan know he approved of his son's mate. Drantos had given her a run-through of things to expect. She bowed her head to show the clan leader respect.

He reached out and brushed her shoulder with his fingertips. "I'm glad you both could make it." He touched Drantos's shoulder next, then stepped back. "Let them come to you," he suggested, his voice barely above a whisper.

"I've got this," Drantos muttered.

Velder spun away, retreating back to the men he'd been speaking to when they had arrived. Dusti glanced around, looking for Crayla. *Where's your mom?*

She's with the women. They prepare the food and the cooking hasn't started yet.

Dusti nodded. Peva strode toward them with a tall, handsome man at her side. She guessed that was the woman's mate. They stopped and Drantos did the talking.

"Hello, Peva. It's a nice evening."

"It is. Dusti, this is Maku. My mate," Peva confirmed.

"It's nice to meet you." Dusti smiled.

He had seriously dark eyes and his nostrils flared. "You smell totally human."

Peva elbowed him. "I told you that."

"No offense." Maku glanced at Drantos. "Are you certain she carries any bloodline?"

"Yes. She's part VampLycan. Her mother was one of us."

He looked her up and down. "I see."

Peva elbowed him again. "Knock it off." She winked at Dusti. "Forgive him. He's over two hundred years old and gets a bit grumpy when it comes to humans. He remembers when they used to chase him with sharp sticks as a youngster. He liked to roam into their territory."

The big guy grumbled under his breath. "It's not funny."

Peva laughed. "He also should appreciate someone finding their mate since he had to wait so long to find me. He watched generations being born and grown before I was brought into this world."

Dusti tried to keep her mouth from falling open.

"I had to chase him." Peva turned into her mate, hugging his waist. "He thought he should give me a few more years to mature since he was so much older. I knew he was mine when I hit sixteen but we waited to mate until I was the age of consent."

"That's eighteen, right?"

"Yes. Some knucklehead made that law." Peva rolled her eyes. "Tell that to a horny teenager when she has the hots for a guy and knows he's hers. He'd leave our village when I went into heat because I'd go to his house and climb into his bed. I told him if he touched someone else while *he* was in heat that I'd hunt them both down and kill them, since I was more than willing to break the law to be with him. My Maku isn't one to break rules."

"I'm an enforcer. How would that look?"

Peva rolled her eyes and sighed. "It was two years of hell." She suddenly grinned again. "Just before midnight on the last day of my seventeenth year, I grabbed my packed bags and ran to his house. I got there about a minute after I hit eighteen. He knew me so well. He had the door open and was waiting on his porch."

Her mate chuckled. "You had warned me that's what you'd do."

"As if you weren't happy about that."

"I was. It was hell for me too. Especially when I'd come home after you'd been in heat to find your scent all over my house—and you'd always leave your vibrator on my nightstand. You left it there for me to find on purpose. You'd send *me* into heat. I never touched another woman though, after I knew you were mine. I had to suffer through it alone."

"Payback is a bitch." Peva hugged him tighter and focused her attention on Dusti. "I know it's going to be difficult for you to adjust to life here but remember that we're people. Don't let anyone intimidate you. That's the plus side of being mated to an enforcer. No one will dare touch you or be overly unkind. They know your mate will make them regret it. Maku was one of our fighting instructors when I was a teen. There was a boy who wanted to nail me, so he'd planned to come after me when I was in heat, thinking I might accept him since Maku avoided me."

Maku growled deep.

Peva nodded. "You made him rethink that, didn't you?"

"Damn pup thought he could take what was mine while you were vulnerable."

Drantos chuckled. "I remember. You took him with you when she went into heat and tied him up in a cave. To this day he hates small enclosed spaces. He's a damn good fighter though since you really tore into him during training."

"I enjoyed my work especially well with that one." Maku's eyes brightened in color, glowing a bit. "He never looked at her again."

"He wouldn't even talk to me and still changes directions when we cross paths." Peva snickered. "He's terrified of my Maku."

"He wanted you. I'm never going to forget that."

Peva rose up on her tiptoes and kissed his cheek. "I'm all yours. Don't go beating him up for old times' sake. You have that glint in your eye." She looked at Dusti. "Just be who you are. Our clan is curious about you. Just show them you accept us and they will do the same."

Maku nodded. "They're all worried that you'll scream or burst into tears. Don't do that." He peered at Drantos. "You should teach her how to fight. It would make them respect her faster if she at least tried to learn our ways. Let me know if you need help. It will be difficult for you to be the one to train her. I always took it easy on Peva, since it's impossible to hurt the one who's yours. I had to allow another trainer to work with her and walk away during their sessions. Otherwise my instincts made me want to attack him to protect her."

"Thank you." Drantos reached out and touched the male's shoulder. "I appreciate that and might take you up on it."

"Come find us when we eat." Peva waved. "That will help too. It will let the clan know we've accepted her."

Maku inclined his head. "See you soon." The couple drifted off to talk to others.

"They're really nice." Dusti squeezed Drantos's hand.

"They aren't. That's the point. Maku is one of our most feared enforcers and Peva can be a terror. They want us to eat with them to send a message."

"That they like me?"

"Mess with you and it will piss them off."

"Oh. Well, that's still really nice."

Drantos grinned. "I'm glad you think so. Peva is like family. I'm not surprised by her offer but I don't know how she managed to talk Maku into openly accepting you so quickly. He *really* doesn't like humans."

"He loves her."

"Yes, he does."

"Is he really that old? I pegged him at about thirty-one, maybe. And only because he's so tall and big."

"He's first generation."

"What are you?" She was afraid he'd say he was one too. That would mean he was about Maku's age.

"Second generation. My father is a first generation." He seemed to study her eyes. "Do you want me to tell you my age now?"

"I don't know if I'm ready for that."

"If it helps, my father wasn't what you'd consider young when he met my mother. He'd already taken over ruling our clan."

"Okay. Just hit me with a rounded figure." She braced, watching him back.

"Eighties."

She had to force her lungs to work. He didn't look that old. Not even close.

"How do you feel about that?"

He probed her mind. She could feel it now. It was like a gentle tap against her skull. She tried to shield against it and it seemed to work. A thought struck and it made her grin. "Can I call you my old man?"

Drantos softly growled and lowered his head, brushing a kiss on her lips. Amusement showed in his eyes. "No."

"Kraven is younger than you?"

"By two years."

"Oh boy. I hope Bat takes that information well."

"He won't tell her until she's ready to hear it." Drantos pulled her closer. "Are you freaking out? I know you like that term."

She shook her head. "No. I'm just glad you're not a few hundred years old. See?

Bright side."

"I'm glad."

"Me too. So it's just you and Kraven? No more siblings that I don't know about?"

"My parents had only two sons."

"I'm surprised there aren't more kids, considering how young your parents look and it's been that many years since they had you and your brother."

"It was a very calm time in our history when my parents mated. They wanted children right away, so they had Kraven and me. There were issues with Decker after our births. They decided to stop having children until there wasn't a threat."

"What issues?"

"A few assassins from his clan tried to take out the other three clan leaders. They failed and lost their lives. My father said he woke when someone entered our home and he attacked the bastard as he came down the hallway toward the bedrooms. He wasn't certain at first if the assassin was there to kill him or his family. He placed a call to the other leaders to tell them what happened, only to learn two others had the same experience. They confronted Decker, prepared to have him pick one of them to fight to the death. But the coward swore his people had acted on their own. There was no proof otherwise so they had to let it go. He claimed they were unhappy members who must have wanted to lead their own clans when they'd left his."

"Is that when he began wanting to take control of all the clans?"

Drantos nodded. "It was the start of the trouble. He'd do small annoying things, like test the borders to see if they were protected well. My father and the other clans needed to watch his every move. My parents might have more children in the future but that would be only if they decide it's safe. Women are the most vulnerable during pregnancy and right after, when they're caring for the very young. He wants her to be able to fight and defend herself to the best of her ability if the need arises."

"VampLycans have birth control?"

He nodded. "It's a Lycan thing most of us inherited. The women can go into heat without dropping fertile eggs. They can only get pregnant when they will their bodies to do so."

"That's freaky but kind of cool. How do you will your body into not getting pregnant?"

Drantos paused in thought. "It's tough to explain. When I'm in danger, I grow claws to protect myself. My body just reacts instantly. I shift and my fangs drop. With Lycan women, it's kind of like that but they can tell their bodies when it's all right to get pregnant and when it isn't."

"Natural birth control."

"Exactly." He looked up, glanced around, and then held her gaze again. "I can feel my father glaring at me. He's probably annoyed that we're talking and not focusing on making eye contact with others to encourage them to approach."

"Okay. Let's do this."

She suddenly had another thought and halted him when he started to lead her to a group of people.

He turned his head. "What?"

"I'm mostly human. What does that mean for us? I can't will my body to do that."

He hesitated before answering. "You'd have to be ovulating...and accidental pregnancies *have* occurred with humans."

She let that sink in.

"We'll talk about this later," he whispered.

She had a hundred questions but Drantos led her to more of his people. They looked wary at her approach but she tried to avoid looking as nervous as she felt. It was important that she make friends.

Drantos felt great pride. Dusti masked her fear well. He couldn't smell it but he felt traces of it through their bond. She'd been introduced to almost everyone present. He knew his people were unsure of her but they were polite. When his mother entered the clearing with her group, loaded down with food, he took Dusti to Peva and went to help. He hated to leave her side but knew she'd be well looked after.

"How goes it?" His mother scanned the clearing until she spotted Dusti. The creases in her features eased. "She's with Peva. Good."

"We're eating with them."

"Did you fight Maku to make that happen?"

"No. Peva worked her mate magic."

His mother laughed. "Ah. That always works. Now *you* have a mate who will be able to make you see reason too. It's impossible to remain stubborn when the one you love expects compromise. You will want to give it to her."

"You lead Dad around by his nose."

She chuckled. "It's not that body part I grab when I want him to follow me down any path."

"I was trying to be polite."

"Your manners have already improved. I like seeing this new side of you."

Drantos scanned the area again and lowered his voice. "Thank you for backing me up with Dad. I know this can't be easy for you either, as my mother."

She leaned in closer and reached up, laying her hand on his shoulder. "She's not the mate I would have chosen for you but that's not our way. You felt something for this Dusti and the bond was there when you touched her. I'm grateful you found her and didn't have to settle for something less. It happens and it's always sad to see. That would have broken my heart. You deserve a true mate, and the love that goes with it."

"Dad is worried that our children will be weak. I tried to tell him that won't happen but I can tell he's still apprehensive."

She released him and waved her hand in the air, a gesture to state she wasn't concerned. "Let them be healthy and give me lots of grandbabies. That's all I ask. Your bloodlines are strong and she's not fully human. I have faith it will be fine."

"Thank you."

"You do need to speak with her about how life here is different from the world she came from. One day your father will wish to hand over leadership to you. That means you'll need her to stand strong at your side. I know you could handle it alone but the women prefer being dealt with by another woman."

"They would hurt or even kill her if she fought one of our women."

"She won't have to do things my way. I'm more hands-on than other clan leaders' mates. I enjoy a good fight. Teach her how to earn their respect and it will never come to violence." She paused. "You said she's more Vampire than Lycan?"

"Yes."

"That's a pity."

"Why?"

"It's possible that carrying your young enough times could activate the Lycan traits to emerge, if it were the stronger of the two. That would have meant she had a chance at shifting in the future."

"She needs my blood sometimes."

"Does she have fangs?"

"No."

She suddenly grinned. "She could use her ability to drink blood as a weapon if she had them. It would weaken her opponents if she bit them, while making her stronger."

"I never want my mate to have to do that."

"We'll discuss this later. It's time to cook. Go to your Dusti and show our people your love for her, and hers for you. No one will dare go after her. They'd have to fight *you*." She winked. "None in our clan are that stupid."

He made it to Dusti's side and was about to take a seat when motion out of the corner of his eye caught his attention.

Marna ran into the clearing, her eyes wide, and the youngster appeared afraid. She waved her arms, too out of breath to speak.

Drantos straightened and rushed at her. He was the first one to make it to the seven-year-old.

"What is it?"

She pointed toward town. "Trouble," she panted.

He crouched, gently gripping her thin arms. "Calm and tell us what is going on."

The girl caught her breath enough to speak. "A human stopped in town. He saw one of us running in shifted form and Lake wasn't able to wipe his memory. The human wants to call the state troopers to report it and came to use the store phone. Lake is stalling him so he doesn't go to another town to use theirs."

More of his clan had surrounded them, including Dusti. He sensed her right behind him. His father growled low.

"Lake is one of our strongest with human minds. The human must be immune. We need to prevent him from telling anyone what he saw or others will come to investigate. Our clan will be at risk. I need to kill him."

Dusti gasped. "What?"

Drantos released the girl, stood, and faced her. "There's no choice, Dusti. My father is right. Lake is a first generation with strong Vampire traits. He would have erased the man's memory and given him a new one if it were possible. We can't allow this human to tell others what he saw. More of them would come."

She scowled. "You can't just kill someone. He might have a wife and kids. I'm sure he has family."

"We need to be safe."

"She's human," someone muttered. "She's siding with them."

Drantos snarled, glaring at the men around them to identify the source. He found him and flashed fangs. The man stepped back, sulking out of his sight. Drantos looked back at Dusti.

"This is our home. Our children play here. Hunters will come. We've seen this happen before. In nineteen seventy-one someone reported seeing one of us and thought it was a bigfoot. A bunch of drunken hunters trespassed on that clan's territory for months. Four VampLycans were shot, one nearly died. And the world is easier to share stories with now. All those humans came from one town. Imagine what would happen if they used the internet. They could come from all over the world. We can't allow this human to tell others. Do you understand?"

"I do."

"It's a law to protect our secrets from the world for a reason."

Dusti nodded. "I get it. Let me take a crack at him though."

"You can't wipe his mind."

"I don't need to. Just let me talk to him. If I can't spin this, he's all yours. I get it."

"You can't tell him the truth."

"I wouldn't do that." She peered up at him in a way that tugged at his chest. "Please let me talk to this guy. I think I know how to handle this mess."

"He saw one of us."

"I know. Take me to this guy. I have a plan."

"What is it?"

"I need to find out what he saw and get a look at him first." She reached out and gripped his hand. "Let me at least try."

"Let's see what she can do," his mother stated loud and clear.

Drantos was stunned when he looked at his mom. "What?"

"She's human. She might know better how to deal with one. No one wishes to kill today." His mom crossed her arms over her chest. "The last thing we need is for someone to go missing in our area. That would cause us problems too. Let's see what your mate can do, Drantos."

He had a sinking feeling in his stomach that this was going to be a disaster. He turned his gaze to his father.

He nodded, looking equally grim. "We can still kill him afterward. Let her try. There's no harm in that."

Shit. He grasped Dusti's hand and tugged her toward town. "Let's go."

She had to almost run to keep up with him. He should have felt guilt but didn't. He was angry. His father followed but the rest of the clan hung back.

"What are you doing?"

She didn't answer so he glanced at her, using their link instead.

Did you hear me? What are you doing?

Trying to save a man's life.

He saw too much. We must protect the clan. You should have said nothing. Now they might question your loyalty to our people for your own. You're one of us now, Dusti.

That doesn't mean I have to agree to murder without at least trying to prevent it.

Anger came through the bond from her. He felt some himself. *Damn! This is a disaster about to happen.*

I heard that. She shot him a dirty look.

Chapter Seventeen

Dusti entered the store with Drantos on her heels. She spotted the visitor right away. He stood at the counter loudly arguing with a dark-haired VampLycan. It was easy to guess who was who since one of them was noticeably buff and big.

She took the time to snag a bottled water from the cooler before approaching them.

"I want to call the state troopers," the out-of-towner complained. "You're like legally required to let me have access to a phone."

"Sir," Lake shook his head, "I told you. The phone is down. It happens. Storms come through and we can go weeks before it's fixed."

"What's going on?" Dusti stepped up next to the stranger.

"Do you have a cell phone?"

She shook her head. "No. Sorry. I don't even think we get cell signals around here," she lied. "Are you okay?"

"I saw something."

She set the water down and held out her hand. "I'm Dusti. What's your name?"

"Brad." He shook her hand. "Do you live around here? Can I use your phone?"

"What did you see?"

"I don't know. It was a big creature. I think it's some kind of new wildlife. It's really remote out here so it's possible."

She bit her lip and studied him. He seemed a little scared and excited at the same time. "Was it kind of hairy but not? Big body? Moved real fast?"

His eyes widened. "Yes!"

She grinned. "You saw George."

"That wasn't a man."

"You're right. It's not. George is kind of a celebrity around here. He's a bear with about the worst case of mange ever. Poor thing." She turned and shook her head at Lake. "You're at it again, I see. Messing with the tourists isn't nice."

She sighed and met Brad's gaze. "It gets boring around here. Let me guess. He pretended he didn't know what you saw? Or worse, told you that you didn't see it at all?" She hoped she was close.

"Yeah," Brad confirmed. "But that wasn't a bear."

"Trust me. It was George. He's big and you can see parts of his skin. He doesn't have much hair left. He looks really freaky like that. Someone even thought he was bigfoot once." She chuckled, forcing her expression to hopefully look amused. "He was up on his hind legs and yeah, I thought that poor lady was going to have a heart attack."

"It wasn't a damn bear."

She reached out and patted his arm. "Tell us what happened."

"It was running through the woods. I almost wrecked my car when I saw it out of the corner of my eye. It was big and was all kinds of messed up with patches of dark fur."

She nodded. "Yeah, that's George. About two years ago he showed up in this area. He knocks over our trashcans and scares the crap out of people who see him while driving along the highway, since jerks toss out garbage from their windows. We call that littering but George thinks it's like ringing a dinner bell. Everyone around here thinks it's a riot when people like you come in after spotting him." She shook her head again and pointed at Lake. "Shame on you. Letting this poor man get all freaked out over that mangy bear. I know you think it's funny but look how upset he is!"

Lake raised both hands and backed up. "Um, sorry?"

Dusti sighed and turned her attention back to Brad. "To be fair, we don't get cable this far out. There's not a lot to amuse us. It would have made his day if you'd left here thinking you saw some monster and word spread. He's always hoping some tourist will think he's spotted bigfoot again and he'll make a ton of money off all the morons who show up looking for a monster. He's the only store and gas station within miles, if you haven't noticed. He made bank the last time."

She shot Lake another glare. "It isn't happening. This man is too smart to fall for your shit." She shifted her body to stare at Drantos. "This has *got* to stop. You heard Brad here. He almost wrecked his car! It's time to put George down. It would be the humane thing to do. Someone is going to get hurt."

She motioned him forward. "Brad, this is Drantos. He's kind of the mayor. The town isn't big enough to have an official one but he's the man in charge."

Drantos inclined his head. "Hello."

"See what I've been saying? That messed-up bear is a menace. It's not some tourist attraction. This man could have been hurt. I *demand* you put down that bear. He's got the worst case of mange ever and I'm tired of him coming onto my property."

Dusti patted Brad's arm again, making eye contact. "The crazy-ass bear also loves to roll in the mud when he gets hot. Thank goodness you didn't see him after that. He looks like the creature from the black lagoon or something. It scared the shit out me too, and I already knew it was George since he did it right in front of my cabin by the river. I'm just glad I came in here when I did, or Lake really would have had you going."

Brad's face turned a little red and she could see he was pissed. "It's really just a bear?"

She nodded. "Yep. He's one screwed-up looking bear, to be fair. He's scarred up pretty bad too. I think he hit every branch of the ugly tree he must have fallen out of."

"Fuck you, man." Brad jerked out of her hold, glaring at Lake. "You're an asshole."

"Sorry." Lake didn't sound it.

Brad looked down at Dusti. "Thanks for telling me the truth."

"You're welcome. And I'm going to make sure that George is euthanized so this doesn't happen to anyone else. It's better for that poor bear too. He's got the worst skin condition I've ever seen on an animal. It's probably painful. I'm going to ride the mayor until it happens. I promise."

"Thank you." Brad flipped Lake off. "Up yours, man." He spun away from the counter, giving Drantos a nasty look next. "Listen to her. That shit's not funny and

I would have sued this town if I'd wrecked my car. You know that damn bear is a hazard. I'm never coming back to this shithole again."

He stormed out and left tread marks when he pulled out of the parking lot to drive away.

Dusti smiled at Drantos. "See? You didn't have to kill him."

"I can't believe he bought that." Drantos scowled.

"It's human nature." Dusti shrugged. "It was a believable excuse for something he saw that he couldn't explain. Add in the fact that he thought we were trying to make him look foolish and we have a winner. Now he won't be talking about a monster. He'll be saying the people in this town are assholes and to avoid this place at all costs. Problem solved and nobody died."

Drantos closed the distance between them and grinned. "I see."

"I don't," Lake grumbled.

Dusti turned her head, smiling at him. "Sorry I made you the bad guy, but do you really care that Brad is mad? He's gone and won't be back."

He shook his head. "I don't have to clean up blood."

That killed her humor. He seemed serious. "That's always a plus." She looked up at Drantos. "Is he kidding?"

He nodded.

She blew out a relieved sigh.

"He would have snapped his neck. That doesn't make a mess."

"You could have left off that second part," she pointed out.

Drantos chuckled. "I'd never lie to you."

"Fantastic."

"You're going to *ride me*, huh?" Drantos's hands slid down her back and cupped her ass. "I look forward to it."

She reached back and yanked his hands off her butt. "Behave. You don't want to shock poor Lake here."

"It wouldn't," the clerk announced. "I'd have something interesting to watch, but it could be off-putting to any humans who come in. They might be offended to see you both naked and going at it."

Dusti rolled her eyes. "We're out of here, on that note."

"You sure?" Drantos deepened his voice. "I could carry you into the back." He shot a dirty look at the other VampLycan. "You're not going to see my mate naked. I'd have to kill you."

They strolled out of the store hand in hand but stopped as soon as they reached the line of trees. A large group of VampLycans waited in the shadows. Velder stepped forward.

"We watched the human drive away." He kept his focus on Drantos. "What happened?"

"Apparently, we have a mutant bear with severe mange and are attempting to fool humans into thinking they've seen a monster to bring in business by drawing more tourists. She verbally chastised Lake in front of the human for scaring him and not just telling him the 'truth'." Drantos shook his head. "The human bought her story, and he's pissed. He swore to never return and said that he'd have sued our town if he'd damaged his car. Dusti promised him we'd euthanize the bear before someone got hurt." He paused. "She made me the mayor, too."

Velder's lips twitched but he didn't smile. He lowered his gaze to Dusti. "Very smart."

"Thank you."

She glanced at the faces around her. They weren't glaring at her with suspicion anymore. Some seemed amused, others impressed. She gripped Drantos's hand a little tighter.

They look a bit surprised that I pulled that off, she thought at him.

They underestimated you. So did I.

Humans are good at bullshitting other humans. It's a gift.

He smirked. *I'll remember that.*

I didn't mean I'd bullshit you. You're in my head. That would be tough to do.

Don't ever try. Mates don't lie to each other.

Good.

Velder turned, motioning everyone back toward the clearing. "The food will be ready soon."

Drantos returned Dusti to Peva. "I need to feel the mood of everyone."

"What does that mean?" Dusti frowned.

"To see how they feel about what you just did," Peva explained, reaching over and patting her leg. "Drantos will one day lead our people. It's important that everyone feels secure that he didn't mate someone who will weaken our clan."

Dusti hated politics. "Fantastic."

"It will be fine," Drantos assured her. "Sit here and I'll be back soon."

She watched him join a group of men talking around one of the fire pits. Peva patted her leg again and Dusti turned her head, holding her gaze.

"It would have been easier if you hadn't mated someone so highly ranked in the clan, but it isn't a matter of choice when it comes to mates. Drantos chose you."

"I am so out of my element."

"You're doing well. It's always difficult when a woman mates someone from another clan. I was lucky to find mine here. Most don't. They have to attempt to fit in with strangers and adjust to their ways. I'm impressed how you're handling everything, Dusti. You should be proud."

"Because I'm not crying and hiding under Drantos's bed?"

Peva laughed. "Yes."

"I was tempted to but I don't want him to regret loving me." She scanned the clearing and watched the man she loved laugh with a new group. He fit in with his clan. Those were his neighbors and friends, people he cared about.

"It will work out. I see the way you look at him."

"He's everything to me. I'd always dreamed about finding someone like him." Dusti paused. "Well, not like him exactly, since I never knew about this world, but you know what I mean."

"I do. Your love is strong and so is his."

"I'm still freaked out about the mind-reading thing." She studied Peva. "How do you handle that?"

"You learn control. It's difficult at first. I once hurt Maku's feelings when I thought too hard about his feet."

"What about them?"

"Look at my mate's feet. They are huge!" Peva laughed. "We were newly mated and I was watching him sleep. He woke to overhear my thoughts as I studied his body. He's perfect except his feet are too large. He took that to his heart. I felt bad. And I once caught him thinking about my cooking. He had a lover once who made better deer stew than I can. He thought about contacting her to get the recipe and wondered if I'd be upset if he gave it to me. I was. He shares my bed so he can deal with eating my bad stew."

Dusti chuckled. "Damn straight."

Peva grew somber. "I don't want him to speak to any woman he bedded before me. It makes me jealous. He's the only lover I've had. I used to wonder if I pleased him enough in bed. I didn't have the experience those women had."

"I totally understand that. Drantos isn't the first guy I've slept with but I got the feeling he had a lot of lovers."

"I still feel jealousy because I hate the thought of someone once touching Maku, but I learned that nothing compares to a mate, Dusti. It's why I don't track down Maku's past lovers and kill them. I'm the one he loves. He didn't have a bond with them. You mentioned reading minds. Your bond is in place. You know what I mean. You feel what he does and he feels what you do. *Nothing* compares to that."

"That's true."

"If ever a woman from Drantos's past approaches you to throw it in your face that she was once his lover, don't allow it to hurt you. Feel pity. They are jealous that you are his mate and not them."

"It's already happened. Yonda gave me the impression her and Drantos were dating, and that he cheated on her with me. I was pissed at him and that's how the whole rejection thing happened. I said I didn't want to go home with him. I thought he was a cheater."

"So that explains it. I wondered why you'd hurt him that way. You think like a human does. Yonda wanted Drantos to settle with her. They were just lovers but without a bond. Do you understand? He was free to bed anyone he wished and so was she. As a matter of fact, she visits another clan regularly to see one of their males. It isn't to say hello. She spends the night there and returns the next day still carrying his scent. She wants a mate and keeps a few men in her bed in the hopes one will agree. It would have been different if they'd agreed to share a home. Then it's implied they are off-limits to others. That they're testing to see if they're compatible enough to have a lasting relationship. Drantos never allowed women into his home."

"I get that now."

"Good. Feel pity for Yonda. Drantos is quite a catch for a VampLycan. He has high standing as the next leader when his father steps down and he's an honorable man. His looks don't hurt either. The women consider him quite handsome." Peva chuckled. "So I hear. I see him like family. He and some of the others were really good to me when I lost my brother. They stepped up and kind of adopted me as their little sister."

"I'm sorry about your brother."

She nodded, her expression growing somber. "We're hard to kill but not impossible. It happens sometimes. Not near as much as it does in the human world. Their bodies are more fragile than ours and they don't have the ability to heal as fast."

Dusti wanted to ask how it happened but didn't want to be rude. Peva seemed to guess at her thoughts.

"He was an enforcer and not mated yet. He hadn't found the woman who was his. Our kind polices those who aren't human. We hear of a problem and sometimes our enforcers are sent to handle the trouble. Well, there was a rash of disappearances in Anchorage. It was making the human news. A few bodies were eventually discovered and they'd all been drained of blood. The human authorities believed it was a serial killer but we suspected it was a nest of rogue Vampires. Those are the ones that break the laws and put us all at risk. It's one thing to feed off humans, but they aren't allowed to kill. It draws attention.

"Rener offered to go hunt the Vampires down and take them out. He was always so proud. He refused to take another enforcer with him, felt he could handle it alone. We lost contact with him so two more enforcers were sent to find him." She paused. "The nest was larger than expected. There were over fifty of them and they'd boasted about killing a VampLycan to other nests that weren't rogue."

"I really am sorry, Peva."

"Drantos and his cousin Redson were the ones who went after my brother. They annihilated that nest and avenged him. I consider them family and I became their little sister. Kraven's too. I'm just closer to Drantos and Redson than him." She paused. "Nests aren't usually that large. They keep their numbers lower to avoid detection, but they were all crazy Vamps who apparently didn't care if humans discovered what they were."

"I admit I'm a little freaked-out now that I know Vampires really exist. I wonder if I've ever met one but didn't know it."

She shrugged. "It's possible. You're lucky a Vamp didn't decide to make a meal out of you. They probably would have tasted your blood and known you weren't fully human. You wouldn't have woken up in your bed the next day with your memory wiped. They would have killed you. They fear VampLycans. We're their enemies. It would have been a great bragging right for a Vamp to kill one of ours."

Dusti shuddered.

"That's why we live in clans. It's safer in numbers."

She thought of her hairy neighbor. "What about Werewolves? Would they have killed me if they knew what my mother was?"

Peva looked thoughtful. "It depends on the pack. We're friendly with some. They've actually called us to request an enforcer help them if they have human or

Vampire trouble. Some just fear us and want to avoid our kind at all costs. They worry we'll take over their packs. It would be easy for one of our men to kill their alphas in a fight. They admire strength but they want full-blooded Lycans to lead them, not mixed breeds. They know our history."

"What about it? I don't understand."

"The one time Vampires and Lycans aligned together, they created VampLycans. Most of those Lycan women who gave birth to our kind were mentally controlled and tricked into conceiving by Vampires. We inherited that ability. Some are afraid history would be repeated. It's why Lycans hate Vampires and they don't get along. They fight sometimes over territories and we step in when we're asked to try to keep the peace."

"How do you do that?"

"One of our enforcers will order that nest to leave the area. If they refuse, it's the last thing they do. We can't compel them to leave by messing with their minds. That's an ability we get from them. They're immune."

"What kind of human problems do packs have? I'm curious," Dusti admitted.

Peva's smile returned. "They're shifters. It gets annoying when poachers invade their territory and start shooting at them in wolf form. Some have died that way. An enforcer can hunt the humans down and have a little mind chat with them."

"Mind chat?"

"You know; tell them they no longer want to hunt in that area and suggest there's nothing to shoot. They go into their minds and place commands."

"Can one VampLycan mind-control another?"

She hesitated. "They'd have to be pretty weak for it to work. You've got a lot of human blood. Are you worried someone might mess with you? It's possible but Drantos would hand them their asses big time if they did. He's feeding you his blood. That will make you stronger."

"He froze me."

Peva arched her eyebrows.

"You know, his eyes got all glowy and I couldn't move."

"Were you able to think?"

"Yes."

She nodded. "That's good. It's very rare for a human to be immune but you aren't a full-blood. If you had been, you wouldn't be aware of anything he'd done unless he ordered you to remember. You wouldn't have been able to think unless he allowed it. You would have effectively gone to sleep and woken up with whatever suggestions or commands he'd put there, believing them one hundred percent."

"I'm back." Drantos took a seat next to Dusti and leaned in, kissing her cheek.

"How goes it with everyone? Are they accepting your mate?" Peva lowered her voice. "Or do I have to take a stroll around to do a little public relations?"

Drantos chuckled. "They want to make her our ambassador for humans we can't mind wipe. She can handle any of them who become a problem."

Dusti grinned. "Awesome. I have a place in the clan. I'll become the official bullshitter."

Drantos gripped her hand, pleased. "It's going to work out, Dusti."

"I have faith since I have you."

He picked up some of her thoughts. The bond between them strengthened every hour that passed. She'd eventually learn to mute them enough to stop broadcasting but for the moment, he knew she worried about her sister.

He pressed his mouth closer to her ear. "She's going to be okay. Kraven won't allow anyone or anything to hurt her."

I just wish they were here with us.

They will be as soon as it's safe.

Bat's not going to take any of this well. What if she tries to run away from your brother? She'll believe he's as nuts as I thought you were.

Drantos frowned. *He'll track her down if she gets away from him. I have faith that he'll find a way to prevent that from happening a second time if there's a first. He's a good fighter, Dusti. He's smart. He knows how to avoid detection.*

Bat doesn't. She's loud and draws attention.

Drantos chuckled.

"What are you two thinking to each other?" Peva let her presence be known. "You both suddenly look so grim."

"She's worried about her sister." He kept his gaze on Dusti as he answered. "I'm assuring her that Kraven will keep her safe."

"He's right, Dusti. Kraven is what you would consider one tough hombre. He'll protect her."

Drantos nodded. "You'll see her soon."

"Food is ready," Maku yelled.

"I'm so hungry!" Peva rushed to her mate.

Drantos got up and pulled Dusti to her feet. "Have some fun. You saved a life today. I'm really proud of you."

"Thank you."

"It will be fine."

"I hope so."

He led her to the banquet setup and they filled their plates. His thoughts drifted to their siblings too. He wished he knew his brother's plan. It was possible that Kraven had Bat hidden somewhere in VampLycan territory, maybe even his den. Drantos silently promised to check it out later after he took Dusti home.

Otherwise, Kraven would have likely taken her far from the area. There were a lot of remote areas in Alaska that two people could get lost in.

"I'm about to eat elk. My life has drastically changed."

He smiled at Dusti. She was adjusting to her new life surprisingly well. He was so proud and grateful that he'd found his mate.

Chapter Eighteen

The door shook from the force of someone pounding on the solid wood. Dusti rushed to it and paused. "Who is it?"

"Crayla."

She twisted the lock and opened it, wincing over her mother-in-law's snarled tone. The taller woman looked as angry as she'd sounded when she got her first glimpse of her standing on the porch. Drantos had turned on the exterior lights so there was no missing the death glare directed her way.

"Lesson number one: We don't lock our doors." Crayla entered without being asked.

Dusti jumped aside so she wasn't pushed. "Well, Drantos locked it when he went on patrol." She closed the door, watching the VampLycan take a seat on the couch. She paused but then followed, choosing the chair opposite her.

"You're already changing my son. This isn't good."

"It might have had something to do with the fact that your husband walked in on us when we were making out. What's wrong with knocking before just letting yourself in? Doesn't common courtesy exist here?"

"Friends knock and wait for admittance but not close family members. We welcome our mates' parents and siblings into our homes as though they are our own. We don't have crime here the way you have in your world. VampLycans are not thieves. We have honor. Stealing is beneath us."

"That's good to know but nobody wants someone walking in when they're about to have sex."

"It's part of nature."

"It's rude."

Crayla studied her. "I see. It's a human thing. Are you ashamed of your body without clothing?"

"I wouldn't say that. Do I want anyone to see me naked besides Drantos? No. Do I want someone to catch me having sex? That would be a hell no."

Some of the other woman's temper seemed to die down. "You don't shift. You didn't spend a lifetime learning that being naked is acceptable around others. Clothing isn't always available if we've shifted and return to skin."

"I figured that it wasn't a big deal to your kind when Yonda strutted around naked in the woods."

"Had she just shifted?"

"Yes."

"We put on something when possible but no one views it as a sexual act to be naked in those circumstances."

"Okay."

Crayla hesitated. "You live in our world now. You need to change your way of thinking. It's an insult to lock your doors to family members. Velder would have turned his back if he'd caught you and our son having sex. It's not as if he'd have watched. That *would* be rude."

"And so wrong," Dusti added.

Crayla grinned. "I like your humor. And you're standing up to me. That's brave." Her smile faded. "It's an internal family matter. I guess we can compromise. You are allowed to lock your doors. We will knock first if it makes you feel more at ease."

"Thanks." Dusti managed to avoid rolling her eyes. She'd have done it anyway.

"You must have a lot of questions as you learn more about us. Ask."

"Mainly, I just want to figure out a way to fit in so things are easier on Drantos. I don't want anyone to give him any crap."

"You do love him."

"I'm giving up everything I know to be with him. That would be a yes."

Crayla's features softened. "This must be a bit difficult for you. Your mother never told you what she was?"

"No."

"What was her name? I tried not to know much about Decker's clan and he kept his daughter close to home. He'd make her stay inside when anyone from another clan visited his. He probably feared they would target her to get back at him…and then she left while still so young."

"Her name was Ann."

Crayla's eyebrows arched. "I don't think so. That's not a VampLycan name."

"That's what she went by but her full name was Antina."

"Ah. It makes sense. She would have wanted to fit in with humans. I'm surprised she gave her daughters VampLycan names."

"She did?"

"Have you ever met other human children with names like yours?"

"No. Not really. I just thought she did it to be cute. She was an A. Batina is my older sister. Our father was Christopher. I got named Dustina. A. B. C. D. My mother joked about it."

"Some women like to name their daughters after them. She gave both of you part of her name. She must have loved you greatly."

"She was a terrific mom."

"You're sure your mother is dead?"

It felt like a slap. "Of course I am. Do you think she faked her death and abandoned us? She'd never do that. She and my father were killed in a car accident."

"We heal fast. It would be tough to die the way some humans do."

"They got nailed by a semi. It cut the car in half. They both had closed casket burials."

"I'm sorry."

The sympathy she heard in her tone helped soothe some of Dusti's anger. "Thank you."

"VampLycans can die if the injures are severe enough. Beheadings, crush injuries, or massive falls will kill us every time."

Dusti had a mental flashback of seeing Aveoth kill the jerk who'd kidnapped her. She pushed that memory away. It still made her feel a little sick over watching his head roll away from his body. "Why are you telling me that?"

"You keep glancing at the door. I assumed you were worried about my son on patrol. You shouldn't be. We're very sturdy."

Dusti wasn't aware she'd been doing that. "It's not locked. I half expect someone to just walk in."

"Kraven is gone and Velder is at a meeting with a few of the other clan leaders. Those are the only ones who would, besides your mate or me."

"Not quite." Dusti stood and bolted the door. She sat back down.

"Why did you do that?"

"Decker could send men after me."

"He'd never make it this far into our territory without being captured. We increased the number of our men on patrol for that reason."

"I'd rather be safe than sorry."

"You don't like Decker?"

"That would be an understatement. I only met him a few times in my life and it was never pleasant. We moved when he found us. He didn't like me and it was mutual. I only agreed to come to Alaska with my sister because I thought he was a pervert, and I didn't want her to have to face that possible truth without me being there. Bat wouldn't trust a stranger as far as she could throw them but she has a blind spot where family is concerned. I knew it would upset her, so I wanted to be there for her if I was right."

"A pervert?"

"He showed an unnatural interest in my sister, and my mom ran away from home to get away from him… Do I need to spell it out?"

"Ah." Crayla leaned back. "You didn't know he'd use them to form an alliance with the GarLycan leader. Do VampLycans frighten you?"

"I'm not stupid. Of course you do. You can shift into another form. I don't."

"There would be no honor in attacking you since you're so much weaker. And your mate would seek vengeance if anyone did. Everyone fears my family. You're safe, Dusti."

That didn't really put her more at ease. "Thanks."

"We just need to get the clan to accept you. It helped today when you dealt with the human in town. Everyone is talking about it. At first they assumed you were weaker than previously thought because you seemed upset about having to take a life, but you handled the problem well. That made them respect you."

"*Everyone* should be upset when it comes to taking a life."

"Will you mourn if we have to kill Decker?"

"Except him," Dusti amended. "I'm not a fan. I think I made that pretty clear. I don't care what happens to him."

Crayla regarded her. "I'm still concerned. You're mated to my son. We're enemies of Decker. Do you feel split loyalties between your mate and your family?"

"*Bat* is my family. You are my family since you're Drantos's mother. Kraven, Velder, and this clan are now family because they are to Drantos, too. I don't see Decker as family. Blood means nothing when it comes to him. Is that clear enough? I'm not going to shed a tear if he dies. He wants to hurt my sister. Being given to that scary Aveoth guy I met would be a death sentence for her. I love Bat but she's a nightmare to men. He'd kill her."

Crayla leaned closer. "That displeases me since Kraven told us Batina is his mate."

Dusti thought about it, remembering the interaction she'd seen between the two. "Kraven handles her better than anyone I've ever seen. She's attracted to him and he doesn't take her shit."

"Is she like you?"

Dusti grinned. "No. I'm the mellow, easygoing one."

Crayla nodded. "I understand. I have a sister and we are nothing alike. We barely see each other and I'm glad. I was grateful to leave my clan to come to this one. We fought often."

"I love Bat. We get along great but we're just different."

"She's the stronger of you two."

Crayla's words rubbed Dusti the wrong way, as if it were an insult. "Bat deals with lowlifes all the time with her job. She's abrasive. That's a kind way to put it. She makes it difficult to allow anyone to get close to her by being a shit-starter. I'm the calmer one, a mediator type who tries to avoid trouble. We even each other out. She blows things out of proportion and I smooth things over. Does that make sense?"

"You work well together as a team."

"Yes."

"I wanted to meet her but Kraven took her away before I could."

"That's probably a good thing."

"Why?"

"You know how you threatened to punch me out when you were giving me the lecture about how I needed to tend to Drantos when he was hurt? I backed down. I don't want to make waves with you because you're Drantos's mother. It's important that we get along and I'm also willing to admit you'd kick my ass in a fight. But Bat has a temper. She'd have told you off and probably gone for your throat, regardless of knowing she couldn't win. She'd regret it later but she's...impulsive. She wouldn't like you telling her how to act with a man she's with."

Crayla sighed. "She doesn't sound like the mate I had in mind for Kraven."

"Life rarely turns out the way you think it will. I bet she's in for a shock when Kraven tells her he's her mate. I know I was thrown when Drantos told me. We deal."

Her mother-in-mate nodded. "True. It would be boring if there weren't surprises, wouldn't it?"

"Exactly."

"What did you do in the human world? Let's start there."

"I worked in an office as a secretary."

"That implies you have useful skills. It's why you're good with speaking to humans."

Dusti shrugged.

"And your sister? What does she do in the human world?"

"She's a criminal defense attorney."

Crayla's eyebrows shot up.

"She's really good at what she does. I know what you're probably thinking. Why does she try to keep bad guys out of jail? I can relate but Bat believes everyone is innocent until proven guilty. She's assured me many a time that not all of her clients actually committed the crimes they've been accused of. She's saved some innocent people from going to prison."

"That's not what entered my mind. She knows human laws. We have to hire outsiders if there are any issues that arise that deal with human authorities. Your sister will be useful to our clan. That's a good thing."

"Do many VampLycans get arrested?"

"No. Of course not. They would wipe the memories of the humans they dealt with to avoid it. Our legal issues arise with land dealings. We buy up territory surrounding ours to expand as our numbers rise."

"Bat doesn't do that kind of law."

"An attorney is an attorney."

Dusti decided to let that go. She didn't want to be the one to explain that wasn't true. Bat could burst Crayla's bubble.

"I was told your sister has more Lycan blood than Vampire. Does she have any abilities?"

"No."

"Are you certain?"

"Definitely. She can't shift. I've seen her pissed plenty of times. The only sharp pointy things she attacks with are her high heels. She can tear those off her feet in a heartbeat and nail someone with them."

"You said she has a temper."

"She does."

Crayla smiled. "That's a Lycan trait. I can work with that. I love a good fight myself. Both of you will need some training. That might help you bond with the other women if I ask them to assist. You may make friends and they can take you under their wings."

"Great." Dusti inwardly winced. She pictured lots of bruises and pain in her future. Her parents had signed her up for karate when she'd been nine. A week later they'd pulled her. She just wasn't a fighter. "Maku already offered."

"He did? That's wonderful."

"Yeah. It seems like everyone wants to kick my ass. I can't say I'm as thrilled about that as you seem to be."

Crayla's cheerful expression faltered.

"I'm not really into violence. That's more Bat's thing."

"I see."

"I don't want to lie to you."

"You *should* be honest."

"Isn't there a way I can fit in without having to punch someone or getting hit?"

"I'm here to help you figure this out. You're good at dealing with humans but we don't have too much interaction with them."

"That's too bad."

"It is. Drantos believes just being his mate will make everyone accept you. I'm sure he's right but that could take many years. I'd like to hurry that process along. What kinds of other skills do you have?"

"I'm great at movie trivia. I love television shows too."

Crayla just stared at her.

Dusti sighed. "That was supposed to make you laugh. I can't fight. I'm not the best cook. I wouldn't know how to make a quilt to save my life if you have some kind of sewing circle or whatever they're called. I'm a city girl. I'm so far out of my element here that it's not funny. I admit it. I'm at a loss."

"Get pregnant."

Stunned, Dusti knew her mouth fell open. She recovered fast. "That's the best advice you have for me?"

"Yes. To birth Drantos's children would endear you to the clan. They could forgive a lot of your flaws if you happen to have a son first. I know that's out of your control but we could always hope. They would rejoice a girl too. Have a baby."

Dusti had no words. She felt insulted.

"It's what I did when I became Velder's mate. I was from another clan and my status wasn't high enough for most to consider me worthy of being with him."

"Are you part human too?"

"No. It's just that my father isn't an enforcer. He is a craftsman."

"What does that matter?"

"Enforcers are fighters who protect our clan and possess much strength. Craftsmen are of lower ranking. My father helps the clan by building homes and furniture." She paused. "We all have our own skills. We just need to find yours."

"I don't think I'd be good at building stuff either."

"Take my advice then. I got pregnant right away. They forgot all about where I came from and my father's standing in our clan once I presented Drantos to this clan. They were grateful that I'd birthed a future leader."

"Don't you think that's kind of..." Dusti failed to find a polite word to describe it.

"Old fashioned? Yes, but it's effective. You'll become the mother of a future clan leader. That will earn you instant admiration. Does that insult your human side? It shouldn't. Women have been breeders for men for all of history. VampLycans are just more honest about it. It's a respectable way to make yourself a useful part of the clan."

"By popping out children with Drantos?"

"Yes."

"Okay." Dusti shot to her feet. "I forgot to get you something to drink. How rude of me. Let me rectify that." She fled into the kitchen, remembering where she'd seen the bottles of booze. "I know I need one," she called out.

Where is Bat when I really need her? Shit. This is worse than I thought it would be. Drantos? Can you hear me? Please come home and save me from your mother.

She closed her eyes and focused but she didn't hear his voice answering in her head.

Just my luck. Damn it!

"I've upset you." Crayla followed her into the kitchen.

"Good guess," Dusti muttered.

"I didn't mean to. Being a mother is very honorable and it has brought me much reward. The clan accepted me on my own merits later. Does that help?"

Dusti poured herself a drink and took a sip. "Yeah. Sure." She wasn't going to argue.

"Do you drink often?"

She met her mother-in-law's narrowed gaze. "Nope, but I think now is a good time to start."

"You need to toughen up, Dusti. You're my son's mate."

"I'm your son's mate who wants a drink, and do you know what?" She lifted the glass to her lips again and took a sip. "I'm having one. Accept that."

Crayla sighed.

* * * * *

Drantos scanned the woods and caught movement to his far left. He eased behind one of the thicker trees and unleashed his claws, waiting. The wind shifted and he inhaled. His tense body relaxed and he stepped out.

"Over here," he whispered.

His cousin changed direction and approached him silently. They were both on duty. Red stopped next to him. "It's all quiet."

"I know. That's good."

"Kraven's plan worked."

"What exactly was that?"

"To take the other sister out of here and make damn sure they were seen by some of Decker's people, to lead them away from our village."

"Where did he take her?"

"All I know is they were heading for Washington State and he planned to keep them moving for a bit."

Drantos nodded. It was a good plan, as long as they could keep ahead of the enforcers sent after them. He just hoped Aveoth found Decker fast, and swiftly gave him justice. He had a feeling that Decker Filmore would end up like the man he'd sent to steal Dusti. He deserved to die.

"How goes it with your new mate?"

"Our bond snapped into place."

Red sighed.

"What?"

"She's so human."

"Don't start that shit too. I found my mate. I got enough of that from Dad and a few of the clan. Some of them have been giving me pitied looks but I'm actually glad she's exactly the way she is."

"Why?"

He considered his answer. "Life isn't boring. She amuses the hell out of me and makes me laugh. I'm happy with her. The fear she sometimes feels is the downside but I'm proud of how well she's taking all this. She knew nothing of our kind before we met."

"She can't shift."

"It's not a problem."

"I bet you thought otherwise while you were traveling with her. I hate walking far distances."

"She rode my back home last night."

Red chuckled. "Seriously?"

Drantos grinned. "Yes. It didn't slow me down by much. I just had to be careful she didn't fall off. I like that she needs me to do more for her than most women. That doesn't mean she's timid or helpless. She makes up for her lack of VampLycan traits with her personality. She's funny, Red. Sweet."

"She won't slap you with her claws if you piss her off. I can see where that would be a bonus."

"Piss many women off, cousin?"

Red shrugged. "Sometimes."

"I can believe that."

"Fuck you too."

Drantos scanned the woods again. "I could use your support with Dusti."

"You have it."

"How do you think everyone is handling her being my mate?"

"They are waiting and watchful. It amused some that she dealt with that human by telling them Jarred was a bear with mange. Lake has told everyone exactly what she said."

"He was the one spotted by the human?"

"Yeah. Your dad handed him his ass for going that close to the main road and being spotted. He should have known better."

"What was he doing there anyway?"

"He was coming back after leaving our territory."

"Why the hell did he leave?"

"Remember old Thomas?"

"Remind me." Drantos drew a blank.

"He helped with that mess back in the seventies when the town over decided to start some shit with us."

It came back to Drantos. "He's the one who warned my dad about the trouble brewing. I used to do the mail runs at that time. Their women would come outside to stare at us. Some of them even drove in to watch us load the truck. Their men didn't like it one bit."

"It's our Lycan traits. They're naturally drawn to our hormones."

"I disagree. It's because we're in good shape. You should have seen some of those human men. They looked as if they were pregnant." He shoved his hands out to mimic a large stomach, then ran a hand over his face. "You'd think they were Lycans with the amount of hair on their faces. They didn't seem to own razors. I understood why the women liked to watch us."

Red chuckled. "That's funny."

"It wasn't when those assholes entered our territory with guns, trying to shoot a few of us in some stupid attempt to get payback. That's why Dad forbade us from sleeping with humans from any of the surrounding towns. He didn't want a bunch of drunk, jealous men coming after any of ours again."

Red's amused look faded fast. "I remember."

"So what does this have to do with Jarred running by the road? Thomas died last year."

"Word spread that the granddaughter finally came to clean out the house. We'll buy it when she puts it up for sale since it borders our lands. That's what she plans to do."

"I still don't understand. What does one have to do with the other?"

"She's the girl who found and hid Jarred in Thomas's barn after he'd been shot. He'd been out hunting and got too close to someone's property. The jerks thought Jarred was there to fuck their women or some such shit. You know they hate anyone from Howl. Humans can be stupid and unstable. They were determined to kill him. As if we've got nothing better to do than steal their daughters' virginities or tempt their wives into cheating." Red snorted. "I've never bedded a human. Only a few of ours did back when it was allowed. It sounded too troublesome and it seems I was right."

"So why did Jarred go there? What was the point?"

"He just wanted to check on her. He'd lost a lot of blood that night and those bastards might have killed him if she hadn't found him first. Anyway, your dad ordered him to stay away from her from now on. There's a real concern that seeing him might undo the mind wipe. It's best if she never remembers that night. She saw too much."

"Did she recognize him?"

"He swore he didn't speak to her or let her know he was there."

"Good."

Red shifted his body and leaned against the tree. "How is it having a mate?"

"Everything we've always heard. Dusti is afraid I'll be able to read her every thought. I told her she'll learn to stop broadcasting and can shield them."

"That's one thing I dread about mating. I don't want someone else inside my head."

"The sex is amazing. You'll get over it."

"Really?"

"It will blow your mind."

"I'm thinking about asking Cavasia to live with me."

"You said she wasn't your mate."

"She isn't, but I'm lonely. I don't think I can take another winter like the last one. She's too far away to visit when the snow sets in and you know I avoid any of our women here."

"You're going to settle?" Drantos curled his lip. "Don't do it."

"I'm not mating her. We're thinking about just sharing a home for a while. She's lonely too."

"I won't judge you but it's going to be hard to find your mate if you're living with Cavasia."

"I've tested all the women from the other clans who drew my interest. I'm not attracted to anyone here. That means no living generations are right for me. I don't want to be like Maku. He was alone for over a hundred and twenty-some years before Peva was born. They didn't even realize what they were to each other until she hit puberty. I don't want to have to feel the way he did by being attracted to someone so young. It tore him up trying to avoid her so he didn't feel as if he'd stolen her youth. He still believes he should have waited until she was in her late twenties before they sealed their bond."

"Peva disagrees. Don't give up and settle for someone who isn't your true mate, Red. I understand. I contemplated the same things you must be but then I met Dusti. It was completely unexpected."

"I bet. Were you horrified at first?"

He hesitated. "Surprised. I worried about how she'd take to me but I wasn't upset that she's not what I'd anticipated. I just wanted to get her home to seal the bond. Bottom line, I don't care what she is, just that she's mine."

"I get it. I have a lot to think about."

"Yes, you do."

"Perhaps Cavasia and I should put a limit on the number of years we share a home."

"You mean like promise to live together for ten and then see if any women who've come of age are your possible mate?"

Red nodded. "Like that."

"And what do you plan to tell this mate when you find her?"

"About what? I don't understand."

Drantos stared at Red. "It hurt Dusti when I admitted I'd bitten other women during sex to even test a mating. Imagine your mate's reaction when she finds out you slept next to a woman every night for years and bonded in the ways a couple does when they live together."

"Damn." Red sighed.

"I just want you to consider the consequences."

"I appreciate that."

"We're family. We look out for each other."

"I'm just lonely. Last winter was the worst. I thought I was going crazy after two months of being snowed in. I envy the ones with mates and kids. It didn't bother me so much before but I'm getting older."

"I understand."

"I know you do."

"Just don't do anything without putting a lot of thought into it. That's all I ask. We live a long damn time and regrets stay with us. I'd hate for yours to be to find your mate and have to soothe her pain. Ask my father about that sometime."

Red nodded. "I remember."

Movement to the right caught his eye. "Break time is over. You go south. I'll take north."

Red inclined his head and they parted to cover more ground. Drantos hoped there weren't any problems. He just wanted to get home to Dusti. He found the animal that had drifted into his zone. It was harmless.

Chapter Nineteen

Dusti staggered into the bathroom and debated on running a bath. She changed her mind when she had to lean against the wall to stay upright. She carefully made her way through the house into the kitchen, deciding food was in order. She hadn't meant to drink so much but Crayla's meeting had encouraged her to have a few too many.

The front door opened and she clenched her teeth. "Oh, you're back. Fantastic." She turned.

It wasn't her new mother-in-law who entered the house. It was Yonda. The woman hesitated inside the open door and stared at her.

"You're not family so you have no right to walk into this house."

Yonda scowled. "I'm not in it. I'm standing in the doorway."

"I'm learning about your tactics." Dusti pointed at her. "You don't like me. Get out."

"I came to ask you to do the right thing by Drantos. I'm not his mate but you shouldn't be either. He deserves a strong VampLycan woman."

"I get it. You hate me and don't think I'm good enough for him. I heard you the first time. *Get out.* You're not welcome here." Dusti waved her hand dismissively. "Bye."

Yonda didn't budge. "I don't hate you. It's true that I don't think you're blooded enough to be a good mate to Drantos."

"We're already mated so you're too late."

The other woman paled.

"True mates. I can read his thoughts and he can pick up mine too. It's a done deal. Now get *out*. I've had a hellish evening already with his mother pointing out all my flaws. She said I need to get pregnant. Like that's my only redeeming quality. Do you know how insulting that is?"

"I do."

Dusti was Surprised Yonda agreed.

"It's never easy coming into a new clan. Crayla has always been very protective of her sons. She threatened to rip out the throat of any VampLycan woman who got pregnant by either them. She worried someone might try to trap them into settling to take a mate if that happened. At least she'll welcome a baby from you. It means she's accepted your mating."

"That's gruesome. What is it with you people and throats?"

"It's an effective way to kill." Yonda took a step inside the house. "I didn't know you'd already sealed the bond when I came here to speak to you. I take my words back. You'd hurt Drantos more if you left him. As you said, it's a done deal. You must make the best of it."

"I'm trying."

"It will take time but everyone will accept you if you try to fit in and don't make Drantos tone down who he is to please you."

"Tone him down?"

"Make him act human. He's not. You probably have a set idea of how a man should present himself. He's an enforcer of one of the strongest and most feared VampLycan clans. We hold that position because Velder and his sons are tough on lawbreakers. You might be squeamish over him doing his duties."

"I watched a guy get his head ripped off by Aveoth. I didn't puke or faint. I'm pretty proud of that."

"You met Lord Aveoth?"

"In the graying flesh."

Yonda's features became animated. "Tell me everything! Is he as handsome as they say? As fierce? He's never visited the clan when I was around. We're not allowed to trespass on GarLycan territory."

"He's very attractive but scary as hell. Big." Dusti noticed that her visitor was a few more feet inside the door. "Are we pals now or something?"

"My protests about you becoming Drantos's mate weren't personal."

"You've slept with him, Yonda. We are *not* friends."

"I've slept with a lot of men. I'm a VampLycan."

Dusti frowned.

"I go into heat every summer. You probably don't suffer from that, being so human, but it's hell. You wouldn't understand how strong the urge to be fucked becomes but we always find someone to spend our heat with. Even when I'm not suffering from it, I love sex. We all expect to meet our mate one day and then be locked into one partner for life. It's acceptable in our culture to have many lovers when we're young and single. It's healthy and normal. Drantos was one of the better ones I've known but I wasn't jealous over you. I was angry because he's going to lead the clan I live in one day and I didn't see that turning out well if he took you as a mate. You can't shift, and I don't pick up any VampLycan from you. None. You aren't even vicious, or you would have gone for my throat already." Her gaze darted around the room. "I spot at least six weapons you could use to come at me but you haven't moved for any of them."

"You can shift. I'm not an idiot." She glanced at the counter. "This block of knives wouldn't even save me if you wanted to kill me." She looked back at Yonda. It surprised her that the other woman smiled.

"You could at least try. Drantos would slaughter me if I laid a finger on you. I'm not suicidal. At least bluff, Dustin."

"It's Dusti."

"Isn't that a boy's name?"

"My full name is Dustina but everyone shortens it. It's with an I."

Yonda groaned. "A human with an I at the end of her name. How cliché. I'm trying to like you but you're making it difficult."

"You're another VampLycan woman with an A at the end of *her* name. Crayla. Peva. My mom was Antina. She named her daughters Batina and Dustina. Is that like a requirement here or something? I think I'll stick with being called Dusti with an I."

Yonda chuckled. "A lot of our names do end with A's. It's tradition in some families to have that in the name of at least one daughter. It's considered good luck. Tell me about Lord Aveoth. I've always wanted to meet him. Does he look like he'd be fantastic in bed? He needs a lover. I'm not sure how I'd do living at the cliffs but he might be worth it." She sobered. "Especially if this clan's future is resting on Drantos making you fierce. I'm not holding much hope of that happening."

"Has anyone ever told you that you're a bitch?"

"All the time. Is that insulting in your world? Call me human." Yonda flashed a grin. "*That* would sting. Now tell me about Aveoth. I'm serious! I've never gone to bed with a GarLycan and the ones sent here with messages are in and out before we can flirt with them. They are all business. You could get rid of me if I volunteered to go live with their clan. Tell me about him."

"He's about six feet four, massive chest and arms, classically handsome but with a touch of seriously scary too. He looks really dangerous. I didn't see any wings but he dressed in a lot of leather and his voice reminded me of thunder when he got angry. His eyes and skin color changed right in front of me. It was eerie. He beheaded someone superfast and didn't seem bothered by it at all. His tone didn't even really change. You'd think he'd just swatted a fly."

Yonda licked her lips. "Did he seem really cold and distant?"

Dusti shrugged. "I guess."

"I'm going to request an audience with him. That's incredibly arousing."

"Did you hear what I said?"

"Of course I did. You made him sound like a wet dream."

"I think I need another drink." Dusti shook her head. "You people are too weird."

"Why do you think that way?"

"I couldn't wait to get away from him but you want to go meet him? I thought you said you weren't suicidal?"

Yonda advanced into the kitchen and snatched away the bottle Dusti had grabbed. "I think you've had enough. You're slurring your words. You don't want your mate to come home from patrol to find you passed out on the floor. It will be just one more reminder of how weak you are. You can't even hold your liquor well."

Dusti looked up at the other woman. "I really don't like you. You're so rude."

"We're honest. Lies are a waste of time. You are Drantos's mate so that means I have to accept you. Feign violence if you are ever insulted. No one would actually strike you since it would be a death sentence if they hurt Drantos's mate in any way. You'll at least appear stronger than you really are and earn their respect for courage. Stay away from the booze too." Her gaze lowered to Dusti's stomach. "I can see why Crayla advised you to get pregnant. You might want to consider getting in that mindset so your ovaries start producing viable eggs. Everyone loves a new baby and it will distract them from your flaws."

Dusti blurted out the first thing that came to mind. "I seriously hate you."

Yonda leaned forward a little. "That's better. Honesty. You're sounding more like a VampLycan. Keep it up." She turned and walked out of the house, closing the door behind her. The bottle went with her.

Dusti sighed and decided to take that bath after all. It would be hours before Drantos returned. Her talk with Yonda had sobered her up enough that she felt certain she wouldn't fall asleep. She had too much on her mind.

Drantos spotted Yonda coming and made his presence known by walking up behind her. She didn't sense him until he was a few feet away. She turned. He stopped.

"What are you doing out here?"

"I came looking for you."

He tensed. "Why? Did you want to insult my mate again? I thought we were friends. How could you pull that shit, especially in front of my father?"

"I was taken aback. I didn't expect you to go on a mission and return with a human who smelled like you'd just climbed out of bed with her. We don't mess with humans. I was reasonably concerned when you made it clear you planned to mate her."

"She believed it was an act of a woman who had a claim to me. I had a hell of a time explaining we have no emotional ties."

"It's not my fault humans date and try to form bonds with whoever they have sex with."

"Did you come to apologize?"

"Yes."

"I appreciate that. Don't cause me more problems, Yonda. Avoid Dusti if you can't be nice."

"I just left your home."

Rage exploded inside him. He lunged and grabbed her by her throat before he could get a handle on it. He didn't squeeze but he let his anger be known as he snarled, glaring at her. "Did you hurt her?"

"No." She reached up and held her open hands near his nose. "I didn't touch her. Smell."

He inhaled and released her, stepping back. "Stay away from her. Did you tell her to leave? Insult her?"

"I went there to explain what you needed in a mate because I consider myself your friend but you're already linked to her. I'd be more concerned with what your *mother* said to her than any advice I gave."

"What in the hell does that mean?"

Yonda grinned.

"Don't play games."

"What is the only way a weak mate could be useful?"

"Shit. She told her to have a baby right away?"

"Your little human'ish hit the bottle. I took it away from her. She can't hold her liquor either, Drantos. I admit I made her angry just to see how she'd react. She has potential."

He growled.

"I expected her to flee into your bedroom to lock the door but she held her ground. I like her but she needs some work. You're probably telling her not to worry about anything and how you'll deal with any problems that arise. It's the wrong approach. She needs to earn the clan's respect by *her* actions, not yours."

"No one would dare hurt her."

"You're right. You'd kill them. That doesn't mean you can force them to like her or be happy she belongs to you. It will cause resentment."

"Why do you care?"

"We grew up together, Drantos. You mated a weakling. You'd look out for *me* if I found myself in this position by offering to teach him how to fight and toughen him up. You have a good heart. So do I. She doesn't have the potential to effectively kill but we can work around that. Lying to another human to avoid future trouble for our clan showed them she had at least one purpose, but it's not as if we come across too many of them that can't be memory wiped. She didn't seem thrilled with birthing babies to prove her worth to the clan. I don't blame her. Talk her into working with some of the women. We'll teach her our ways and how to work around her lack of physical strength."

Drantos debated it.

"Some of us want to help you. I do." She cocked her head. "You might be Crayla's son but she's a terror to most of us. Don't depend on her to be softer on your mate than the rest of us once the shock wears off that you've brought your Dusti home. It's her duty to see to the harmony of the entire clan. She can't afford to play favorites. You know it's true."

"I'll think about it."

"Do that." Yonda suddenly grinned. "You can thank me by asking your father to request an audience with Lord Aveoth. I'd like to meet him."

"Why would you want to do that?"

"He lost his lover." She ran her hands down her body. "I have a lot to offer him if he's as sexy as your mate said."

Jealousy rose. "She—"

"Fears him. Relax. She isn't attracted to him. The opposite. I figure if he can instill that kind of reaction in her that he's pretty impressive." Yonda peered at something behind him. "I'll leave you now. I'm willing to help if you decide you need it."

Drantos watched her stalk away before he turned. He saw the reason she'd left. Red approached. His cousin and Yonda had never gotten along well. She'd wanted to test a mating but Red had refused.

Red closed the distance between them. "What are you doing talking to her? Your mate wouldn't like it."

"Tell me something I don't know."

Red sighed. "Fine. I talked to Kraven. He called."

"How are he and Bat?"

"Safe so far. He kept it short. His message was that he plans to talk to the doctor. He said you'd know who that is and where he went. He didn't want to say over the phone."

Drantos nodded. "It's the one who treats Dusti. He's in California."

"For what? Your mate is ill?"

"Forget it. Did he say anything else?"

"He'd call afterward to share the details. I told him you'd gotten your mate back safely. He was relieved. He said he wouldn't have to watch his balls anymore, whatever that meant."

Drantos found that amusing. "The sister he's with likes to threaten to remove his when she's angry."

Red growled. "Why would he put up with that?"

"You'll understand one day when you find the right woman."

"It must be something they learned being raised human." He let his disgust show. "Why did you even test a mating with one?"

"I didn't see this coming, Red. I was just curious how much of her mother's blood she carried since I couldn't pick it up by scent. She takes shots for anemia. It made me think she might have a need for blood."

"And?"

"I was right."

"I hope you didn't tell your father about that. What if she's unable to breed? He expects you to have children one day."

"It's not an issue." He remembered what Aveoth had said about having Dusti drink from him when she was pregnant to have strong VampLycan babies. "I think their mother might have drank the human father's blood during her pregnancy, and that made her children weaker when they were born. She must have known Decker would want to use her children, the way he had attempted to do to her. They'd have been of no use to him that way."

"That's insane. Who would want to purposely create weak offspring?"

"A desperate VampLycan living in a human world who probably figured she'd never be able to return to the clans. What is our rule when we go out into the human world?"

"Blend and fit in. Don't do anything that will draw attention."

"Exactly. I was once told that Decker forced one of the elder Lycans who survived the war to stay with him for the first ten years as an advisor when he took control of his clan. She was the Lycan midwife, so she didn't stay behind to fight when the younger ones fled the Vampires." His mind worked. "What if that Lycan had told Decker about sharing blood while a mate was pregnant? It's possible that Antina could have been passed that information as well. Decker would have demanded all his children give him strong grandchildren."

"What are you talking about?"

"Never mind." Drantos looked up at the sky. "I can't wait for my shift to end. I just want to go home to my mate."

"Go." Red waved him off. "I'll cover for you."

"Thank you."

Drantos started to walk away.

"Hey!"

He stopped and glanced back. "What?"

"I want my jacket back."

Drantos nodded and sprinted home. He found the front door unlocked and entered. The lights were on but Dusti wasn't in the living room or kitchen. He sniffed the air and followed her scent through his bedroom and into the master bathroom. She was in the tub with her head tipped back along the rim, eyes closed.

"I'm home."

Her eyes opened and she sat up. "You're early."

"I missed you." He opened the link between them and a wave of sadness swept through him. He crossed the room and crouched next to the tub. "What's wrong, sweetheart?"

"I want to fit in but I don't ever see it happening."

"It will. Give it time."

"Your mother thinks I should have a baby but I want us to get to know each other better first. No marriage should start off with a baby. We have enough stress without adding in sleepless nights and changing diapers."

"I agree." He caught her word. "Do you want me to marry you? I know that's important to humans."

She lifted one of her hands from the water, staring at it. "A band would be nice but I honestly don't want the whole ceremony thing." Her gaze met his. "Or maybe we can buy matching necklaces. Just something we both have that shows we're a couple. I noticed none of your mated couples wear rings. You could hide a necklace under your shirt."

He didn't want to remind her at that moment that he shifted into another form, and how jewelry wasn't a good idea to wear during the change. "We'll smell the same as we keep strengthening our bond."

She looked away and tried to lower her hand. He snagged it and curled his fingers around hers. "I'll get us rings." He could just remove his when he was on patrol, then put it back on when he came home. That way he wouldn't lose it when he shifted forms.

She smiled and stared into his eyes again. "Thank you."

"Don't thank me. You're giving up a lot to live in my world. I can compromise, Dusti. Your happiness is important to me. How did it go with my mother?"

"She tried to be nice. She got an A for effort. We're just really different."

"Did you talk to anyone else?" He wondered if she'd tell him about her other visitor.

"Yonda stopped by."

He clenched his jaw at her unhappy tone. "It won't happen again."

"I thought she'd come to kick my ass at first but she was just mildly insulting. I will never be a fan of hers but it was okay. She wanted to give me pointers."

"I just hate that it's so difficult for you."

"It's not too easy living in my world either. You'd stick out like a sore thumb."

"I've been in your world before. I made sure I fit in."

She grinned, her mood lightening. "Baby, you stand out. Trust me."

"How so?"

Her gaze lowered and he felt arousal came through their bond. "You're hot, tall, sexy…they'd have to be blind not to see you."

He stood and grabbed a towel, holding it out for her. "Come out of there."

She rose and he admitted enjoying the sight of her naked and wet. Her nipples pebbled from the cooler air. He wrapped the towel around her and lifted her right out of the tub, carrying her to the counter and gently depositing her there. He spread his legs and leaned in, putting his lips close to hers. He wanted to kiss her but resisted. She needed more than sex at that moment.

"I love you. That's the most important thing of all. We're together. Don't let bullshit clan politics get to you, Dusti. I don't give a damn what anyone says or thinks. I won't have you unhappy. I own some land that borders the territory. We can move out there before the winter sets in if you want space from my people. I can't imagine anything better than spending months snowed in with you. We'd be alone in our cozy cabin. It's not this big but I think you'll like it."

She smiled. "Wouldn't we get bored?"

He shook his head. "We'd keep each other occupied. Open up to me. Let your inner guard down."

She did. He felt it instantly, as if she'd opened a window and her emotions and thoughts breezed through him. She wanted to touch him, kiss him, but was holding back.

"I want you too, sweetheart." He stopped fighting his urges and took possession of her mouth. Passion exploded inside both of them. He groaned and reached down, shoving the towel out of his way so he could play with her pussy. She spread her thighs wider apart, hooking them around his hips.

She was already getting wet from the sexual tension between them so he used his thumb to rub upward, using the pad of it to tease her clit. The little bud hardened as he stroked it up and down. Her moans urged him on but mostly it was the needy thoughts he could pick up. She wanted him inside her. His dick stiffened painfully.

I want you, Drantos.

Easy, sweetheart. I want you to come for me first. That's it. You're getting so wet and hot for me. Don't tense up.

I can't help it. I need!

He could feel how close she was to coming. Broken moans tore from her parted lips and he clenched his teeth, shutting down their link since he knew he'd end up coming in his pants if he didn't. He applied a little more pressure against her clit, strumming it faster. Her inner thighs squeezed his hips, her breathing turning choppy and harsh. He loved the way her fingers clawed at him where she clung.

She threw her face forward and her body shook. He glanced down to see where the towel had fallen, loving the sight of her nipples beading as she climaxed. They were tight little pebbles he wanted to suck on and nip with his teeth.

He eased his thumb away from her pussy and reached down to open his pants. The next hours he'd spend fucking her were going to be heaven. He opened his mind to her again, sending flashes of images of the things he wanted to do. He said them as well, just in case their bond wasn't strong enough yet for her to get those visions.

I'm going to bend you over in front of me and fuck you until we both collapse, then I'm going to keep going until we can't move. You want me, sweetheart? You're going to have me. I can't wait to—

"Drantos!"

He snarled, enraged at the interruption. Dusti's irritation was felt inside him too, or it was possible she was mirroring his. She released him with her legs and he eased her off the counter. He kept hold of her for a few seconds since her legs seemed shaky.

"I'll be right back. That was my father bellowing."

"I know. I'm so sick of them walking into the house."

"I'm sorry. I'll get rid of him. Meet me in the bedroom." He stormed out of the bathroom, through the bedroom, but took a moment to close the door. His father waited in the living room. "What?"

"You're supposed to be on patrol."

"I was. Red relieved me. My post is covered."

His father glanced down and inhaled. "Sorry."

"Whatever it is, it can wait. Now is not a good time."

"We have trouble. I just got a call from Decker's clan. He and a few of his enforcers returned to their village. They kicked in the door of someone's home and stole a young child."

His passion cooled quickly, replaced by anger. Only Decker would use a child. It was a cowardly thing to do. He had no damn honor. "This shouldn't surprise me anymore but a child is low even for him."

His father glanced toward the hallway, then back at him. "Get your mate. This involves her family."

Drantos spun and found Dusti in their bedroom, putting on one of his t-shirts. "You need to come out. My father wants to speak to both of us. Decker has kidnapped a child."

She appeared shocked. "*What?* Why?"

"I'm not certain. That's probably what my father wants to discuss."

"Give me a minute." She rifled through a drawer in his dresser.

He opened the one that contained his sweatpants, secretly pleased that she preferred to cover herself in his scent, and then helped her by crouching and rolling the bottoms of them. They were far too long for her shorter legs. He straightened and held out his hand, leading her into the living room.

"What has my asshole grandfather done now?"

Drantos saw his father's eyes widen slightly at her question. It amused him. His mate was direct and to the point. He put his arm around her to keep her close.

"Lake's niece was kidnapped by Decker. His sister mated to a member of Decker's clan and lives there. He told her to contact us. He's willing to trade the little girl for Batina and has threatened to kill the child if we don't make the exchange. He left a phone number for us to call, so I did. He obviously believes his enforcer really had grabbed Batina at the ambush, and he thinks Kraven took Dusti away, in an attempt to fool him. He's also aware that Lord Aveoth is hunting for him but he clearly thinks that'll change after Aveoth gets a whiff of Batina. As if scenting her blood will appease the GarLycan leader." Velder snarled. "It won't. I talked to him too."

Drantos clenched one of his fists. He wanted to kill Decker. "What did Aveoth say?"

"He was with his clan handling some internal matter, but he's taking to the air to search for the child and Decker with some of his enforcers. He ordered us to stay out of it." His father looked and sounded frustrated.

"Where's Lake?" Drantos wouldn't be surprised if he'd left to go track the child.

"I told him to wait outside. He's beside himself with worry. The child is barely a toddler. She's defenseless. Damn Decker. Lake's sister said he and a group of his strongest enforcers disappeared after they attacked us on the road yesterday. Then they just showed up and took her child half an hour ago. She also said some of her clan were outraged and left to try to retrieve her daughter, but Decker has a head start. He knocked her out but she wasn't down for long. Her mate wasn't there at the time or they probably would have killed him. I've notified everyone to be on high alert in case that son of a bitch tries to come in here himself and take who he thinks is Batina."

"We should send trackers out to help search for the child." Drantos would volunteer.

His father shook his head. "Lord Aveoth was clear. Our job is to protect your mate and keep her where she's safe. The GarLycans can cover a lot more ground than we can. Decker is desperate. He sounded paranoid on the phone. I don't blame him. He wanted a war and he got one by pissing off Lord Aveoth. It just wasn't the war he wished."

Drantos mulled over the situation. "Why don't you call Decker and tell him we'll make the exchange? That way we can inform Aveoth where he'll be. We'll have a location."

"They could kill the child at the first sign of betrayal. Decker would be caught but at the price of that child's life. I think we should do everything to avoid her death."

He agreed. Decker was a vindictive bastard. "You're right. I'm so mad I can't think straight."

"I've had years of experience dealing with this son of a bitch, Drantos. I have a plan...but you aren't going to like it." His father shifted his attention to Dusti. "I noticed a strong resemblance between you and your sister. Do you believe you could fool Decker into believing you're Batina, even for a few minutes? That will give us time to grab the child and attack once she's clear."

Drantos released Dusti's waist and pushed her behind him, drawing his father's focus. "Hell no! My mate isn't bait. He'll kill her when he realizes she's the wrong granddaughter."

"Calm," his father ordered. "Decker won't harm her if he thinks she's Batina."

"What if he doesn't buy it? He has no use for Dusti." Drantos snarled, enraged. "*No.* I won't risk her life."

"I could do it," Dusti stated.

He spun, glaring at her. "Dusti!"

She put her hands on her hips and scowled at him. "Bat and I *do* look a lot alike."

"I don't agree." They both had blonde hair, blue eyes, and a similar build but Drantos would never mistake the sisters. They weren't twins.

Dusti reached up, placing her hands on his chest as she stepped closer. "Decker Filmore hasn't seen us since we were young girls. I think I was ten and Bat was twelve." She licked her lips. "I can do this. Do you know one of the most annoying things I dealt with, growing up with my sister? I'll tell you," she rushed on. "It was answering the phone. We sound alike. Our friends could never tell us apart until we'd talked to them for a little bit. Bat's only recently talked to our grandfather on the phone a few times. I'll just talk like she would. I can mimic my sister for a few minutes."

"No." Drantos shook his head and cupped his hands over hers.

"You're being unreasonable. You heard your father. I'll go pretending to be Bat so the little girl is set free. You guys can come to the rescue then and arrest him."

"We don't arrest," his father clarified. "We capture."

"Whatever," Dusti murmured. "You'll have Decker and the little girl will be safe." She peered up at Drantos. "I can pull off playing Bat. Who knows her better than I do?"

He studied her features. "Sweetheart, you don't look that much alike."

"Did you miss the part about how he hasn't seen us since we were kids?"

"What if Decker has seen photographs of your sister? She's an attorney. Doesn't she participate in cases that draw media coverage? It's possible he knows what she looks like."

Dusti seemed to consider it. "He hasn't seen her since she's been in a plane crash and had to spend days in the woods, without access to makeup. My sister is always really put together—so I won't be. I can fool him. It's not like I have to pull it off for a long time." She leaned to the side, staring at his father behind him. "Right?"

"Yes. We just need time for Lake to grab the child and get her clear."

Dusti smiled at Drantos. "See? I'll just act snooty and butt hurt for a few minutes. I can do a Bat rant for that long."

It *could* work—but what if it didn't? Drantos considered it.

No. Decker would kill Dusti if he detected the lie. "I can't risk your life. You're my mate. My first priority is your safety."

"It's a little girl," she reminded him, as if he could forget.

"I can't lose you." He tightened his hold on her hands braced against his chest. "Don't ask that of me."

"I'm not asking, Drantos. I'm telling." She leaned to the side again, looking at his father. "I was told mates are allowed to argue in private so you need to step outside because I think that's about to go down."

"Did she just order me out of your home?"

Drantos ignored his father. "I've made my decision."

Dusti's eyes narrowed and she tugged her hands free. "It's not your decision to make. It's *mine* and I'm doing it."

"It's too dangerous! Do you ever listen to me? How did you survive in your world for so long?" Drantos felt his fangs elongating out of annoyance and anger. She could drive a man insane. "I love you. We'll think of another way to get the child back that doesn't involve putting you in danger."

"Wow, that wasn't insulting at all." His mate rolled her eyes. "Your people think I'm useless already. Would one of your women do this? I think they would. Don't even bother answering that."

The matter was too important for the luxury of being sensitive to her feelings. "Our clan women grow claws to fight off an attacker and can shift to run for their lives, if need be. They are able to defend themselves long enough for help to reach them. What are you going to do? Glare at them and yell insults? Perhaps threaten to have them arrested by your human law enforcers? Decker will *kill you*. You admitted he has no use for you. He'll know who you are!"

She surprised him by lunging forward and smacking her hands on his chest. "You're wrong! I'm going to do the same damn thing I've done my entire life—which I survived without you, by the way. I'm going to use my brains and bullshit my way through this." She shoved but wasn't able to move him. "You're pissing me off."

"I know the feeling. I forbid you to do this."

Her mouth opened and she backed away, releasing him. "As if you can. You might be my boyfriend but that doesn't mean you can order me around."

"Mate," he snarled.

"Whatever!" She backed off and defied him further by addressing his father again. "I'll do it. Count me in."

"No!" Drantos spun on his father. "She's not."

His father glanced between them, finally holding his gaze. "It will only be a few moments. We'll follow them at a distance so the lookouts don't detect us and surround the area. Lake only needs to grab the child and run. We can attack then."

"With Dusti in the middle of it without any defenses."

His father took a deep breath and blew it out. "Your mate thinks she can fool Decker. He won't want Batina dead. His life is in danger and he believes the only way to avoid Lord Aveoth killing him is to use the sister as a bargaining chip. You're being unreasonable, Drantos."

"Yes, he is," Dusti huffed.

He turned to her. "Stay out of this. You thought I was insane when I told you about VampLycans. Your thinking process isn't always clear. This is a clan matter."

"You can't have it both ways." The anger drained from her face and he hated to see the sadness in her eyes. "I'm either a part of this clan or I'm not. Let me do something useful. Geez, Drantos. It's a little girl we're talking about. I'd rush into a burning building if I knew one was inside. I'd have to be a total selfish asshole not to. I convinced a freaked-out guy that something looking like a hell hound was actually a bear with mange. I can do this. It's not as if I'm going to have to pretend to be some stranger. It's Bat." She put her hand on her hip, cocked it out, and threw back her head, jutting her chin. "Don't make me take off my high heels and beat you to a pulp, you big ape."

His father snarled. "Ape?"

"That's how Bat speaks," Drantos explained, watching Dusti. "That's what her sister calls Kraven when she's angry."

Dusti eased her tense body and softened her voice. "I *can* do this, Drantos. Give me a chance. I'm not totally useless."

Her need tugged at his heart. "This isn't how you prove that to the clan. This is too dangerous."

"Yeah. I'll get pregnant instead." She snorted.

Drantos sighed and shook his head at his father. "We'll think of another way."

The front door opened and his mother walked in. "What's the holdup? Lake is pacing outside." She nodded at Dusti. "Is she too afraid to go?"

"No. Talk to your son. I said I'd do it," Dusti replied.

Drantos winced when his mother gave him a dirty look. "We'll think of something else."

Dusti glared at him. "You do that. I'm going in the bedroom, away from *you*. I need to cool down." She left the room and slammed the bedroom door.

"Damn." He hated to fight with his mate but he couldn't live with himself if something happened to her.

"She agreed," his father argued. "It will help her be accepted into the clan."

"I don't give a damn about that. I don't want to bury my mate!"

His mother softened her gaze. "I'll go talk to her. I understand." She paused next to him and patted his arms. "The mating is new and she is weak."

Fuck! It was a no-win situation but at least Dusti would be alive. He'd get her to calm and see things his way once his parents left.

Dusti eased open a drawer and found her new shoes. She sat on the bed. The bedroom door opened and she jerked her head up, ready to continue the argument with him.

It was worse. Crayla came in and shut the door at her back, sealing them inside the room together.

"Great," Dusti muttered. "Just what I need. Did you come to tell me I can't pull this off too?"

"No. What are you doing?"

"Exactly what it looks like. I'm putting on my shoes. I'm not a complete idiot. I've already walked around barefoot in the woods and I'd like to avoid doing that again."

"Drantos doesn't want you to go anywhere."

"I heard him. He heard *me*, too." She stood when her feet her covered and hurried into the bathroom, flipping on the light. She stopped in front of the mirror to assess her appearance. She reached up and started to use her fingers to rat out her hair.

"I'm certain there's a hairbrush in one of the drawers."

Dusti shifted her gaze in the mirror and spotted Crayla hanging out in the doorway separating the two rooms. "That's not the look I'm going for. I plan to be the anti-Bat."

"I don't understand what that means."

"Maybe our grandfather saw pictures of my sister. It's possible. She's really neat and tidy. Her makeup is always flawless and she wears expensive clothes. I'm going to give him the version that's opposite." She focused on her reflection again, leaning in and turning her face as she used her fingers to mess up her hair more. "No bun. No makeup." She glanced down at the borrowed clothes. They dwarfed her. "He knows we've had some hellish days and lost everything in the plane crash. He won't expect her to be looking her best unless he's a complete fucking moron. I'll point that out if he says anything."

"Your mate refused to allow you to go in her place."

Dusti sighed. "Is that a law too? Total obedience to your mate? No one's here to watch me defy him so I don't see a problem—unless you plan to tell everyone." She turned and stared into Crayla's eyes. "I can play my sister. All I have to do is stall until the cavalry arrives. Right?"

Crayla arched her eyebrows. "Drantos said no."

"Your husband is the clan leader. So that makes you Mrs. Clan Leader. Don't you overrule your son?"

The other woman smiled and leaned against the wall, crossing her arms over her chest. "My son will be furious."

"He can get over it. Can he unmate me, like a divorce?"

"No."

"That's what I thought. So are you going to help me get that kid back or listen to your unreasonable son? I need you or your husband to help me do this since I have no idea where my grandfather wants me to go, and someone needs to grab the girl at the exchange."

Crayla pushed off from the wall and slowly advanced. She came forward until only a few feet separated them. "Are you prepared to piss my son off that much?"

"I've done it before. Trust me. He didn't enjoy me calling him a nut job and insulting him when I thought he needed medication for his wild imagination. We got past it. Best case, I can tell him I told you so when I come back safe. Worst case, I'll never get to hear him yell at me. That's hard to do when I'm dead."

"Why are you willing to risk your life for a VampLycan child?"

"I'd do it for *any* kid. It's human nature." Dusti hesitated. "And I'm human. Besides, you have to be a total dick to sit on your ass and not try to save a child if given the chance." She bit her lip. "I also really hate my grandfather and always have. I came to Alaska with Bat to give her emotional support once she'd discovered he's a waste of space. It was going to be a bonus to tell him off. I want him caught and stopped. Nobody fucks with my sister—and he planned to big time. I want to take him down. Are those reasons enough?"

It surprised Dusti when Crayla reached out and brushed her fingers against her cheek and smiled. "I like you, Dusti. You have courage and inner strength."

"Thank you."

"You're also willful and stubborn." Crayla dropped her hand and stepped back. "I'll help you. Just don't die. My son would never forgive me."

"I don't plan on it. I'm kind of addicted to breathing."

Crayla chuckled. "Stay here and I'll send my mate and son to our house. They can plot another way to save the girl while us women get this done."

"Nobody is going to whip Drantos if I disobey him, will they? I don't want him offering to take my punishment again." It was her only concern.

"No. I'm in charge of the women and you have my permission to do this."

"Good enough." Dusti faced the mirror again, messing up her hair more.

Crayla left her and Dusti returned to Drantos room. Without claws or fangs, she'd need a weapon. A quick search of his bedside drawers was helpful. She might not have ever fired a gun but she'd seen a lot of movies. The weapon was heavier than she thought it would be. She made certain to point it toward the outer wall as she learned where the safety was, how to remove the clip, and ensured it had bullets. She snapped the clip back in and double-checked the safety again, using her thumb to move it a few times to get a feel for it.

She removed the sweatpants, put on Drantos's underwear, and then put the pants back on. It gave her a place to hide the gun down the borrowed briefs. The gun sagged a bit but she rolled the waist of the sweats to help support the weight. She closed her eyes, thinking about what she was about to do.

It was crazy. It was probably stupid. It might not work...but she needed to try. Everyone thought she was cowardly and that she needed to be protected. Her sister would have the nerve to pull a stunt like this.

That thought gave her the courage to walk out of the bedroom. Crayla waited in the living room but Drantos and his father were gone.

"Are you ready to do this?" Crayla didn't look convinced.

"Yes."

"Be certain, Dusti. This is a dangerous situation. Decker has no honor and he's vicious."

"He wants Bat alive to use her. I'll just *be* her."

"Lake is still outside. I motioned for him to stay when our mates left. I'll go tell him our plan."

"What is that, exactly?"

"I'm going to have Lake call his sister. She'll have the number to reach Decker. Lake will tell him that he grabbed you from our village and wants to make the exchange for his niece. No VampLycan would dishonor another by stealing their mate, but it's behavior that someone like your grandfather shouldn't question."

"Because he's an asshole with no morals. That's something he'd probably do."

"Exactly." Crayla smiled. "Lake will tell me where Decker wants him to take you. I'll give you a head start before telling our mates. They'll rush to save you. Lake will hand you over to Decker, grab the child, and run back in this direction, but by that time, our mates will be on their way to you. Is that clear enough?"

"Crystal." Dusti felt fear but she refused to let it change her mind.

"It's possible that Decker could take you, if they don't reach you in time. We have no idea how many enforcers are protecting him or what kind of escape plan he's made in case of a trap. I'd have one if I were him. Are you prepared for that?"

Dusti understood. "He'll want to take Bat to Aveoth." The memory of meeting the GarLycan leader flashed in her head. "At least Aveoth knows who I really am. He'd let me go and give me back to Drantos. I feel confident about that. He's definitely a badass and I wouldn't be bummed if he beheaded my grandfather. I've seen him in action already."

Crayla regarded her sternly. "Hide your fear. That's important."

"I'm going to be channeling Bat. She doesn't get scared. She gets pissed off and mouthy. Trust me. I've got her down."

Crayla nodded. "Be strong and courageous for your mate. He'll be furious that you defied him but his anger will be lessened if we pull this off without a hitch."

"How pissed is Velder going to be at *you*?"

"He's my mate. He knows me well so he shouldn't be surprised by anything I do. You're a woman in our clan and that child is a VampLycan girl."

"Good enough."

"I appreciate that you're concerned for my relationship with my mate."

Dusti forced a smile. It was more a matter of how angry Drantos would be if she was the reason his parents weren't on speaking terms—on top of going directly against what he'd told her to do.

Chapter Twenty

"Lake?"

Dusti peered around the dark woods behind Drantos's home. Crayla said the VampLycan would be waiting for her there. Movement to her right drew her attention and the big guy from the store stepped out from behind a massive tree. Enough light showed from the house for her to distinguish his grim expression. He didn't look happy to see her.

"I'm desperate to save Asha but this goes against my better judgment."

She could respect that. "Is that your niece's name? Asha? It's pretty."

"She's a pretty girl."

"How old is she?"

"Almost two."

Dusti *really* hated her grandfather. He'd kidnapped a baby, not a little girl. It made it so much worse. "I know the risks. Let's do this, okay?"

"I wouldn't be doing this if Crayla hadn't ordered me to. She said Velder would agree with her. Your mate is going to want to kill me, isn't he?"

She decided to change the subject. "Did you call your sister and were you able to reach Decker?"

"Yes."

"And?"

"He gave me a place to meet. I don't think this is a good plan."

"Not you too." She sighed, feeling frustrated. "Focus on your niece. I can handle myself. Just get me there, grab that baby, and haul ass to get her back here. That's the plan. Crayla said she told you what we had in mind when she came back from talking to you."

"She did. I just don't think this is going to work."

"I can pull off being my sister to a man who hasn't seen us in twenty years. Give me some credit."

"Decker could hurt you if he figures out you're the wrong sister."

"I'm wearing Drantos's clothes for a reason. I smell like him, don't I? It masks my scent. I learned that when I met Aveoth. I can do this. Just get me there and save your niece."

"I don't know if you're brave or stupid."

"Let's call it a bit of both. Do you need to tie me up or something? Crayla said you could move faster if you're carrying me."

He shifted his stance some, his shadow moving. "Drantos is going to kill me for this."

"He'll be too busy yelling at me."

He snorted.

"Let's get this show on the road. We don't have a lot of time." She glanced back, spotting Crayla watching them from the back porch. "We're wasting what little time we have." She faced Lake again. "We need to get going before Drantos and his dad come back to the house and notice I'm gone."

"I told Decker I couldn't get a vehicle so he agreed to meet us close to the border of our lands. It might be uncomfortable for you but I can move faster if you're over my shoulder."

"I didn't expect this to be a picnic." She stepped closer.

He stripped out of his shirt. "I'm going to put this over your back to further hide your scent. There are guards posted that we'll need to pass. If they scent me, they'll just think I'm out for a run to rid myself of nervous energy. They'll contact your mate if they pick up his scent you're carrying, wondering why you're out in the woods. They know he's with his father right now."

"Smart." She reached out and felt the big man's broad shoulders when he crouched down in front of her. He gripped her hips gently and pulled her closer to his body until she bent, her pelvis against him. He released her hips and hooked one arm over her legs as he stood.

Memories of when Drantos had carried her returned. This time she was willingly letting a man treat her like a sack of laundry. He threw his shirt over her, covering as much of her as he could.

"Be very quiet." He paused. "What is that pressed against my chest?"

"Gun."

He sighed.

"I don't have claws. I stole one of Drantos's."

"Do you know how to use it?"

"Of course," she lied.

"Good." He spun, moving fast.

Dusti closed her eyes since she couldn't see anything anyway. All her recent conversations with her sister replayed through her mind. She mentally repeated the way Bat spoke, mimicking her. Her sister could be condescending and bitchy. It extended to her tone of voice.

The practice helped pass the time as Lake ran with her. She had to give him a lot of credit for using his hands to cushion her body from a lot of jostling around. It wasn't exactly comfy but it wasn't painful either. His breathing hardly changed. VampLycans were really fit.

Lake finally stopped running and Dusti opened her eyes, lifting her head. He bent and helped her ease away from him but kept close.

"We're near. I smell strangers," he whispered.

"Game on," she whispered back and cleared her throat. "Do you know who I am, you big gorilla?" She raised her voice. "I'll have you arrested for kidnapping, and hell, offensive groping. I'm an attorney. You chose the wrong woman to fuck with!"

Lake turned his head and she could feel him staring at her. She shrugged, shoving his shirt at him. "Grab the baby and go as fast as you can," she breathed.

"Shut up," he loudly snarled. He gripped her hand and yanked her none too gently forward. Dusti startled but didn't stumble.

"Let me go! Did you hear me, you Neanderthal? I know dozens of judges who will throw your ass in the slammer and toss away the key. It doesn't mean shit that we're in Alaska. You kidnapped a resident of California. I'll have your pathetic ass extradited there to stand trial. Get your hands off me!"

He pulled her out into a clearing and the moon helped her see a bit. He stopped there. "Shut up or I'll knock you out. You're unpleasant."

"Fuck off, dickhead. Where's my grandfather? That poor man is sick and you drag him out here for some ransom scheme? That's a federal crime. You and that band of thugs are going to be lucky if you don't get the death penalty for everything you've done. And my sister Dusti better be alive! I don't know what you idiots did with her but I'll see you in hell if you touched a hair on my baby sister's head."

Movement came from the tree lines in at least four directions and Dusti's heart hammered. Fear rose but she tried to push it down. They could pick it up with their freaky sense of smell. Lake moved behind her and gripped her throat. He didn't hurt her but was putting on a show. He had sworn to break her neck if Decker didn't bring him his niece.

"Where is Asha? I brought you Batina. I'd love to kill her if you lied. She's been insulting me ever since I took her." Lake forced her head up with his hold on her throat. "My claws are out. I'll rip her head off."

She was glad he lied. Just his fingertips pressed against her skin.

"Don't," a deep voice ordered. "You can have the brat. I'm sending her out to you. Take her and go. My enforcers said you weren't followed."

Dusti got a fix on the voice and shifted her eyes in that direction. Decker Filmore had to be the dark shape across the small clearing, near the trees. A smaller form appeared from the woods.

Lake's hand on her throat flexed. "Asha! Come to me now. It's Uncle. Run, baby."

Dusti pressed her chin against his hand and watched the small body rush at them. She couldn't get a real good look at her since it was too dark. The child reached them and slammed into her and Lake. The kid sounded upset with her ragged breathing.

Lake leaned in and pressed his lips against Dusti's ear. "Help will come soon."

She reached back and surreptitiously patted his leg. He released her throat and gave her a shove forward before snatching up the kid and pulling her into his arms. Dusti turned her head, watching him disappear into the woods. She could hear him running. He wasn't being quiet.

"Asshole! You better run!" she yelled, then spun. "Grandpa? Are you out there? It's Batina! You don't know the hell I've been through. Those bastards took Dusti!" She needed to keep him distracted and convinced he had the right sister for as long as possible. It would give Lake a chance to get away. She lifted her hand and placed it on her forehead. "It's been a nightmare."

* * * * *

Drantos sat across the desk from his father. Both of them stared at the silent phone. It hadn't rung to let them know Decker had been captured by the GarLycans or that the girl had been found by the members of Decker's own clan searching for her.

His father sighed. "I hate waiting. I feel useless."

"I know what you mean. I should go check on Dusti." He sat up straighter and gripped the arms of the chair.

"You need to give her time to cool down. It's something you'll learn being mated. Sometimes a little space is a good thing. Your mother is with her. We'll wait for word together here."

"We don't sit shit out. We should be out there searching for that child."

"I agree but Lord Aveoth made a request. For whatever reason, he doesn't want our clan involved."

"We already are. Decker stole that child because he thinks we have what he wants."

"I agree with that too, but he was clear. Stay put and out of it. He must have his reasons."

Drantos couldn't remain seated anymore and stood, pacing the floor. "Aveoth must be really pissed at Decker."

"It's understandable. Decker is trying to use his weakness against him. And you should call him by his title."

Drantos paused and stared at his father. "He'll always just be Aveoth to me."

"They are very formal, son. It's their way."

"We were friends once."

"I remember. That was before he challenged his father and became the GarLycan ruler."

"So what?"

"We have Vampire blood running in our veins. Gargoyles are never going to forget that. We might be allies but that doesn't mean his people would welcome a close association. Some might question his ruthlessness if he showed any favoritism to you or Kraven."

"That's such bullshit."

"You don't know them the way I do."

Drantos studied his father. "Right, you had a GarLycan lover before you mated, didn't you?"

"Yes. I learned a lot about them from her. She feared some of her people would find out about us. It was taboo."

"GarLycans can take VampLycans as lovers."

"Their men. Not their women. She feared reprisals for both of us if her clan found out." His father shrugged. "It only lasted a week but it was memorable. She was very sweet. Her mother was a Lycan and her father a Gargoyle."

"I take it she took after her mother?"

His father hesitated. "She physically took after her father. She had wings and could shell out her body. Inside she was Lycan. She had to hide it from her father. They see emotions as a defect. I got the impression her life was a struggle because she did feel so much."

"No wonder she took a VampLycan lover."

"She said her father had arranged for her to mate someone inside her clan. Daughters don't get to chose who they're paired with."

"That's depressing. What about finding a true mate?"

"They are expected to ignore the Lycan side."

"Damn." Drantos sank back into the chair.

"Yes. She didn't want her first lover to be a cold one. Those were her words. Their clan is very formal. You should have seen the way she dressed. Every part of her, from the neck down, had to be covered. Mates sleep in separate bedrooms and only share a bed during sex. Afterward the man leaves. They often restrain their women so they can't touch their men. It's too intimate otherwise. They have titles and call each other by those, even with family members. It's a deep show of disrespect not to. The only exceptions are mates, but only in private."

Drantos tried to imagine that but failed.

"I just told you what *sex* is like between GarLycan mates. Imagine how distanced they are from the concept of friendship. The fact that you're VampLycan would have made some of that clan nervous if their leader spent time with you. So far they've kept the alliance between us but that doesn't mean they look at us as equals. I don't think they ever will."

"I almost feel sorry for Aveoth."

"I had dealings with Lord Abotorus when he still ruled." Velder paused. "Ice cold. He spoke to his son with contempt. He'd bring young Aveoth to meetings to show him how to deal with us. I wasn't surprised when the boy grew into a man and challenged him. I saw no compassion or love at all when he looked at his son."

"I'm glad we don't have that kind of relationship."

His father snorted. "We don't see eye to eye on everything."

"I respect and love you. I'd never challenge you. You're my father."

"I love you too. We show our emotions and welcome close bonds in families.

GarLycans aren't like us."

The door opened and Drantos's mother entered. He shot to his feet at her forbidding look. "What's wrong?"

She held his gaze but then averted it to his father. "You need to gather your enforcers quickly and rush to the clearing to the northwest. It's the small meadow with the yellow flowers in summer. You know the one." She looked at Drantos. "I agreed to allow Dusti to try to save the girl. Lake and her should be arriving there at any moment. Go quickly. She's waiting for you to rescue her."

Drantos lost his mind.

He bellowed, his claws ripping out of his fingertips and his fangs painfully wrenching from his gums.

"She wanted to do it," his mother stated calmly. "She's trying to prove she's worthy of being a VampLycan in this clan. You *will* respect that, even if you don't agree. She's a woman, and one of mine. Have faith in her abilities to survive."

Drantos refused to hear any more. He started to shift, moving fast toward the door. His father cursed, following.

He needed to get to Dusti before Decker realized he had the wrong sister.

* * * * *

Without warning, someone snuck up behind Dusti and gripped her upper arms. "I have her."

The voice was new and male. Dusti would have just gasped but she was playing Bat. Her sister would have hated to be touched. She twisted, smacking at the guy. "Get your hands off me, dirtbag! What part of 'I'm an attorney' and 'will see you in hell' do you not understand? I'm fed up with you assholes groping me." She smacked him again and he actually released her, stepping back.

"You're safe now, Batina."

Dusti clenched her teeth and turned back around. Her grandfather stalked across the clearing, coming right at her.

"I thought Los Angeles was bad." She reached down and smoothed the shirt, a

Bat move if there ever was one. It also put her hands closer to the gun hidden in her underwear. It had shifted so part of the handle or barrel dug into part of her inner thigh. "You need to call the police and the FBI! Dusti's been kidnapped by a bunch of crazed lumberjacks. I don't know where they've taken her. To add insult to injury, they gave me these horrible clothes, my suit was ruined, I don't know where my briefcase is..." She huffed. "And those jerks broke my phone too!"

"It's going to be fine, Batina. I'm here now."

She turned her head, glaring up at the dark shape of her grandfather's thug. "Back off, barbarian."

He did it. Decker came closer. "Let me look at you."

She faced him. "Don't you people own flashlights?"

"Get one," Decker ordered. "She can't see." He reached out and took her hand.

She wanted to yank it away but that might let him know she was aware he was a bad guy. She grasped it tight instead. "What in the hell is going on? Who was that kid? Thank you so much for rescuing me."

He sniffed. She hoped all he picked up was Drantos.

"I smell, don't I? They forced me to wear some guy's stuff. My suit was torn in the plane crash and we were dragged through the woods to some backward town." She tried to sound outraged. "Do you have a phone? I'll call my legal assistant and have her send me clothing immediately." She wasn't sure if Bat could do that but she was willing to bluff. Every second put Lake and that child farther away and out of danger of being captured once the jig was up.

"I'm going to take you to a friend of mine who lives near here. He'll have a working phone and women's clothing for you to wear." He released her hand.

She let him go. He was probably speaking of Aveoth. They weren't friends and she wasn't stupid. "But we have to find Dusti! She's probably terrified. The poor thing gets frightened easily and she's sick. My law firm will pay whatever they demand if they want money. I just need to contact them."

"They are cowards. They wouldn't harm her." Decker cleared his throat. "You can also bathe once we reach his home."

"Good." She peered around, spotting four man shapes close to them. She lowered her voice. "Who are they?"

"My employees," he lied. "One of them will carry you. I see you don't have decent shoes."

"They stole my four hundred dollar Italian pumps! And I don't want to be touched. I've been manhandled enough. I'd actually just like a few minutes to calm down after being toted through the woods like a sack of potatoes over that gorilla's back. Do you have any idea how traumatic this has been for me?"

He hesitated.

"I've been through hell! You have no idea, Grandfather. I don't trust anyone after the last few days I've had. I just want to decompress and not have everyone looming around me. Can I have some breathing room? I need them to back off! What is it with people who live here and invading personal space? It's so damn rude."

"Of course."

The shapes moved away. Dusti lifted her hand again and rested it on her forehead. "Thank you." She dropped her hand and did a little pacing. She glanced around, watching the dark figures blend into the woods, and noted their locations.

"We really should get you to my friend's home, Batina. It isn't safe out here. Those criminals could be searching for you."

"Just give me a moment to meditate." That sounded totally Californian. She slipped her hands down her body and gave him her back. She dug the gun out of her underwear. "I'm going to throw the book at all the assholes involved with what was done to me."

"We'll sort this out later. We need to go," Decker urged.

She turned her head, peering at him. She wished she could make out his features. It would be nice to know what he looked like. It didn't really matter though. "Mom never talked about you. Why is that?"

"She was a foolish teenager when she ran away. She didn't understand about duty and family loyalty. Now isn't the time to discuss this."

"I disagree."

"I'm your grandfather." He sounded pissed. "That's all you need to know, and that I'm going to do what is best for you. Right now, that's taking you far from here."

"And giving me to Lord Aveoth?" She figured Lake had likely had more than enough time to get a good head start. "Maybe I don't *want* to become the lover of a GarLycan. Do you even care?"

He sucked in a breath.

She hid the gun along her hip and slowly turned to face him. Her thumb found the safety and rested there. "I know you have a phone on you. They have these nifty lights on them. Pull yours out and show me your face."

He didn't move at all.

"Are you even Decker Filmore?"

"Of course I am."

"Show me your face, Grandpa. I want to see you."

"What the hell did Velder say to you?"

"Show me your face and I'll tell you."

He moved and she saw his hand fumbling with something. It surprised her when he actually turned on the phone and the faint glow of light lit his face. It had been a long time since she'd seen him but recognition hit. She stepped closer, studying him. He appeared no older than his mid-thirties.

"You look amazingly good for what? Two hundred years old?"

"Give or take a few years." His tone grew cold. "I'm glad you know what we are. Velder lied to you. They're a bunch of idiots who are going to get our race killed. They hide from the world like the cowards they are. We're VampLycans, feared by all! We're at the top of the food chain."

"Is that what you told my grandmother before you killed her?" She expected him to deny it.

"That stupid bitch was always making me appear weak in front of my clan, with her nagging ways and sympathy for those who broke the laws," he snarled. "She went behind my back one time too many. I have no use for anyone who stands in my way. She didn't deserve to live."

Dusti stepped closer to him. "I guess I take after you in at least one way. I don't think *you* deserve to live, either. You're a piece of shit."

His nose flared and she saw his eyes narrow.

"You were always an asshole to me, Grandpa." She flipped off the safety of the gun. "You shouldn't call other people idiots when you can't even tell your own granddaughters apart. I'm *Dusti*—and I'm not going to let you hurt Bat."

Rage registered on his face and his mouth opened. His fangs grew as he snarled.

"You know what else you were wrong about? I'm not totally human. I smell like it but I take after the woman you mated and killed. I'm not sick. I just needed some blood."

Another growl came from him.

"You could have used either of us to give to Aveoth," she went on. "I met him, by the way. He really hates your ass. That's one scary guy. I already have a mate, so he let me go. I guess I should thank you for luring Bat and I here. Drantos is the best thing that has ever happened to me."

"I'll kill him and Aveoth will accept you then!"

"No, you won't. You've hurt enough people. I always knew you were an asshole but you're actually a monster. Bat defends criminals for a living because she feels some people might actually be innocent. You're not. You just like to hurt people and step on them to get your way. Someone needs to stop you."

His arm shot out and he grabbed her throat. "No one can. You think those cowards from Velder's clan are capable of taking me out? I'll slaughter them all and make you watch!"

"It's never going to happen."

"It will. And Aveoth will help me."

"You're delusional. Aveoth wants you dead."

"He's addicted to the blood. I'll bleed you in front of him and he'll agree to *anything* to have you. He has a weakness—and I intend to use it against him."

"He was told about Bat, and do you know what he said? 'Keep her away from me.' He doesn't want her either. It's *over*. He knows what you're up to and he's a badass son of a bitch. I watched him kill one of your men. He didn't even break a sweat. Boom. It was over that fast. He moves like the wind."

"Smelling the blood will change his mind. I'll *own* him."

"You're a moron." She actually leaned closer, glaring into his eyes. "People say I'm the sweet one but they're wrong. Go to hell, Grandpa."

She lifted the gun and shoved it against the front of his shirt over his heart. He looked down right as she pulled the trigger.

She fired at least four bullets into him as he staggered back, releasing her and dropping the phone in his hand. She could still make out his shape when he hit the ground from the dim light of the moon. She targeted his chest and fired two more bullets, striking him again.

A loud snarl came from the woods. She turned and pointed the gun in that direction. "He's dead! It's over! You can kill me for that but if I were you, I'd save my own ass. Look up. Incoming GarLycans, assholes! That was the signal," she bluffed. "Here they come."

She heard something crash through the woods in a few different directions but nothing came out into the clearing. She did a fast turn, expecting one of them to attack from behind, but nothing did. Her pounding heart slowed after long moments passed and none of her grandfather's men attacked. She walked over to the phone and bent, picking it up. A touch of the screen lit it up brighter and she turned it, getting closer to the man on the ground. She pointed the gun at Decker Filmore, ready to fire again if he tried to grab her.

Blood soaked the blue dress shirt he wore. It looked as if she'd shot him in the stomach at least twice and he'd taken four to the chest. He wasn't moving and his eyes were closed. She couldn't detect him breathing.

Decker Filmore was dead.

Dusti wasn't sure what to feel about that. She backed away and turned, holding up the phone for the limited amount of light it put off. She was alone with her dead grandfather in the clearing. The men working for him had taken off.

"Now I wait," she surmised. The wind blew and the gun in her hand felt heavy. She wondered how long it would take Drantos to arrive.

She turned around, staring at the body on the ground. "I don't feel guilty. You killed my grandma and made my mother so afraid she left everything she knew. I bet that was terrifying for her." Emotion choked her. "You would have used my sister without caring how miserable she would have been. That Aveoth guy would have ended up killing her at some point. You didn't care about us, so why should I care that you're dead? I don't. Never fuck with a Dawson."

Chapter Twenty-One

Dusti backed away from her grandfather's body. It unsettled her, being close to it.

A howl tore through the woods and she faced the direction she believed it had originated from. It was where she'd come out of the trees with Lake.

She opened her mind, trying to feel Drantos. She caught an emotion that wasn't hers. Rage.

She winced, figuring he'd be mad and hadn't been wrong. He was coming for her. She sensed him getting closer.

Dusti touched the screen again to activate the phone and used it like a flashlight to enter the woods. "I'm over here," she called out.

Something crashed through the woods at a frightening speed. She found a fallen log and climbed up on top of it. The phone light wasn't good at showing her more than about four feet in front of her. She held it up, searching for any sign of movement.

She spotted a big beast just as it leaped over a bush and crashed into the ground in front of her.

It skidded to a stop and sat on its hunches, just staring up at her with black eyes.

"Drantos?"

He shook his head.

Fear came instantly but he didn't attack. He just stayed in front of her, close to the ground. He watched her with those eerie eyes until more noises came from behind him. He turned his head and lifted up, walking a little to the right of her.

Another shifted beast bounded over the same bush and it almost struck the log she stood on. All four legs of the big furred body skidded on the loose leaves covering the ground until it came to a stop. It didn't stay put. It snarled and lunged at her.

She gasped and almost fell off her precarious perch. Emotion flooded her though and she froze. The furry body hit hers but she didn't hit the ground. One of the

VampLycan's limbs wrapped around her and she landed on Drantos's big body after he twisted in the air.

He shifted forms, his fur receding to be replaced by skin. His other arm wrapped around her, almost crushing her to his big body. Something dark sailed over them then stopped. She lifted her head. The phone and gun had been torn from her grasp when she'd fallen. The dark shape of another shifted VampLycan stood near their heads.

How could you go against my orders?

She flinched as Drantos yelled inside her head.

She braced her hands on his chest and lifted up. "Did Lake make it back to the village with his niece?"

"Yes," his father answered. "We passed him on our way to you."

She jerked at Velder's harsh tone.

Dusti? Drantos yelled at her again. *Answer me!*

"Where's Decker?" Velder snarled.

That's what I want to know. How did you get away from him? I was told he had you.

"Is she alright?" She recognized Red's voice.

"Answer," Velder demanded.

Dusti? I told you not to go, damn it. Are you injured? Hurt? Where the hell is that bastard Decker?!

"Enough," Dusti shouted. "You're all talking to me at once. I just had the wind knocked out of me from being tackled." She took a deep breath and blew it out, staring down where she knew Drantos's face was from the sound of his heavy breathing. "I'm okay. Everything is fine."

"Where is Decker?"

She flinched. Her new father-in-law still sounded furious. She stared up at his hulking shape. He wasn't on all fours anymore. He stood tall and was just a big silhouette in the shadows.

Dusti wiggled her hips and Drantos released her. She stood. "I killed him," she admitted.

"What?"

"Um, I took the gun from your nightstand drawer. I shot him. Trust me. He's dead. I hit him in the chest four times, and twice in the stomach after he had fallen down."

"No fucking way," Red gasped.

"Way," Dusti muttered, turning to try to make out Drantos's cousin. She could barely see anything at all so she gave up, blindly turning to Drantos again. "He didn't know about the gun until it was too late. I hid it. Then I bluffed so his men ran away instead of killing me."

"*What?*" Drantos gasped again.

"What part of that is confusing you or so hard to believe? I shot my grandfather and then yelled at his men that the GarLycans were flying in, told them the shots were my signal for them to attack. I can't see a damn thing but I heard them running for their lives."

"Son of a bitch," Red muttered.

Drantos yanked her against him, nearly crushing her in a bear hug. "You could have been killed!"

"He thought I was Bat at first. He needed her alive. He didn't know it was me until I told him—by then it was too late and we were close enough for me not to miss him when I fired the gun. I would have shot him more but I didn't know how many bullets were in the gun. I didn't exactly count them. I think there's eight, right? I wanted a few to spare in case not all of his men ran away."

"Unbelievable," Velder rasped. "Where's Decker's body, Dusti?"

"In the clearing. It was freaking me out, standing so near it."

Drantos shifted his hold on her and lifted her up his body. They left the trees and her vision got a little better with the moon to help. She saw two large shapes next to them. Red and Velder, staying close.

Until Velder suddenly sprinted forward.

She could make out enough to see her father-in-law wasn't sporting any clothes. The sight of his bare ass wasn't something she wanted to see but she couldn't help it. He walked over to a spot in the longer grass and crouched.

"Damn it," Drantos hissed.

"What?" Dusti gripped his shoulders.

"His body isn't here."

"I smell a lot of blood." Red walked away to go to Velder.

"What do you mean his body isn't here?" Dusti shook her head. "He was dead! He wasn't breathing." Drantos eased his hold and let her slide down his body. He clutched her hand, holding on tight.

Velder rose and walked a little. Red followed him.

"What is it, Dad?"

Velder paused. "There's a blood trail and two sets of prints. It looks as if an enforcer returned for him." He started walking again and then bent, lifting something from the ground.

"What is that? I can't make it out." Dusti hated being at a disadvantage.

"Clothing," Drantos whispered. "Someone shifted." He sniffed the air. "Not Decker's scent."

"I shot him six damn times." Dusti refused to believe he might be alive. "Six! He wasn't breathing."

"We're hard to kill." Drantos tugged her closer.

"It's possible he died and they just took his body. Get her out of here, Drantos." Velder fell to his knees. "Shift back, Red. Help me track them to be certain. Let's end this."

Drantos let go of Dusti's hand and gripped her hips, lifting her. He flung her over his shoulder and proceeded to carry her back into the trees.

She placed her hands just above his ass to brace her body so her face didn't slam into his back. "I can walk."

"Shut up. I'm angry right now." He stopped. "Find my gun. It's around here."

"I can't see a damn thing," Dusti admitted.

"I wasn't talking to you, mate. More of our clan just arrived. Be silent."

She tried to hold back her irritation as Drantos gave orders to people around them that she couldn't see. He had a right to be upset with her but he was taking it to the extreme. He told some of them to go help his father, others to spread out and search the area for any of Decker's enforcers. Then he marched through the woods with her. His mind was closed off when she tried to sense what he was thinking or feeling.

"I really hate when you carry me like this," she finally sighed.

"You're lucky I don't spank your ass. What were you thinking? You could have died."

"I told you I could play Bat. I totally faked him out and he didn't even know it was me until I threw it in his face. I sounded just like her when she's pissed off. I have it down pat. Can you please put me down? I hate feeling like a sack of laundry."

"Goddamn it." Drantos snarled. "Take this seriously. Do you understand that he could have killed you?"

"I knew that but I'm not useless."

He came to a jarring halt. "I never thought you were."

"They do," she whispered. "I needed to show them I'm a part of your clan, Drantos. Tell me one woman who wouldn't have willingly done what I did if they'd been in my shoes. I know you're mad but you wouldn't even listen to reason."

He growled and began walking again.

"I'm okay. Lake got his niece back. That's all that matters, right?"

"Damn it, Dusti."

She heard his tone soften, some of the anger fading. It encouraged her to try to lighten his mood more. "Think I'll get that official clan title after this stunt? Dusti, the Master Bullshitter."

He snorted. It almost sounded like a harsh laugh. "Shut up."

She closed her mouth. He took her home, slammed the front door after entering, and then eased her onto her feet. She couldn't help but stare at his naked body. A smile played at her lips.

He reached out and clasped her jaw, lifting it. "Don't you dare try to distract me. Sex isn't going to calm me down."

"I wasn't going to do that. I was just admiring the view."

"You shouldn't have left our home." He eased his hold and caressed her cheek. "You drive me crazy."

"It's more human nature and I *am* mainly that."

He frowned.

"We generally have this overriding desire to help someone, Drantos. My grandfather kidnapped a little girl. The easiest way to get her back was to give him what he wanted."

His lips pressed into a firm line, relaying his displeasure.

She studied his eyes. They were beautiful and dark blue at that moment. "Don't be mad. It did work out. That little girl is safe and so am I. Look on the bright side."

"I'm afraid to ask what you think that is."

"I shot him. Bat and Kraven can come home. She's safe now."

"You could have been *killed*. That's all I can think about. Do you know what that would have done to me? You're my life, Dusti. My mate." His voice deepened. "It's my job to protect you. I can't do that if you defy me and put yourself at risk."

"Do you want a mate or a trained pet?"

He scowled.

"I have a mind of my own. I don't take orders well. You don't either, or you would have let me go in the first place."

"Are you blaming me for this stunt you pulled?"

"No. Don't get bent out of shape. I'm just saying we're two people in a relationship and we both have our own opinions. We're not always going to agree with each other. You can't expect me to always do what you say."

"I can when it comes to your safety."

"You said it yourself. You live in a dangerous world. I'm living here with you now."

"God! You drive me crazy."

He suddenly lunged and took possession of her mouth, kissing her hard. She pressed her body against his, clutching his waist.

The sound of the door opening broke them apart and Dusti twisted her head to see who had interrupted them. Crayla entered.

"You're alive."

"No thanks to you," Drantos grumbled. "She's my mate. Don't ever pull rank when it comes to her again. You have no business helping her do something foolish."

"Stop!" Dusti turned, blocking Drantos's body as best she could from his mother.

Crayla crossed her arms over her chest. "Asha will be returned to her mother alive and well. We can thank your mate for that."

"You helped her leave my home and talked Lake into going along with it."

Dusti sighed. "Did *anyone* hear me say stop? I meant don't argue, if that wasn't clear." She turned her head to stare up at Drantos. He moved closer, wrapping an arm loosely around her middle. "Please don't do this. Be mad at *me*."

He held her gaze. "I *am* mad at you. I'm *furious* with her."

"Where's your father?"

He broke eye contact to glare at Crayla. "He and some of our men are tracking the enforcers that are with Decker."

"I killed my grandfather," Dusti added.

Crayla gaped at her. "What?"

"She took my gun." Drantos held her tighter. "It's a miracle he didn't smell it on her or take it from her."

"Where did you hide the weapon?"

"In my underwear. Actually, Drantos's underwear. I had to borrow his."

"Close to your body and hidden under a few layers of clothing. That was smart."

Praise from Crayla was nice and appreciated. "Thanks."

"Don't encourage her, Mom."

"She did well. She survived and the child is safe." Crayla's tone softened. "How are you handling your first kill, Dusti? I'll assume you've never taken a life before."

She'd been running on so many emotions that the reality of shooting Decker Filmore really hadn't sunk in yet. She admitted as much. "He was a bad guy though. I doubt it will keep me up at night."

The door opened again and Velder strode in. He sported a pair of faded jeans and nothing else. He went to his mate and pulled her into a hug. They held each other close.

"What happened?" Drantos was the one to ask.

Velder nuzzled Crayla's cheek with his nose before he looked at his son. "They had a zip line rigged. They got away. I wasn't willing to risk our men following them in case they cut the line from the other side. It was a steep, rocky ravine below. The fall could have killed them…but I do have worse news." He dropped his gaze to Dusti. "We saw signs that Decker survived."

"No way. I shot him six damn times!"

"I found a bloody set of prints near where they crossed. They were his. They carried him for a ways but he definitely walked to the edge of that cliff."

"Son of a bitch," Drantos cursed.

"Unbelievable." Dusti was in shock. "He wasn't breathing. I'm sure I got his heart or his lungs. Four of them were chest hits!"

"We're really hard to kill." Crayla sighed. "You should have placed every bullet in his head."

"I would have had to lift the gun up higher to hit him there. I kind of hid it between our bodies so he didn't see it until I'd already opened fire. I didn't think to keep shooting once I thought he was gone."

"We also heal fast," Drantos reminded her.

"From being dead? It's not my fault you VampLycans are freaks of nature. Don't give me that aggravated tone, Drantos. Nobody takes four hits to the chest and two to the gut, then gets up. That's just wrong."

"Regardless," Velder stated. "Decker is alive and got away. I need to make a lot of calls. I'll report to Lord Aveoth what direction Decker took. I'll also alert his clan that the girl is here with us and make arrangements for her parents to join her here." He looked at his mate then. "You and I will talk afterward."

"She's one of mine. Don't give me that look, Vel."

"Not this again," Dusti muttered. "Let's just clear the air now. I wanted to do it. You wanted me to pretend to be Bat. The only one who had a problem with it was Drantos. My mate, my problem. I refuse to be the reason my mate-in-laws argue."

Both of them looked at her.

She shrugged. "I hate bullshit."

"Obviously not, master of bullshitting," Drantos drawled.

Dusti laughed, turning her head to grin at him. "I do like that title."

"What title?" Velder didn't sound amused.

"Never mind." Drantos shook his head. "It's a private joke between my mate and me. She's fine. You both should go. We have our own argument to finish."

They left and Dusti turned in his arms, wrapping hers around his waist. "Are we okay? I love you."

"I love you too but you're going to drive me insane."

"You're a tough guy. I think you can handle me."

"I can think of many ways to do that." Desire flooded the bond they had, the emotion filling her.

"Make-up sex?"

"Make-up sex," he confirmed. "You have a lot to atone for."

"Sounds sexy."

"It does."

"Good. And I can't wait until Kraven and Bat return."

"I know you miss your sister."

"I do but she's really going to piss your parents off." She grinned. "Tag, she'll be it. I almost feel sorry for your family. Almost."

He laughed. "I want to make love to you right now."

"That sounds like heaven."

A slight noise sounded from outside. Dusti immediately tensed, prepared for someone else to walk into the house unannounced. "Why don't you lock the door? I'm so sick of interruptions."

"So am I."

She let him go and he stalked over to the front door, bolting it.

Chapter Twenty-Two

Dusti entered the bedroom first. "Alone at last!"

"Yes." Drantos followed, closing and locking that door too. "I'm going to shower. I've been running in the woods and I'm covered in sweat. I'll be right back."

"Hurry."

She watched him go but then decided to join him. He'd already turned on the water and was standing under the spray by the time she'd stripped and entered the bathroom. She enjoyed the view of his body through the steamy interior of the shower stall. He had his head tipped back but quickly sensed her, turning his head and smiling.

"Do you have room in there for me?"

He shoved open the door and held out his hand. "Always."

Dusti stepped inside and tried to open her mind. Waves of passion hit her and she reached out, grabbing hold of Drantos. He chuckled and hooked an arm around her. "Open up to me."

"You're the one who closed me off. You've been guarded since you found me. I could only pick up that you wanted me a few minutes ago."

"I was angry but I'm not anymore."

"So I feel." She caressed his skin.

He groaned, lowering his mouth to hers. "You make me so hot. You burn me up, sweetheart."

Dusti closed her eyes and could relate. She loved the way he kissed her. It went from mild to an overdriving need to be inside her. She wanted him so bad it hurt. He dominated her mouth with his tongue, picking her right up off her feet and pinning her against the stall tiles. She lifted her legs, hooking them around his waist. Lust rolled between them, reflecting off each other until he shifted his hips and entered her. Dusti cried out at the feel of his cock filling her.

Drantos tore his mouth away from hers and went for her throat. His tongue swiped over her skin, right before he bit. His fangs caused a slight amount of pain but he thrust up into her at the same time, distracting her with more pleasure. Her gums began to throb but she wasn't sure if it were really her sensation or his. The taste of blood wet her lips and Drantos moaned against her throat. He moved faster, fucking her hard and deep.

She clawed at his shoulders and knew she wasn't going to last long. The climax tore through her in the next instant and she shouted his name. Drantos came with her. She could feel it both in her body and through the mental bond between them. He clutched her tighter and sank to his knees with her still wrapped around him. Water poured down them both from the showerhead, dousing their upper bodies. It didn't matter.

Drantos removed his fangs from her neck and licked at the spot he'd bitten. He chuckled. "That was a quickie. Ready to go to bed and do this a hell of a lot slower?"

Dusti became aware that she had her mouth still pressed to his skin when she tried to talk. She opened her eyes when she pulled away and saw that she'd bitten him too. There were no puncture wounds from fangs but the familiar twin crescents from her smooth row of teeth. She'd broken the skin in a few places but it wasn't bad.

"I'm so sorry."

"Don't be. You can always bite me. I heal, remember?"

He shifted so the water wasn't pouring down on them and she met his gaze. "That was something."

"We're newly mated and we had a scare. It's normal."

"I've never gotten off that fast before."

"You've never been mated before either." He changed his hold on her. "Stand. Let me turn off the water."

She hated to untangle their bodies but did with his help. He rose up to stand next to her and twisted off the flow of water. He threw open the door and stepped out, just running a towel quickly over his body. He dropped it and grabbed another, opening it for her.

"Come here."

She stepped out and he dried her body as quickly as he had his own. He threw that towel aside as well and surprised her by sweeping her off her feet. He carried her to the bed and gently laid her down.

"Now that we have the edge off, I'm going to make love to you."

She smiled. "I felt pretty loved."

He chuckled and gripped her ankles, lifting and spreading her legs. He climbed onto the bed with her, pushed her legs up, and she bent her knees. Drantos released her before coming down on top of her. He didn't kiss her lips this time but instead surprised her by going for her right breast. His mouth was hot when he focused on her nipple. She moaned and threaded her fingers through his hair, holding him close.

"I can feel that all the way to my clit."

He growled and suckled her breast harder. Dusti moaned and shifted her legs, hooking them along the back of his thighs. He released her nipple and focused on the other. He braced one arm on the bed and reached down, running his palm over her leg, under it, then cupped her ass.

You're my everything, sweetheart.

Dusti loved hearing his voice inside her head. "I feel the same way about you. You're torturing me. I don't need foreplay. I can feel how much you want to be inside me. I want you there."

I want to play with you.

Sadist.

He chuckled and released her breast, scooting down. "Never. I just love how you respond to me. I promised we'd go slower. I'm just keeping my word."

He brushed soft, wet kisses down her stomach. He slid lower, released her ass, and pinned her thighs open with his arms. He ran his lips over the inside of her thigh and nipped her with his fangs.

"Now you're just being mean."

He laughed. "You're already ready to come again. I'm giving you a little time to cool down."

She arched her pelvis at him but it was tough to do with him holding her open, legs apart. She tried to read his thoughts but they weren't there. "You cut the link between us. I can't feel you."

"I did it on purpose or I'll come when you do again." He rubbed his jaw over her pelvic bone, teasing. "Let's try to last longer than thirty seconds this time."

He lowered his mouth and teased her clit with the tip of his tongue. Dusti moaned and unwove her fingers from his hair, grabbing at the bedding instead. His lower teeth raked over the sensitive bud.

"Torture," she moaned.

"I haven't even started, sweetheart. I plan to be here for a while."

He ran his tongue over her clit, slowly licking her with light strokes. She squeezed her eyes closed and bit her lip, the pleasure slowly building. Every so often he'd use his teeth to gently slide across the swelling bundle of nerves. Sweat began to coat her body as she writhed on his bed. Every muscle strained from how wound up she felt.

"Drantos, please!"

That's all it took. He became aggressive with his mouth and tongue, applying more pressure. He snarled against her, adding vibrations into the mix. Dusti yelled his name, the climax hitting so hard that she worried her heart might explode and the top of her head seemed in danger of blowing off.

Drantos released her legs and crawled up her body. Dusti opened her eyes and stared into his glowing ones. The blue was absolutely stunning and near neon. He opened his mind to her and she could feel his pain. He hurt with the need to be inside her. His cock was painfully hard and he wondered if the skin would actually split open. It felt as if it could, from needing her so much.

"Why wait so long?"

"You deserve to be worshipped."

His words melted her heart. He gently entered her, his cock filling her pussy. His eyes closed as pleasure gripped him. She could read how perfect she felt to him. Tight, really wet, and so right. *So mine.*

"Yes, so mine," she repeated.

Drantos opened his eyes when he was fully seated inside her. She hooked her legs around his waist, resting her heels on his ass. She wrapped her arms around his neck to hold him tight. He wanted to fuck her fast and hard but he was holding back. He wanted to show her tenderness and part of him worried he'd be too rough.

"You're not going to break me."

"I'll always worry," he admitted. "I'm much stronger than you."

"We're linked. You can feel me and how much I want you, can't you?"

"Yes."

"Trust us together. I do."

"Open up all the way to me."

She did.

He grinned. "You think I have a big dick."

"You do."

"And you love how I feel inside you."

"Guilty. Are you going to keep reading my thoughts? Read this one." *Make me come again. Move, baby. Give me all you've got.*

I aim to please.

You're turning me into a dirty mouth. Next I'm going to be demanding you fuck me like an animal.

He kissed her. *I love your mouth. I love everything about you. And I can totally do that. I'm not human.*

She dug her heels into his ass and squeezed her vaginal muscles, rocking her hips. He liked it and the move broke the last of his restraint. He spread his knees a little to get better leverage and began to thrust.

Dusti closed her eyes, reveling in bliss. He felt amazing inside her. They fit together perfectly. He was right. It was as if they'd been made for the other. He was thick and hard. He picked up the speed before they both exploded together.

Drantos eventually rolled them so she ended up sprawled on top of him as they tried to catch their breaths.

"Like an animal, huh?"

She grinned. "You won't just let that slide?" She lifted her head and stared into his eyes. The glow had faded until they were a pretty dark blue again.

"Nope. So, do you want to get on all fours and we can do it doggy style?"

She could sense he was teasing her.

"Only if you don't shift forms. That's so never happening."

"Agreed. I don't even think we're sexy in that form. I've accidentally come across a couple or two in the woods going at it in shift."

"Have you ever tried it?"

He hesitated.

"I'll take that for a yes."

"I was young and horny. We'll try damn near anything once. I didn't find her quite so attractive with fur."

"Does it bother you that I can't shift?" That was a concern to her.

"No." He stopped hugging her middle and reached up, cupping her face in both his hands. "You're perfect to me. I wouldn't want you any other way, Dusti. Don't ever go there with your thoughts again. I'm never going to regret mating you. I don't see you as weak or inferior. I know you get that shit from the clan but they aren't me. They don't know you the way I do." He paused. "I actually like that I can be so protective. It makes me feel very manly." He grinned.

She laughed. "I see."

"I get to carry you around. Most VampLycan women would slap me with their claws for that offense. You let me get away with a lot of things they wouldn't."

"Like what?"

"You didn't protest when I dried you off with a towel. They'd be annoyed but the truth is, I just really enjoy doing intimate things for you. I find it sexy."

"I think it's sweet."

"Then we're both happy."

"Yes, we are."

"I'm so grateful that we met."

She remembered how crazy she believed he'd been. "I wasn't so thrilled at first. You grew on me."

"I never thought I'd have to kidnap my own mate and force her to spend time with me."

"Yeah, that's not really something you plan for."

He chuckled. "I know I didn't see it coming. I would have bought furry handcuffs if I'd known."

She laughed. "Only you would say that."

He stroked her hair and his expression grew somber. "I know what my mother said about having a baby right away. Don't listen to her. She means well but that doesn't make her any less annoying. I don't give a damn what they think or want. All that matters is that we're happy."

"You never did properly explain that whole birth control thing so who knows. I'm not exactly able to see my doctor to get more shots when I need them. I guess we should just see what happens when it does. I'm not going to worry about it either way. I was still unsure of how this mate thing worked but now I realize we're going to be together for as long as we're both alive."

"Yes, we are."

Dusti braced her hands on his chest and lifted up, straddling his lap. "Just tell me one thing."

"What's that?"

"Do you guys have hospitals? Because I so do not want your mother to be my midwife."

"We don't have hospitals but she isn't the one who would be at the delivery."

"That's one good thing at least. Why don't you have hospitals? The blood work stuff?"

"Yes. They'd realize something was different about us and you do carry some of your mother's genes."

"Right."

"And I'm going to feed you my blood often when you do get pregnant so our children can shift." He paused. "Is that alright with you?"

"I've spent a few days here and I don't want our children to be seen as weak and too human. It sucks."

"I'm so sorry, Dusti. I hate that you've felt that way."

"It's okay. They'll learn to like me or we'll go live in that cabin you told me about. It will help a lot when Bat arrives. We'll at least have backup."

"I completely forgot. Kraven called Red. He mentioned it during patrol and then stopped at my father's to update us further while we were waiting for word from Aveoth. They're fine, and he's taking your sister to see that doctor you told me about."

"Dr. Brent?"

"Yes. He's going to get information from him. We'll learn what he knew and perhaps why your mother never told you both the truth."

"Bat's going to Los Angeles?"

"It seems so."

"Wow. Poor Kraven."

"Why do you say that?"

"She's not going to want to leave. You have no idea how many years I begged her to take an actual vacation with me. It never happened until she thought our grandfather might leave us big bucks in his will."

"Kraven will manage her."

"I hope he doesn't take her to her place."

"Why?"

"You should see her closets and the amount of shoes she owns. It's her favorite weapon of choice when she gets mad. She'll be able to toss hundreds of them at him."

Drantos laughed.

"I'm serious."

"I think he can handle her."

"I hope so."

"He will." Drantos sat up. "Are you hungry?"

"I thought you promised me animal sex."

He growled and suddenly rolled over, pinning her under him. "I always keep my word. We'll eat later."

Drantos stared into Dusti's eyes, grateful that he'd found her and for the future they'd have together. Life would never be boring. She would keep him on his toes. "You ready for some growling and fangs?"

"Bring it, baby." She stroked his skin, urging him on.

He lowered his mouth to hers—just as something banged on the window from outside.

He stiffened, twisting his head.

"Is that someone at the *window*?"

"I think so."

Dusti softly cursed and grabbed the bedding to cover up. "Are you kidding me? We locked the door to keep from being interrupted."

"Drantos..." His father pounded on the glass harder. "Drantos!"

"Goddamn it," he muttered, untangling his body from his mate's. He yanked on the bedding, better covering her. "What the hell?"

"We *really* need to go to that cabin you told me about."

He agreed with Dusti's frustrated assessment as he stalked to the window, spotted his father standing just outside, and opened it. "What?"

"I couldn't get in the front. Why is your door barred?"

"I'm bonding with my mate. We didn't want to be disturbed." He'd never found either of his parents overly annoying before but he was learning new things every day. His smaller cabin was looking better and better to move into.

"The three clans are holding a meeting. You need to get dressed and be a part of it. We're discussing ways to track and capture Decker. The GarLycans are attending as well."

"Damn."

His father nodded. "Lord Aveoth will arrive within half an hour. Hurry up."

Drantos glanced back at Dusti. She sighed, clutching the bedding to her chest. He knew she could overhear everything. He looked back at his father.

"I'll pass. It's going to be a long time before you're ready to step down and have me take over. Humans have these things called honeymoons, and my mate deserves the best. That would be me spending at least a week alone with her. You have this, Dad."

His father appeared stunned.

"Don't come to our window again. And I'm buying curtains." He closed the glass between them, locked it, and returned to the bed. Dusti smiled.

"I can't believe you told him no."

"You're my priority, Dusti. Did I ever tell you that VampLycans keep dens? They're safe bunkers hidden in the ground. We built them in case we ever went to war with the GarLycans or humans. It's not the most romantic place but no one but Kraven knows where mine is located. He helped me build it, and I did the same for him. We could lock ourselves inside and no one would be able to find us."

A glint of excitement sparked in her eyes. "Really?"

"Yes. How would you like to see our den?"

She looked tempted but shook her head in the end. "Bat and Kraven might come back. We need to be here."

"They won't return until Decker is no longer a threat. He's stupid and crazy. I can take a cell phone and Red can text me when he hears from Kraven."

Dusti grinned. "It sounds like a plan."

"Yes, it does." He leaned in, brushing his mouth over hers. "You're always going to come first to me, sweetheart. My family is just going to have to adjust."